The Richest Girl in the World
AN AMERICAN ODYSSEY

By Nona Coxhead

Fiction

THE MONKEY PUZZLE TREE

SIMON WEST

HOUSE OF MIRROR

THE HEART HAS REASONS

THOUGH THEY GO WANDERING

Biography

GRETA GARBO

AMELIA EARHART

Non-Fiction

MINDPOWER: THE EMERGING PATTERN OF CURRENT RESEARCH

The Richest Girl in the World

AN AMERICAN ODYSSEY

BY NONA COXHEAD

Doubleday & Company, Inc., Garden City, New York 1978

Library of Congress Cataloging in Publication Data

Coxhead, Nona.
The richest girl in the world.

I. Title.
PZ3.C83967Ri [PS3505.0972]   813'.5'4
ISBN: 0-385-13380-4
Library of Congress Catalog Card Number 77-82619

The Richest Girl in the World
AN AMERICAN ODYSSEY

Chapter 1

"You're extra quiet this morning, Lil. Up all night watching, I bet." Thomas glanced around from the driver's seat of the chocolate Rolls-Royce Phantom, amused shrewdness on his swarthy face. "Don't blame you—some binge, huh? And I thought I'd seen 'em all."

The maids, in their churchgoing hats and dresses, smiled at Lily in anticipation.

"Miss Lily," corrected Maudie. "And that will be enough of *that*." Red eyebrows raised high above metal-framed glasses, she looked into Lily's freckle-dotted face. "Did you get up and go to that window again, dear? After giving me your word?"

Lily kept her light, brilliant eyes on the glittering Long Island Sound. With Maudie wearing the smart navy cloche Mummy had given her that covered her netted red hair and made her not so plain or old or familiar, it was hard not to tell the truth, that she did, and that she had heard and seen *everything*.

"It's just so hot," she said, puffing wisps of light glossy hair from her damp forehead. "As soon as I've seen Mummy, I'm going right up to my pool."

"Best not disturb *her*, lamb," said Dora, the black-haired maid from Ireland. "They was all still cavortin' when we come to serve breakfast."

"It will be time for your lunch," said Maudie, her British voice clipped and final.

"I don't want any today." Lily handed Maudie her Bible, her white straw hat and gloves. "I just want a cool swim."

"Afraid you'll miss something, eh?" Thomas winked at her in the rearview mirror.

"Forty more coming to lunch—and their chauffeurs." Irene, the gray-haired maid from Scotland, mopped her face with a folded handkerchief. "I wouldn't wonder if the cooks quit, all four."

"It's the bootleg booze, if you ask me. They say it's straight off the boat, but I say it's poison." Thomas drove the car through the white iron gates, along the half mile of fir-lined, white-graveled driveway to where the chauffeurs stood in the shade of the great red-brick mansion, gossiping or polishing their employers' cars. "Not that it bothers *him*. He was out there with the horses, not a wink of sleep. The guy's made of iron!"

"But herself is *not*," said Dora.

"Amen." Gertrude, the dark maid from Alabama, rolled her eyes upward.

"This conversation is thoughtless," said Maudie, with a sharp glance around. "It must not happen again."

Because of her high position, there was brief silence.

Lily felt like touching her hand. She'd never really understood the talk, until lately. As Thomas stopped the car and jumped out, she edged to the door.

"Dear," said Maudie, "I shall have to come with you . . ."

"Maudie! It's four feet deep at the *deep* end—child-size!"

"Nevertheless . . ."

Suddenly, before Thomas could open the door and get his possessive grip on her arm, Lily was out of the car, sprinting off towards the hill, her long thin legs carrying her quickly past the garage with its endless line of cars looking out at her like mechanical horses in a stable, on past the croquet lawn and on up the rose-arbored pathway to her own chalet at the top. Although the sickly sweetness of the massed roses and the closeness of the buzzing bees made her dizzy, she didn't stop till she got to the front door.

And then, she only stopped because the sound of voices floated up to her, far across the lawns, beyond the sprinklers arching and bowing and sweeping the green velvet grass like tall silver dancers, across the wide, layered terraces and glass-domed tennis house to the tremendous sunken pool, shimmering blue-green and empty in the midday sun.

Her heart tripped. Were they coming out at last—Mummy, perhaps Daddy?

But it was only the Filipino boys, calling out in their soft singsong as they worked, still straightening up turned-over chairs and tables, stacking bottles and glasses in wheelbarrows, and hosing off the terraces where the food had been spilled from the long supper and cocktail counters. She saw one of them hold up some kind of underwear, pink and satiny, and there was soft giggling.

She was hotter, thinking about it; her white organdy dress with the low-slung blue sash clung to her body. She wanted to turn away, but couldn't . . .

It was all coming back.

Pressing her hand to her mouth, she watched what seemed to be the guests arriving again—all their cars piling up the whole length of the driveway, the butlers in their white ties and tails, the footmen in the Boeker blue-and-gold livery, the maids in their neat black-and-white uniforms everywhere at once—and Mummy, wearing her lovely lavender georgette dress with the long pink-beaded fringe that hung down low in the back and from under her hips, her brown curls bobbed very short, a silver band around them, her diamond loops in her ears, and waving her long ebony cigarette holder as she greeted everyone, hugging and kissing them, her powder-blue eyes with big gobs of mascara on their lashes, looking enormous and glowy.

. . . And Daddy, too, beside her at first—in his white flannels, gray shirt and dark gold tie, his dark-brown hair jutting up from where it had been brushed flat, looking enormous and smiling and suntanned, shaking hands and slapping backs, bowing over ladies' hands with his joking "Continental" manners . . .

. . . And she herself had been there in the beginning, looking almost grown up in the pale-blue crepe-de-chine with the floppy rose on the shoulder, meeting all the guests Mummy or Daddy remembered to introduce her to as they poured in and went to their rooms or gathered around in the Williamsburg "salon." There were stars from Broadway who called her "precious lamb," golf and tennis stars, earls and lords and princes, lawyers, architects, dress designers, senators and generals, poets, authors, stock-exchange people, and lots of neighbors from Palm Beach and around here—and, of course, the newspaper pests who always put things in their papers about "The Wealthy Boekers," whatever that meant . . .

Her head had reeled, and she'd felt like an idiot with her silly smile and saying the same things over—it was a thing she was used to, but she was relieved when they forgot her, and she drifted about listening to little conversations about "The Scopes Trial"—the effect of radio on young minds—the Ku Klux Klan—a book called *Soundings,* a play called *The Green Hat,* and the star of it was coming later, someone said . . .

Then the sun had gone down into the Sound, and though the whole house was full of breeze from the whirring fans, it was warmer than the outdoors, and everyone gradually moved out to the terraces, and hundreds of colored lights and magic lanterns strung in the trees and around the pool began to look bright, to make a fairyland as far as she could see.

The guests' voices started to get louder and louder, and they made up changing groups and put their heads close, then gave those noisy, hoarse sounds she knew were for "risqué" jokes. The glasses from the butlers' trays disappeared as fast as they were filled; it was like watching magicians in the dusk—all you could see were the trays, the hands, and the butlers hurrying back for more.

The big orchestra from New York began to arrange all its instruments on the special platform—and soon they were playing and everyone was dancing. She longed to join in and do the fox trot and tango, to try swaying back in her partner's arms the way the girls did, looking snaky-eyed at the same time and not falling over. When they played "I Want to Be Happy" and "Tea for

Two," she tapped her feet, sang along with the sweet-sounding saxophone . . .

But that was when Thomas had appeared, sent by Maudie to haul her off to her own supper, and bed.

Only she'd fooled them. The view from her window was much better, anyhow, and she'd pulled up a chair and watched and watched . . .

By then, people were doing "acts" and stunts on the stage—a brother and sister called the Adairs did a tap dance and sang, and twins dressed like Kewpie dolls sang funny lisping songs that made everyone howl and clap for more. A tall, thin man in a black sombrero played an accordion that hung from his neck, and sang in a very romantic voice about moonlight and roses.

Then minstrels put on a whole show, and Japanese jugglers with white-painted faces and bare chests walked around among the people doing their tricks—and a line of beautiful girls in feathered and fringed dresses did a kicking dance that showed their rolled stockings and fancy garters.

Somewhere below her window, she heard a voice say, "If they don't bring the real food soon, I'll be drunk as a monkey."

She would have laughed, except that Mummy was beginning to lean on everyone and look as if her legs were made of something soft, and she kept looking up into Freddie Osborne's face with that gaga smile, and he kept filling those glasses like bowls with champagne, giving them to her, and holding her close to him. (He wasn't even handsome, she'd discovered. There were bags under his eyes—his shoulders were narrow—and in a bathing suit, his stomach looked like a basketball!)

There was a big commotion, then, and supper was served—but that was dull to watch—just a lot of back and forth with plates—and it didn't last long because another orchestra came out and began to play, softer, jazzier kind of music, and the leader, who sat at the piano, sang songs in a very meaningful, significant voice everyone wanted to hear—so they got all around close, and she couldn't make out the words . . .

She'd jumped when suddenly Maudie was there, pushing her off to bed, saying, "Down with you and no nonsense," and then, "Now promise me to sleep tight, dear," as she left for her own room in the suite.

"Promise," she had murmured sleepily.

Of course she was up again in a minute and back to the window . . .

But it was different out there now. A lot of lights had been turned off, and the people who were dancing couldn't, not properly. They stumbled around, holding on to one another, or helping one another up when they fell. Mummy had her arms around some man's neck, but her legs were not working at all. A girl did a dance by herself, snapping her fingers and pushing her tummy around, and different people got behind the drums, or sang in awful, out-of-tune voices through the megaphone.

She kept on watching, her lids so heavy they wouldn't hold up —only she made them, in case she could see what Mummy did— and Daddy . . .

It was harder now, because the lights were low over the pool, but she could make out people splashing about. They jumped in and out of the pool, screamed, yelled—and she could hardly believe it . . . They were naked! There were dozens and dozens of faces in the black water, too, like white puddings bobbing about . . .

Then—at last, she heard Daddy's voice from the dark side of the pool; she'd have known it anywhere. "I'm the Sheik of Araby," he was booming out. "Your heart belongs to me . . ."

In a minute, a lot of other men were singing with him, and she could hear the plink-plink of his banjo. *Naturally*, then, he sang "Show Me the Way to Go Home" and "It Ain't Gonna Rain No More . . ." His voice got hoarser, and sillier—so did the others . . .

Under her window, she heard a soft voice say, "No more, *no* more—thassanuff. Gotta go to bed, sugar—gotta . . ."

"Come on, come *on*, baby—open up . . ."

"Don't do that—my dress . . . ! Ouch—you're hurting me . . . I'm drunky, sugar—gonna pass out . . ."

There was a scuffling sound. The voices got thick and blurry, and she couldn't tell what they were saying, or what was happening, but she began to shiver all over, as if it were ice-cold winter.

There was only silence then. She had waited and waited, till the lanterns were pale spots. A phonograph was stuck in a part of "Ain't We Got Fun," and no one fixed it. Birds began to stir around . . .

She'd gone to bed, a lumpy feeling in her chest, like when she watched Mummy and Daddy drive away for weekends to other people's houses, or off for long trips to Europe, but there was something more scary as well . . .

. . . Now she put her palms to her eyes to blot out that whole scene, and went on quickly into the house, through the big, brightly colored rooms done like circuses and zoos to amuse and interest her as a child—which she was not any more, and she wished Mummy would hurry up and redecorate more sensibly as she kept promising . . . and on to the largest room of all, with its mirrored walls and smooth, springy dance floor.

But it would have been too hot for even Isadora Duncan to practice today, she thought . . . She didn't even feel like putting on the music. If only she had a friend, a best friend her own age —perhaps they could have talked about secret things, found some fun things to do—not like playing Ludo or Little Casino, or other silly games with the maids (they always let her win—only Thomas gave her a good battle at checkers!). Even Mr. Gilson, if he wasn't stern and tutoring, would have done.

Her image in the mirrors caught her eye. She moved over to one, inspected her face closely. If only the hateful freckles would go away—if only her hair were some color—not almost white. She turned her arrow-straight nose to view, studied it a moment, then stuck out her tongue and pressed her nose upward into the tip-tilted version she yearned for.

And what about *those?* Undoing the top of her dress and slipping down the shoulders of her petticoat, she scrutinized her breasts. They were small, with very sharply defined but light pink nipples—but the sight of them froze her expression with horror . . .

They were *bigger!* She'd have to talk to Mummy quickly about getting a tight bandeau. It was revolting, so unfashionable— Mummy would understand. Maudie, of course, wouldn't—but this was not her business.

Rushing from the room, she went to her bedroom and grabbed one of the bathing suits from the long row of them in the wall-length closet . . .

"Of course, you must not go in swimming—on those certain days, Miss Lily."

"Nuts!"

Lily grinned at the word picked up from cousin Andy Dundell —it had a good, satisfying sound. Maudie would give her "Tch-tch, now . . ."

But as she started to take off her panties, she paused. She had read in a book of Mummy's—you could get very bad cramps in your stomach—and even drown!

With an angry snorting sound, she threw the bathing suit aside, put her clothes on again . . .

All right—then she'd read the new Gene Stratton Porter novel the bookshop had sent in the last big batch of books to read. She went out into the sloping, tree-shaded garden and flopped into her favorite hammock, with its view right down to the house and all its surroundings . . .

Suddenly her eyes widened. At last they were coming out. A man in a bathing suit with a red-striped top was winding the phonograph, and only a little thinned by distance, she heard "Lady Be Good," the piece that Freddie had played so many times to Mummy it nearly made her sick.

"Babe in the wood"! Lily's mouth folded inward. Andy Gump was more like it! How *could* people say he looked like Rudolph Valentino, who, next to Daddy, was the handsomest man in the whole world (she had his pictures pinned up inside the doors of all her closets. And Maudie even liked him, though she pretended not to) . . .

. . . Honestly, the way Freddie dived! She laughed at the big smack he made—*she* could have done better than that. His black hair floated out from his head like a Japanese wig, and his swimming looked like a girl's compared to Daddy's, with that splashy breaststroke.

He was only getting wet, really—because he got out before anyone saw him, and called the butler (old Nobby) to get him a drink. Then, natch, he looked all dignified again, with his cigarette held like the advertisements in magazines.

Now he was baring his teeth and standing up—and there was Mummy coming towards him, wearing her pale-blue negligee with the marabou fur all around it, and looking very tired and miserable, with her soft brown curls all mussed up, and kind of slapping her high-heeled marabou slippers behind her across the terrace.

Lily jumped out of the hammock and ran quickly down to the rose arbor until she could hear them clearly through the leaves without being seen.

"Cigarette me, big boy," she heard Mummy say, in her husky, early-morning voice, as she flopped into a wicker armchair. And while Freddie got his gold cigarette case open (Mummy had given him that, and put "from your ardent student" in the inside), she picked up his drink, swallowed it down and made a face as if it had been castor oil.

Oh, Mummy, why did you do that! Now you won't feel better at all today, and you won't want to talk to me . . .

Lily sighed, squatted lower, wrapped her thin arms around her legs and rested her chin on her knees. Why didn't Daddy come out—why didn't he see or notice or do something about . . . ?

Ah, there he was. Maybe now he *would* . . .

But, of course—Freddie stopped sitting at her feet and looking up with his goo-goo eyes before Daddy got there . . . She watched Daddy kiss Mummy's forehead, then go and make a neat straight dive from the high board, shake his hair from his eyes and swim swiftly with his big, strong brown arms from one end of the long pool to the other. "Water's like hot gin!" he called out as he turned around and swam back again.

Lily giggled. Oh, if only he knew how much she loved him! She could hardly wait for next week. He'd promised solemnly this time, "on the Bible, Lollipop," to spend a *whole* day with her. He wanted to check her tennis form, watch her ride her new horse (she loved the horse, but didn't dare tell him how she hated riding!), look at the new dance she'd made up herself and take her to see *Abie's Irish Rose* in New York . . .

. . . Once, in the days before Mummy had got so squiffy, they had all gone to the theater together. She had sat between them, and they bought her chocolates and kept looking at her and asking her if she liked the play. And afterwards they had walked out to the Packard arm in arm, and Daddy had told Edwards to drive through Central Park. They had stopped to watch some riders,

Mummy on one side, Daddy on the other, each one holding her hand, all squeezed together and close. "Poor horses," Daddy had said, "they ought to have a law against riders like that!" and she and Mummy had giggled so hard at him! And then they had gone back to the Fifth Avenue house and had tea, still all together . . . It had been the happiest day of her whole life . . . !

Well—it was no use getting too excited. If Daddy did remember, though, and kept his promise, she had a huge lot of things saved up to talk to him about—things you couldn't ask Thomas, who didn't know anything about the world, or Mr. Gilson, because he only knew books and studied nothing about business and planes and ships and foreign places; and she wanted him to tell her the story again of his boyhood, about Grandpa and the huge farm—about how Grandpa started as a peddler in the old days and made a great fortune . . . And, of course, her favorite thing—how he'd met Mummy at that ball in Newport and fallen in love at first sight . . .

And then, there were serious things she never could mention to anyone else—like about life, and who she was, and about becoming a great dancer, and why there were so many people living in little houses with no servants at all (or even cars), while they had such big houses, so many servants and cars . . .

"Good morning, Beth snookums! How are you feeling?"

"Oh, just Jim Dandy, sugar. Like a new man."

Lily heard the enormous woman columnist with the gray shingle laugh out at her mother like a hyena, saw her bosoms heave like sandbags under her jersey suit. Then she put on her bathing cap that pressed deep wrinkles into her low forehead, pulled the skirt over her huge fat bottom and plonked into the shallow end like a hippopotamus.

Lily's eyes crinkled at the corners, as she saw Daddy splash her and duck her head. He was such a *tease* . . . ! How she would like to be there and tease him right back, have a lovely big water fight the way they used to when she was younger . . .

Other guests were wandering out now, filling the terraces again. More cars drove up, and she named them as Thomas had instructed—that was a Daimler, that a Packard, that a Pierce-Arrow . . . There were Chrysler and Maxwell tourers—and even another blue Bugatti Royale just like Daddy's . . . !

Servants trotted around, and Freddie kept winding up the phonograph in the big cabinet, playing the wretched "Lady Be Good," and Daddy came back all dressed in white and greeted the new guests. One of them, she heard, was a very famous song writer—and another, who looked like a worried boy, was an English prince Mummy curtsied to—and everyone laughed because she nearly fell over sideways . . .

Lily squeezed her eyes shut. Please, Mummy, get *dressed!*

"This is *my* lunch!" she heard her say loudly to the butler who whispered to her. "Bottoms up, everyone! Down the hatch!" She tripped over the hem of her negligee, once, twice . . .

Freddie caught her each time, because he was always with her, and all Daddy did was to look over as if he was worried . . .

Now the beautiful girls were coming out, dressed in perky white sports dresses, finding Daddy as if by accident and gathering around him with their cigarettes in long holders like Mummy's, and those bored expressions . . .

Lily practiced it . . . But it was too goofy . . .

Why didn't they all go to lunch—it was so bad-mannered! Maudie never let *her* forget the right things to do; "Manners are consideration of other people's feelings, Miss Lily—not just a set of rules."

"Some sight, huh, Lil!"

Lily nearly screamed as Thomas took her elbow. "You scared me half to death," she told him, shaking off his hand. "You've got to stop coming after me as if I were a two-year-old, Thomas!"

Thomas laughed. "Thought you'd hear my boots squeak—you usually do. Anyhow—you know it's Maudie sent me. You said you were going for a swim."

"Ssh—be quiet."

Thomas, squatting down beside her, peered with her through the bushes, a look of disgust on his face. "Haven't you had enough, Lil? Turns my stomach looking at the rich getting sloshed from Thursdays to Tuesdays . . ."

"Ssh . . ."

"To Beth and Dick—a happy anniversary!" a man shouted from a tabletop. There were shouts, laughter, a small sea of lifted arms and glasses.

"Anniversary of what?" muttered Thomas. "Their first drunken orgy?" He tapped Lily's arm. "Come on, kid, this is no place for you."

Lily scowled, cocked her head, listened.

"Here's to good old Calvin!" someone shouted.

"To my Jocko beating Man o' War!"

"To Babe Ruth!"

"All right—to Helen—Queen of the Courts!"

All glasses turned to a woman with a suntanned face, who looked sober, and embarrassed as they toasted her.

Chefs in their tall white hats came out, stood frowning.

"To Repeal!"

There was a sound like thunder as everyone roared and spoke at once.

Lily sighed. Mummy kept on tilting up her glass, hanging on to Freddie. Once, her knees bent right down to the ground. He lifted her up again, kissing her cheek, smiling that spoony smile as if she was being so adorable.

"She's sodden with the stuff," said Thomas. "It's a crying shame what's happened to her. He ought to see that she dries out . . ."

"To Freud!"

There was the loudest laughter of all—and some man in white flannels and blue blazer was pushed into the pool.

Lily heard Mummy screaming with laughter, staggering up to the edge of the pool to look in, with big, goggling eyes. She clutched Thomas, as her mother seemed to crumple forward, her arms dangling . . .

"Jesus!" said Thomas, half rising. "Doesn't that bastard know she don't swim!"

Lily stood up, her hands going to her head, her eyes stark . . .

Her mother hit the water with such a light and gentle splash that for an instant no one seemed aware, even Freddie, who was standing laughing at the man emerging in wet clothes . . .

Lily burst from Thomas, ran around the arbor. "Daddy!" she screamed. "DADDY!" Her long legs went like a deer's across the lawns, through the sprinklers, over the flower beds . . .

In the commotion, no one heard her. She saw her mother's blue robe billowing on the surface of the pool as her flailing arms vanished, reappeared, vanished . . .

"Out of the way—out of the way!" she heard her father yell, saw him shove people aside, nearly knocking them down.

But already another man was struggling with her mother, hauling her towards the rungs at the shallow end, helped by dozens of other hands.

As her father plunged at them, scooped her mother into his arms as if she were a large doll with a broken neck, she felt Thomas grab her arm hard.

"Stay out of it, Lil," he said. "He'll know what to do."

Lily struggled wildly in his grip, tried to hit at him. "She's dead, she's dead!" she gasped, her slender face chalk-white.

Thomas's grip was a vise. "Look," he said reassuringly as her father bore the limp figure quickly off to a rubber mattress in the shade, but his face was grim as they watched him kneel over her, begin artificial respiration. "Christ . . ." he breathed.

"Let me go—let me GO!" Lily jerked and twisted wildly.

But after a moment more of futile struggle, she was suddenly still . . .

Her mother was moving! Squirming, beginning to giggle, she sat up, hooked her arms around Daddy's neck. "Am I blotto!" She laughed hysterically against him, coughing at the same time. "I'm just so blotto . . . Did I fall in, Dickie?"

Picking her up in one powerful movement, her father strode off towards the house. "Okay—she's all right," he called back over his shoulder.

The crowd that hovered stopped following, except for some of their closer friends, and, of course, Freddie . . . They all disappeared into the side entrance of the house. The ones left behind started talking among themselves, drinking again . . .

Lily sank to the grass.

"All right, Lil?" Thomas's big, blue-uniformed figure bent down over her.

Her heart was hammering too hard to speak. She pushed him away, got up, started to the house.

"*You* can't do nothing." Thomas strode along at her side. "She'll sleep it off and be right as rain, you'll see."

"Thomas—will you please let me *alone!*"

"So I will—but you ought to take it easy."

"Thank you." She took off, running up the shallow marble

steps between the tall pillars and into the vast, dim, fan-cooled hall that smelled of wax polish and scent from the enormous gardenia plants and giant urns of cut flowers that stood everywhere.

"And where do you think you're going *now*, Miss Lily?" called Maudie, appearing from the back of the house, half jogging across the gleaming floor.

Lily kept on. "I'm not your child, Maudie," she said. She marched up the wide rectangular staircase with its delicate wrought-iron balustrade, and on down the thickly carpeted halls lined with closed or half-open doors that led away from her parents' wing, on to her own. Passing the sitting room, she went on across the full length of the pink-and-gold bedroom, then flung herself on the rose-patterned silk bedspread under the frothy organdy canopy and pressed her face into the pile of flower-shaped satin pillows.

Almost immediately, she heard the door she had slammed, open. There was the firm, flat-heeled tread, unmistakable . . .

Lily dug her face harder into the pillows, pulled them around her ears.

"Miss Lily—there's something I think it's time we should talk about.

"Miss Lily—I think you'll feel better if you hear this."

Lily felt the bed sag, but did not move.

"I've been wanting to tell you, but I thought it might best come from your mother herself. Unfortunately, she hasn't got round to it, and I don't feel it fair to simply—"

Lily opened her eyes into the darkness. Something familiar was in the tone . . . She held her breath.

"I'll soon be leaving you, dear," said Maudie.

There was silence, with only the whirring of fans in it, the faraway drone of voices and music.

Lily turned slowly, pushed herself up.

Kathleen Maude's hand went to the top of her white starched collar, pressed it. "You're surprised—of course. But . . ."

"Because I've been rude and stubborn?" Lily asked, her head tilting.

"No, no, no. You're growing up—I understand that, dear—though I did my duty as directed."

"Mummy?" Lily lowered her eyes, not liking to speak of her to a servant.

"No—not actually. Not that it hasn't been difficult. Liquor's a terrible thing—but your mother is a very kind person at heart."

"Then . . . Daddy?" Lily kept her voice "tidy," the way Maudie's always was.

Maudie poked at her net, which had a way of slipping sideways, and lifted the nosepiece of her glasses from the pink stripe it made. "No—he's a wonderful man in many ways—but . . . Well, he *can't* slow down. They're both on a merry-go-round. They get bored if it stops for a moment. No doubt it's the money, the times."

Maudie stopped. "I'd not meant to discuss your parents. I've no right."

Lily blinked, tried not to show that she minded.

"But there's more to it with me anyhow, Miss Lily." Maudie's brow puckered, drawing her net downwards. "You see, I'm not one for the size and grandness of a household. I never felt right here—it's wee tots I'm fitted for, where the real need is." Her eyes had a meditative softness. "But I was taken with you, your proud little ways. And you had no one to—" She pressed her lips together.

Lily looked at the floor, followed the complicated twining of roses and green squares with her eyes, but saw only Maudie who'd made her dolls' dresses, knitted outfits for Oskie, her favorite bear, now wearing her blue cloche, her brown Sunday dress, going down the front steps, Thomas putting her bags in the car, driving her away down the long driveway . . . out of sight . . .

"You'll be better off, Miss Lily. All the coming and going in and out of your life—it's not a good thing. And as you very well know, you're much too big a girl to need a governess any more. Should be going to school, learning about the world, making friends."

Lily turned her face away.

Maudie rested her small, liver-spotted hand on one of Lily's. "It's because of you, Miss Lily, I've stayed, not, as Thomas always says, because of the money. There *are* people who set store by other things."

What did it matter, Lily thought, what a *paid* governess said she felt! They acted like mothers, fussed, seemed to care—for a *wage*. Thomas was right. Because, when they didn't feel like doing it any more—they just left. She shrugged her slim shoulders, kept her face averted.

"You must develop your own good values, Miss Lily, and stick to them," Maudie was saying. "It's not what you *look* like or *own* that counts—it's what you think and feel inside that makes people love you.

"Goodness—" She patted Lily's hand. "Here I am delivering a sermon, and so final, when I shan't be going for a week."

She sat on a moment, leaving it to Lily to break the silence. When Lily didn't, she drew in a breath, started to rise . . .

"Maudie?" Lily swung slowly around to face her. "Maudie?" Maudie paused. "Yes?"

Just for a moment, Lily hoped the black feeling in her would move away, that she could say "Oh, nothing . . ." and that would be that.

But, suddenly, as Maudie's familiar, bespectacled eyes met hers inquiringly, a big sob came out of her throat. "Oh, Maudie!" She flung herself into her arms and clung fiercely. "Don't leave me—*please* don't leave me!"

Maudie sat stiffly. For a while she stared over the blond head against her chest as if stunned. Lily clung harder. "I love you, Maudie, really. Love me, too—*please*. I'll be good, work at my lessons, act like a lady, develop character . . ."

"Ssh." Maudie shook her head at the excess, but her arms went around the tense young body in slow, automatic response. "Ssh." She rocked her, patted her back.

"Will you, Maudie—oh, say you *will!* Please—*PLEASE!*"

Maudie was still. She blinked once or twice, as if clearing her vision. Then she sighed, put her cheek to Lily's head. "Oh, dear," she said. "Oh, dear me."

Chapter 2

Beyond the tall, pillared archways of the loggia, the Florida sun
lay like yellow fire on the multicolored stone floor of the patio,
with its forest of exotic potted plants and shrubs. Further on,
past the brilliant green lawns scattered with towering, leaning
palms and the pristine nine-hole golf course, the white carpet of
beach shimmered like finely ground gems before a sea of rippling blue steel, blinding to the vision even in dark glasses.

Behind the archways, within the wide crescent containing a
series of oval tables for eight its full length, under the high
mosaic-work ceilings and Florentine frescoes, there was a monas-
tery-like dimness and coolness, and the people who sat at breakfast were untroubled by the humid tropical heat of the morning.

Lily sat next to her father and listened to the talk around the
tiled, flower-laden table, hardly able to contain her excitement.
This very afternoon, at least, it was definite—she and Daddy
were going to play tennis; he was going to give her some

pointers, and afterwards, they might have time for a swim and talk.

"Of course," her Aunt Miriam was saying, "now that the house is finally finished, Palm Beach has just about seen its day. You'll have to admit, Beth, it's gathering up hoi polloi at a frightening rate. You see the most ghastly people everywhere, not just tourists—though God knows *they* infest the place! But at the Everglades, the Breakers, the Bath and Tennis, at the best parties."

Beth Boeker, wearing a white satin robe that drooped off one shoulder, nodded, her myopic eyes focusing the subject and the strong, handsome, glowing face of her older brother's widow with equal difficulty. "Mmmm!" she murmured. "Nouveau riche?"

"You're right, Beth!" said Freddie Osborne, as he took more of the scrambled eggs the butler offered. "That's just what it is." His dark eyes flashed their intimate, admiring message.

"Poppycock," said Richard Boeker, wiping his mouth vigorously on a large, crested napkin and throwing it onto the table. "What do you think *we* are, any of us! This old-guard talk gives me a pain. And who are *you* to talk, Freddie, anyway? *A bridge teacher*—a professional roué, a social *parasite*." The glint in his eyes and his grin, belied the harshness of his words, though too late for their object's discomfort.

"*Anyway*," he went on, "this is 1927! Who wants the same old worn-out pack of face cards reshuffled and redealt season after season. Let's have a *new* pack."

Lily smothered a laugh; she did not want to be relegated to a child's role today. She assumed a thoughtful, adult expression.

"Besides, Mirry," he continued, smiling at Miriam Dundell Hower, sitting straight-backed and regal in her yellow linen dress, "how would you ever fill this great palace without equally great hordes of riffraff? It's mathematics."

Miriam laughed, showing even teeth devoid of gold (there was a saying that it was the only place she *didn't* have it), and fanned her face with a small, exquisitely carved ivory fan. "You're quite right, Dick. And I intend to fill it. I'm going to do the most lavish and imaginative entertaining ever attained in the Palmetto State. I shall reign here in my palace, as you call it, a monarch supreme, enjoy every minute of it—*and* go down in social history!" She patted the shining gold braid that wound her immaculate head, and winked.

Andrew Dundell, her tall, lanky, thin-faced son, crossed himself rapidly.

Lily put her hand over her mouth, but the giggle burst through.

Exhilarated, as usual, by her susceptibility, Andy made a dome of his long-fingered hands, put them to his narrow, cleft chin and lifted his large, deep-set gray eyes piously. "It is easier for a camel to go through the eye of a needle than for a rich woman to enter into the kingdom of God," he intoned. "But Mother will make it—she'll slip him a couple of million."

"Andy!" Miriam's chief house guest and possible next husband, General William Court, a stocky man with gray streaks in very short black hair and heavy eyebrows, scowled with disapproval. "That's pretty impertinent, young man!"

Miriam put a hand on his arm. "It's all right, Willie dear. He's just showing how much he worships me—aren't you, Andrew?" She gave her son a smile of humorous indulgence. "Anyhow, it wouldn't work—so that's why I'll spend the lot while I live. Oh, don't worry—you'll have what's left."

"Beth—did you drink before breakfast?" asked Dick, more thoughtfully than accusingly.

"No . . . oo." She looked up, her eyes round with offense. "It's just the long ride, sweets. A private Pullman's still a *train*, and trains exhaust me." She spoke to Miriam, smiled appealingly, made her voice small and childlike. "Mirry—you wouldn't mind if I had a teensy bit of shut-eye, would you—just till lunch?"

Freddie nodded his gleaming black head wisely. "She should, Miriam, my dear, she really should. She hasn't been . . . well." His hooded lids descended, lowering heavy black lashes like a veil of double meaning. Under the table, Lily saw his hand move onto her mother's knee and press it hard.

"You slept most of the way down, and you've done nothing *but* sleep since we got here," said Dick. He shifted his big, heavy frame restlessly in the ancient Spanish chair. "Mirry's got a whole schedule revolving around us!"

"Don't worry, Dick," said Miriam. "I can get my secretaries to manipulate a few things if Beth's not up to them."

"She'd be up to anything if she'd lay off the hooch. What I'd like to know is, where's she getting it when it's not being served? It's very strange." He leaned back, stared at Freddie, blew smoke slowly down his nostrils.

Freddie's sleek black brows winged into question marks of total mystification.

Dick kept on staring for a moment—then suddenly ground his cigarette in a black quartz ashtray and rose. "Well, if I'm to get in any trading—" He looked at the thin gold watch chained to his belt. "Now, Mirry, am I correct—cocktails twelve-thirty, small luncheon following?"

"Right." Miriam opened a needlepoint notebook and put on horn-rimmed glasses. "Then—bridge, which you can't make, and cocktails at the Andervens', which you can, but I can't—but you'll come back here in time for cocktails, and dinner—formal, by the way, at eight forty-five. After that, *I* shall go to bed—but you and Beth are invited to at least two late parties, one or both or neither of which you need attend unless you want to."

"*One* of them I do," said Dick. "The Bournywinns'. Haven't seen them since the Beaux Arts Ball. Swell people." He looked at Beth, who sat with her shoulders slumped, her face propped in her hands, a distant stare in her heavy-laden eyes. He grunted with impatience. "I can see I'll go alone."

Lily's heart strained towards her mother, but to her father, too. If only they would try to understand each other—if she could talk to them, make them see . . .

"All right, Lollipop," he said, dropping his big hand on her head a moment. "Two-forty on the dot, racquet in hand. Okay?"

She smiled up at him jauntily. "And ready to beat you."

"Two-forty!" said Miriam. "Why, Dick—you're playing *polo* at three! That's why I've ordered lunch early!"

Dick frowned—then clapped his hand to his head. "My God—how in hell could I have forgotten *that?* I must be going loco!" He turned to Lily, lifted her face and looked into her eyes. "I swear—the very first thing I thought of when I woke up this morning was—I'm playing tennis with Lolly!" He looked at Miriam. "You know—I didn't realize till I saw her hitting the ball with Andy yesterday that she's got a really great stroke—I'm going to work with her!"

Miriam's dark-blue gaze showed speculative interest. "Well—so you shall. We'll see to it. And—she's going to have a lovely fifteenth-birthday party in a week."

The fury in Lily spread like a storm, too fast to control. She jumped to her feet. "I don't care, really, Daddy," she said. "I haven't even seen all the house yet."

"Andy," said Miriam quickly, "go with her so she doesn't get lost."

"Yes, Mother—dear." The tall, stoop-shouldered boy got up. "Forthwith the *grand tour!*" He sauntered after Lily.

"She's hurt, poor baby," murmured Beth, watching Lily move off, her light bobbed hair, her white pleated skirt, her thin freckled arms in the navy-blue sleeveless middy swinging vigorously. "She's always like that when she's hurt." She blinked, her eyes murky with tears.

"Come and watch the polo, Lollipop," Dick called. "*Please*—you'll bring me luck!" His hearty tone was sincere, hopeful.

"*I'll* play tennis with you, Lily," called Freddie.

Lilly didn't halt or turn.

"You really want to see all of this crazy place, Leelee?" asked Andy. He lifted a wrist, made it flop, and studied his watch. "We'll hardly make it before lunch, even with my shortcuts and cheating." He peaked one eyebrow, to express his ennui.

"Andy, I'm not in the mood for your jokes." She dug him lightly with her elbow, and he pretended to slide across the highly polished stone floor into a Roman bust on a stand.

"Dear," he said, "*that* is sixteenth-century—irreplaceable—and I'm not joking. There are precisely one hundred and twenty-eight rooms, forty bathrooms, a Versailles ballroom, a sixty-foot tower with God knows how many steps to the top, a panoramic view, Chinese, Mexican and tropical gardens, citrus groves, meditation cloisters, nine-hole golf course, four clay tennis courts, a covered tunnel to the Rotunda Club. Apart from that, there's the furniture, rugs, ceilings, walls, floors and ornaments, each with a special history that must all be explained en route."

"Help!" said Lily. She stood still in the entrance hall, casting a

trapped glance up and around its immensity, its exotic, complicated splendor.

"Ah, indeed." Andy sighed. "This 'veritable palace' contains
many of the world's greatest treasures, art, sculpture, whole
rooms taken from Roman palazzos, from Spanish, Moorish,
French, English castles and monasteries, or copied and incorpo-
rated with brilliant precision by Mrs. Dundell Hower's resident
artists the Chiardi brothers, together with that architectural genius of the stage set Barthold Boas, and a host of other expert ad-
visers and artisans, guided, of course, by the unimpeachable
good taste and bold vision of Mrs. Dundell Hower herself."

"How could you do that without reading?" said Lily.

"Practice, dear. We're all onstage here."

Lily felt a puzzled awareness. "It's kind of—not real. And lonely,
somehow."

Andy wrinkled his long nose. "You're supposed to be awestruck,
dear, all oohs and aahs."

"Really? Is *that* why Aunt Mirry built such a place?"

"Oh, I wish Mother'd heard that! *Not* that it would faze her
. . . Come!" He moved on, leading her through several vast, high
rooms with pink-tiled arches into another that stretched to a
painted horizon of massed white clouds in a sky the color of
Lily's eyes, aqua, pale and translucent. "No, Mother's motives
are quite uninhibited." Andy gestured about. "She just wants the
best of everything money can buy, that's all."

"Yes—but if I were wealthy, I wouldn't spend so much on *myself*. I'd want to give most of it—maybe all of it—away. I'd try to
help all the poor people everywhere, without letting them know
who I was or anything."

Andy's cautious glance showed he wasn't to be caught nap-
ping on innuendo. "*If* you were wealthy," he repeated. "You're
not, of course. Ha-ha-ha!"

Lily's bright gaze was just as cautious. "Why, Andy—are we
very rich—the Boekers, I mean?"

Andy looked sidewise down his nose. "Who's joking now?"

"I'm not. Oh, I know we're *rich*, that Grandpa Boeker made a
fortune in dry goods—and Daddy makes heaps on the stock exchange. What I mean is, like Aunt Mirry."

Andy moved on, his angled face and big eyes still warily averted. "I'm not in the mood for *your* jokes, either," he said.

Lily tugged at his shirt sleeve. "Andy—come on, I want to know."

He looked down at her, and peaked his left eyebrow (Lily often practiced this trick of his in the mirror, without success). "You know—you know very well when you're twenty-one you come into the whole caboodle."

Lily squinted at him blankly. "I will? Well—even so . . ."

"Even so—you'll be the richest female in America—maybe in the world. Oh, come on, you know that's why you're always guarded—why you don't go to school—why they never let you mix with 'ordinary' people."

"But *you* didn't go to school—until two years ago—and *you* had guards."

Andy shook his head pityingly. "For the same reason, dear, of course. They don't want us kidnapped—held for ransom, whoever *he* is." He rolled his eyes. "Not that I'm in your league. If Mother hadn't parlayed her inheritance with *two* millionaire husbands, she'd have been very small potatoes, barely eighty million, *and* with strings. When she dies, I'll have to share it with all kinds of step-relatives. Not that I'll be poor—there'll be enough to make a joke of working or being serious about anything."

Lily looked as puzzled as she felt. "But I don't want so much. I simply won't have it!"

"Idiot! As if you had a say."

"Well—anyhow—I don't want to talk any more about it." She peered up at the great vaulted ceiling as if absorbed by it.

"Well, I like that! It was *your* idea. Anyhow, *that* is a replica of the 'Flight of Birds' motif in the main gallery of the Santa Marietta palazzo in Tuscany—Gonzaga—fifteenth century. The settees are of Genoese velvet, and that gilded console with the falcon was brought from Prince Pamplona's summer villa in Naples, circa 1530. That stupendous Venetian glass chandelier was shipped from some other palace on the canal in Venezia." Andy showed his prominent teeth as he mocked an Italian accent. "Can't think why. Let's skip the rest, go to your room. I want to try on your clothes."

"Oh, Andy—be serious."

"But I *am!*"

Lily hoped she wasn't turning pink. She walked away into the main dining room.

"That is the largest table of its kind in the world. Seats forty. Can't be duplicated. Took artists years to make. This is lapis lazuli, those are red and green jasper, and that is peachstone marble, and over here, white alabaster from Egypt."

"Golly!" Lily followed some of the gold tracery, the intricately blended inlays of soft-tinted flowers, fruits and birds with a fingertip. "Think of the patience it must have taken. I wonder why they would do it."

"Because it pleased them—made them happy. If you're a real artist, you just forget all about everything—you just work, and then someday it gets finished, and it's all worth it."

Lily looked up at him, her vivid eyes wide and thoughtful. "That's wonderful! That's the way I feel about dancing. I want to be a really great dancer—I don't care *how* long and hard I work!"

"Fat chance." Andy beckoned her imperiously. "Let's go—here come swarms of electricians and handymen."

Lily followed him through another vast room with large tiger skins and Persian carpets on a black-marble floor, great white-marble columns, tapestries and murals too immense to decipher, and another, with alabaster urns taller than people, whole trees filled with brilliant stuffed parrots, hanging glass lights like hundreds of rosy flames even without being switched on, a huge lighted fountain and waterfall, a green sunken pool with floating white lily pads and countless varieties of tropical fish, and a jungle of huge, spiked plants and ferns, a ceiling of giant interlaced palm fronds.

"What did you mean by that?" Lily asked, overwhelmed by all she saw, but determinedly catching up with him near a closed black oak door covered with Spanish grillwork. "I'm pretty good, you know!"

"That's nothing to do with it. You could be Pavlova! No one's ever going to *care*. They'll only be interested in your mazuma."

"Mazuma? What's that?"

"Money, ninny. Wampum. Dough." He waved his hand

through the air in disdain of her naïveté. "You'll be telling me next that you've never even *seen* the stuff."

"Well, of course I have. But I haven't got any—not of my own."

Andy held his flat, thin stomach with mirthless laughter. "Oh, I've got to put that in my play," he said. "That *is* droll!"

"But it's true!" Lily's eyes were bright with defense.

"Never mind, Leelee. I'll give you some. Here . . ." He reached in the pocket of his white knickerbockers, took out a wad of green bills and thrust some in her hand.

She pulled her hand quickly away and several hundred-dollar bills fluttered to the ground. "I don't want it," she said. "What would I do with it?"

"Spend it, of course," he said, retrieving the money.

"On what?"

"Oh, Lord—I'm going to *die* laughing." He put his long, thin arm around her, shook her affectionately. "Never mind, Leelee dear. Someday you'll wise up. Meanwhile, keep your ears flapping."

"I haven't got such big ones as yours," she began.

"Ssh," said Andy, as another voice seemed to cut right through hers . . .

She was still. Only occasional words penetrated the heavy door . . .

"Consolidated Can Common—P and O rails—if it goes bearish —Rails Preferred—Montgomery Ward—Cities Service—plateau—if split up—merger—Wright Aeronautical . . ."

"It's Daddy!" Lily whispered.

"Yes—piling it up." Andy shook his head. "That man's a Whirling Dervish. He hasn't stopped since he got here—no wonder Aunt Beth's fizzling out! Someone should put a crimp in his sail before it's too late!"

"How do you mean too late, Andy?"

He put his arm through hers and walked her out of earshot. "Divorce—all that. Like everyone else around here."

"But they wouldn't—not my parents. They love each other!"

"Did, maybe. Thank goodness my father went down on the *Lusitania*. Still, I hope Mother will marry old Court. Otherwise I might not get away from here."

Lily was quiet. What can I do, she was thinking, what can *I* do!

"Come on, Leelee," said Andy, "let's go up to your room—be a sport."

"Andy—no. You're awful. Anyhow—Maudie'd find us."

"Drat Maudie—you baby!"

Lily leaned back from her hips trying to look older, a match for him. "I think that's infantile, anyhow," she drawled. "Let's take bicycles on the trail."

"With that big ape Thomas tagging along?" Andy scratched under his armpits, made his lower jaw protrude.

"It's his job, Andy. All right, how about Mah-Jongg?"

"What a bore—completely passé. But if you insist." He yawned as he sauntered on, his long face set with pique at being denied.

Lily followed him to a large room with a checkered floor and several areas arranged for special games. The Mah-Jongg was set on a green baize table with chairs around it.

Lily set up her bamboo-and-ivory tiles with the usual pleasure at their smoothness, their etched oriental "flowers—South Wind—Seasons—Red Dragon," though her heart was not in the game today.

When Andy had called "Pung" or "Chaw," or broken the wall, several games in a row, he said, "You should learn to play contract bridge. Get that answer to a maiden's prayer to teach you—ready Freddie."

"Him! No, thank you!"

"You mean you don't swoon when he looks at you like that?"

"Like what?"

Andy lowered his lashes and leered at her.

Lily slid a tile into place. "He does not. That's the way he looks at Mummy."

"Ah—poor, innocent Leelee—you'll find out."

"You've got a terrible mind, Andy Dundell." Lily looked at him with exaggerated distaste.

"I'm observant, dear—which is more than I can say for you." He looked with silent glee at his latest tile.

"Andy?" Lily frowned casually at her tiles. "Do you want to go and watch Daddy play this afternoon?"

"Not me. Wretched sport. Forcing the poor animals after a ball till they practically drop. I'm supposed to play bicycle polo—with some 'young friends.' " He lifted his eyes ceilingwards.

"Don't you want friends, Andy?"

"Of course—but not the vacuous little beasts around here."

Lily looked thoughtful for a moment. "I want friends," she said. "I don't have any real ones. There was one girl, Amy—"

"Tresserton—the sugar people?"

"I don't know. But she went to France to live. Then there was another girl—but they wouldn't let me go there."

"Obviously Jewish, Irish, Negro, Catholic or insufficient income."

"Andy! Why are you so cynical?"

Andy laughed hoarsely, throwing back his head. "*Cynical*, dear, *cynical!*"

"Well—I've only *read* the word!"

As he was about to answer, two enormous Great Danes burst into the room, followed by Miriam, dressed in a white pongee trimmed with brilliant red silk and wearing large rubies at her throat and ears.

"There you are!" she said. "Where have you been?"

"To hell and back. Filling in time—what else?"

She looked at him with an amused smile. "Enjoyably, I presume. Well, luncheon's about to be served. Please change, dear—put on your striped flannels and smooth down that cowlick."

She turned to Lily, who was patting and hugging the dogs. "Don't push your hair behind your ears, dear—it makes you look like a boy. And put on something a bit more suitable to the occasion."

Lily stood up. "Yes, Aunt Mirry." She could hardly meet her aunt's eyes—she was so regal, so handsome, so perfect! It was hard not to be frightened of her.

Miriam smiled briefly—then, with sudden preoccupation, went off to talk to some maids who hovered nearby, the dogs, their claws sliding on the stone floor, racing after her.

Andy and Lily went dutifully upstairs, parting with a wave at the landing. Lily did not like to ask him again how to find her room, and after losing her way, finally caught sight of Maudie sitting by a window sewing.

"Maudie," she said, hurrying in, "I'm to wear something more suitable to the occasion—what?" She started dragging her middy over her head.

"Your pale-blue linen with the drawn thread. I'll get it."

"Maudie," Lily said as she took the dress. "Why haven't you ever told me that I'm to be the richest female in the world?"

Maudie's face turned pink. She wet her lips. "Well. Wherever did you hear that? Better speak to your daddy."

Lily's look softened. "I suppose it isn't your fault. Anyhow, then—that's something else I'm going to get straightened out with him."

She washed her face, slipped on the dress, brushed her hair. "I'm glad you wouldn't let those maids in here, Maudie," she said. "They're like bugs, everywhere. And I hate such a huge bedroom. I wish I was home in my own cozy room."

Maudie smiled as she did up the snaps of the dress. "Your bedroom at home, my dear, is many times larger than the whole house I grew up in."

"Really, Maudie—you never told me that. Tell me now."

"There's not much to tell. It was dingy, damp in the winter. Our bathtub hung on the back wall, and when we wanted a bath, we boiled the water in a huge kettle on the coal stove and brought in the tub and filled it—usually once a week."

Lily listened intently, her eyes bright with wonder. "Go on."

"Well—it was attached to other houses on both sides, and was right on the street. The rooms were tiny, and when I was a child we didn't have electric light, only gas lights in the parlor. We took candles up to bed, and it was pitch black and cold. My parents would go ahead of us children so we wouldn't be afraid of the dark. There was no running water, and we washed in a marble basin on a washstand, in lukewarm or cold water."

Lily tried to picture it, but it was as if she were looking through a glass the wrong way.

"But it was a very decent house, Miss Lily," Maudie added. "With so many of us, and so little money, we were very lucky. I hated leaving—but when I was twelve I started looking after little ones for other people. I worked up to nursemaid in a big important house in our town. It had fourteen rooms."

Lily saw that Maudie was very proud of that. There were ten very big ones in her tiny chalet, her *playhouse* . . .

"Never mind all that," said Maudie, as if waking up. "On with you or you'll be late, and that will never do with Aunt Miriam."

Lily sighed, then turned to complete her dressing. "Am I pretty at all, Maudie?" she asked when she was ready.

"I wouldn't think about it," said Maudie. "Nothing does us more harm than vanity. Get a move on, now."

"I've decided to watch Daddy play polo this afternoon, by the way," Lily told her as she started away. "Be ready after lunch."

"Oh—I thought you were going to play tennis with—"

"Daddy forgot."

Maudie checked a comment.

"I hope he loses," said Lily suddenly. "It's about time someone put a crimp in his sail."

"Now wherever did you pick *that* up?"

"Before it's too late." Lily walked quickly from the room.

Daddy was not at her table out in the crescent-shaped loggia, but she could hear him laughing and talking, and see how everyone paid attention to him. He was easily the handsomest man there. Glancing around, Lily noticed for the first time how many of Aunt Mirry's friends were quite old. Their skins looked like scratched brown leather, making all their lovely jewels a waste. Freddie was there, and once she caught him looking at her in a way that was somehow secretive. She looked through the huge, shallow bowl of yellow and orange flowers at Andy.

But Andy hadn't seen. He had his eyebrow lifted, and was saying, in a very false and affected voice, "Yes, I hope to have it produced next season."

Ordinarily, she would have giggled, but it was so hot and the butlers moved around so slowly that she yawned instead, had to cover her mouth quickly so no one saw.

The voices droned on. Lily sat in a daze of perfume, flickering jewels, dark-red nails and lips. There was much too much too rich food. She didn't want the wines Aunt Mirry winked to her to taste. She longed to be excused, to be somewhere alone with her parents, just the three of them . . .

She jumped as a voice said, "And are you having a lovely time, dear?"

"Oh, yes—thank you."

The lady leaned forward, and Lily saw past her pearl necklace to where her bosom hung like brown leather bags. "And what do you think of your aunt's house—isn't it like something out of the *Arabian Nights?*"

Lily looked into her eyes. She felt sorry—she knew the woman could not help looking like a dressed-up witch. "Yes, exactly."

"Your aunt is an extraordinary person. You can learn a lot from her. Seventy servants to organize, the cooking, ordering and entertaining to supervise, apart from the charities she gives her time to—why, the etiquette, protocol, table settings alone frighten me—and I've only got *half* the staff and size house."

"Talking about Mirry?" said another man, with a brilliantly polished bald head and a yellow coat. "Isn't she something! Why, that woman's a walking encyclopedia, a connoisseur—and the most charming and gracious person in the world!"

Lily nodded sympathetically, sagely, thinking that in a moment she'd fall off her chair with boredom.

But Andy was rising with a sickly-polite smile. "Very sorry—must run—appointment with the Duke."

Everyone smiled in vague bewilderment, and Andy looked over at Lily. "All right, Leelee," he said. "We must go."

Lily tried not to look startled. With a rush of relief, she stood up. "Oh, yes, we must. Well, goodbye then. Nice to meet you." She smiled at each face, made a small curtsy, and followed Andy away into the house.

"What a delightful child," she heard someone say.

Andy grinned down at her. "Thought you needed rescuing," he said. "You looked like an owl in daylight. Aren't you used to such things?"

Lily gave a soft groan. "Not too. Mummy and Daddy have mostly *parties*, you know . . . And I was too young when they . . ."

"All right—only now you're on your own. I'm off. Better find your nursemaid."

"You meany," said Lily. "Maudie's my friend!"

"Well, bully for Maudie. Anyhow—see you later." With an

offhand wave, Andy vanished into some part of the house she didn't know.

She wandered slowly through the vast rooms, already feeling lonely for him. If only there was something definite to *do*, not just playing all the time. At least at home she could practice her dancing . . .

Recognizing the door to the room where Daddy had been working in the morning, she walked over and went in. It was a full library with ceiling-high rows of books and a great black oak desk such as a king might sit at. The telephone Daddy had been using stood on it, tall and silent, as if waiting. She went to look over some two hundred of the books, remembering titles from her schoolwork or Mr. Gilston's reference.

Perhaps Aunt Mirry wouldn't mind if she borrowed a few. Reading was fun. What she liked best were the histories, about Marie Antoinette, or Queen Elizabeth, or the early days when George Washington beat off Lord Cornwallis and his redcoats . . . And those with a great and handsome duke or prince, who was kind and brave. But she also liked books she wasn't allowed to read, had stolen from the maids, like *Jurgen* and *The Sheik* and *Flaming Youth* . . .

Anyway, she'd better ask Aunt Mirry before she took any of these.

She went to the desk and sat in the tremendous leather chair and imagined she was conducting business over the telephone. He sometimes went to an office, he'd told her, and knew a lot of other men who worked—it would be interesting to know what they did, people who *worked* . . .

She glanced down at a note pad with some writing on it— Daddy's. Bending closer, frowning, she tried to decipher the scrawly words . . .

"Do something about Lily," it seemed to say. What did it mean? There was one other word . . . U-r-g . . . "Urgent."

She sat back, tapping her teeth with a pencil. Urgent? It made her heart go fast, though she didn't know why. What did "do something about Lily" mean?

After a while, she put down the pencil and started off to find the stairs. Perhaps Maudie would know. Perhaps he was cross

with her for being gruff this morning—he was going to give her a
lecture on her behavior in front of Aunt Mirry.

Suddenly she saw him, striding across the hall with his extremely busy look, a bundle of clothes under his arm. She saw
the helmet he wore for polo. She wanted to call out something—
she tried to think what—but nothing came because she wasn't
sure how she should treat him. She'd been angry—now she was a
bit afraid . . .

He went on, not seeing her, and the butler opened the big
front door for him, closed it behind him.

Lily went quickly now, to get Maudie . . . But Maudie wasn't
in her room, or her own. She went looking through the house,
and eventually discovered the great kitchens and pantries.
Maudie wasn't there, but the maids told her she was in the servants' dining room having lunch. They all looked at her, the maids,
the cooks, the butlers, as she ran in the direction they gave.

Maudie was sitting at a long table, with two other women in
uniform and three chauffeurs, being waited on by a butler with
his jacket and waistcoat off.

"Whatever is it?" Maudie asked, putting down her fork and
looking worried.

"We must go, Maudie—Daddy's left!"

"Well, now—calm down, Miss Lily. There'll be plenty of time."

Lily saw them all looking at her with little smiles, and she
turned and ran quickly back the way she had come.

She heard Maudie following her. "All right, all right," she
called. "But I thought you were angry with him, Miss Lily."

Sometimes Maudie aggravated her, and this was one time:
when she teased, or reminded her she'd said the opposite thing.
"People can want to hurry without changing their minds," she
said.

"Tut-tut. Well, I hope Thomas is ready."

"He'd better be." Lily moved on, half running.

"You're going the wrong way, Miss Lily."

Lily made a grimace as Maudie took her arm, swung her to
the right and led her to the exit where the garages were.

Thomas was sitting in one of Aunt Mirry's sports cars away
from the other chauffeurs, reading a paper, his feet up on the opposite door.

He moved slowly when Lily rushed up. "Now what, Lil?" He eyed her blue dress with obvious admiration as he set aside the paper.

Lily glared at him. "Which car?" she asked. "I want to get out to Delray as fast as possible."

Thomas winked at Maudie. "You do, eh? All rightee—hop into the Mercedes-Benz—your aunt said it was at your disposal."

Lily walked along the line of cars, and didn't wait for him to open the door before getting in.

"You ought to have a hat or scarf for the sun," Maudie said, following her.

Lily sat back, her arms folded about her, and didn't bother with conversation on the ride to the polo grounds.

"They're all coming out, Lil, you know," Thomas observed. "You're not the only one. There'll be quite a crowd. Your daddy's got a match ahead against Alberto Vicini on the other team."

"I *know*, Thomas."

At the polo field, when they drove up to the rope, many people had already arrived and were sitting on benches or bumpers waiting for the game to begin.

"That's where Aunt Mirry's crowd sits," said Thomas, pointing.

"Thomas," said Maudie, "her name is Mrs. Dundell Hower."

"She don't use the Dundell in speaking," said Thomas. "That's from her first marriage."

Lily got out of the car and walked away from the controversy. But Maudie moved after her, and Thomas got back in the car.

Looking at the people sitting in her aunt's benches, all talking together so intimately, and most of them years and years older, she didn't feel like joining them, but hovered in the back. She wondered if Mummy were still sleeping. Once upon a time, she'd have been here, with that eager, loving look on her pretty face— she was still pretty, but it wasn't the same . . .

"It's certainly not the place it was," said a very ancient lady with white hair sticking out of a large pink leghorn hat with flowers on it. "Give me Newport anytime. At least there, you know who everyone is, and every house isn't a Mizner atrocity."

"Exactly," said another lady with brilliant red hair and a white straw hat with blue and pink ribbons. "*Everybody's* making so much money nowadays—they crowd the right people out. It's spoiled the place. Why, I can remember the Royal Poinciana Hotel when—"

Lily's attention was caught by Aunt Mirry arriving, together with her luncheon guests. Trailing behind was Freddie wearing a panama hat turned down all round, with his hand under Mummy's elbow.

Lily wanted to hide at the way Mummy looked. She had on a white crepe-de-chine dress and long ropes of pearls and amber around her neck, but her stockings were baggy, she still hadn't combed her hair and her mascara was like two big bruises. She smiled very foolishly at everyone, so foolishly that there was a buzz-buzz of talk.

"It's a sin, such a lovely girl she was. I remember her at her wedding—breathtaking. They seemed such a perfect couple that day."

"They say he's got a case on Meg Bournywinn."

"Among others! Of course, Johnny Dundell spoiled Beth rotten after Emma died—she was always a wild, flighty little thing. I suppose the child will get all *her* money, too, if anything happens."

"It won't—these drunks outlive the best of us!"

Lily wished she could shield her ears.

"Why, hello, baby!" Mummy called, in her hoarse, broken voice. "You *did* come—that's nice. Good girl!" She walked with exaggerated straightness towards her.

Everyone on the benches turned to look, to watch.

"You come an' sit with us, sugar. Ooh!" She grabbed Freddie's arm as she swayed a little. "With me and Freddie?"

Lily pulled back from the smell of whiskey on her breath. "I'd rather stand here, with Maudie. All right, Mummy?" She smiled, as if she saw nothing unusual about her.

Beth Boeker focused Maudie's face. "Oh—good—you're still with us—good." She nodded. "That's *very* good."

Freddie kept his wide, appreciative smile, as if everything she said was amusing and endearing, but led her purposefully away to sit down.

People made room for them. "Glad you could make it, Beth dear," Miriam said. "Are you feeling better? She wasn't too well, dizzy from the train ride, you know." She nodded, turned to her group.

There were murmurs of polite, doubting condolence.

Maudie's face was a white freckled mask, and Lily did not want to meet her eyes.

Suddenly there was a stir among the spectators, and the ponies came out onto the field. There was clapping as the helmeted, booted riders, carrying their mallets behind them, rode into position.

Lily's heart jumped as she saw Daddy on his booted dun pony, sitting straight, looking big and strong and stern, with the helmet shadowing his eyes. "Hooray!" said Beth, and several people went "Sssshh!" but Freddie laughed, and she did it again.

Lily sighed, felt shame and sadness at the same time—but then the shrill of the whistle and the sound of ponies' hooves beating the turf made her forget . . .

"Dear me," said Maudie, "I wish I could follow this."

"It's not very complicated," whispered Lily. "They just try to get the ball away from each other and make goals."

"I know that much, Miss Lily."

Lily shielded her gaze with her hand so she could concentrate on her father. He seemed to be everywhere at once, riding hard, his mallet swinging and hitting and tangling with other mallets—and then he'd thunder off in another direction . . .

"Boeker's in good form," she heard some man say. "He's rattling them already."

"If he can keep it up."

Suddenly, Daddy's strike had lifted the ball so that it rose and rose like a white bird and seemed to soar between the goal posts.

"Glorious," someone said, "a sixty-yard penalty hit."

There was applause.

The riding and hitting began again, and it was sometimes hard to pick him out when they all closed in—there was another man always fighting him. Probably that man Thomas had mentioned, she thought.

"That's a good pony Boeker's got," the same man observed.

"But Vicini's is faster."

Lily squinted, trying to follow what they meant. To her, it

seemed that Daddy was the star player, as if a spotlight of sun were picking him out.

Now—all the sweating ponies were turning and trotting off the ground. "That's one chukker," she explained to Maudie.

Then the players came out again, Daddy on a chestnut pony this time, his new one, and it backed as it came, as if furious. She saw the nonchalant way Daddy gave to it, shook his wrist to tighten the loop of his mallet for a better hold.

"He's got trouble with that pony," the man in front of her said.

"He says it hates going out on the field, but then moves perfectly."

"I hope so."

Lily did not want to hear their comments—she wanted to see Daddy with her own eyes. She wasn't angry with him any more —she was proud. Everything would be all right between them, she was sure, even the "urgent" thing he wanted to "do about" her . . .

How adorable the eight ponies were, with their ears cocked towards the sideline as one umpire cantered out beyond them on to the ground, and the other calmly towards them, groping for a ball in the pockets of his saddle . . .

There was a great confusion. The ponies galloped hard this way and that about the field, their riders following formations that Lily did not really understand . . .

"I still say that's a hard-pulling pony of Boeker's."

"Afraid you're right."

She saw Daddy moving forward in his saddle, his gloved hand go to the mane of the glistening-wet pony and pat it . . .

Then he was hitting, turning after to race at full speed back the way he had come, his mallet ready to swing again, his body forward in the saddle . . .

Suddenly the man, Vicini, was cutting straight across his path, mallet swinging . . .

"Dear God!"

The entire crowd was on its feet.

Lily put her fists to her mouth, and Maudie moved close to her side as the chestnut pony tripped full force, went down, the rider hurtling through the air, the pony rolling over and over on the ground . . .

A shocked gasp went through the spectators.

Lily couldn't see what was happening now. She jumped up, tried to push her way through, but no one moved to let her—it was as if the whole world was standing completely still.

"Bad—rolled right on top of him—nothing he could do."

Lily heard her mother screaming without control.

People's voices began to break the momentary hush, and a man pushed through to where Aunt Mirry and Freddie were holding Mummy . . .

She heard what he said, plainly . . .

"It's serious, Mrs. Boeker, Mrs. Dundell . . . He's . . ." The man couldn't say the word.

They held Mummy closer, Aunt Mirry and Freddie, as her sobbing got louder and louder above the quiet voices.

Everyone moved forward to watch the doctors who had come running out . . .

"The ambulance is on its way," a man called.

Lily pushed, struggled through the crowd. No one seemed to notice her—only Maudie, who tried to hold her back, and kept repeating, "It's no good, dear—don't. You don't want to see him like that."

Lily didn't listen—and finally she broke from her and got to where he lay . . .

She didn't feel the strong arm holding her back. All she knew was that Daddy looked strange and terrible, his big, sprawled body half turned, bent, awkward—and that his wide-open eyes seemed to be looking right into hers, saying something . . .

Chapter 3

Freddie Osborne did not see Lily, in a white tennis dress, push open the doors to the big, glass-domed garden room and come quickly across to him, her shoulders back, her eyes like blue ice.

Wearing crash-linen trousers, a white silk shirt with a mono-grammed pocket, his black straight hair brushed smoothly back, he lolled in the deep cushions of a large wicker chaise longue, cigarette in hand, gin rickey beside him, an amused expression on his sun-darkened, high-boned face at what he was hearing in the radio earphones.

When he did see her, he took off the earphones and looked up with a slow, delighted smile, his lids half covering his eyes. "Hello, Lily pet," he said, reaching for her hand.

Lily jerked her hand behind her. "You have no *right* to fire Thomas. Daddy hired him to look after me—and only Mummy could do that."

"Mummy?" Freddie laughed happily. "Here." He patted the gilded bamboo loveseat next to him. "Let's try to understand

each other. Unlike your daddy, I've got all the time in the world
for you."

Lily kept standing. Her cheeks were bright pink. "Daddy
looked after us, and worked, too," she said.

"Better sit," he said, looking at her steadily.

Although he smiled, his tone compelled her to obey him.

"Look here—my lovely girl." He put a hand on her slender,
bare knee. "I've given you every chance to be—well, at least civil
to me. If you won't, then I'll have to make you. See?"

Lily put her legs under her, covered her knees. "If you fire
Thomas I won't stay here. I've got my own money." Her chin rose.
"I can do anything I want."

His smile broadened. "Is that so? Well. However—you're not
sixteen yet, baby—you're a *minor*." He pressed her knee again, as
if in emphasis, and let his hand rest on it. "Ah, come on, Lily pet,
be intelligent. Let's make this trip *fun*. The house is going to be
a wow, Venice in miniature—and you can give me—us—ideas for
redoing the yacht. How about it?"

His hand sent strange, unpleasant alarms up through her insides, and she pulled away from it. "I'm *not* coming to Palm
Beach," she said. "It's the wrong time of year—I've got my
schoolwork to do."

Freddie drew on his cigarette, his gaze passing slowly from
her shielded knees up to her slim body, to her flattened but still
perceptible breasts, to the bare smooth V of her throat, to her
mouth . . . "Oh, about that," he said, "your dear tutor's taking
leave of you, off to the cafés of Montparnasse and 'intellectual
freedom.'"

Lily tried not to show her shock. ("They're *all* ships that pass
in the night—only an idiot cries for servants," Andy said. And
Mr. Gilston was only a bald, skinny little man who nagged her to
study. Still—there had been those nice times when he didn't,
when he talked with her as if she were his grown-up friend
about "Imagistes" and D. H. Lawrence.)

"Well—I want to go to school, anyway," she said, shaking back
her pale, shiny bob.

"We won't get onto that again. Ah, come on, Lily pet—don't
be blue. I'll make you a whiz at bridge and the Charleston—with
your other accomplishments, it will be more than enough!" He

looped his thumb and forefinger around her ankle, and slid it slowly up her slim, freckled leg, keeping his smile.

Lily jumped up so abruptly that the earphones slid off his knees to the floor. "I'm going to tell Thomas he's staying," she said, starting quickly for the door, "and talk to Mummy about school, definitely."

"It won't get you far," he called, his voice smoothly patient. "And I will see that difference in you, won't I, Lily? By the time we leave tomorrow?"

Lily didn't answer. As she reached for the door handle, she felt almost sick with hate, wanted to rush and hit him with all her strength—but in her dreams, when she did that, beat on him with her fists, it never hurt him, there was never any force in her arms and he only stood there with that one-sided smile—and then he would start touching her body in that soft, sliding way.

"I won't be going with you," said Lily, opening the door, closing it sharply behind her.

Mummy would *have* to see this time, *have* to believe her, she thought as she started up the wide stairs three at a time—no matter what!

The big pale-blue room, with its French brocade draperies and satin bed, was filled with maids in black-and-white uniforms packing the large wardrobe trunks that stood open everywhere. She hardly knew any of Mummy's personal maids now. Even Mrs. Jennings, who had run the house for Mummy and Daddy so many years, and the nicest secretary, Miss Watt, hadn't been able to stand Freddie's bossiness, the way he questioned and interfered with everything they did. They'd been sorry to leave Mummy with him, but there was nothing they could do for her nowadays, either . . .

"Your mother's in the sitting room, dear," one of the new maids said. "Feeling better," she added meaningfully.

Lily pretended not to understand. "Thank you," she said, smiling, and went past the great piles of beautiful Paris models, the silk and satin underwear, the lines of shoes (so many of them never worn) fitted together for packing, the big stacks of pretty hat boxes, the fur coats and capes and velvet and brocade evening wraps, the trays of silver and gold compacts, French perfume bottles, dozens unopened . . .

"She leaves the jewelry in the safe till the guards come," said one maid to another. "She only wants the small pearl-and-emerald rope and the emerald bracelet and earrings for tonight—if she goes!"

Lily looked questioningly into the sitting room beyond.

Beth sat in an armchair beside the telephone, her hand resting on the receiver. Even in the low-waisted striped sports dress with the wide collar and necktie, her figure looked spread and floppy, and when she turned and Lily saw her blotchy, white-powdered face, her bloodshot eyes without mascara looking naked and forlorn, it made her want to cry.

"Darling," Beth called, in the voice that was so husky it wheezed, "come here—quickly!"

By her gesture, Lily understood she was to sit at her feet, as she had since she was small when they had time together.

"No—close the door first." Beth pointed, then put the finger dramatically to her lips.

Yes, she was "better," thought Lily—more sober than usual. But when she settled close to her, she could feel her shaking body right through to her own, and when her mother's arms went around her, and her cheek was pressed to hers, the quickness of her breathing was like small sobs.

"Sugar, listen—you've got to help me, help your mummy. Freddie won't let me have—anything—you know. He's ordered the servants not to give it to me—and they won't—they're too scared, even old Nobby. Now, look—I'll tell you where some is. I know how you can get it."

"Mummy!" Lily grasped her hands, as if *she* were the mother. "How can *I* give you that stuff!"

"I know." Her eyes were sad, apologetic. "But, baby, you're my only hope. You can stand up to him—you're not afraid. And I only want *one* bottle, one teensy bottle." She tried to make her face pretty and appealing in its old way, but to Lily it was so ugly and pitiful she had to look away.

"The doctor said you could still be cured, Mummy, if you'd really try." She looked up at her, her large light eyes bright with zeal. "Mummy, listen—you're all right now. Couldn't you just *stay* like this, keep on? We could go off by ourselves somewhere —take a nice sea voyage, or go to some lovely island. You'd get strong and forget all about—I mean be your old self again. Oh, Mummy—it would be so *wonderful!*"

Beth was still, her eyes held to Lily's, her mouth slack. After a moment, she let go of Lily, sighed heavily and pushed at her graying brown curls with her palms. "Oh, dear God," she said.

Lily started to say something, then stopped. It was as if a thick veil hung between them—they could *see* through it, but that was all. She held her mother's hand to her cheek like a denial.

"Poor baby." The lavender blue of Beth's eyes was a washed-out gray. She wet her lips slowly. "But just this once more. I can't stand it, you see, darling. It's too sudden. He's always given me all I want—never scolded or lectured like Daddy and everybody else."

"That's true." Lily looked at her searchingly. "Why not any more?"

Beth was still. After a moment she opened her eyes and tried to give a bland, casual smile. "For my good, of course, baby. So I can be . . . Attractive again. A wife to him." Her smile became tentative, false.

"Mummy—what is it, really? What does he want *now?*"

"Lily! Sssh!" Shuddering, Beth looked around. "I wish you wouldn't say things like that, in such a loud voice."

"I don't care. You shouldn't have married him, and you shouldn't let him spend all your money. You've *got* to listen to me, Mummy—he's *terrible!*"

Beth closed her eyes and grimaced. "You're not going to start all that again, darling—I can't *stand* it. I think you wanted me to stay alone and go on grieving for Daddy the rest of my life. You don't understand that I'm still a young woman, that I love Freddie!"

"How *could* you!" Lily took her hands and shook them. "Do you know what, Mummy—he gets funny with *me*—like that . . ."

"Mmmm?" Beth's forehead creased as she tried to focus the significance in Lily's tone. "Funny?"

"Yes, Mummy. Honestly. He follows me around, everywhere, like into the cabana when he knows I'm getting out of my bathing suit—and he comes in swimming with me and kind of presses close, and when I dance, he . . ."

Beth expelled a deep shaken breath. "Oh, sugar, my head aches so!" She closed her eyes, a pained smile on her mouth.

"Mummy, Mummy, Mummy!" Lily shook Beth's hands hard against her lap. "Stop looking like that—you've *got* to think about this! I'm not a child any more—I know what I'm saying. He's always after me, touching me, putting his hands on me—and he knows that I know and that I can't do anything about it, or get away!"

"Baby—don't try to frighten me. I know Freddie's fond of you —he *loves* you. And he's trying to take an interest in your—"

"Damn!" said Lily, releasing her hands, and sitting back.

"Lily—that's not nice language for a young girl."

Lily folded her arms. "You've *got* to send me away to school," she said. "I won't live here. Not with him."

Beth stared. Slowly, her face seemed to crumple, as if it were made of soft rubber. Tears welled and flowed from her bleak eyes. "What am I going to do?" she said huskily. "Get me a drink, baby—just so I can pull myself together."

"Do you know what he did because I wouldn't be nicer to him —fired Thomas! And—he says he'll fire Maudie!"

Beth shook her head slowly. The tears kept coming. "Sugar," she said suddenly, leaning forward. "You know that new maid, Lorna? Maybe she'd do it. Please—you ask her?"

Lily stood up. "No," she said. "You do it yourself, Mummy—if you have to. But you should be ashamed."

"Lily—you're so *hard*—so young. Don't you see I *am* ashamed?"

Lily hesitated before walking away. For a moment she was immobile with confusion. "I don't know . . . Oh, if only Daddy were here—or *someone!*"

Beth was still. The pallor under her mottled face seemed to gray as she gazed miserably into Lily's eyes. "All right," she said, the huskiness squeezed to a near-whisper. "Go tell Freddie I will —I'll do it."

Lily's head tilted slowly. "What, Mummy—you'll do *what?*"

Beth shook her head, looked down at her inert hands, was silent.

"Tell me, Mummy—you must tell me what it is."

Beth shook her head again. "Just say all right. He'll bring me something then."

The sight of her mother sitting beaten, with no pride left, gave her a sharp sense of desolation, tinged with fear.

"Oh, well—you might as well know," Beth said abruptly. "It's my will—he wants it all left to him."

"You'd do *that*, Mummy?" Lily asked with a quick intake of breath.

Beth barely nodded.

"Mummy." Lily went over to her, knelt, took her by the shoulders. "You mustn't," she said. "I won't let you."

"But it's mine—not for you to say."

"If I did get that bottle—this time, *just* this time . . ."

Beth's gaze caught to hers, as if facing a bright glare. Then she closed her eyes and shook her head slowly from side to side. "No—it wouldn't be just this time, baby. You were right."

Lily waited a moment, but when Beth didn't look up, she sighed, got to her feet and went slowly from the room.

The maids were still busily folding and wrapping, but she passed them without a word.

Freddie was no longer in the garden room. She went about the house looking for him, then caught sight of him out on the driveway. He was, she discovered, as she listened from the steps, taking delivery of his new Duesenberg.

"The gold basketwork turned out well, sir," the man who had brought it was saying, "and that West of England upholstery's real elegant."

Freddie, standing with hands on hips, nodded. "It is a humdinger, isn't it? It's the length—puts other cars in the shade."

"You won't see many like it, I guarantee."

"That's the idea."

Lily saw the way they looked at each other, slyly.

"You understand about the bill, Joe?"

"Yes—there won't be any question?"

"None." Freddie's smile was all long teeth, as he shook hands with the man. "Thanks."

"Thank you, sir—anytime. We can always work *something*."

The man grinned again, then walked over to a cream-and-green Nash with another man behind the wheel.

Freddie waved as they drove off, then slid into his long, low, gleaming blue machine and studied the powerful-looking dashboard absorbedly, unaware of Lily or the gardeners and chauffeurs watching him.

Lily went up to the car—not too close. "Freddie," she said, in a terse, cold tone, "Mummy says all right—she'll do it."

Freddie looked up with his immediate, knowing smile, his intense gaze. "Aha—well well. Thanks, Lily pet." He reached out and placed his hand on her hipbone before she could back off. "Hop in, my lovely, I'll take you for a fast spin—that's what you like, isn't it?"

She eluded his grasp at her elbow, and backed out of reach. "I'm going to tell Coggy," she said. "He has charge of things like that—he won't let you have it. And—I'm going away to school. It's settled."

Freddie stared a moment, then broke into laughter. "Just stop and think about that," he called out as she moved off. "Get it all thought out, Lily pet. Only don't forget anything—know what I mean?"

"Well, Lily pet," Freddie said when they were seated in the private Pullman car and on their way, "what do you two think of the new name I've given it—Befred?" He gestured expansively around the long, rosewood-paneled observation salon, sat back in the big floral-plush armchair under the whirring fan, gave her a frankly taunting smile.

Beth lifted her glass, smiling worshipfully at him. "I'll drink to that, Freddie boy. I think it's the cat's meow."

Freddie looked past her without acknowledgment, to where Lily sat reading a *Saturday Evening Post*.

"Lily?" he insisted.

"Answer Freddie, sugar," said Beth. Her heavily mascaraed eyes lost some of their jollity, widened in furtive message under the brim of her pink straw cloche.

"Everyone knows its real name is Bedick," said Lily without looking up.

"Lily! Don't be fresh!" Beth sat up anxiously.

Freddie motioned her to be still. "That's all right—let her have her say. She's old enough to have her opinions, aren't you, Lily pet?" Freddie threw his straw boater onto the opposite seat, took off the jacket of his light-gray suit, removed his striped bow tie

and resettled in a position for a better view of Lily's long thin
legs, pressed tightly together and dead straight in front of her.

"*Don't* call me Lily pet," said Lily. "I *despise* it!"

In answer, Freddie took a pink carnation out of the gold vase
affixed to the wall, threw it onto her lap.

Beth giggled. "Laugh, sugar," she said to Lily. "Come on,
have some champagne instead of that gooey lemonade."

Lily ignored the carnation, and her mother. She didn't want to
look up, to see her flushed, bloated face, her dark crimson lipstick like two blobs of melting grease on her small, bowed
mouth, or to catch that horrible, meaningful stare Freddie was
certain to have. She could feel it—and the nasty tingling went
right up between her legs, like the time she had seen a mouse
and had to jump on a table and clamp her thighs together. But
whatever happened, he mustn't see she'd grown afraid of him.
He even liked her rudeness—she'd come to understand that—but
it could go too far, then for sure that would be the end of
Thomas and Maudie.

"Want a refill, baby?" he was saying to Beth.

"Mmm!" Beth lurched over to him, and Lily caught a glimpse of
her kissing him long and hard on the mouth.

"Go sit down, precious," Freddie said to her, pressing her
away, and pushing a mother-of-pearl button on a panel above
his head. "Seems strange to be going in August—it'll be hotter
than Hades in the swamps. But never mind—if Zordan cottons to
the plans, we'll have our Venetian palace by next year, water-
ways and all."

"You're a whiz, big boy. Who'd have thought of gondolas—by
the hundreds—in little old Palm Beach!"

"We'll have more champagne, Harry," Freddie said to the servant who came in, "and some pâté. Got any worth having?"

"Yes, sir—the best," said the Negro servant in the short white
jacket and braided "Boeker blue" trousers.

"I want caviar, sugar," said Beth, pouting. "I don't like pâté."

"All right." Freddie nodded at the man. "Both."

"Cookies, Miss Lily?"

"Good Lord, no—she's not a little girl, Harry. She'll have what
we have. Won't you, Lily pet?"

Lily looked up briefly. "I'll have some Fig Newtons, please, Harry."

He smiled, nodded, hurried off.

"That was rude," said Beth. She reached over and shook Lily's arm. "Why don't you put that book down and talk to us, anyhow?"

Lily could smell the familiar odor that always hung around her, more pungent than ever in the humid fanned air. "I'm reading a good story by Booth Tarkington," she said, turning her face away.

"She's a bookworm, Freddie—don't let's pay any attention to her."

Lily knew he was staring. She wished she hadn't worn the skirt with the tiny pleats that wouldn't stay down around her knees. As she read, she kept the magazine **up** across her front, another place he was always looking.

"Come and help me do this crossword puzzle, Lily pet," he said.

She shook her head.

"Then how about a bridge lesson?"

"Give *me* a lesson, sugar. I've got to improve my contract bridge—no one wants to play with me any more." Beth giggled, got up, sat down heavily on his knees.

Harry came in with another servant, and the two of them laid food out on a lace-cloth-covered table, poured champagne from the new bottle, then withdrew.

Lily heard Beth's laughter grow gradually louder, and Freddie's jokes coarser. She knew, and dreaded the look he would have when Mummy couldn't tell what was going on any more, as if she shared something secret with him.

She got up quickly and went into the lounge. Sitting in a wide-armed, leather-seated chair, she stared into the countryside until it became light-dotted silhouettes of trees, hills and houses —into a world totally removed from her knowledge.

What was to happen to her—what was *her* world to be? Her lips pressed in resistance to bewilderment, to apprehension . . .

She got up and went forward to the modernistic bathroom Freddie had had installed with its geometric (hideous, she thought), black, white and purple fittings and tried to cool off.

She splashed quelque-fleurs cologne on her face and let the fan dry it, then undid her blouse and sprinkled talcum powder under the square collar and on her neck.

There was a pounding on the door. "Let me in, sugar!" she heard her mother call.

Lily opened the door, and Beth swayed inward. "Got to pee-pee." She smiled impishly, beginning to lift her crushed pink linen dress as she plunged towards the enclosed toilet.

Lily felt slightly giddy, as if the lurching train had left the track and bounced her into space.

"I love you, baby," Beth called, "and I love Freddie—and I want us all to all three love each other—so you be nice. No mean face. Spoils your beauty. Gonna be a beautiful woman, sweetheart—know that? Only you got to smile. Freddie wants to make you happy—that's why he keeps after you, baby. See? Unnerstand?"

"Yes, Mummy." Lily went out and closed the door.

As she stepped into the passageway, she looked back to the car where some of the servants sat. They had a Victrola playing and they talked or shuffled cards. She saw Maudie, off by herself, her bobbing netted head turned to the dark countryside; her familiar face like a small island of safety. She wanted to go in, be with her, and all her friends there . . .

Slowly, reluctantly, she went the other way, through the jerking, swerving cars back to the salon. Dinner was about to be served. A centerpiece of sweetheart roses had been placed on the table, along with crystal candlesticks and glasses and silver-embossed china.

The servant, Harry, and Freddie were discussing the Pullman, how it was costing another thirty thousand for overhauling of draft gear and brake rigging—and another fifty thousand for the new decor Freddie wanted. The maids, and the new butler Freddie had brought along, were hovering with silver-domed serving dishes.

"Ah, there you are, Lily pet!" Freddie grinned with welcome. The lock of straight hair fallen low across his forehead, the high flush in his face made him seem wilder, less a "gentleman."

Lily took the opposite chair, and felt the immediate pressure of his knees. She drew her own back with a jerk. "If you do that again, I'll leave," she said, her eyes a sudden blaze of vivid blue.

"What?" he asked. "My, you're a snooty one—all ready to fight your poor loving stepfather!"

Beth came in smiling, her hair brushed up unevenly with water, powder spilled over the front of her dress, and with the soft, vague look that couldn't quite focus where she was. She missed the chair Harry held, and he slid her gently back to it by the elbow.

Freddie laughed, then nodded to Harry. "This isn't a bad menu under the circumstances, but we should have a more European cuisine. Let's hire a top chef—someone experienced with royalty."

"Yes, sir—right, sir," said Harry, and nodded to the new butler.

"I'm not hungry, Freddie boy," said Beth, smiling up at him, her head lolling back. "I'd like something to drink, more champagne."

Harry looked at Freddie, and Freddie nodded. Her glass was refilled, and Beth toasted them all before she drank the liquid in long, practiced gulps.

Lily watched her helplessly. "Why do you do that," she asked suddenly, "keep making her drunk?"

Freddie and Beth looked at each other in wide-eyed surprise, then broke into mutual laughter.

"He doesn't *make* me, darling silly—he *lets* me—isn't that right, big boy?" She bent over to kiss him.

Freddie pushed her away. "You've got the wrong idea," he said to Lily with his one-sided, mocking smile. "I just want everyone to have a good time."

"Hear, hear!" said Beth—and suddenly slipped off her chair to the floor.

Lily moved back, not trying to compete with the rush of assistance.

Freddie beckoned to one of the maids in attendance. "I think Mrs. Osborne would like to go to bed," he said.

The small, gray-haired maid nodded.

Lily watched her mother borne off between two pairs of arms, her head hanging limply, her feet barely stumbling along.

"She was very tired to begin with," Freddie said to Lily. "And this weather . . ."

Lily got up, turned and walked abruptly from the car.

She went to her own sleeping room this time, and drawing the heavy green baize curtains across it, she stood still, afraid he might follow even here. The fans only stirred the enclosed heat, and in sudden total exhaustion, she lay down on the bed in her clothes.

The next thing she knew, Maudie was shaking her gently and holding out her nightgown. "It's after ten," she said. "Better get properly in bed. Here, I'll take that dress—you can wear the green or blue shantung tomorrow."

Lily stared sleepily, her mind hazy, her throat parched. "I'm thirsty," she said, "it's so *stuffy*."

"It's a terribly hot night." Maudie got water from a bottle on the little built-in dresser and poured it in a glass.

"Thanks." As she gulped down the water, Lily looked at Maudie's heat-drawn face, the red hair plastered to the forehead under her flattened net, and took her hand. "Do you wish you didn't have to be with me any more, Maudie?" she asked.

Maudie raised her brows over her glasses. "Now, now. None of that. We won't bother the maids—give me your undies, dear."

"I could easily learn to look after myself, you know—learn where everything was, and how to care for my clothes."

"Then what would *I* have to do?" Maudie gave Lily's chin a little squeeze, gathered up her discarded clothes and said, "Sleep tight—"

Lily smiled after the door had closed. Every single night she said that. Going to bed wouldn't be the same without it.

She turned off the light and stretched out on the bed. She felt better. It was even good to be rolling along the tracks in the dark, feeling the rumbling wheels under her, watching the black, mysterious shapes of the countryside move so quickly past. She only wished Maudie was nearer, not at the other end of the cars. Still, at least she was somewhere on the train . . .

Becoming sleepy again, she drew the fringed blinds together so that she wouldn't be seen from the platform in the morning, and settled her head into the comfortable soft linen pillow . . .

Suddenly Maudie was back. Lily heard the curtains "whoosh" softly across their runners as she tiptoed in.

"Maudie," she whispered drowsily, to let her know she was still awake.

"No. It's me."

Lily's lids shot upwards. She sat up quickly. "What do *you* want?" She pulled the sheet quickly up to her chin, shrinking back as Freddie sat heavily on the bed beside her.

"I want to talk to you, Lily—don't be afraid," he said. "I just want to *talk* to you."

Lily held her breath. Her heartbeat was louder than the wheels.

"Lily—listen to me. I want to love you. Is that so terrible—is that such a crime?"

In the darkness, she saw the paleness of his pajamas, the white parts of his eyes, the wide line of his teeth. She didn't move.

He bent closer, and she could smell the toothpaste he'd used, the hair tonic, his perspiration. "Why won't you let me? I'd do anything for you, my lovely girl—*anything!*"

She felt his hand on her cheek. "You're so pretty, so soft and slender—like a soft boy with a girl's face. But a real girl—young, sweet, tender." His taunting voice was gone. He spoke thickly, breathing hard.

"Go away," Lily said. "Go away!" She barely contained a wild scream.

"I will—I will." His hand slid gently over her cheek, down her neck. "Just let me sit here a minute, just a minute. I only want to be with you awhile without all those prying eyes. We're always surrounded, Lily—we can't get to *know* each other."

"Please—go away," Lily said. "You're frightening me." Her heartbeat was like small thunder now, hard in her head.

"Ah—don't be frightened." He rested a hand reassuringly on her shoulder a moment. "I want to love you—and you want love —so *badly* you want it. We need each other, don't you see—so much!"

Lily could hear *his* heart now, hard and heavy, like a hollow drumbeat.

His hand began to slide downward again—was suddenly on her breast. "Ah—you haven't got them flattened—oh God!"

Before she could switch from his grasp, his hands were pressing and kneading her breasts, moving down over her flat, bare stomach, pushing up her nightgown with great powerful movements, while he gasped and groaned.

"Oh, beautiful—soft little thing, lovely little thing . . . I knew it . . . Touch me, hold me!" He grabbed her hand, pressed it tightly against something low on his stomach . . .

The stone-hard length of it shot stark terror through her.

"Don't, don't struggle, don't. I want to kiss you all over and put that inside you, darling girl . . . Oh, let me suck those darling nipples, those soft little tits . . ."

Lily let out a shrill scream at the top of her voice, and another, and though she was pinned down, kicked and pushed furiously with her knees.

"Don't, don't—" He threw himself full-weight on top of her, and holding her shoulders down with one arm, tried to insert himself between her writhing, resistant legs.

"Maudie! Maudie!" she screamed again and again, but the sound of the wheels half muted its shrillness, and he brought his mouth down on hers, pushing his tongue hard between her lips.

"Give in," he said, raising his head an instant, and covering her mouth with his hand. "I've seen you shudder—I know you'll like it . . ." His hands were rougher now, pinching and pressing with abandoned force. "Open up, open . . . or I'll tear you apart . . ."

Another scream came from her, so hoarse and piercing that it seemed to shrill like a siren about the small closed space.

He gave her a hard slap across the face. "Damn you, damn you . . ." he muttered, shaking her back against the bed.

Suddenly the curtains jerked back. A figure pushed in. The rose-colored lights went on.

"I thought I heard a . . . What on earth . . . Oh—dear Lord!"

There was a moment of absolute silence, except for the whistle of the train as it rushed heedlessly on through the night.

Freddie groaned, raised himself heavily, shook his head as if emerging from the sea, then reached to pull up his pajamas.

Beth stood there, watching him, her face a soggy gray-white, her violet eyes dilated with stunned sobriety. Then she turned to look at Lily, and her mouth moved as if to speak, but instead hung loose, without sound.

Lily covered herself, shook back her pale, disheveled hair, drew a long, shaken breath. With tears in her eyes, she met her mother's gaze—squarely.

Chapter 4

"My dear girl, will you please read the clipping, and come and pay attention." Miriam Dundell Hower Court's voice, as she called from the large desk across the immense Regency Period room, was unusually impatient. "After all, this is *your* debut, not ours."

At these words, both her secretary and her secretary's assistant looked up with veiled interest from their separate desks and chores.

Lily knew she owed much too much to her aunt to be as resistant as she wanted to be, more than ever today. "That's not really the truth," she said, not daring to turn from the bay window of Aunt Mirry's third floor where she peered down onto Fifth Avenue, hoping to see Thomas pull up to the curb with Whitey.

"Well—I see. Then whose is it?"

Lily did not answer—how frozen people looked, their heads down, their shoulders hunched as they scurried across the avenue, or stamped their feet waiting on corners. Not to have warm clothing, furs, money for furs . . .

Her aunt's voice rang out again. "Lily—you've been most unpleasant ever since that girl accepted your invitation."

"Her name is Pamela White, Aunt Mirry, my best friend. You couldn't say I graduated from Fairglades if it wasn't for her."

"I've never spoken a word against the child—Pamela. I'm sure she's very nice, and I admire your loyalty. But I hardly think she would expect an entire household to pause for her arrival."

"She was the most well-thought-of girl in the school, Aunt Mirry, even if she was on scholarship, and *wasn't* in the Social Register. In fact—no one seems to remember that I'm not, either. Only the snobby girls at school were—they never stopped reminding me, after I arrived with eight trunks, two chauffeurs and a governess and maids . . ."

"That was a mistake of your mother's, dear girl, not mine. Now, let's have no more of this. The trains from New England are obviously delayed. Simms will announce her as soon as she arrives."

Lily still didn't turn. Her jaw set with the anger that sometimes went through her without warning. "I'd like to meet her—in the hall. I asked Oliver to get me."

"All right, all right, I haven't got all day to give to the matter. Something that you *well* know. Now—the clipping."

The reminder of her aunt's dinner party for thirty people brought Lily back to control. Grudgingly she turned from the window, looked at the paper in her hand, the clipped and annotated society page, with the column by that awful Reggie Blount.

"*Beautiful Boeker heiress,*" she read again, "(*that's the dry-goods dynasty, of course), to debut December 30th at the Ritz-Ambrose with four orchestras and fifteen hundred guests, to the tune of $75,000. 'We have avoided extravagance in deference to the times,' says Miriam Dundell Hower Court, who is presenting her niece in lieu of her mother, Mrs. Frederick Dundell Osborne (prevented from participation due to a long-standing illness).*"

Naturally, then, he had to go on and tell, as they all did, *every* single time they mentioned her, that she would come into $200,000,000 and the whole story again of how Grandpa had started as a peddler and gone on to build up an "empire" of department stores that not only covered the nation, but were now extending into other countries, and on and on about the Long Island mansion, the Palm Beach "palace," the Fifth Avenue mansion (Aunt Mirry's and hers), "which is kept fully staffed, though seldom used," the yacht, "which is often anchored alongside her aunt's at Lake Worth," the amount of servants and crew, in "aggregate" several hundred, and all the other personal details they repeated so disgustingly, like their clothes and what they spent on them, their jewels, cars, collections and treasures— to say nothing of her aunt's fortune and how it had "accrued," and the "feud" between herself and her stepfather. (*"The independent-minded girl refused to accept a replacement for her beloved father, and simply left home, leaving her mother torn between the two, and her aunt the difficult role of assuming guardianship."*)

"That frown spoils your beauty," Aunt Mirry was saying. "And by the way, I was misquoted there. I didn't say I was avoiding extravagance. That was Reggie's way of offsetting criticism. Well-intended, but unnecessary."

Lily stared a moment. There was actually a pleased glint in her aunt's eyes. She walked over and threw the clipping on her desk. "It's all so crummy," she said.

The two other women cast a quick look at her aunt, but Lily went on.

"If what you and Coggy and your banker friends say is true, that the worst is over, that the nation will soon be back on its feet just as President Hoover says—then why are there more unemployed instead of less, more factories closing down, more banks failing every day, more stocks collapsing and ruining people, more and longer breadlines, more pitiful people selling apples, more terrible suicides!"

Miriam was not disconcerted. "Even so—what good could it possibly do anyone for *us* to economize, dear girl!"

Lily made another vow to herself to know more about the mathematics of her money. The only answer she could make

would, as usual, be considered "naïve." "It's just so unfeeling, so
. . . callous." She blinked at the strong word, not entirely without fear, even at this age, of the magnificent, commanding
woman before her. "How would *you* like it, Aunt Mirry, if you
lived in a cold-water apartment and had nothing to eat!"

The other women dissembled a sudden busyness with envelopes and letters.

Miriam's smile was a study of tempered wisdom and humor.
"I wouldn't. But I don't. And no one would benefit from my
guilt. Nor will they from your idealism, my darling. You'll have
to come to grips with your position—the sooner, the better, for
your own sake. Because, whether you like it or not, it's unique.
Your whole life will be lived in public. And if you don't learn to
cope, you'll be run to the ground—by the press, by anyone with a
grain of envy—which, truth to tell, is just about everybody. People only complain about those with money until they have it
themselves. Then they don't give it away, they hang on to it."

"You've said all this before, Aunt Mirry."

"Apparently it bears repetition."

"Oh, Aunt Mirry—you know I'm never going to accept it, ever.
It just won't be like that at all when I live on my own."

"Let's talk about that a moment." Miriam looked at the mahogany clock on the marble mantel. "I'm afraid we've wasted
the time allotted for your debut plans. Anyway, just what *will*
you do, apart from moving into the Boeker house—which I've
only agreed to as long as you have it suitably altered and take
the staff and bodyguards I insist upon."

"I've told you, Aunt Mirry. I'll work. I'm perfectly capable of
earning a living."

Miriam pressed a hairpin firmly into the back of the thick coil
of hair she still wore tightly braided about her head, while she
overcame amusement. "At *what*, for instance, darling?"

Lily was amazed. For the first time in her life, her aunt
seemed less than formidable, less than unconquerable. Why,
Aunt Mirry was actually helpless, she thought, utterly dependent
on her inheritance! All she really had was the gift of imagination
in spending it! "Well, for one thing, I can *dance*." Her chin
lifted. There was nothing but pride in her face now, because if

there was anything she was sure of, it was that she could dance as well as anyone she'd ever seen perform.

"All right. You do dance reasonably well. But *where* would you dance, child? In a musical show? A speakeasy? One of those modern dance troupes? And who do you think would employ a girl who could buy the entire theater in which she worked? And what do you think girls who need their salaries to survive would feel about your—*experimenting* with hardship?"

"But you don't see! I wouldn't *have* the money. I wouldn't *be* rich!" Lily threw out her arms, swung and took a few steps away from the desk, then back, her bias-cut black dress with the white collar and cuffs moving gracefully on her slim, maturing figure, a light cloud of Fleur de Rocaille wafting from her, her light hair, fresh from the hands of Carlo the resident coiffeur, bouncing from its smooth backward sweep. "I'd have to work!"

There was a silence in the big room. Miriam tapped a gold tasseled pencil against the seating chart in front of her. From a distant area of the mansion, the clock-winding man could be heard on his weekly round, adjusting chimes. A tap at the door interrupted whatever Miriam had been considering in her mind to say.

"It's General Court's coat from Revillon, madam," a butler was saying. "He wonders if you would like to look over the mink lining."

"Yes, indeed I would."

Lily watched as they all inspected Uncle Will's birthday present, Aunt Mirry running her expert eye over the rich brown skins inside the heavy black coat. "Nice," she said. "As good as my new one." She turned to Lily. "Would you like a cape or coat made up in these quite superior skins, my dear?"

Lily shook her head. "I don't really like mink—and I've got too many furs, Aunt Mirry. Thanks, anyway."

Aunt Mirry nodded. "All right, Bertrand, give it to the General's valet to keep out of sight. Where is the General, by the way?"

"With the wine men, madam, decanting."

They smiled at each other.

"My husband's lost all trust," she explained to the two women, "since someone put Madeira chains on the Port decanters. I can only pray he doesn't use his *fouet* on the Moët et Chandon.

Without its bubbles, it tastes like very poor Chablis. Hard to explain to guests without ulcers."

Everyone laughed.

Bertrand withdrew, and Miriam returned briskly to her desk. "Now, Lily," she said, "have you studied this chart as I asked?"

Lily sighed, but it wasn't noted. "Yes, Aunt Mirry."

"And could you now achieve the same results with a similar guest list? Did you note the positioning of Ambassador McKinley?"

"Yes."

"And did you know it was because he was a former ambassador?"

Lily nodded.

"Good. These things are of the essence. You can sink or swim on your ability to seat the right people side by side."

"Doesn't it matter, Aunt Mirry, that Jean McKinley was responsible for my vile initiation at school, that she was . . . well, funny with girls, and if Whitey hadn't explained to Miss Blair I'd have been expelled?"

"It's in the past, child. I've put you next to him. You must make conversation with him about her—tell him you were fond of her. He's still a pivotal man in Fifth Avenue society, and important to us both just now."

Miriam picked up the chart. "All right, Mrs. Hamp—put the monetary requests and RSVP's aside, and concentrate on the debut. I'll talk to you sometime this afternoon. Come, Lily! She'll understand. This is instruction you can't afford to postpone any longer. Be glad of the opportunity."

With the set face of recurring anger and oncoming boredom, Lily followed her tall, regal figure from the room.

"Those who don't know more than their servants," her aunt said, as they rode downward in one of the gilt and mirror elevators, "soon lose them. How is the French coming along?"

Lily made a slight grimace. "Very *comme ci, comme ça*," she said.

The trace of levity was lost on Miriam's tightly programmed mind. "You must get to Europe at the first opportunity. Your lack of sophistication could be a calamity. Oh well, we've done our best to mend bridges."

Lily felt an old touch of childhood hypnosis with the masterful woman beside her. How beautifully she held herself, making even the fawn-silk morning dress seem grand. How she rustled and breathed her jeweled, scented superiority, as if in her life she had never held a doubt of it, even in sleep. Had she ever questioned her rightness, her absolute wisdom and authority? If so, it was impossible to imagine. What was it Andy said? "Money makes the opinion of a fool infallible." He'd made it up, he said. He could have, she thought, almost smiling.

Her aunt moved swiftly from the elevator. "You must watch again how the men go about preparing the table. Hurry, dear, I mustn't fall behind schedule."

Lily hid her reluctance from the four shirt-sleeved butlers in the vast, high-ceilinged, oak-paneled room, cast them the bright smile that came easily to her with servants, who always seemed more like her friends than those they served.

"Miss Lily wants to observe my method of setting again," Miriam said, bringing her forward by one heavily ringed hand.

The men paused to nod deferentially, to smile back at Lily.

"Carry on," Miriam said.

Lily folded her arms across her chest, and watched, feeling like a prisoner in chains.

The big, high-backed tapestried chairs had been pulled away from the long table, and a stage-type spotlight trained onto it. Two men had yardsticks and were measuring the overhang of the white Venetian lace tablecloth, to make sure, apparently, that it was the same length on all sides.

"Remember, dear, everything must be centered," Aunt Mirry said, her eyes keenly narrowed on the procedure. "And when the places are set, each dinner plate must be exactly sixteen inches from the other. Have you learned why?"

"I forget . . ."

"Well, you mustn't. It's the right amount of space for easy, smooth serving, of course. Then everything else on the table must be lined up, for the sake of absolute symmetry. The silver vases will be four feet tall, so that they don't block the view—the centerpiece low for the same reason, and very tall candles will intervene."

Miriam turned, glancing upwards with her narrowed gaze. "I

see the chandelier man's been at work—the crystal's sparkling the way it should again. What about the gilt service?"

"Being polished now, madam. Tunman had a problem with an incomplete set of dessert forks, which held him up—but they've been found and everything will be well on time."

"Tunman . . . Tunman? How long has he been my polisher?"

"It's his second year, madam—a very good man, if I may say so."

"Strange—I seldom overlook an employee. I'd probably know him on sight."

"Yes, madam. Would you like to check the menu and place cards while you're here?"

"I certainly would." Aunt Mirry took her glasses from a brocade case dangling from a gold chain on her belt, put them on, studied the menu, nodded and handed it back. Then she opened up the seating chart she had carried in under her arm.

Lily shifted weight from one foot to the other, barely stifling her yawns, or the agony of not being able to tell if Whitey had arrived. Engrossed by the spelling of stuffy old people's names, as if all of life depended on it, her aunt seemed satanic, and the immense, brilliantly lighted room, with the quietly moving butlers, the velvet and damask, the thick, richly woven carpet, the great mirrors and paintings of olden times and long-dead ancestors, was a torture chamber in which she would slowly smother to death.

"You can see how important it is to do your own checking, even with a top-flight social secretary! Imagine what a blunder that would have been—Judge Dawson next to Roy Mortimer the lawyer after that famous tangle in court!"

Lily gazed at her blankly. It won't be long, she thought. I shall do my own cooking, the way Whitey's mother did that wonderful Thanksgiving holiday. There'll just be Maudie—perhaps Thomas, because he'd be lost without me—but I'll go everywhere alone. Store people won't know who I am, and I'll be able to shop without any fuss. Waiters won't act like fawning goats, won't even notice me. I'll get the kind of service everyone gets, even if it's bad. I'll make my own bed, get to work on time like the maids do, and . . .

"Yes," said Aunt Mirry, pausing for a sudden, thoughtful gaze at her preoccupied niece, "those eyes will be famous."

"Oh, Aunt Mirry, *honestly*. May I go now?"

"Not just yet." She took her by the elbow commandingly. "I want you to look over the floral arrangements with me. You've never taken note of the fine points. I'm having American Beauty roses through the main salons, but I've left the table creations to Mrs. Koster. Never do this, dear, unless you have someone of her genius to rely on."

"Another day, Aunt Mirry—please. I forgot to tell Maudie where Whitey's sleeping . . ."

"What has Miss Maude to do with it?" The arched, blond-gray eyebrows rose high. "I've already ordered that the child be taken to the Delph suite by the maids who attend it."

Lily pushed at her hair, blew a breath. "Well, then—may I just go? Whitey's never been here, and it'll be so cold and ungracious not to . . ."

"About that." Her aunt's tall, full figure blocked the foot of the second-floor staircase. "I want to say, once again, that I think it's a foolish mistake to include her in all the events before the debut. She's hardly likely to have the clothes, and will only be embarrassed. Water seeks its own level—it's a law of life to remember."

Lily's anger spilled at last. "If you think Whitey's going to be left out of anything, you can leave me out, too, Aunt Mirry. And if you think she cares about such things, or will be impressed by this huge old museum, you're all wrong again. *Nothing* impresses Whitey—*nothing*. Only values—real ones."

Before her aunt could answer or demand an apology, Lily was off, starting down the stairs, her heart racing. She'd have to apologize, of course—would want to—but not now. All she wanted now was to see that bright, cheery face, hear that jaunty voice again, and feel the fresh air of laughter, fun, being loved for herself and that alone.

Suddenly the butler, Oliver, was calling to her. "Your guest has arrived, Miss Lily."

Before his words were out, she was running, half sliding down the huge circular stairs, careering around the newel post and on down the next flight, across the great polished marble hall.

"Whitey!" she shouted.

The familiar compact figure of her friend was standing just inside the doors beside Thomas, who held her one imitation-leather suitcase as if it were full of jewels. "Here she is, Lil," he said, grinning. "All in one piece."

Pamela White's smile broadened as Lily rushed up to her. Her dark eyes sparkled, almost brimmed. "Hiya, Boke!" she began—then the exuberance faltered. "Hi, Lily." As if in suddenly evoked deportment, her hand shot out and gripped Lily's in a formal shake. "Gosh," she said, "I hope I haven't inconvenienced anyone or anything, being late. But there was snow on the tracks."

"Lord, no—it was just awful for you, though. I was watching—I could hardly wait. I can't believe it—you've actually materialized!" For some reason, her tongue hesitated over the "Whitey," yet couldn't settle for Pamela.

They looked at each other, their smiles of equal brightness.

"Gee, you've changed, Boke—Lily." Pamela's gaze had a searching uncertainty, no hint of nonchalance.

"Have I? How *perquillear*. Is it my hair style, maybe?"

Pamela didn't rise to their old term. "No—you've . . . grown up."

"But I'm not—that's the trouble."

"Give me the young lady's case," Oliver said to Thomas.

"I'll take her up in the elevator, Oliver," Lily said.

"Anything else, Lil?" asked Thomas.

"Yes—call me Miss Lily. Aunt Mirry's about to fire you."

He chuckled, unimpressed, and went whistling off towards the kitchen.

"Same old Thomas." Lily smiled. "Come on—we can have a quick chat in the elevator."

Pamela was following, but her gaze traveled the stairways, the ceilings, the partly visible main rooms beyond, with furtive awe. When they stood in the elevator, she was quiet, stole several glances at Lily's dress, and her own brown coat, which, together with the brown velour hat, Lily remembered from school.

"How's the family?" asked Lily quickly.

"Fine. They sent their love, of course."

"I'd love to see them again. I'll never forget that Thanksgiving you took me home. It was the most real fun I ever had!"

Pamela's smile was uncharacteristically polite, unconvinced. "You know, they lost everything," she said. "We may lose our house. Dad's been ill with worry—Mom's teaching for nothing, and Rob's had to leave school and get a job—so has Sis. I won't be able to go to college, of course . . ." She stopped. "Brother— get out the violin!"

"I'm sorry, very sorry," Lily said. "Oh, dear . . ."

"I think I'm going to look awfully hickish, too, Lily. I got a few new things—but with the fare—well, I just couldn't—you know . . . Ask them for more . . ."

The unsaid word hung between them.

"I didn't stop to think about that—I wish you'd let me . . . I mean, I *should* have . . ." Lily felt the warmth in her cheeks.

"Oh, shut up, Boke!"

The phrase was the same, but Whitey's tone and expression were not. Lily thought of the little suitcase, the round of parties, dinners and dances ahead. Could she offer to lend her clothes, one of at least a hundred gowns hanging uselessly in that tremendous dressing room, any of her furs, her jewels? Would she let Starenze (who had nothing to do now that the debut dresses were designed and made) create something to bring out her peachy skin, the reddish glints in her dark "Dutch-cut" bob?

She stole a glance at her as she opened the gilt gate. Not a prayer, she thought.

"Don't worry," she said to her. "Just wear your smile—it's your crown jewels."

For an instant, "Whitey" was back. "You *remember* that! Dad's old chestnut!"

"Of course. And something else he said, too. Do you remember the morning after Thanksgiving, at breakfast, when I asked him if he would adopt me?"

"Vaguely. What did he say?" Pamela's smile hovered, giving her squarish, even-featured face its more familiar irreverence.

"He said, 'Child—*you* might better adopt *us!*'"

"*He* would," she said.

They walked along the wide, deeply carpeted corridor a little apart. Lily could think of nothing to break the silence.

Chapter 5

On each side of the red-carpeted entrance to the Ritz-Ambrose, the dense crowds were getting edgier.

"Come on, your highness," a repeated joker called, "your peasants are freezing!"

There was boisterous laughter, yelled replies.

"We ain't got no ermine coats to keep us warm, baby," someone shouted louder than the rest.

"You're right, buddy! None of old man Boeker's millions, neither!"

This, loudest of all comments, was followed by a growing uproar of discussion and laughter with an undercurrent of disorder.

The police casually braced their cordons.

Sauntering down the steps from the doorway, a small group of special plainclothesmen convened at the curb, ignoring other cars that drew up, watching for one.

Inside the hotel, there were other forms of readiness for Lily. The square pillars of the long foyer leading to the ballroom had been covered with mirror and sequin stars, banked with living magnolias brought from the South (nurtured in hothouses to full bloom) and arranged with Easter lilies and camellias surrounded by silver-painted palm fronds, all of this bathed in aquamarine-blue spotlights—to match her eyes, of course.

In the ballroom itself, last touches to what seemed a vast exotic garden under a full tropical moon, an ingenious arrangement of light and glass, had been completed. Here, again, were magnolias together with a great profusion of white gladioli, bushes of lush white roses, calla lilies, tall, silvered trees hung with brilliant tropical fruits.

To one side of the room, where Lily would stand to receive, was a brilliantly lighted fountain with floating water lilies below, a slim gilt maiden breaking through a curtain of golden rain, which may well have been champagne. Suspended from the high ceiling were hundreds of faceted-mirror stars, glittering and twirling with dizzying effect just above where soon would glitter and twirl fifteen hundred or so of the nation's social elite.

The first of four orchestras which were to play, the famous Leslie Marvin's Society Favorites, had finished setting up instruments on the bandstand and was prepared to strike up at the relayed word of Mrs. Miriam Dundell Hower Court, who, together with General Court, had just come in to cast a final glance over the glowing maze of candlelit tables, the riotous bank of bouquets still swelling with additions, against the wall where the guests would enter.

Wearing cream-colored satin with deep ostrich-feather hem, her Marie Antoinette emerald-and-diamond necklace with matching earrings and bracelet, and on her golden-gray, regal head her world-famous diamond tiara (beside which all other tiaras within twenty feet would be blighted), Aunt Mirry stood at the foyer entrance with the General, looking his most splendid and distinguished in white tie and tails, a decoration in his buttonhole instead of the usual flower, members of his family, Miriam's designer of decor, Dag Skeerber, with his assistant "Dickie," and, naturally, Reginald Blount.

"This debut will make history," she said with a contained smile.

"I'm not sure what kind, dear." The General looked at his

watch from the shadow of black brows. "You'd think she was facing the gallows."

"Oh, she'll cheer up when she sees how really divine it's all turned out," said Dag Skeerber, winking a thickly lashed eye at Miriam.

"Yes, Dag, dear—I'm sure she will," Miriam said.

Reginald Blount, a mountainous penguin in his tails, patted the top of his stomach. "Even if she doesn't, Miriam dear, you're right. More stock disasters notwithstanding, she hasn't a competitor for tomorrow's headlines."

"Quite." Miriam rested an emerald-ringed hand on one solid, square-cut diamond of her necklace (rumored to be, stone by stone, the biggest in the world), a quiet, almost secret satisfaction on her pink, solidly planed face.

"And only slightly due to you," the columnist added with the quick twitching smile so feared by most of "Society." "Apart from Lily herself—and that's another matter—her position in the saga of American wealth not only is, but will be unique."

"You speak as a prophet?" She cast him a sidewise glance.

"As a historian, darling." He patted his stomach again, and looked impatiently at the big doors. "You've taught her the nasty art of a late entrance, I see."

"Quite unintentional. We started out together, but there was some kind of commotion en route and we lost them."

"That, Mirry my dear, was an uprising of the unemployed—or did you think it was a parade?"

Miriam's smile was undisturbed. "Here she is," she said as a heavy-shouldered guard moved suddenly away from his post, calling to a companion.

Down at the curb, the new pearl-gray Rolls Miriam had insisted Lily use for the occasion had drawn up. Through its windows could be seen two young men on the small seats and, in the back, the very light shining head of Lily herself. In front, along with Thomas, were Maudie and a maid, both in dark coats and hats.

The police pushed back the jostling crowds, and Thomas, forced to relinquish his protective role to escorts, guards and doormen, sat where he was.

Andy Dundell and General Court's young nephew Rick

jumped out quickly, reached back to help Lily emerge. Maudie and the maid squeezed through the men to settle the bouffant skirt of her dress under the chinchilla wrap.

There was a hushed instant, then the crowd's murmur and the miniature explosions of photographers' bulbs broke in unison.

She seemed unreal as she moved forward, her wrap falling back, a hazy materializing brilliance, a sparkling, candescent form on the semi-darkness.

But only too factually the "form" was the chalk-white velvet-and-tulle dress Starenze had designed to dramatize her slenderness, small waist and high rounded bosom—spectacular eardrops of pear-shaped diamonds—her mother's incomparably lustrous pearl necklace—a bracelet of baguette-cut diamonds made to Miriam's specifications as her debut present—her platinum-colored hair, as fabulous as the jewels in effect, long, loose, softly curved over one eye, and a brilliant but rigid smile of reluctant self-display.

"Hey, Lily—you look like a million dollars, baby!" a female voice called.

"A two-hundred-million-dollar baby! You'll be okay, kid!"

"Hello, Miss Boeker—thanks for not spending more than a hundred thou tonight, real considerate!"

"Hiya, honeybunch—you're *beautiful!* How about a couple of million you wouldn't miss, darlin'."

There was an outbreak of laughter, and Andy and Rick and the detectives, trailed by Maudie and the maid, moved in around her.

Lily stared straight ahead, met no eye, as Aunt Mirry had instructed—but it did not close out the contempt on the faces, the shabby, unshaven and shivering among the people looking at her as the flashbulbs steadily popped.

She remembered long rows of shacks where people who had not been able to pay rent now lived, the proud, good people without enough to eat because "the bottom had dropped out of the market," as the papers had said.

"Move!" Andy said, pushing her by the elbow. "Ignore them!"

She could do nothing else—and suddenly the sad, dreary outer world and all its ills were behind her—she was in another of soft and subtle splendor, of brilliance, warmth, intoxicating fragrance, rich fabrics and dazzling jewels, dreamlike flowers and flower-beautiful faces all around her, smiling, smiling.

Solicitous hands removed the chinchilla wrap from her slim white shoulders. She was drawn into a group, surrounded, kissed, praised—for her beauty, her dress, her hair, her figure, her very existence, it seemed.

"All right, my darling," her aunt cut through, with constrained pride, "let's take up positions to receive."

Lily followed after the glittering, imposing figure, her inner turbulence overlaid by the sheer opulence of the ballroom.

"It's . . . heavenly!" she breathed, her eyes as softly brilliant as what they gazed on. But the impact of such lavishness on her behalf, the principle behind it, hit her with new force. It was so wasteful, so false, so unjustified! Still—she smiled at the waiters who smiled at her, at the musicians who waved and bowed, chatted lightly with the members of her entourage who lined up with her by the massed bouquets. She felt like an offering to pagan gods, beyond deliverance.

"Pull up your gloves, dear. Think of yourself as a princess. It's really what you are, in American terms. Be charming, gracious, radiant—give everyone what they're expecting, and then some."

"People must be terrible fools," Lily said. "Perhaps I should hand out money."

Suddenly her never-before-perturbed aunt swept her with a cold glance of exasperation. "For heaven's sake, girl," she whispered, "wake up! I've had enough of it."

Their eyes met in brief, bare recognition. Lily understood that her "sentiment and naïveté" were to be openly terminated with this public alignment. That she now dedicate herself to social rule was not Aunt Mirry's fond hope—it was her command!

She felt the sudden ache of her mother's absence, turned, involuntarily, to look for Maudie.

"And I've asked Miss Maude to stay in the background, in the dressing room," her aunt said, "along with the other servants."

Lily's eyes, made to look larger than usual with a touch of mascara, stared widely into hers. It was all she could do not to walk away—run out on everything, the whole revolting show.

"And one more thing, Lily," Aunt Mirry whispered. "Just because I've let you have relatives as escorts doesn't mean you can ignore the fine young men here tonight. It's time to forget the past in *that* regard, too."

Lily drew away from her, the last of her gratitude dissolving in betrayal.

Andy came up and thrust a bouquet of lilies of the valley into her left hand. Leaning close, he said, "You look like a dying duck in a thunderstorm, sweet pea. By the way, Count Vittorio de Santi couldn't make it, so I've put a college pal of mine, Joel Maitland, next to you at the table. If you freeze him, I'll step on your dress—I promise." He smiled, showing more of his narrow, crowded teeth than necessary.

"Go 'way," she said, but she was instantly cheered, as usual, and managed to smile benignly, to sniff her bouquet with exaggerated bliss.

"She has no idea how truly beautiful she is," someone whispered, "and so natural."

"Lovely posture. It's unfair—she should be pimply or fat, at least."

"Ssh!"

Now, like the final signal of a firing squad, the orchestra struck up "A Pretty Girl Is Like a Melody." With the dulcet lilting notes, the first guests were starting towards her, faces glowing with admiring, affectionate, congratulatory smiles, to be greeted by her aunt with the ultimate of dignity and grace, who, in turn, announced—"My niece—Lily."

"How lovely you look, dear!"

"A dream, Lily!"

"Wonderful to meet you!"

"Your flowers are divine—so are you!"

"Beautiful dress, Lily!"

"Known you since you were so-high—you've grown into a beautiful young woman!"

"Angelic!"

"Great to see you, Lily—remember Fairglades?"

In final surrender to the inevitable, Lily emitted the easy responses of hard training. "Lovely to meet you, Mr. Hogg. Thank you so much. Wonderful to see you again, Lady Radtree. Oh, hello, Roy. Hello, Prue. How do you do, your excellency. Nice you could come, Lydia. Hello, Chip, thanks—so do you. Divine dress yourself, Polly. Good evening, sir. Yes, isn't it heaven."

She heard her own soft, lilting voice like the echo of a schooled parrot. One tune went on to the next, and still they came, every age, every shape, every style of gown, every variation of young men in tails with freshly slicked hair and careful manners, looking at her in keen, diffident or sophisticated delight, older ones, straight or bent, large, small, bald, gray, bespectacled, mustached, bearded and plain-shaven, with the same gallantry, a wistful amorousness, as if she alone in the world shone out, had fatal feminine allure.

Her gloved hand grew sore, her back ached, her feet in the high-heel satin shoes swelled and her jaw cramped with smiling. "Have you noticed her eyes?" she heard a voice behind her say. "Like blue fire!"

She blinked at the idea, but forced them wide with appropriate spark. Now and then she giggled at a comment with proper melodiousness, or gave a quick, rippling laugh—as if she loved it all, found the orgy of attention delicious.

As the room filled, and still more came, she felt like a stuffed mannequin coming undone at the seams. She wanted to peek down to see if she was decent about the chest—Starenze had insisted on the half-naked, precarious neckline.

The outstretched hands at last came to an end, and Uncle Will, who had been hovering like a genial shepherd to fifteen hundred sheep, came over, bowed, bore her off to the first dance.

Instant applause greeted her appearance, and the orchestra swung into "I've Got a Crush on You," followed by a medley of tunes all implying her singularity and desirability.

"You carried it off magnificently," her uncle by marriage whispered. "Isn't it fun, after all? Admit it."

The approval in the pink-veined blue eyes under the black brows was the most spontaneous she had ever seen. "Yes, Uncle Will," she said, "of course." What else could you say to him? He was such an old fogey, like an ancestral portrait come to life. She followed his stiff, dated dancing with dutiful enthusiasm, half lifted from the floor by his corpulent stomach.

Andy took over. "Sensational, dear." He peaked both brows tonight. "The press is running wild. Bessie Dixon's making two columns of the guests' names alone, apart from the decorations and your gown and hair. Legghardt Westby says you're the most, quote-quote, beautiful debutante ever presented to American society, apart from the richest."

"Goody Two-shoes, Andy. Great for the country. People who haven't eaten lately will be thrilled."

"You're making me cry, cousin." He wrinkled his long nose, blinked his large-lidded eyes. "And a bit sick."

"Even you haven't got a heart. You think you're above it all, don't you, Andy-Pandy?"

"Honey chile," he said in his Amos 'n' Andy voice, "you is regusted."

She pushed him away with a furious smile, and turned quickly to Rick, who was preparing to cut in.

Rick, a tall, stout young man with tightly waved red hair, leaned over her, engulfing her in awkwardness, his feet finding hers with every step. "I'm sure lucky being related," he said ardently.

She smiled at him. "Ditto. But, phew, I'm so hot—would you mind if we sat down?"

"Oh, sure—I know I'm a lousy dancer, too."

The roar of voices, rising to the ceiling and vibrating the stars, precluded a reply. Smiling, shoulders straight, eyes bright as if with enchantment, she pressed past the massed dancers into the arena of candlelit, flower-laden, champagne-dotted tables to the biggest table, in the center. She felt afloat, vaguely nauseous.

At the table, the circle of remaining people looked up delightedly. Young men leaped to their feet, and the girls with them smiled and called pleasantries to her in cultured, suitably bored voices. Diabolically, inevitably, Aunt Mirry had placed her special favorite, Chip Kenelm, there, like a bull waiting to stampede her back to the floor in one of his suffocating clinches.

"Think of my poor feet," she said, sitting down quickly, "and my *hand*—ow!" She puffed exaggeratedly as she removed her gloves.

The young man next to her watched with amusement. He did not offer his name, or attempt conversation, but sat listening to the cross-talk between her and others around the table. When she got up to dance, he did not ask one of the other girls to dance, but followed her actions, her every move on the dance floor, with close attention.

Supper was served, champagne glasses were lifted in toasts to her. From her nearby table, Aunt Mirry rose and made a short, charming speech about coming out, with all its commitments. This was followed by many toasts, amusing to serious, from several members of the socially prestigious and "four hundred." A light was turned on her, and though she could only think of "Thank you, thank you for all your kind wishes—I hope I can live up to them" (said quickly and a bit too faintly), the impression she made was one of becoming modesty and confidence, as befitted one with spectacular beauty, youth and two hundred million in the offing.

"Eat," Chip commanded when she sat down, and white-wigged waiters with Boeker blue exchanged for their maroon hotel uniforms served capon and foie gras, while close by the Roving Gypsy orchestra played hauntingly. "You need fuel—I can tell."

She hadn't eaten since yesterday, but after a mouthful or two put down her fork.

"Then drink." Chip now forced the glass upwards to her lips. "To the most charming deb in captivity," he said, clinking his glass to hers.

"How can *I* drink to that!" She put down her glass.

The young man next to her laughed in easy accord, nodded and lifted his glass. "I can," he said, looking at her and downing the liquid.

Lily noted him reluctantly. Some of Andy's friends had strange ways, like his, only not as endearing—but this one seemed different. He was almost as solidly built as Chip, and as tall, she guessed—but unlike Chip's bland, winter-tanned face, bearing the imprint of his thoughts like ticker tape, this person's had to be guessed. Obviously intelligent, she thought—old for his age—quiet, but forceful in some unusual way.

Furtively, she scanned his face, feature by feature. Brown hair, thinnish, faintly waved—would recede early from the high, wide brow. Nose, high-bridged, bumped, as if once broken—but distinguished, pleasing. Mouth, good shape, firm—probably more often serious than smiling. Eyes, at least by candlelight, hazel, searching, comprehending.

She smiled back, wanting suddenly to talk to him.

But Chip Kenelm practically lifted her to her feet. "Here's Harvey Morrisby's band—time's wastin', gal." He pressed her ahead of him, his big hands possessively about her waist, his glance taking note of whether they were being duly recorded by columnists, photographers, his social contemporaries.

How you do *lumber*, she thought, as he pushed and heaved her around the jammed floor, hiking her dress in the back with his sweating palm, breathing heavily against her hair, flattening it to her cheek. She gritted her teeth, prayed for quick interruption, but Chip was an immovable force.

"I shall marry you someday, gal," he told her, crushing her against his tremendous chest. "I hope you're grateful. At least seven females in this room have already set their caps at me."

"How flattering, Mr. Kenelm. I'm simply atwitter."

He patted her bare back, smacked it playfully. "You'll have no worries with me, little girl." He grinned down at her patronizingly. "Together, we'll hold the reins of this little old nation!"

She set her lips, said nothing.

Luckily, the music stopped, and she started away from him at once, but another young man was waiting at the table for her, and with growing impatience, she was forced to rejoin the great whirling mob under the moon and giddying mirror stars.

And even after that, others waited. She could not have counted the young men in whose arms she continued to swirl and dip and hop in unison, into whose assorted eyes she looked, with whom she laughed and made inane chitchat and future dates (most of which she promptly forgot).

A ceaseless stream of spectacularly gowned girls her own age, or young married women, kept stopping her to comment on her dress, her hair, the success of the ball. Tiaraed matrons and dowagers, some of whose paint-stiff pink-and-white faces cracked with the sweetness of their smiles, or who were so totteringly ancient, so precariously preserved, that their grandest jewels for the occasion all but bore them to the ground, complimented her on her loveliness, wished her happiness unlimited!

She thought of herself as a goose, gorged and stuffed to the point of death to make foie gras, and longed for escape.

At last, Rubi Lavalle, with his bush of chestnut hair, wry, off-center face and spaniel eyes, appeared before the band and began to croon into his megaphone. To the horror of the older audience, the ecstasy of Lily's contemporaries, he "breathed" the popular songs, poured them from "velvet-covered tonsils"— "Singin' in the Rain"—"My Silent Love"—"Ain't She Sweet" . . .

"Ssh," she whispered to the arrogant young customer's man from Wall Street, who, with an arm draped on her chair, sang along into her ear, "please." He stopped—but there was a curious silence in the room, and suddenly Rubi Lavalle was singing her name in a totally unfamiliar song . . .

"Lily—Lil-Lily-Lily—she toils not, fellas, neither does she spin. But, oh my—consider how she grows! Lil-Lovely-Lily-Lily— a field of hearts she's bound to win. Oh, my—heaven knows! Lily —Beautiful Lil-Lily-Lily!"

Rubi had stopped, and with his famous sad smile was pointing towards her. A blue light cast its brilliance on her uplifted face.

There was a startled burst of applause, growing in volume. With a rumble of chairs, guests rose. At least a thousand champagne glasses must have clinked.

"Oh, no!" With a mortified glance at the people nearest to her, she got up, thinking: How could Aunt Mirry have done such a tasteless thing, *paid* for a song! But she turned slowly to smile "radiantly" all about the huge room, over the whole ghastly sea of staring faces, wishing only that she could dissolve, become invisible.

The applause simply increased. (In the press the next day, one columnist described this moment as "Breathtaking—the slim, graceful swan of a girl, modestly aware of her soon-to-be role of the richest girl in the world, accepting it with a calm radiance that reached every heart in that vast ballroom. What a pity her grandfather Wilbur D. Boeker could not have witnessed this culmination of all his labors, sacrifices and dreams. He would have been the proudest man in America.")

Not knowing how to withdraw (Aunt Mirry's schooling had failed to prepare her for this), she raised her hand (foolishly, she thought) and motioned the band and singer to continue.

It did the trick. Everyone sat down, and presently the attention of the room was focused on the famous Spanish dance team, Carlo and Carlotta. In the safe interlude, she slumped in her chair, let her smile descend.

"What's wrong, princess?"

At the hard grip on her hand, she looked up in surprise. Andy's friend was not smiling now. "You're not enjoying all this, are you?" he said.

"Enjoying it!" She did not draw her hand away. "It's stupid. And immoral!" The ambitious word came easily with him.

As applause for the dancers burst around them, he drew his chair closer. Ignoring the young man on her other side, he said, "I'm glad I let Andy talk me into filling in for some count or other."

"Oh—Vittorio de Santi. You didn't *want* to come?"

"No more than you, I guess."

She looked into his eyes, and her heart jolted in a strange new way. "Why did you, then?"

"Want the truth?"

She smiled, lowered her whisper. "If it's not too awful."

His smile was warm, knowing. "To see what the richest girl in the world would be like—to observe her in the full plumage at the height of the season."

"Oh, *no*—like a specimen in a zoo!"

He chuckled, and his grip on her hand tightened. "Such a lovely one."

She found it almost difficult to meet his eyes. No person of the opposite sex had affected her like this; she had been sure they never would. She drew away a little, only because it seemed too fast, too good to be anything but questionable. "I wonder what you expected. Someone spoiled and vain, full of herself, hateful? Do you despise the rich?"

"Now, now. Let's say I didn't expect you to be *you*." There was more than banter in his tone, a kindness in his long look. "And I don't despise anybody. The effects of wealth interest me, though—its insidious molding of character and experience."

Fascinated, she forgot her caution. "Has it molded me, Joel? What am I like?" She leaned to him again, wanting to hear his every word.

"You *do* know my name." His smile teased, but only briefly. "You've got me on the spot, princess. You mustn't take me seriously—I'm just an over-intense pre-med student with psychiatric aspirations—hardly qualified to . . ."

"Really!" She gazed at him in such ardent admiration that he touched her cheek gently, laughed.

"A stranger bird than you," he said. "Now *you* can observe."

"You didn't answer me," she said, wanting even more urgently now to hear his thoughts.

He gave her hand a squeeze and released it, but only while he deliberated. "You're very dear and vulnerable," he said. "It hurts to think of it being you."

"Then I *am* molded? You think I'm a gone duck, that I'll never escape the money and be a real person? You might as well say it."

He looked into her eyes a few moments. Then his hand came back and gripped hers again, even harder. "I know you'll *try*," he said.

Before she could answer, the music had stopped and the dancers were taking bows. Lily looked up as if awakening, and with a sense of loss. But to her relief, the famous "street singer" troubadour now emerged, sombrero in hand, rose in mouth, and the music swelled and pounded again.

Under its cover, she returned to Joel. "You're right about that," she said. "But not the other. I shall soon be on my own— and from then on . . . Well, you'll see."

He smiled, lifted a fallen strand of her hair, replaced it carefully. "You might just do it," he said. "I'll be rooting for you from the sidelines."

"Will you?" As she met his eyes, her heart gave the strange jolt again. "But not from the sidelines . . . Please?"

"You wouldn't want it any other way—there's nothing to me but study. I'll be dull grind for years to come."

"Never dull—if I could just *talk* to you . . ."

He shook his head. "My world is as remote from yours as the North Pole. My parents were hit by the crash. I'm working my way through, along with the rest. Needed textbooks will be my whoopee, princess."

The thought crossed her mind that she could provide them all.

She could pay his tuition, help him. Then she stopped. This was the whole point.

"What did you think of Andy's song for you?" he was saying, his large body shifting in the chair, his tone lighter.

Her eyes opened wide. "Andy wrote that!"

"Yes—I thought you knew. Maybe I wasn't supposed to . . ."

"Oh, that *fiend!*" She put her hand to her mouth, covering the sudden giggle. "Wait till I get him alone!"

"He's a riot, that man. He used to keep us howling. I gather that aunt of yours is a formidable lady."

"Aunt Mirry!" Lily sobered, nodded. "But wonderful, too—in her own way."

"Which obviously isn't yours."

How blissful it was to be understood, to have a *real* conversation. "I suppose you know . . . Well, how Andy likes to . . ."

"Dress up? Yes—he likes to, without a doubt. But a very good kid—I say kid, though he's my age. Well, both of you have had quite some childhood to survive."

"Did you know about me, too—what really happened with my stepfather?" She wanted to tell him everything, in a way that she'd never been able to express before to anyone. "It wasn't the way the press has it."

"Between the lines, I guessed he tried to seduce you, or did."

"He tried. My mother came in. I went to school then, and afterwards Aunt Mirry took over because my mother . . . Well, she's been in and out of the sanitarium—but it's hopeless. She's sort of a—what's that word?" Lily didn't mind her ignorance and innocence with him.

"Dipsomaniac."

"That's right. And Freddie has all these girls . . ."

He shook his head slowly, gazed at her in wonder, in concern. They sat so close that she yearned suddenly to put her head on his shoulder. "Will you take me to a speakeasy afterwards?" she said unexpectedly. "Andy says most of us young are deserting the party to go."

He was quiet an instant, as if silenced by indecision. "Princess —I'd love nothing better," he said presently. "But the sordid fact is, I've got less than two bucks on me. I only expected to eat and run—home to study."

She sat up brightly. "Oh, that's nothing. Andy will give you money."

"I don't hold with borrowing, either."

She was reminded, abruptly, of Whitey—Pamela. How genuine had her sudden "sore throat" been? Hadn't it come suspiciously quickly after Aunt Mirry's visit to the bedroom to "check over" the clothes situation?

"Don't look so sad, princess." He reached for her hand. "The quiet orchestra's back—can I try my three steps on you?"

She got up gladly, going happily for the first time in her life into a man's arms. Being close to him, held tight, she didn't withdraw and freeze like a statue—Freddie was forgotten.

Could it, then, really happen like his—like all the drippy June-moon songs, the gooey love stories she'd never believed?

She felt his arms tighten, his cheek against her hair—she closed her eyes.

"What a clod I am," he said. "You're a brave girl."

"You're not bad," she said, "you keep good time, that's the main thing."

"You sound professional. I bet you're a beautiful dancer."

"That's what I intend to be, after some more training and work."

"Good for you."

"I'll dance for you, Joel, someday."

At the sound of his name, he put both his arms around her, and their steps grew slower, dreamier.

"Well, well," said a voice nearby, "our little deb's coming out whole hog."

"And wouldn't you know—with that medical type of Andy's!"

Her aunt's ringing tone was meant for her ears. Lily grinned against Joel's shoulder. What did it matter? What did any of her old life matter?

"You see, darling?" he said.

His significant tone was lost—all she heard was the "darling." She looked up into his eyes, smiling dazedly. She saw herself sitting quietly beside him as he studied, reading some instructive book he'd suggested—pressing his clothes—cooking his meals—even darning his socks the way she'd read women did for their men. Maudie would teach her. They'd make love—he'd be tender

and knowing, and she would make up for all the lost time of
being dumb and afraid by being a wonderful lover. She would
bear him three—perhaps four children . . .

"Joel," she said suddenly. "Let's go now and meet Aunt Mirry
and Uncle Will, so we can just ooze away when we want to
later."

Uncle Will stood up quickly, as Lily bent to her aunt at the
table. "I want you to meet Joel Maitland, Aunt Mirry," she said,
"because he's going to take me to a speakeasy afterwards.
Thanks very much for everything, and I'll see you at home."

"No!" Her aunt slapped a gloved hand to the table, and
glasses rattled. "Absolutely not! We're planning extra protection
and—"

"Oh, don't worry, Auntie—I've already got that!" She brought
Joel forward, smiling gaily, almost gleefully, as she performed a
formal introduction.

Joel said, "How do you do," to both Aunt Mirry and Uncle
Will, his detached and dignified courtesy allowing them no opportunity to be patronizing. "I'll take good care of her," he
confirmed.

"That was tricky, young lady," Joel said as they returned to
dance. "I see you expect to get your way." But he was smiling
with tender amusement, not reprimanding. "A speakeasy," he
murmured, half to himself. "Well, I never."

Lily was excited, genuinely animated now as they strung out
the remaining time. While she danced with hordes of assorted
young men, Joel watched, still not asking anyone else, observing
her as she did her duty, made social chitchat, gracefully followed
complicated steps.

Love me, oh please love me, she messaged to him with her fre-
quent glances—you could change my whole life!

Whenever she went back to him after a bout with some non-
descript male with nothing better to offer than a "good" name,
good looks or a fortune, it was like coming home.

Looking into her shining eyes and flushed face, he was unable
to shift his gaze. "By what miracle am I thus honored?" he said.

Whenever she was left unsought a moment, they talked, getting quickly to the heart of things. She told him how lonely she
was, and he didn't laugh. She described Maudie and Thomas,

and her life at the Long Island and Fifth Avenue mansions, and he said, "No wonder!"

She asked him about his childhood, and he told her that it had been quite the opposite, standard American home life, very close, but with an unusual amount of tragic incident. It was when his younger brother had suffered a breakdown after a bad car accident that he had started delving into the mental side of medicine, which led on to his present, now obsessive ambition.

She told him that she would like to develop her mind. She had thought about the Russian Five-Year Plan, for instance—but no one would discuss it seriously with her . . .

Looking bemused, Joel kissed her slowly on the mouth.

She forgot where she was, didn't care.

The orchestra was playing "Body and Soul." He took her hand and led her to the dance floor. Many people had drifted away. The photographers had gathered on the periphery of the room to chat and smoke. Joel swung out more daringly.

"You see—you're actually a smoothie."

"It's you—I'm suddenly another Carlo."

She laughed happily, rested her head where it wanted to be, where it seemed right to be.

"Princess?"

Only *he* could make her like that name! "Yes?"

"You *do* understand. Speakeasy or no—we can never make it."

Serene in the power of her new feelings, she smiled. "You're so gloomy."

"I'd never want to hurt you."

"You aren't going to. I'll do everything your way. I love ordinary things, honestly—like walking, riding buses . . ."

"I bet you've never been on a bus—and have you tried all this without bodyguards in tow?"

"Oh—well . . . I wouldn't have them any more, of course!"

There was a silence, a long one.

She looked up, suddenly frightened.

He gathered her close. "Perhaps I don't trust my own immunity. Money can be a disease—you get infected without knowing it. I can't afford to experiment. You might find it selfish, but nothing is more important to me than my work, never will be, I'm sure."

"Oh, Joel." She looked into his eyes pleadingly. "Don't go away from me. Please don't."

He gazed a moment longer, then suddenly he wrapped her in a closer embrace than ever.

Happiness, she thought, is like this.

The tunes got livelier, the dancers more abandoned—but almost suddenly it seemed, there came the strains of "Good Night, Sweetheart." Everyone gathered around the crooner—just barely moving, while the soft, haunting notes fell, and the lights began to dim.

In Joel's arms, Lily felt tears of ecstasy under her closed lids, and knew it was a moment she would never forget as long as she lived.

They left the floor. Good-nights were said. Andy came over to ask them to a party at some actor's penthouse. Lily could tell he was crowing about his strategy in bringing them together—he liked to think that he could beat his mother in breaking down her resistance to men—and this time he'd succeeded.

She kissed him on the cheek, forgave him for the song—she loved everyone now, unreservedly!

They pushed through the remaining throng to the room where Maudie still waited. "I'll be right back," she told him. "Don't move."

Maudie had her wrap, a brush for her hair, a fresh, perfumed handkerchief, a change of shoes. "Miss Lily—you look happy. Have you had a wonderful debut after all, then?" Her eyes had a private questioning.

"It isn't that, Maudie—I still know it was a ghastly mistake. But, oh, Maudie—I've got to tell you—I've fallen in love!"

"But how can that be, dear? It's much too quick. And besides, you're only eighteen still." She looked solemn, gave a warning cock of her head. "Why, you've only just begun to . . ."

"I'm glad! There'll be that much longer to be married to him!"

"Miss Lily!"

Lily laughed, hugged her, took the chinchilla wrap and threw it on.

"What about these?"

Lily didn't turn.

But Joel wasn't there. Her heart slowed, then accelerated as she looked around at the smiling, straggling guests, tried to avoid being scooped into their chatter.

But suddenly he *was* there, striding towards her.

"Oh, thank goodness!" she said. "I thought you'd . . ."

"Princess—I wouldn't. Not like that." He patted his hip. "You undoubtedly forgot the essential. I just caught Andy—who happened, for once, to have some on him. Usually, it costs me a month's allowance to be with him—paying out cash for his tips and whims."

"I thought he always had scads. Did you get enough?"

"He only had hundreds. I took one. God knows when I'll pay him back."

"Oh, he won't even remember. Will it be enough for us?"

Joel laughed, throwing back his head. "What do you think we're going to do, buy the place? We're only going to have a drink or two, then I'm taking you home before you turn into a pumpkin." He tapped her chin, smiled into her eyes.

"Oh, dear—well, let's say our good-nights in a hurry!"

Joel grinned at her defiance and daring as he followed her slender, luxuriously furred figure through the camellia-fragrant foyer, past the heavily banked magnolias.

She smiled back at him, mischievously, her eyes catching the brilliant glints of her jewels. Darling, darling, she thought, here we go into the beginning of everything . . .

"LILY!"

The sudden confrontation of Aunt Mirry, Uncle Will, Rick, her new relations, detectives, interested members of the new and old guard, blanched her face.

"You can't believe I'd *allow* you to do this foolhardy thing," Aunt Mirry said, her face a darker than normal rose. "Without a chaperone! Without guards!"

"Very unwise," said Uncle Will, and everyone nodded.

Lily was quite aware of the order behind the question. But she broke into a smile. Now that she was no longer angry, only sorry for all the wasted effort and time on her behalf, she no longer felt beholden, either. She forgave her, felt fond of her. "Look, Aunt Mirry—Joel has studying to do. We won't even be late. He'll bring me right inside the door."

She pushed on past, reached to slide her arm through Joel's.

"I promised I'd take good care of her, Mrs. Court," Joel said, "and I will. We'll take a taxi, and I won't let her out of my sight." He gave them a knowledgeable, reassuring smile, and clipped Lily's arm to his side.

The doors opened. They went out into the freezing wind that had risen, the brilliant warmth behind them fading abruptly with the closing doors.

To Lily's astonishment, a huge crowd was gathered there. Flashbulbs began to pop like a miniature fireworks display.

Shivering, Lily clung to Joel, tried to escape the renewed focus by hurrying, head down.

"There she is! How was it, Lily honey—get enough pheasant and caviar?"

"Did you drink champagne from your shoe?"

"Did it beat breadlines, Lily Boeker?"

"Yeah—how does it feel to be so lousy rich, Lily?"

"Didn't even have to earn it, did ya? Just spend old Boeker's dough—good old Boeker's-for-the-best profits. To hell with the unemployed and homeless—right?"

Lily stopped, pulled back on Joel's arm, looked about with desperate sympathy. "It's not my fault," she called out, her young voice rising high and clear over the traffic noise. "I didn't want it. I'm going to give it all away!"

There was a great outburst of ribald laughter, swelling ominously louder.

"That's real funny, rich bitch," someone yelled.

Joel's arm around her waist tightened to a forceful pull, but she balked, struggled to speak again. "I hated this debut!" she yelled back. "Believe me! I know how you feel!"

"Could you live on thirteen bucks a week? That's what Boeker's pays, a lousy thirteen bucks!"

"Throw acid in her face—that'll fix her!"

A surge so sudden that it took the police off guard practically swept her off her feet. Joel's arms were around her like a powerful shield, but his effort to shove onward was blocked by men who had broken from the rank, pressed in on them.

Over the top of the commotion, a voice called through some kind of an amplifier. "Break it up, break it up—this is the police. Move back—move back!"

Detectives and guards were magically in a solid phalanx between Lily and Joel and the crowd, and in a few moments the police had regained control.

Aunt Mirry, in her ankle-length sable cape, appeared beside Lily, and Uncle Will, his mink-lined overcoat thrown over his arm, was right behind her, flanked in turn by the special guards Lily knew.

Down at the curb, the pearl-gray Rolls had drawn up, with Thomas sitting beside one of Aunt Mirry's chauffeurs.

Thomas jumped out at once and leaped up the red-carpeted steps three at a time to Lily's side. His face was apelike with fury. "Goddamned bastards!" he shouted at the barely quiescent crowd watching now from a safe distance. "I'll kill 'em!"

"Thomas! That will do!" The ultimate dismissal was in Miriam Dundell Hower Court's penetrating, contralto voice.

Lily felt herself hustled like so much baggage into the car. She tried to hang on to Joel as he was wrenched away from her. Quickly running down the window, she reached out her hand to him. "Joel!"

Aunt Mirry leaned across her. "I'm sorry, Mr. Maitland," she said, her tone as personal as one of her calling cards, "another time, perhaps."

Joel inclined his head to her. He lifted Lily's hand to his lips. "Good night, princess," he said, and quickly tucked the one-hundred-dollar bill into her hand.

Looking into his eyes, Lily pleaded, "Call me, Joel—*please!*"

His gaze caught to hers, lingered—but he did not answer.

The car moved away. She sat rigidly beside her aunt, tears staying in her eyes.

Chapter 6

In the immense room that had once been Grandpa Boeker's private study and was now Whitey's office, there was the sound of a pen scratching against paper, like a counterpoint to the tick of a towering clock in a niche.

"Just a few more of the checks, please, Boke. Mrs. Hamp and Aunt Mirry said it was fatal to get behind."

Lily shook back the green velvet cloak she wore over her leotard and stirred restlessly in the high oak chair. "I mustn't be late for my lesson."

"You've got almost half an hour, Boke—don't worry." Whitey grinned furtively on the other side of the vast desk as her employer scrawled "Lily" and "Boeker" as one barely legible word, impervious to amounts that could keep whole families for months, quite often did, as with the one that had also staved off bailiffs and foreclosure for her own. "I've got some cash for you, if you want it," she said.

Lily shook her head. "What for?"

Whitey shrugged. "Thought I'd better ask." She returned to her task of culling references to Lily from the day's newspapers. "Jeepers . . ." she muttered under her breath. "What bunk—don't they ever let up!"

"Never, Whitey." Lily pushed some pale, waved hair from her cheek. "You shouldn't bother with those morbid scrapbooks—we don't have to follow all of Aunt Mirry's instructions."

"I don't know, Boke . . . They're useful—as records. I think Aunt Mirry's right."

Lily sighed inwardly. Sometimes it seemed Whitey was on the other side of a wall. "Will you please telephone Joel again?" she said.

"Again, Boke! I've already left four messages at the hospital . . ."

"Did you say that it was very important?"

"Of course, Boke—I always do!"

Lily put down the pen and looked up, her wide, light gaze wavering under Whitey's bright scrutiny. "Whitey, I've got to talk to him. I've got to explain something!"

Whitey blew softly at her bangs. "You're only going to hurt yourself more, Boke. And him. He can't afford to have his picture plastered all over the front pages as your great true love—not again—it could ruin everything he's working for!"

"I know, Whitey, I know." Lily spread her ringed hands. "That's just it. I want to tell him it wouldn't—ever. It was a terrible mistake to go out in public, to think two people could go to a theater, go dancing after, without causing a riot . . ."

"Not any two people, Boke." Whitey's mouth tugged.

Lily's gaze flicked away. She felt a rising frustration. "Well—what I want to tell him is that from now on we'll only see each other in private, very discreetly. I want to promise him there'll be nothing more to worry about . . ."

"No?" Whitey drew in a breath. "Look, Boke—be realistic." She tapped her scissors at the newspapers in front of her, indicating various items. "Here—you're between the presidential candidate, Franklin D. Roosevelt, and the airship Akron—because when you tried to do some useful work at the hospital you raised a storm of protest from paid workers, and a lot of ridicule. Here—you're above the Lindbergh kidnapping, below Hoover's talk on his Reconstruction Finance Committee—because you donated a coffee and doughnut canteen but didn't know you had because it was done through Coggy for 'appeasement of the starving masses.' And here—Bessie Dixon's feature about this house gets more space than the one on the Russian Five-Year Plan . . . !"

"The Hippo?" Lily saw the huge woman splashing about with Daddy in the Long Island pool. "What does *she* have to say?"

"Better not ask—she's twisted truth like a pretzel. Aunt Mirry knew she'd have it in for you when you didn't invite her to the housewarming!"

Lily's heartbeat quickened. She sat back in the chair, locked her fingers against her bare thighs. "Read it out, Whitey."

"It'll make you *boil* . . ."

"Never mind."

"Well, okay . . ." Whitey reluctantly flattened the article, cleared her throat. "I'll skip all the who-you-are and how-much-you've-got bits . . ." Her voice lowered to a sly drawl.

"'It's hard to be sorry for the rich at any time, for any reason, and the compassion we once felt for this young multimillionheiress's bizarre childhood has vanished without a trace as we observe her current, unabashed self-indulgences.

"'You will, of course, have read many times how our gilded "Lily-Lily-Lily" was too jealous of her stepfather (who, to his credit, tried very hard to win her love) to live at home, how her mother was not up to controlling her, and of how her "Aunt Mirry"'—Mrs. so-and-so-and-so of so-and-so-and-so—'took on the responsibility of launching her into Society.

"'But that was only a taste of what was to come for this minion of unearned wealth. Not long after that-debut-we-shall-never-forget, the slender, blue-eyed beauty decided she could not live with her aunt, either—that the Palm Beach and Washington rounds were a bore, and that she wanted to set up her own menage in the great mansion on Fifth Avenue left to her by her grandfather—to "pursue her dancing career." (We suspect a likelier motivation was her cousin Andrew Dundell and the more sophisticated society *he* moves in!)'

"Want me to go on, Boke? It gets worse."

Lily nodded. Her fingers laced tighter.

"'There were, naturally, some very essential improvements to be made—plumbing, for instance, complete rewiring—oh, a thousand and one things to raise Grandpa Boeker's standards to his granddaughter's!

"'Thus—when she finally moved in, at the tender age of twenty, with no less than forty-one trunks (I have this on authority within the household!), six new bathrooms had been installed, a laundry to take care of wash for fifty guests as well as the resident staff, two large new kitchens (one smaller one in her own suite for her compulsive late-night snacks), a roof tennis court and putting green, a miniature Versailles ballroom, a huge mirrored dancing studio, and a lighted, full-size pool. The whole, of course, redecorated and refurbished to sparkle like a fairy-story palace!'

"I can bear this, if you can," Whitey said. "She goes on to say that you entertain as if there was no end to the money, and that there isn't, because that wizard 'Coggy' (Cogswell Brent, lawyer and trustee of the Boeker fortune) has quietly bought into markets no one seemed to notice were on the rise, like synthetics, aviation, wide-strip steel, et cetera, and has ways of making Boeker taxes dissolve while the rest of us, lacking influence and genius, pay . . .

"Surely that's libelous!" Whitey paused.

Lily's face was white and stiff. "If only we *could* sue her . . . But Aunt Mirry says it's never worth it. The publicity just makes it worse. Anyway, finish it."

"Well, she ends by saying that your parties feature elaborate dance presentations, with *you* as the star performer . . . Then a little sermon which warns you of what the future will bring—unless something 'pulls you up with a start, and shows you that such greed and selfishness will never make you happy and that you are an insult to the nation which made your fortune possible.'"

Lily looked down at her hands. "I could kill her."

Whitey nodded. "Considering Aunt Mirry commanded and carried out the whole thing, that all you asked for was one repainted apartment and the small kitchen—and that she was going off to Europe, in any case, and didn't know what to do about you . . ." Whitey's eyes brightened. "I know—why don't I write a protest to the paper, telling the real facts!"

Lily shook her head. A small lump seemed to travel down her chest. "I'll just *have* to conquer the art of manipulating the press before they manipulate me."

Whitey grinned. "Aunt Mirry's creed!"

"I know . . . If only I were Aunt Mirry . . ."

Suddenly Lily was on her feet. "But I'm not, Whitey, and I won't ever have to be—not if I keep up the hard work. Tino says I'll soon be professional enough to audition for the Mishka Modern Dance Company. . . . That's another thing I want to tell Joel—you see, we'd *both* be working people then. That *would* be different, wouldn't it? I'd be a real person apart from the money, wouldn't I?" Lily's eyes sparkled with wistful eagerness.

Whitey gazed at her blankly. "Well—I don't know, Boke . . ." She shrugged, grinned uncertainly. "To me, you're real with it. I like you best when you're just being what you are—you know?"

Lily's straight shoulders slackened a moment. In her mind the wall between them seemed to broaden, to rise. "Ah, well." She sighed, feeling the pull of some inward gloom that made her want to retreat to her bed, to bury her face in the pillows and sleep for days . . . "Well, let me know if Joel telephones. Tell him where he can reach me. . . . Where do I go after this?"

Whitey's peach-pink face quickly assumed efficiency and cheer. "Lady Nina Glendower's fashion lunch at one P.M.—you're the honored guest, of course. Then—if you insist, and I think it's a very risky thing—to serve at the canteen. After that, home, to hear the Young Women's League appeal for funds . . ."

"Why can't we just give them a check?"

"They wanted to see you—personally, I think they just want to get a foot in the door with you, and to see the house. Anyway, after that you've got the fitting for your fancy-dress costume, and at six Andy comes for you for the dinner party at Count and Countess Langlere's—and a late supper party with the cast of *Of Thee I Sing*, the leading man's birthday, I think—and Andy's promised he won't stick you with any more money leeches . . ."

"He doesn't know them when he sees them." Lily made a face. Whitey laughed.

Lily looked at her, wanting to say something that would bring them close again, like the days at school—but nothing would come to her. "Well—see you later . . ." She started for the door,

her cloak flying out behind her like dark, voluminous wings to
her thin, perfect body.

"That's good, darling, but unloose the waist more—bend—
sweep the floor with the fingers. Up, over, down—like a rag doll,
like a sensuous woman."

"Both at once, Tino?" Lily broke into a surprised laugh as she
struggled to match Tino's movements.

"Yes, both at once—you are young, supple, without bones!
Like this!" The black-haired man narrowed small black eyes,
raised his short torso from the bulging muscles of his thighs and
rotated it in grotesque emulation of a languid, sinuous female.

She tried again, but, as ever, fitting her movements to that of a
teacher was against her inclination. She longed to break free, to
just dance her own way—but of course she knew that had to be
controlled. If she was to be good, really good, she would have to
acquire the technique and discipline Tino tried so hard to give
her.

"But that is better, very nice—up, over, down—one, two, three,
four—up, over, down. Now—to the right and up—left leg low to
the ground, right knee to the chin—bend deep, deep. The same
to the left—one, two, three, four—pair-fect!"

Lily was surprised at his approval; the tendons of her calves
had pulled and her balance had faltered. But perhaps she was, at
last, getting closer.

"Now I will put on the music and you will do the rest with me
just as you've learned."

She shoved her damp hair behind her ears, her face flushed.
"Tino—if I hadn't been—well, *me*—would I *really* have this chance
to get into the dance company?"

He waved his arms as he moved, feet out-turned in soft ballet
shoes, towards the big mahogany Victrola. "I told you yes, darling, yes. You are a beautiful dancer, and someday you will be
supreme!"

"Oh, Tino—I must work hard, harder than ever before!"

He looked back over his shoulder, blew her a kiss from
bunched fingers. "We will show the world, my darling!"

What would she do without Tino? she thought. He was the
one and only person who took her dancing seriously, who

believed she could achieve something legitimately her own, that no amount of money, no mount of mockery could deny . . . !

"Lily! Lily! What about this famous work!" Tino clapped his white, hirsute hands, beckoned her to take up his position behind him. Sometimes she felt like laughing at his serious, powdered face with the high, black-penciled eyebrows and lipsticked mouth drawn into its pinched, haughty smile. His close-fitting tunic and tights did not become him as they did in the photographs and press clippings of his dancing days, and his raised chin made his neck like a scrawny bird's. But when she remembered that he had given up his own dancing school to coach her, the laugh stuck.

"Tino isn't suffering," Thomas said when she was sorry for taking him away from it. "He's got more dough than he's ever seen in his life!" And when she'd wondered if he was lonely, Thomas said, "He's got a boy friend, Lil—gave him a new Oldsmobile for Christmas!" Thomas, of course, could never believe there were people money could not corrupt.

"No, no, darling—you're dreaming! We will start again, yes?"

"Sorry!" How patient and dedicated he was! She must reward him by excelling herself. Remembering Daddy's face wreathed in amused approval, the voice of the Irish maid saying, "You're a bit of a genius, you are," and all the servants applauding her special performance for them in the studio of her house, she braced herself tall, put her feet in position. In the high, pink-mirrored walls of the ballroom-size studio with its wrought-iron torches in mirrored recesses, its multicolored spotlights and satiny polished floor, she saw her figure like a thousand blackbirds poised for flight through brilliance.

As the first strains of the haunting modern symphony waved through the amplifiers, she felt vibrations of pure energy. Her head went back, her slender arms began to lift and undulate, her body began to weave patterns of movement that welled joyously from some long-known source deep within her . . .

"Lily, pleece—we waste the precious time!"

Lily's eyes were half closed. She heard Tino, but she couldn't make it matter, couldn't stop. She danced away from him, farther, farther across the great room, lost in motion and rhythm, in oneness with the music . . .

"It is lovely to improvise, darling, lovely—but you acquire bad habits. Pleece—do as I say!"

Only a moment more, she thought hazily as she whirled, dipped, leapt, scooped up invisible feathers, released them, arched her back and reached for the sky. Around, around, around —her hair fluttering from its smooth waves and fashionable curls like a pale-lemon banner . . .

I am the earth, the trees, the wind, the oceans, mountains, stars —the planets and all the universe . . .

Abruptly, the music stopped. There was silence. Caught awkwardly off balance, arms raised, head thrown back and lips apart, she tottered, blinked with chagrin. Tino stood by the Victrola, arms folded across his chest, face puckered with severity.

She righted herself, smiled appealingly. "Oh, Tino—I'm sorry, I couldn't help it, honest."

Tino didn't speak or move, and his expression failed to resolve into loving tolerance.

Lily frowned questioningly. "You're angry, Tino—really angry." A dim, unfamiliar doubt edged her awareness. But before she could name it, Tino was throwing out his arms, advancing towards her with his quick, splay-footed walk.

"Darling—I think only of you. Will you be a child of nature— or the true artist?" He lifted her hand, laid it against his flour-white face, then drew her towards the middle of the floor. "Come—I will show you the difference. I will prove to you how much you need Constantino—to listen and follow him!" His voice rose with dramatic emphasis on his name.

Why was she suddenly watching him, looking at him as if she had never really seen him before? Why did he look like a stranger and everything about him suspect?

"Tino," she said, before the terrible thoughts took hold, "I really don't feel like dancing any more. I've got a very busy schedule."

"Ah—I am disappointed, heartbroken, my darling. Before you have even begun—and Tino's so thrilled with your progress!"

"Tino—if you've been lying to me all this time . . ."

For an instant, the tender, almost simpering expression on his face seemed a waxen parody of itself. "What can you possibly mean, darling—lying? About what?"

She kept looking at him. The fear behind the innocence in his small black eyes made the ground wave under her feet. Words of accusation, of cruel revenge, came trembling to be said.

But suddenly, before the ground opened and caved in, she turned and moved off towards the black-tiled dressing rooms. In a mirrored image, she saw Tino standing like a molded statue, hands pressed hard to thighs, head lifted in wariness.

She let the maid who was waiting pat her with towels, brush her hair, change her shoes, lift her cloak onto her shoulders. When she emerged, Tino was hovering outside, the painted eyebrows anxiously raised.

"I see now, darling," he said quickly, "you have the true sensitivity of the artist—I should not have said a child of nature, but untrained!"

"Yes, Tino," she said, meeting his eyes. "Perhaps you should."

He swallowed, ran a narrow white hand across the black plastered cap of his hair. "We will have another lesson soon, darling—yes?"

She drew her cloak around her. In high heels she now looked down on him. "I'll have Miss White get in touch with you," she said.

She was no sooner through the doors than she felt remorse. Pausing, she turned back. Tino was still standing where she had left him, his face stiff with shock.

"Tino," she called. "There's nothing for *you* to worry about." She closed the door.

"Lily, darling, I'm so delighted to see you!"

Lily tried to fend off Nina Glendower's kiss on each cheek with a hand extended, but it fell back unacknowledged. "I just adore the Schiaparelli blue, Lily, and that matching cap's such *fun!* I'm dying to show you the house—as you see, I've had it completely done over in white. Refreshing, don't you think?"

"Very nice, Nina. The flowers look spectacular against it."

Nina Glendower smiled broadly. An ash blonde with blue eyes, a heavy square face running to chins, she had tried desperately to pattern herself on Lily since meeting her at her debut. She walked regally and dieted stringently, but even in simplest black and all the jewels she had inherited with her new husband, she achieved only a lady-in-waiting image beside the princess her-self.

Lily was oblivious. Her royal-blue chinchilla-lined cape was taken. In a white velvet-walled boudoir with a vast black-and-white bed, she removed the tiny, side-tilted hat, and when no maid appeared, reached into her purse to see if a comb had been put inside. Yes, the pretty one with the diamond-chip edge. It was pleasant to do her own hair, though she was clumsy.

"I think you'll like the clothes we're showing," Nina said, put-ting her arm through Lily's and leading her to the lime-white living room where twenty or thirty young women, like a blaze of multihued flowers, were stiffly assembled. "And don't you think it's just the niftiest way to raise money for the unfortunate, darling?"

Lily thought of the persistent telephone calls that had made her accept, and Nina's final plea—"It's your name, darling—if you come, everyone will . . . *and* fork up, don't you see?"

It would have been easier to give her a donation—but Aunt Mirry had admonished her about "playing God at a distance" and shying away from her contemporaries. "You'll need compan-ions," she had advised, "those not too far down from the moun-taintop. So you won't be left up there alone."

"It's marvelous of you to do it, Nina," she said sincerely. "It must have taken quite a bit of work."

"Well, it has—I've only got one secretary, you know—though servants being as cheap as they are these days, I've got more help with the house. Come and meet the girls—though I'm sure you'll have met most."

As they stepped into the large room with bay windows onto Fifth Avenue, there was an outbreak of restrained greeting. Young women with variations of immaculate hair, good looks and recognizable haute couture turned their attention to Lily in wordless concession of sovereignty.

"Darling, Tom and I saw you at Reggie Blount's ball—you were sensational in that apricot lamé with the feathered train!"

"Yes, and that handsome red-headed man with you, Lily, we couldn't place him . . ."

Lily laughed. "Probably Rick—General Court's nephew."

"Oh, yes . . . ?"

Lily pushed at her hair, already feeling stifled. Every woman in the room watched her hands as they rose, fell. (It was said that one of her rings had been found sewn into Marie Antoinette's pillowcase just after the beheading.)

"Why, hello, Lily my dear. The last time I saw you was at the theater with that darling medico . . . !"

Lily turned in swift recognition of the voice. Hilda Housman of *Vogue* magazine was someone even Aunt Mirry spoke to with care; it was one thing to be misquoted, misinterpreted, misjudged, but another to be "characterized," "revealed" for the socially discriminating. All her cause with Joel needed now was the astute discernment of "H.H.," as she was known!

"I thought this was to be a strictly private occasion," she said to her.

"But that's right, darling," Nina intervened. "H.H. is only here to write up the show itself."

The woman with flatly waved henna hair protruding from a black satin sombrero, parted dark-red lips like a jagged pocket and smiled. "Absolutely, my lamb. Only want to *help*."

Lily held her glass carefully. "How generous."

Hilda Housman's black-outlined eyes were etched in benevolent disinterest. "The course of true love not too smooth, darling? Must be very difficult to . . ."

"Lily!" Nina called out. "I'm told the grub is on!"

Laughter at this impropriety relieved Lily of answering, and Nina led her off ahead of the chattering group to the large, equally stark-white dining room. Here, in meager imitation of Aunt Mirry's jungle theme, birds flew out of painted forests and tiger skins covered tall-backed chairs. Large paintings of ebony-skinned natives carrying spears or playing drums were hung at unconventional heights, forcing the guests to raise their eyes and glimpse the ceiling where light filtered like sun through a matting of giant leaves.

Lily could hardly believe the comments.

"Your interior decorator's a genius, Nina."

"So original!"

"Delicious, darling. Makes one actually hungry."

Surely they carried politeness too far. She had had superior decor in the playhouse!

"Thank you, thank you—here, angel, next to me," Nina Glen-dower was saying, smiling as if in triumph.

Lily squirmed inwardly. It was clear why she was an angel in this case, but it wasn't only Nina who paid her unearned hom-age; handsome, pretty or plain, most of the young women here gave her heedful, if furtive glances of regard.

"I wonder if I can count on you for my dinner party in May, Lily?" one of them paused to ask in a low voice.

Lily looked into the vaguely familiar face. "You've invited me?" she asked, trying to place her.

"Oh, yes! Some time ago. My secretary hasn't heard from yours yet."

"Really? I'm very sorry—but you see, mine is quite new . . ."

"Don't worry. I understand only too well. But you're my guest of honor—hopefully, Lily."

"Oh?" Lily smiled uncertainly. "Something special?"

"No . . . nothing specific. It's just that you're fairly new in New York, and we thought you might not know some of the charming people coming, perhaps want to . . ."

"I see." Lily opened her eyes upward into the discomfited but persevering hazel gaze. "I'm sorry again, but please remind me of your name."

"Why, Florence, Lily. Mrs. Glifford Herbert now. My daddy's General Court's old friend. I was at your debut and your . . ."

"Yes, of course! I'm so vague, Florence . . ."

"Not at all—you must meet so *many* people!"

Lily shook her head, although it was true; if quantity meant anything, her "friends" could not have been counted. "Whitey—my secretary—will let you know tomorrow, I promise. Please for-give me."

"Of *course*. Hope you'll make it."

Lily was conscious of Nina watching her as the food and wine were served. There was nothing outstanding about it, but Nina obviously hoped for reassurance. If only she would forget her, relax and be herself.

"What do you think of the fashions this year, darling?" Nina asked now, accepting Lily's smile as seal of approval, but at-tempting to emulate the innocent catlike expression of her eyes.

Lily felt the attention on her, not only of the women at her table, but those nearby, among them H.H. "Well, I haven't bought much this year," she said, as softly as she could. "Apart from Vionnet's bias cut and Madame Gres's marvelous drape, I really hated to see the short skirts go out."

"I agree!" said Nina. "And after the years it took to get them up there! What about hats?"

"I don't know, Nina—I like Rose Descat's little brims, I suppose. But personally I loved the cloche. My mother used to have them made on her head, in all colored felts, by one of Reboux's descendants, you know. She looked so lovely in them!" Too late, Lily was aware of the fascinated silence. Her lashes flickered downward to her watch in an almost unconquerable urge to run.

"Your finger waves are beautiful, Lily. Who does them?"

Lily looked at the plump brunette, not sure whether her name was Sally or Mary Vanderveer. "Gustaf—he's on the staff."

"That's so sensible," the brunette said. "Nothing in the world bores me more than sitting in those stifling places while they hover over you with dryers."

"I can't bear *manicures*," said another girl Lily did not know at all. "But Daddy gave me ten thousand dollars to stop biting my nails!"

"Cheap at the price, Denise. Mine gave me twice that much to give up the violin!"

During the laughter, Lily's right little finger passed in unconscious impatience over the long red nails of her left hand, causing the diamond-surrounded sapphire to sparkle more noticeably.

"We must begin," said Nina, quickly clapping her hands.

Lily touched her arm. "Nina—I may have to leave."

"Lily, you wouldn't!" Nina could barely conceal her stricken look. She bent closer to Lily. "Everyone thinks that you and I—I mean, it would be *embarrassing*, darling!"

"Well—it depends on how long the show is. There're so many things crowded in, you see, Nina—I'm sorry."

"We'll get right on with it. Oh, thanks, Lily—you're an angel!" Lily sighed.

For what seemed hours, now, tall, bored mannequins strutted in and out of the room, announced by an equally tall pale man in morning suit and accompanied by a string orchestra playing the

dansant music. Dresses of Lanvin, Chanel, Worth, Poiret, Moly-
neaux, Lelong and others passed before her in a blur. She had
seen most of them with Aunt Mirry, and already bought what
she considered best of the lines, so that these held no interest
whatever.

She smothered a yawn and tried to look at her watch without
notice, but the face surrounded in diamonds was too small and
pale to see. She toyed with champagne, smiled abstractedly at
the cadaverous mannequins and fought an aversion that gnawed
increasingly at her control.

She was aware that when she politely applauded, others behind her immediately joined in, as if not to be outdone—and
once, in a slight hush as the tall girls drifted—swiveled—drifted
past, and the music suddenly softened for the "new romantic
look of frills and ruffles," she heard a guarded whisper . . .

"What do you expect? Of course she's blasé! She could buy
the collections en masse, and us!"

As if a tide pushed her to her feet, she had stood up, moved
quickly and quietly between the tables, over to the open doors
and into the hall.

Somewhere as she went on, she found a maid, asked for her
wrap and hat. Without putting them on, and before Nina could
catch up to ask questions, she was at the front door, having it
opened for her, beckoning to Thomas down at the curb.

"Take me to the canteen, Thomas," she told him, "and please
don't argue."

Thomas gave her a sharp glance of appraisal, then nodded to
his aide, closed her quickly into the Rolls.

"I don't like the look of this," Lily heard the bodyguard say to
Thomas. "Did anyone tell the papers she was coming here
today?"

Lily could see Thomas grin. "You kidding? Who has to tell the
vultures anything!" Horns hooted as he slowed the Rolls.

Lily sat up and peered beyond his broad, familiar back. For
almost a block ahead, crowds of shabbily dressed men and
women milled along the trash-littered sidewalk near the row of
stores on the far west of the city that had been converted into
the Boeker-funded canteen. "They're probably waiting their

turn, Thomas," she said. "We serve hundreds of people, you know . . ."

"They'd be lined up, Lil—afraid of losing their places."

"He's right, Miss Boeker, something's fishy." The guard turned his big blond head to her, his bony jaw alertly raised.

"Looks like the cops there, Herman. It could be anything—I'm getting out of here." Thomas pulled quickly to the middle of the avenue, put his hand out for a left turn.

"Sit well back, miss," the bodyguard said as the car made its swerve. "Keep out of sight."

"Another second, and they'd've recognized the car," Thomas muttered.

"Thomas!" said Lily. "Turn back at once! I'm due to be there and serve in person, and I intend to do what I promised!"

"Sorry, Lil—know how you feel. But I ain't taking chances."

The bodyguard was nodding. "It could be anything, as you say. Better to read about it in tomorrow's papers."

"You can say *that* again."

Lily clenched her hands helplessly. When Thomas felt right beyond question, she had no power.

She sat back, swallowing disappointment.

"Where do you want to go now, Lil—home?" Thomas asked.

Lily rested her elbow on the padded armrest, her gaze disconsolate. She thought of the Young Women's League, the fitting for the costume, the evening of festivities, of Joel not having called her, receding from her, perhaps forever . . .

A sudden resolve hit her, made her pulse race. Yes, she thought, yes! She sat up. "Take me to Coggy," she said clearly, firmly, "to the Boeker Building!"

"Lil—you're nuts to go all the way downtown, when he always comes to you!"

"This is not your business, Thomas!"

He raised a shoulder for Herman's benefit, was silent.

Lily felt a lift of spirits, a buoyancy. It was *the* answer, one she had often considered, secretly, not knowing quite how or when it might be done . . .

She gazed more alertly from the window, watched the city flash past. How obliviously the spring sun shone, turning the park to carefree green and the windows of the great buildings to blazing gold while hungry men shuffled along in thousands to the breadline diners, swarmed forlornly around employment agencies with no work to give them, or sheltered in the acres of tar-paper "Hoovervilles."

As Thomas slowed at a corner, people stared in at her so dully, so curiously, that she pushed the mink rug from her knees. They did not all, she thought, look "down and out." They weren't *all* without jobs and homeless, even if she had read that about seventeen thousand were evicted every day because they could not pay their rent. But of course good clothes, Whitey said, could last quite a long time before looking shabby, and usually they kept their good clothes for looking for work . . .

Lily averted her gaze and drew her face from sight as a big man with a mustache and angry, mocking eyes moved close to the car saying something she could not hear.

She felt guilty for being glad when Thomas drove on and other cars surrounded them. Ice prickled her neck when she thought of the crumbs she had offered in the way of assistance. No wonder they had called her "Princess Bountiful," thanked her with that sarcastic ardor!

"But you didn't notice them refusing anything, did you?" Coggy had said, his thin lips smiling.

"What would you do if *your* stomach was hurting with hunger?"

His smile had stretched thinner. He seemed to find her words amusing.

Well, today he wouldn't.

"If you ask me," Thomas was saying to the guard, "most of them are shiftless bums."

"I wouldn't say most, Thomas—some." The guard gave Thomas a sharp look. "There are plenty of respectable businessmen, lawyers, teachers among 'em. And men who fought for their country. Don't forget that, buddy."

Thomas shrugged. "And a lot of them got greedy, kept spending instead of laying by. Boeker wouldn't be jumping out of no windows now. Nor would his son."

"Thomas," Lily spoke out abruptly. "What would *you* do now if I fired you?"

Thomas gave her a disdainful look and wink in the rearview

mirror. "I'd be okay, Lil. I haven't stuffed my ears with cotton all these years."

Lily glanced at the guard, wondering if there was bitterness in his averted gaze. "And why haven't you lost it all now?" she asked Thomas.

"That's easy, Lil. I watched Coggy."

Lily frowned. "You've never told me all this . . ."

Thomas turned smoothly, adroitly onto Broadway. "There's a lot you don't know, Lil. Look at that," he said to the guard, lifting a hand from the wheel to gesture towards the block-long queues to the movie theaters. "Twelve noon. You call that broke."

"Thomas," Lily said, her blue gaze sharp on the mirror. "Shall I tell you why? Thousands of people have nothing else to do and nowhere else to go all day. Besides, it's their only fun!"

Thomas burst into a deep chuckle. "What sob sister have you been reading, Lil? You should talk to the movie moguls. Movies is the biggest business in the nation—they're making billions out there in Hollywood!"

Lily tilted the blue cap even lower over one eye and looked from the window. "No more of your opinions, please, Thomas," she said, so curtly that Thomas actually fell silent, as if realizing something unusual was in her mind.

Lily looked at the names of the movies, the stars spelled out in light on the marquees—soon she would see them all, not with Andy or in private homes, but paying for her seat herself and going inside along with all the others—*The Sign of the Cross* with Claudette Colbert and Charles Laughton—Marlene Dietrich in *Blonde Venus—Love Me Tonight* with Jeanette MacDonald and Maurice Chevalier—*Rain* with Joan Crawford—*The Mask of Fu Manchu* with Boris Karloff—Katharine Hepburn and John Barrymore in *A Bill of Divorcement* . . .

And she'd see all the plays and wander all through stores like John Wanamaker's and Altman's and the others Aunt Mirry said sold "nothing worth having." She'd visit the Boeker Emporiums, too, of course . . .

She would change her name, dye her hair black, wear glasses. No one would know who she was or ever had been. No one would connect her with money in any way. There'd be no more bowing and scraping, those sickly fawning smiles and all the nauseating flattery—no more press people following her, spying on her, snapping her picture every time she moved—no more guarding her words, no more of the false rumors and conclusions that had to be denied—no more people hating her for just being rich.

She would get to know herself, what she was really like as a person. If she made friends it would be because she was wanted as a friend, not for her name or money or influence. If a man was attracted to her, it wouldn't be because of the wretched millions, but because he was genuinely attracted . . .

Not that that mattered, since Joel would be there. They would marry in a very small church, with only a few hundred guests—no, less, even including Joel's family . . .

Lily gazed from the Rolls with growing recognition of another world, as it paused by shops plastered with cut-rate "going out of business" and "for sale" signs. A youngish man in a tweed suit sat in a vacant store demonstrating something with a chart and pointer. Watching him, Lily felt her throat tighten. He was so handsome and jovial, so enthusiastic as he made jokes and talked and talked—to only three people, one of them already losing interest. He could so easily have been one of her friends, someone Aunt Mirry cultivated because of his good manners and family name. How thin the line was that divided the rich and poor!

The car moved on, past a restaurant called "Depression Cafe. Meals 5¢ and 10¢." Meals for *cents!* Lily saw mentally into her purse . . . There must have been several hundred dollars in it . . .

"Well, here it is, Lil," Thomas was saying, "ye Olde Boeker Building. Okay, Herman, you cruise."

Lily cast aside her dismal feeling, as she saw the blond bodyguard slip behind the wheel of the Rolls and put a Boeker-blue chauffeur's cap on his head. Looking upward a moment before entering the gigantic, narrow building, whose doors were flanked on one side by a man in a cap selling neckties from an upturned crate, on the other by a lady apple-seller wearing a fur-collared coat, she marveled again at its height. As tall as other buildings around it were, its pointed dome rose above them all to pierce straight into the sky . . .

She swayed, forgetting where she was . . .

"Lil! You're getting enough attention already!"

At the hard, insistent pressure on her elbow, Lily's slim figure in the short-jacketed blue suit and cape quickly straightened. As she saw the familiar recognition and curiosity, the massing of a crowd, she was suddenly glad of Thomas pressing her on quickly through the big lobby and into Cogswell Brent's private elevator.

Riding up in it, Lily got a sense of her grandfather's presence. His pride in this building had been so great that, as a small child visiting him, riding up, up to his huge Napoleonic offices, when she had spoken of him as God and the building as his house in heaven, he had only smiled. Even when she was older and had seen it at night lit up like a giant castle in the Manhattan sky, she had thought of it as a celestial structure somehow made visible through her grandfather's invisible influence.

"You'll wait in the outer office," she said now to Thomas, "and keep away from Coggy's door."

Thomas's swarthy face pinched with reluctance, and he did not fall back until Miss Griffith returned quickly to usher her into the palatial rooms that had been both Wilbur and Richard Boeker's offices.

"Why, she's dear—just like anyone," she heard the receptionist say to the secretary as the door closed.

Cogswell Brent crossed the sumptuous Persian carpet to greet her, putting on his jacket as he came. Behind him, several men looked up in barely shielded curiosity. The sun seemed to billow over the vast expanse of paneled walls and woods, the verdant plush, and dark, looming oils, the glowing depths of mellowed leather, unhampered by intervening structures.

"Good morning, my dear—what an unexpected pleasure! My staff and I have been working on various new ventures. I'm sure they would like very much to greet you."

"Coggy," she whispered, "I'd rather not just now—and this is extremely confidential."

"Well—of course. We'll go to old Wilbur's inner sanctum, as your dad used to call it."

"Thank you." Smiling vaguely in the direction of the other men, Lily followed the tall, narrow-shouldered man to another, smaller room. Here, the papers were piled high, cigar butts and ashes had not been emptied, and there were crusts of sandwiches and black dregs in ringed coffee cups.

"No one's allowed to clean the place," he explained, "nothing's touched. Just the way old Wilbur liked it. He did all of his hardest thinking in here, drove his hardest bargains across this old roll-top."

"I know." Lily declined to have her cape taken and sat down slowly on a scuffed leather chair. "I remember this—it came from his very first office."

"That's right." Cogswell Brent sat behind the desk and studied her quickly as she settled herself slightly forward in the chair, her delicate, lavishly ringed hands clasped gracefully on her knees. What he thought was not apparent on his tightly drawn, golf-weathered face. That most of his life had been spent thinking, except for his deliberate weekend transmutation on the links, was mapped in deep permanent lines across his domed forehead, between his indistinctly blue eyes and under the gaunt chin so consistently lowered to sheets of figures in small print.

"To what urgent matter can I ascribe your sudden visit, my dear?" he asked.

Lily wondered if he meant to keep her at the child level, or whether he simply didn't notice any change. When she was a small girl, she had liked his way of squatting down beside her to say hello, and his quick, sand-dry kiss. But over the years he himself seemed to have dried. She could not remember seeing him laugh, as he had done occasionally with Daddy and Mummy, and even Aunt Mirry said that there was nothing in the world you could talk to him about except money. "He's obsessive, lost in the game—but thank your lucky stars he is! It's that concentration that's made him a genius, a visionary."

Lily drew in a breath, lifted her chin. "Coggy," she said steadily, "it's about my money."

"Again! You're *still* dissatisfied with what you're giving away!"

Her hands moistened. Sitting there so straight, expressionless and detached, he seemed suddenly fear-inspiring.

"This time it's the whole thing . . ."

"The whole thing? What does that mean, child?"

She pressed a stray wave closer to her left ear, touched the horseshoe pin of diamonds on her braided collar. "I don't want to come into my money, Coggy. I want you to start a complete divestiture of it—all of it."

Cogswell Brent did not speak. His left forefinger beat a restrained tattoo on the desk. Part of his jaw moved like a pulse. Then suddenly he threw down the pencil. "Young lady," he said, "you need some of the hard facts explained, and explained bluntly. With due regard to your difficult childhood and lack of proper education, your naïveté is downright dangerous. And I can't allow it to destroy a bequest in good faith."

Lily folded her arms across her chest and set her chin. Her heartbeat was unsteady. She could not remember anyone speaking to her like this, even Aunt Mirry. "My grandfather did not say I *had* to have the money, or *keep* it. If he had known how the people felt about it, how wrong it was to have so much when others had so little, he would understand. And he'd approve, what's more!"

Coggy leaned back slightly in the creaking swivel chair with its huge oak backrest. "Let me ask you one thing, Lily. Just suppose there hadn't been this stock-market decline and its effect, and the people of this country were still proud of their rich and looked at you with smiles and adulation—would you still want to shed your wealth?" He looked at her long and hard, his eyes flinty.

Lily could not help thinking that it was probably in her power to replace Coggy. She sat back and crossed her silk-stockinged ankles, placed her hands flat on the chair arms.

"Well, yes—I would. It isn't natural. I've had no say or choice in my life. And it *is* my life, Coggy."

"Only in the way you conduct it." He sat back, tucked his thumbs into his waistcoat pockets, one of which held his inevitable two cigars. "Assuming you would genuinely like to divest yourself of your money, which I seriously doubt and wouldn't like to see tested—how exactly would you suggest this be done?"

Lily looked at him warily, her delicately shaped lips slightly apart. "Just . . . Well, sell everything."

"And do what with the profits?"

"Oh, Coggy, honestly—naturally I don't know the details. Charities. People who need it most. *You'd* take care of all that."

"I see. I would sell all the investments, the bonds, the property, hand all the money out. And you, I gather, would fire all your servants?"

"See that they were well taken care of first, of course."

Grim amusement passed briefly over Coggy's granite face. "Well, my dear." He took out one of the cigars, lit it concentratedly, put it in the side of his mouth and puffed thoughtfully before he spoke. "Before you cherish these illusions let me inform you that divestiture of a fortune this size is not only too complex to be feasible, but if it were, it would be selfish, irresponsible and ignorant, benefiting no one and creating havoc."

"I don't understand."

"No, of course you don't. It would take an education in high finance, the machinations of law and taxation, of big business, of vast interlocking networks of corporate mathematics. It's taken *me* thirty years, ever since your dad gave me the responsibility, to gauge, maneuver the Boeker fortune in relation to the national economy and vice versa."

"Is that why you don't want to do it, because it would be your life's work gone?"

He considered the young face bright with revelation, then took the cigar from his mouth in suppressed exasperation. "Young lady," he said, "I know better than to expect credit from you, but now I see that you can't come to grips with simple reality."

"It's all you think of, Coggy, though—isn't it? Making money from money. You've forgotten about people, you don't *care!*"

Coggy's sand-colored lashes descended in ennui. "It's an all-consuming pursuit to anticipate trends, to keep an empire of interests under control, to evaluate international monetary shifts, to make decisions and commitments and take calculated risks. Perhaps you're aware of some of the results of faulty judgment and inattention?"

Lily's left eyebrow rose slightly. "You mean the suicides?"

"Well—those, and millions of less spectacular victims." The spring light filtered through the cigar smoke gathering around Coggy's head, haloing him, in Lily's eyes, in godlike authority.

"Now," he recommended, "let's talk sensibly. You could start off by publicizing the charities you already support—there's nothing to be gained by the anonymity you've insisted on, and when you inherit the rest, you can endow a few more foundations, a college, donate land and various collections."

"But people must be clothed, fed, sheltered—now!"

"Ah, welfare is difficult. However, we can make a point of creating substantial and effective assistance. The greatest good you can do, however, is to keep the money *flowing*. There's only one crime wealth can commit, and that's hoarding. As long as money isn't taken out of the currency system, there's nothing it can do but good. Your spending means employment for thousands. It increases production, for instance, when you buy clothes; it keeps the dressmakers in business. When you buy cars, houses, jewels, furs, yachts, foods and wines, flowers, gifts, furniture and so on and on, you keep the economy moving."

"But all for one person, one unimportant . . ."

"Let me finish, child." Coggy held up a dry-palmed hand on the small finger of which gleamed a perfect, muted star sapphire set in white gold. "Try to get it through your head, my dear, that the question of wealth, of some people accumulating a great deal while others go without, has never been satisfactorily equated. No philosophy has ever found a lasting means of equal distribution. Until such time as it is, ninety-five percent of people on earth will scramble to have what the other five percent have. In fact, money provides the chief incentive of almost every human being on earth."

"But what am *I* supposed to do for incentive, Coggy!"

Coggy paused, then shrugged. "That's something I'm not qualified to answer. Your aunt, however, wants to leave behind her museum collections of great treasures—that's one kind of contribution, one kind of incentive. There must be hundreds of others. Contrary to common opinion, it takes more character to be in your unique position than to be struggling."

Lily thought of Joel. "To have the money I need before I even start," he'd said, "that would totally demoralize me. To struggle for a goal, that's a blessing, and the harder it is to achieve, the greater the blessing!"

"You're puzzled," Coggy was saying. "I admit you're much too young to recognize this. Perhaps the ideal situation for any of us would be to have *enough*—enough to want more, enough not to be in want."

Lily looked past his head to the clean-swept blue of the sky. A white bird flew across her vision, and then another, winging strong and free above the city.

"Now, while you're here," Coggy said, clearing his throat and looking at his watch, "there are some suggestions I would like to make to further the opportunities of the moment. For instance, there are several houses in Newport, one or two of the biggest whose owners you undoubtedly know, which have come up for sale. It would satisfy your need to help others, and increase your holdings, to buy at least one. When you feel like it, you could redecorate. A staff of resident servants would increase employment."

Lily stood up abruptly. "I'm not going to discuss things like that now, Coggy. I'm not sure *anything* you've said is right!"

Cogswell Brent nodded, stubbed out the cigar, rose. "I'm sorry if I've upset you, my dear. The facts of economic life aren't easy. For any of us."

Lily was almost eye to eye with him now, thin, straight-backed, a brilliant splurge of blue in the big musty room. "You must be pretty rich yourself," she said with sudden insight, her eyes searching his.

His Adam's apple moved slightly under his stiff white collar. "I don't stop to think about it." He put his hand on her shoulder and patted it. "Someday you'll understand. You'll look back on this day and smile."

"Yes?"

"Yes. The way many years from now the whole country will look back. Long after the dust of panic and fear has blown away, it will see that Hoover was right, that it should have had confidence in him. And it will see that despite all apparent evidence, American prosperity was continuing to expand."

"Oh . . . !" The gasp of futility burst from her. She half ran from this man she thought she had known all her life. Grabbing the door open for herself, she ignored his startled attempt at gallantry and solicitude and moved quickly through the main offices, out to where Thomas, hat in hand, stood waiting.

She walked quickly past him, and under the fascinated stares of typists and receptionists, Thomas strode after her. He moved with her into the elevator, stood close beside her, eyes vigilant.

As people watched them in abandoned curiosity, Lily felt every nerve in her body strain, pull, tingle. She wanted to run, to scream, to jump into a black, bottomless hole.

On the street a crowd stood gazing at the smoothly gleaming Rolls. Lily considered bolting—but it was not, she had discovered one time she had tried it, a sure means of escape.

"Here's Herman, Lil—quick!"

Thrust skillfully through the crowd, Lily found herself propelled and safely closed into the soft-leather, perfume-scented interior of the car, moving swiftly off into the traffic.

Thomas did not ask where she wished to go. "It's no good, Lil," he said, tugging his cap more squarely on his head, "we ain't moving about no more without another bodyguard, without Al as well as Herman."

Lily did not bother to answer.

Chapter 7

"Late, of course, spectacularly late to her own twenty-first-birthday party. Always an eye to the grand entrance."

That was what the papers would say, Lily thought, as she and Chip stepped off the elevator into Andy's new, fifty-room penthouse. Little would they guess that she nearly hadn't come at all. If Andy hadn't planned such an ambitious occasion, she could not possibly have emerged from her soul-black mourning for Joel.

"This way, Miss Boeker, and . . ."

"Mr. Kenelm," said Lily. For once, Chip was amusing. His smothered groans, as he struggled to be heard through his huge Ape Man headpiece, protested her laughter.

The footmen and maids smiled without restraint. When she had followed them past a room already filled with coats to another of shocking-pink alabaster and low-lined black-mirror furniture, and allowed the maids to take her long white-fox cape, she had another moment of acute reluctance.

How could she have let Starenze talk her into this ludicrous impersonation of Florenz Ziegfeld's notorious star Gamelda, the vulgar gold lamé split to the knee, the gold lamé gloves to the armpits, the gold, black and white feathered headdress and the jewels practically weighing her down!

And all that makeup! She peered at her heavily mascaraed eyes in one of Andy's lighted mirrors. The mauve eye shadow and high, thin penciled brows, the dark-red mouth made her a stranger—but Whitey had been ecstatic. "You could be Gamelda—but you're much more glamorous!" Only Maudie had disapproved.

Oh, well—no turning back. For better or worse, here she was.

"Mmm-ahhh dee . . ." Chip said, as she rejoined him and they moved towards the main room.

She pushed at the immense ape teeth leering at her as he bent close. "You can take the thing off as soon as people have guessed," she whispered, thinking that there was poetic justice in his suffering for trying to be the biggest and most outstanding here tonight.

"Mr. Dundell's been waiting for you, Miss Boeker—he's anxious to talk to you. I'll find him."

Lily thanked the footman, who plunged ahead into the massed confusion of milling, costumed guests. A big band was playing jazz with such rhythm and individuality that it could only be Duke Ellington's, she thought.

She felt a sudden excitement, a pull of response in her body. Her costume was not outré at all—and there was an electric gaiety in the crowd.

She peered further into the room, which, last time she had seen it, resembled the garden of an ancient Roman villa with a terrace, a semicircular pool and statues of male Romans copied from originals. Beyond, in an incongruous harmony, had stretched the geometric rooftops of Manhattan and, below, the panorama of the park. Now, all she could see was bodies, faces, a fantasy of familiar images like the maddest of dreams spilled into waking.

"You'll have to hand it to me, sweet pea," Andy had said, "the idea's pure genius. A Guess Who party—your birthday and my housewarming combined—a Come as a Famous Twentieth-Century Personality party. They'll trample each other to death getting invitations. It'll be the party of our day, dear."

"But what about Aunt Mirry!" she had protested, hoping it would be the excuse she needed to forget the odious day of inheritance. "She's planning to have a party for hundreds of illustrious . . ."

"Bores! You know it, dear. Come on, Leelee—you're a big girl now. Tell my mother she can . . ."

"Don't be rude about *her,* Andy. Besides—what about the times and spending so much?"

"I thought you'd finally had that out with Coggy. Anyway, dear, think of all the costumiers and couturiers getting business, the food suppliers, the florists, the electricians, the . . ."

"Bootleggers!"

"Don't be a goose—you don't think I'll bother them for a few hundred quarts of champagne. I'll rob Mother—it won't make a dent in her cellars. Anyhow, you'll never be twenty-one again, sweet pea. Why not forget everything and have the time of your life? Come as someone sensational, someone disgustingly alluring."

"And who would you come as, Andy-Pandy?" she had asked, more in curiosity than to be persuaded.

"Aha—you wait and see!" Andy's big, deep-set eyes had rolled with such coy significance that she had giggled helplessly.

"Just a hint," she had begged.

"Well, then, just one—I don't need your clothes any more." A sideways look then, and that eyebrow peaked and quivering. She had a horrible suspicion . . .

And now, in a moment, she would know.

"Here's Mr. Dundell, Miss Boeker."

"Sweet pea! Thought you'd never get here! Oh, divine, dear—it must be Gamelda! And Ape Man—but who in the world is it?"

"Oogh-chhs-emm," said Chip, starting to remove his head.

"No, no, no—not yet, not yet. Isn't it all too droll!"

"Andy!" said Lily, her incongruously huge eyes aghast. "It's hideous—you look positively beautiful!"

"Don't I? I've never been happier!" He fluttered his lashes, patted his immense wig of blond fuzz, smoothed the hips of his blue sequin costume, gazed down at his long slim legs in the blue tights, pointed the toe of his gold high-heeled slippers. "You've guessed who, of course—everyone has."

"Marlene, natch. I should have known."

He pressed his red-nailed and ringed hands to his padded chest, then strutted for her, swinging his hips. "I had it copied faithfully from *Blonde Venus*," he said. "But best of all, Leelee— she's here herself. You'll have to look very hard. Come on, get into the spirit—make whoopee!"

Andy pushed them towards a vast table with white-coated servants pouring champagne ceaselessly into extended glasses. "Quaff," he said as they were served, "get gloriously stinko, my dahleenks. Oh, by the way, sweet pea . . ."

Andy drew her aside a moment, Gamelda and Marlene in private conference. "At midnight we do our act. Don't get stinko till after."

"Our act?"

"Didn't I tell you—well, dear, it's hilarious. You stand inside this little room—but actually it's shaped like a cake outside. When the band plays Happy Birthday et cetera, the whole thing opens up and there you are! We'll all sing to you, nauseatingly."

"Andy—I'm going right home."

"Don't be silly. There's nothing to worry about—I'll show you exactly what to do. And if you're *very* good, I'll let you dance for us." His cleft chin dimpled sweetly.

"As if I would," Lily said, but he had already gone. She took several large swallows of the champagne and looked for Chip, but he was caught up in a group of people roaring with laughter at him—Joan Crawford, it seemed, as Sadie Thompson in *Rain*, Mary Pickford with long curls, Lionel Barrymore as Rasputin and someone as Nero. Who were they really? she wondered, catching the curiosity of Andy's game.

"Lily, my dear—you're a ravishing Gamelda," said Nero, suddenly detaching himself from the group and coming towards her with arms outstretched.

"Good grief—Reggie!"

Reggie wrinkled his big fleshy nose. "I don't fool anyone. Ridiculous caper."

Lily smiled. He was being his nicest. "You're a marvelous Nero," she said.

"But I'm supposed to be Charles Laughton as Nero—everyone's seen *Sign of the Cross,* but they don't recognize my magnificent characterization." He patted his huge sloping stomach she'd found so fascinatingly awful as a child, and flared the wide nostrils in contempt. "Tell me, my dear, are you enjoying yourself?"

"I've just arrived—but, yes! I am."

"Good. Splendid. Who's your ape escort, my dear?"

"Chip Kenelm. I don't know how long he'll keep his head on—he's smothering alive."

Reggie's close-set blue eyes narrowed, but he didn't turn. "Well, this is a great occasion, our little Princess Dry Goods coming of age. What are you going to do now you've got the key to the palace?"

"That's a key question," she said pertly, and finished her drink.

"Joel Maitland . . ."

Lily sipped, tried not to jerk the glass. "Where did you get his name, Reggie?"

He shook his head. "I've shown admirable restraint not heralding your romance. Out of respect for your aunt's dismay, you understand." He laid a finger against his nose, smiled playfully. "If there is anything serious, however, I hope you'll tell me first, so we can print the proper facts."

"Joel is my friend, and that's all."

"You look strangely sophisticated in that makeup, my dear. Almost shrewd."

"Reggie? You haven't really been interviewing me, have you? You're not here to report the . . ."

"Well, of course! What else would bring me out in the dead of winter to watch this dreadful mishmash cavort? But don't worry—I'm your friend, too—you know that." He pressed her shoulders, ambled away, his nose alertly raised.

"Meet me darling cousin," Andy said, bringing up Charles Atlas, another huge man dressed as a ballet dancer, Clara Bow as the "It Girl" and Mae West.

"Guess who, you dear creatures," he drawled, and left them.

"It's easy—Gamelda," the ballet dancer said. "You sure picked someone in the news! That awful thing about her lovers killing each other. You're much prettier, of course."

Lily smiled at the muscular man in the elaborate tutu, the black plastered hair parted in the middle and the dead-white makeup. "Pavlova," she said.

"You hit it. Boy, though, the more I drink, and the more I sweat . . ."

"Perspire, boy," intoned Mae West suggestively.

"This is my wife," the man said, grinning. "Lilyan Tashman."

"Oh, no—you're Edmund Lowe . . ." Lily's amazed glance went from one to the other.

"Always wanted to meet you, Miss Boeker," said the strong man, Charles Atlas. "May I shake your hand? My name's Weissmuller, Johnny."

"I've heard of you," said Lily.

The others laughed, and Pavlova made a piercing cry, pounded on his chest and said, "Me Tarzan—you Jane."

Lily looked appreciative, but did not get the joke. She had seen far fewer movies or plays than she wanted to; and only through Andy had she been introduced to what Aunt Mirry called "café society," coined from Reggie Blount's grading of "the old and new guard," and which she found so much more fun than the society she knew. "I recognize you, though," she said to Clara Bow. "Tell me who you really are."

"My name's Betty Compton."

"Oh, yes. How do you do?"

There was a short pause before Lily realized her quick recognition was based on a scandal, some connection with Jimmy Walker, the mayor of New York.

"Come dance, girl," Chip said, appearing at her side.

"Your head—where is it?"

"Someone's holding it—come on."

Lily looked at the people she had been talking to, unaware that her smile was sultry and seductive, that coupled with the makeup expert's simulation of Gamelda's features and her own exotically blue eyes, she bore little resemblance to herself. "Excuse me," she said, her soft, formal voice unchanged, "hope we'll see you later."

As Chip bore her into the thick of the dancers, she saw them watching her, talking. "Do be careful of my dress, and my feathers," she said as his clammy hands crushed her against his huge fur chest.

"This is a great binge," he said. "Glad to see you're coming down off your high horse."

"Am I?" She frowned as he barged into Frankenstein dancing with Jean Harlow, whirled her past W. C. Fields with Elizabeth Barrett, Kate Smith with Einstein, Emperor Jones with Amelia Earhart. But the music was thrilling. She closed her eyes and it blended with the dizzying images in her lids, the effects of quickly drunk champagne. "You ain't been blue, no, no, no—you ain't been blue—till you've heard that Mood Indigo." Oh, if only she could be dancing with Joel, or someone who felt the bone-stirring rhythm . . .

"This is too slow for me, gal," Chip said. "I don't like these Harlem darkies."

"Let's stop then," Lily said quickly, breaking from him and starting to weave through the weird swaying mélange of recognizable characters. She caught sight of Pavlova beginning to wilt, the black middle-parted wig slipping sideways, and Charles Atlas draped over a rather too small Greta Garbo in a too large plumed hat.

"Make for the booze," Chip commanded.

He drank the champagne thirstily, like water, and Lily had another glassful. Andy came to them with some of his special friends. One was Ginger Rogers, another Nazimova, another Tallulah Bankhead. One stood close to a man who carried an accordion around his neck. Lily guessed easily—Adele and Fred Astaire; they'd come to a party in Long Island!

Apparently not many had recognized them; they expressed their pleasure with her in penetrating drawls somewhat like Andy's.

"You look divine, darling—I just adore the gown and feathers!"

"You're much more beautiful than your photographs!"

"Goddamn fairies," muttered Chip when Andy bore them off. "That fag cousin of yours should be shot. If his mother saw this . . ."

"You were anxious enough to come, Chip—you actually pestered me. I had to refuse many others!"

"I wanted to stand by you on this memorable occasion."

He blinked down at her, almost spoke, but lapsed into scowling silence.

Suddenly the band had stopped playing. People filtered back for drinks. Lily listened to snatches of their conversation with interest; she had never heard what people said when they were oblivious of her, particularly people out in the world.

"America's crawling with these Viennese analysts!"

"Lost all my elms, dammit . . ."

"If you ask me, *Ulysses* is a perfectly clean book."

"They say she's got this hold on him—a vagina like a vise."

"Doesn't *anyone* want to buy my yacht! I'll have to *give* it away!"

"Put me wise—is it true about Doug Fairbanks Senior and Mary? They seemed spliced for life."

"Clara's forty if she's a day—she was a star when I was a kid!"

"I went to this nudist wedding—we all covered our privates for the ceremony!"

"H. G. Wells says by 1940 no important person will be without a bodyguard."

"I wasn't born yesterday—she's drying out again. The bridge teacher brings his chorines to live in the house . . ."

Lily's realization that it was gossip of her mother she was hearing came in dull shock. She turned away, her smile of amusement fading.

"Dance?" asked Chip, but another man was smiling at her eagerly. "Miss Boeker, may I have the pleasure? I have been looking for Andy to introduce me to you, but . . ."

"You must be John Gilbert." She finished the champagne, put down the glass. "You don't mind, Chip . . ."

"Suppose I *do* . . ." Chip's voice trailed off.

The dark-eyed, curly-haired man gazed at her ardently as she accepted his arm and they pushed through the now more boisterous crowd. "I don't know who you are supposed to be in this costume," he said, "because I have not been very much in your theaters. But I know who *you* are, and I have been trying to meet you since your debut."

"Really? What's your name?"

"Count Vittorio de Santi."

"Vitti! Andy's friend. You were supposed to be at my table."

"What a memory. A girl who meets so many people—I'm flattered and grateful. Do you mind the tango?"

Only if my partner knows how, she thought. "Not if you don't."

"I like it very much." He turned, took her hand, drew her neatly past a lumbering Babe Ruth and somewhat drunk Claudette Colbert in Columbine cap and ruff, and close, but not too close, to his braided, gold-buttoned chest. "You hold yourself splendidly," he said. "I can tell at once you will dance like a dream."

"I feel awkward in this headdress," she said. "I'd love to take it off."

He looked at it, at her, his white teeth bared in delight. "It is charming, but I will gladly . . ."

"No, no—it's too early to spoil the effect. Andy wants everyone to stay as they are until midnight. Then the real people will meet their impersonators."

"Bizarre—brilliant! It is the most original party I have been to in your country!"

As she felt the effortless harmony of their movements, the longing for Joel slipped away, not to become less, but to wait. Oh, it was good, so good to dance like this. "Beautiful," she said, her head moving back and her whole body responding. "How beautifully you dance!"

"You dance like a . . . What? A professional? No—better, more from the soul. Excuse me if I talk bad English—you are a joy. I am already in love with you!"

She closed her eyes. She could believe him. It was a sort of love she felt for him, too. If only there weren't so many people and they could let go. It would be even more satisfying than dancing alone—in fact, it was like being alone, doubly.

"All these people," he said, "it's madness—but so wonderful. Oh, no—it can't be the end!"

"There'll be more," she said, before she realized she had not yet been asked.

"Dance the rest of the night with me," he said, putting her hand to his lips. "Every dance—ah, no—I'm asking too much. Every man in the room will want a chance."

"But I don't want to dance with every man in the room!"

"Your eyes sparkle and shine like a beautiful Persian cat's in the night. I would like to see them without all that black stuff."

"Isn't it ghastly? They insisted it was right for Gamelda."

"Aha—I've heard of this woman. But you should not lower yourself even in fun."

"She's very successful—who am I?"

He laughed knowingly, joyfully, as if her wit enchanted him, and led her with forceful ease, dipping, wheeling, stopping short, and then moving on again in exquisite timing to "Stardust."

It was such relief to forget everything, to be so absorbed that only her body existed, no mind, no self to feel empty or longing. Now and then she looked at her partner. Smiling, always smiling, he seemed blissful in a way she had never encountered. His smooth, olive skin, his dark, expressive eyes, his white, strong-looking teeth, the springiness of his black curls had a vigor both rough and refined. In the high-necked uniform he wore, his figure was far more masculine and youthful than the man he impersonated, more confident, less arrogant.

"It was Andy's suggestion," he explained later, when they paused for refreshment. "He said I was handsome enough."

She couldn't help smiling at his frankness. After all, why shouldn't he accept his handsomeness as a fact?

When Chip and many others asked her to dance, she gave artful excuses. Why, in this at least, go through the torture of second-rate gyrations when she had the best? Besides, Vitti's enthusiasm, his excessive declarations, began to make American men seem dull and uninspired.

"I have fallen so in love at sight—you will marry me, yes? You could not say no and break my heart!"

Lily laughed soundlessly. This was the famous Latin ardor, she thought as she followed his smooth, ever-varying steps.

"Ah, but I am serious," he said, "very serious, *mia cara*. You will live in a palazzo as old as Rome and grace it with your beauty. My family will adore you *molto*—and someday you will give the de Santi name an heir."

Lily shook her head, smiled. There was no need to answer such extravagance. How pleased Aunt Mirry would be, though—

if he *did* happen to mean it and she *did* happen to marry—a count!

When the music stopped, the present bandleader's big round face with the thin black mustache smiled benignly on the mass of upturned faces. "Ladies and gentlemen," he said, "I am asked to announce that supper is being served in the loggia through the archway. There, you will be regaled by a cornucopia of talent, from strolling players to the super-colossal Dundell Vanities."

There were shouts, applause, laughter. How shocked Aunt Mirry would be at the "lack of decorum." It was just as well she had decided not to be associated with this "riffraff."

"*There* you are, sweet pea!" Andy grasped her hand as they strolled into the taper-lit, many-pillared gallery, with its maze of sharply clipped yews and small water steps. "You must preside, dear. Next to me. Drape yourself on that *banco*, Helen-like." He waved his thin, shaved arm with the sequin wristbands towards a long table on a raised platform.

"But I'm American-made, Andy-Pandy."

He looked at her in wary approval. "A topical joke, Leelee— you're actually tipsy!"

She smiled happily.

"Vitti—you're a good influence. You may sit next to her on the other side."

"What about me?" said Chip, barging up to them righteously.

"I'm sorry, Vitti," Lily said regretfully, "but I did come with Chip. Perhaps you could sit on the other side of Andy."

"No, dear—that's reserved for a very good friend of mine. There's a place reserved for you, Vitti—farther along."

Vitti laid the back of Lily's hand tenderly to his lips. "*Mia carissima*," he murmured, with an intense glance. "I will feast my eyes on you and wait impatiently our reunion."

She smiled vaguely, nodded. Perhaps he was really too soppy . . .

"That dago may be a count," said Chip as Vitti moved off, "but he's a lot of hot air, and you'd better not encourage . . ."

"And who are you, Mr. Kenelm—my guardian?"

"Sure, gal—anytime." Chip gave a hearty laugh at his wit.

Lily shrugged off his hand. Aunt Mirry's sponsorship had

made him insufferable. Thank goodness Andy would be on her other side. Sitting down, she noted with amused wonder the huge mounds of black and white grapes basketed in gleaming emerald leaves, the eye-height pottery wine vessels, the luxuriant lily garlands that festooned not only this but all the tables. Andy's Roman decor mocked the trend in piecemeal importation, of course, but the details were his own bits of genius.

"Dahleeng . . ." Andy pouted his dark-red mouth, patted the immense fuzz of blond hair and turned to a slight young man in tails and top hat. "I want you to meet my friend, dear."

Lily's expression faltered between recognition and skepticism. Was it a man, or was it . . . ?

"My cousin, Gamelda," Andy was saying.

The small man leaned forward. "How do you do, Miss Boeker. We are all mad, yes?" The voice was low, softly guttural.

"Of—of course!" Lily laughed as she leaned forward. "And I've always wanted to meet you, Miss Dietrich. Andy doesn't do you the least justice."

"But he's a genius—such a party!" Marlene Dietrich leaned forward. "We must have a dance later." The famous wide-cheekboned face and large-lidded eyes had a somnolent humor.

"Ah—well, yes." What would Aunt Mirry's Mrs. Hamp advise on this occasion? Lily thought.

Servants dressed as Roman slaves wove their way between the tables bearing great silver platters of food. Lily recognized some of the dishes served as Aunt Mirry's, the *bisque nantua*, the *caneton rouennais* (she would leave it, of course—it was disgusting to think of the duck's blood in the sauce!), the *pois exotiques*.

"When we get to the *bombe Miriam*, sweet pea, leave the table and wend your way to the back of the proscenium. You're first on. I'll be there to instruct you."

"It's idiotic, Andy . . ."

"Nonsense, dear, the drollery will be supernal."

"You should save your talents for a play, cousin."

"Ha-ha. You should become a legend in your own time, a rich bitch to crown 'em all, cousin."

She showed a new dimple, the result of slimmer, maturer cheeks. "Perhaps I will. Who knows?"

"Start off by becoming a countess." He gave her a sly glance under purple-painted lids and turned to his prototype before she could answer.

"Great grief," Chip was muttering, "what next?"

Lily saw that the first wandering musicians had begun to play, a small band of fiddlers and flutists for whom Andy, their leader announced, had written "a rhythmical dirge for chanting," called "I Was a Vestal Virgin."

During the loud laughter at the witty intoning, Lily's gaze traveled the gallery of half-reclining figures. As in paintings of bacchanalian orgies, certain figures stood out. She saw Baby Le Roy, Charlie Chaplin, Scarface Al Capone, Will Rogers, Hoover, Noël Coward, Gertrude Lawrence, Helen Wills Moody, Groucho Marx, Al Jolson, Gertrude Stein, Nancy Cunard, Erich von Stroheim, Lady Mendl, Jack Dempsey, President-elect Roosevelt.

They ran together, whirled in her head. She felt an exultant sense of release, of escape from prescribed boundaries of being, from herself . . .

"Miss Boeker—excuse me."

Lily looked up. A servant handed her a folded note on a tray. "Thank you," she said, smiling at him. The man backed away with a bow, his expression registering appreciation.

Lily opened the note out of the range of Chip's sharply curious eyes. "*Mia amore—te amo molto, molto!* You are so beautiful sitting there, my hearts melt. As soon as the dancing starts you will be in my arms again, and I will never let you go. Vitti."

She smothered a giggle, dug Andy under the table and slipped the note into his hand.

He read it, smiled delightedly and cupped his mouth with his hand. "As long as it isn't his parts that melt," he muttered.

"Andy!" Lily looked quickly to see if Chip or others along the table had heard.

"You're not supposed to understand, sweet pea." He put a kiss on one fingertip and wagged it in her direction. "Congratulations, Contessa."

"Who's sending you notes, gal? That dago, I bet."

Lily pressed Chip aside. "That fur of yours has an odor," she said. "Actually, it stinks."

"Lily—you're getting coarse. It's that cousin's influence."

"It's better than yours. You think about nothing but making
more money and impressing people."

"Say—that's unfair. I play golf, sail the yacht, race horses, belong to clubs—and I'm not interested in your fortune. Someday
you'll appreciate that!"

"So why *are* you interested in me, Chip Kenelm the Third?"

Chip's solid face tilted to hers in bland confidence. "You've
got everything, gal. Terrific gams, marvelous orbs, great chassis—
and you're a lady."

"What about my mind?"

"Pshaw! You don't need to be smart!" He grinned down on her
magnanimously. "I'll take care of the brains department."

She felt a sudden, unexpected pain of loneliness. What was
she doing here? Oh, Joel, Joel, I need you so!

"Now, sweet pea. Now, slip away quietly with me. Move closer
to Miss Dietrich, Chip—fill the gap."

Chip grunted reluctantly as Lily and Andy withdrew. They
were hardly noticed as they circled behind the laughing, talking
diners. "Follow me," Andy whispered. She disappeared from
view behind a tall archway curtained in white velvet. Inside was
a giant "cake" made up of movable "slices," and topped by
twenty-one electric candles in red, white and blue.

"To show our patriotic fervor," said Andy. "An all-American
cake for an all-American princess. The press will like it—the people will like it." He patted her comfortingly. "No need for that
guilt, dear." He fluttered his hands and several maids moved forward. "Stand up there, dear—now, girls, see that the split in the
skirt shows, fix her hair. Hurry, hurry. Dear, you really should
have worn more whim-wham for the natives."

"I'm staggering with it," Lily said, groaning. "Practically everything in my New York safe!"

"Next to being presented, what more suitable time to bring
out the collection? After all, I haven't wined and dined forty detectives for nothing. Well, never mind—as Gamelda, you'll do."

Lily stood while she was dabbed, patted, her hair combed, her
tall headdress reset. Detectives examined her wide throatpiece of
striped rubies, pearls and diamonds, her two-inch eardrops of
rubies and diamonds, her pearl, sapphire and diamond neck-
laces, her above-elbow bracelets of oriental jewels (Daddy's gifts

to Mummy on their Far East travels) and below-elbow bracelets of emeralds and diamonds from the will of her grandfather. They checked clasps and their notes and retired to a discreet distance.

Suddenly Colleen Moore ran in breathlessly. "Can I do anything to help, Boke?"

"Whitey! You changed your mind!" Lily smiled delightedly. "And you found the dress."

"Yes. Boke—I couldn't miss this occasion. Happy birthday from me, okay?"

Lily blew her a kiss. "Very okay. Have a good time—come home anytime you feel like it."

"Thanks. I brought—you know . . . That boy from home."

"Do run along, Whitey," said Andy, "it's such a crowd."

"Sure." Whitey stood for a second in the short black chiffon-and-lace dress of Beth's that Lily treasured, her dark eyes sparkling, her dark bangs straight across and slightly curled, one bare shoulder raised.

"The image." Lily nodded.

"She's here somewhere," said Andy, brushing her aside irritably. "We're going to match everyone up later—so see if you can spot her."

"Oh, *peachy!*"

"Oh, vomit," said Andy, as Whitey vanished. "She's such an incurable Girl Scout, dear!"

"Shut up, Andy—or I won't do this."

"No skin off my nose!"

"All set, sir," an older maid said.

The mustached bandleader peered in. "Ready, Andrew—good evening, Miss Boeker—a personal happy birthday!"

"Thank you, Mr. Whiteman."

"Ready, Paul. Now, then—on with the lights, start the platform up with the music, straight and tall, Leelee—that's it, throw out those nauseating things . . . Tra-la . . . !"

There was a slight jerk and Lily felt herself rising. The music started with a great burst of "Happy Birthday to You!" and blazing light engulfed her while singing exploded in one concerted roar.

Flashbulbs popped like hissing stars, lighting smiling faces about them. Lily responded automatically, every reflex tensing to regal grace, her feather headdress seeming six inches higher, her stomach board-flat, her thin arms almost lifting, white as marble under blue light, her face a classic statue's brought to life, exceeded in timeless beauty.

There was applause like the sound of a subway crashing through the room. The singing rose to a crescendo of vibration that set the taper lights flickering, trembling.

"For she's a jolly good fellow!" the band played now, in an abrupt switch, and the response was overwhelmingly tumultuous.

Why? thought Lily. Why? All I am is *rich* . . .

"Now, if you please, ladies and gentlemen!" Andy was holding his own thin bare arms high over his head, showing armpits as smooth as Lily's. "Guess who! Guess who!"

"Lily!" roared the assemblage. "Lily!"

"Not Gamelda?"

"NO! LILY!"

Andy nodded. "No one else. Today, good friends, my dear cousin has achieved her majority."

He waited while laughter rippled a staccato tide. "She has the key to the front door. And, my dears, the back, front and sides. Grandpa Boeker's little granddaughter is a WOMAN!"

There was glass tapping, table thumping, shouting.

"Please!" said Andy. "This isn't a paper convention. This is a celebration of unusual significance. Leelee dear won't like this—but we have before us the living symbol of American economic progress. Let us wish her many happy birthdays on her unique throne. I give you—Princess America!"

Lily felt the blush coming upward from her toes. As glasses were lifted like a mass of flashing half-moons, her face turned from white to rose, then to deeper rose. Her knees weakened; for just an instant she swayed . . .

But a sudden silence had fallen. The servants had stopped moving. The piercing blue light bore down. As if the executioner's ax were poised, she knew there was no reprieve.

She drew in a breath. "You are all so wonderful to me," she said. "I don't deserve it—but thank you. Thank you for your wishes, for your generosity." Her soft tones, assisted by the excellent acoustics, reached out in sweet waves of clinging sound. "I

hope that you will continue to enjoy yourselves at Andy's marvelous housewarming, and find this party and the entertainment
as brilliant as Andy himself." She looked fondly at Andy, who
put a hand on his hip, a leg on a platform of the cake, and called
out:

"Cahn't help eet . . ."

In merciful rescue, as the voices rolled and echoed over her, the
platform began to descend and the slices of the cake to close.

"You looked beautiful, Miss Boeker!" said a maid, and the
others chorused agreement.

"Phew . . . Thank goodness that's over." Lily smiled at them
and at the assistants. Allowing the detectives a last look at her
jewelry, she retrieved her purse and started back to her table,
dimly aware that the detectives followed, that they had probably
been nearby from the beginning.

"Good gal," said Chip, "good gal." He pinched her arm,
rubbed a heavy hand across the back of her neck.

"Very charming," said Marlene Dietrich, leaning to her. Now
that she had taken off the top hat, Lily saw that her golden hair
swept from her high brow in fine smooth waves, her blue eyes
under the thin arched brows were enormous, the hollows under
her cheekbones more glamorous than anything she had ever
seen. "Andy said you were to sing for us, Miss Dietrich," she
said.

"Yes—one song. I see Andy's young man signaling now."

"Andy's young man?"

"Yes, darling—Howie. The one who plays the piano." She got
up and with a laconic wave wandered off.

Lily looked across at the young man. He was thin, willowy,
dressed in silver tails. His yellow hair was long and tucked behind his ears, and he moved towards the back of the stage with
tightly undulating buttocks. It struck her as curious that she was
never disturbed by Andy's strange ways and friends. With anyone else she would have felt . . . well, sort of uneasy. But Andy
was just too much fun. Without him, she would never have
known really interesting people, gone to speakeasies, nightclubs,
crazy parties like this.

"I'm sober again," she said, turning to Chip. "Fill me up."

"You sure?" A frown cracked the gleaming tan of his brow.

"Pos." She looked mischievously along the table for Vitti. He was there, ardent-eyed, alert for a sign. She laughed aloud, lifted her glass to him.

"You encouraging that . . . Latin? I tell you, you'll be sorry, gal."

"Oh, dear," she murmured. Vitti was standing up, toasting her. She waved a hand downward through the air, shook her head. He sat down again, looking rueful.

"You're power-mad, Lil."

She drank gaily. "You sure, Chip?"

"You know *I'm* crazy about you."

"Really?" Her eyes teased. "Who else is?"

"Just about every guy you meet."

"Name three."

"Three! I could name at least thirty."

"But it's my money they love, Chip—isn't it? That's what you said. Anyway, ssh—the curtain's going up."

At a white Steinway sat the young man, Howie, his silver tails divided and tucked up. Standing against the piano, his foot on a chair, his elbow on his knee, his palm supporting his chin, was Andy.

There was a burst of clamorous applause, and the pianist began to play "Falling in Love Again."

As he began to half talk, half sing in Marlene Dietrich's inimitable husky tone, Lily clasped her hands tensely. Perhaps he would go too far, look ridiculous . . .

But, no, his guests were loving it, loving the very fact that he failed—and after one verse, in strolled the slight man in top hat, white tie and tails, Marlene herself. She had to hold up her hand to quiet the semi-drunken audience. Then she took Andy's hand and began to sing to him with exquisite nonchalance, "Men flock around you, like moths around a flame—and if their wings burn—I know you're not to blame. Falling in love again, never wanted to, what am I to do . . . ?"

Andy joined her, and they chorused, "Cahn't—help—eet!"

The applause was so loud that Lily wondered if the people thirty floors down were hearing it above the traffic. She thought fleetingly of them, of the desperate times still going on—but now Marlene and Andy were doing a brief encore, and ending with their arms entwined and blowing kisses to the cheering guests.

"Obscene," muttered Chip.

Acting as master of ceremonies, Paul Whiteman appeared now in front of the curtains. "The next act in the Dundell Vanities, ladies and gentlemen," he announced unsmilingly, "will be that incomparable trio—the Boswell Sisters!"

There was a gasp of surprise.

"Isn't Andy extraordinary?" whispered Lily. "He's got the most famous entertainers in the world here!"

"You know why," answered Chip. "Publicity—crashing society."

"Bosh! This isn't society."

"To them it is, gal."

"Quiet." Lily nodded towards her glass, and Chip, scowling his disapproval, saw to it that it was filled.

Sitting back, feeling the pleasant dizziness increasing, Lily wallowed in the freedom from attention, the dreamlike sequence of music, talent, wit that delighted her senses. After the Boswell Sisters came Ethel Merman, belting out "Edie Was a Lady," the chorus of which she invited everyone to join, and Veloz and Yolanda, the dance team.

Helen Morgan sat on the piano and sang "These Foolish Things" and "What Is This Thing Called Love?" with such mournful emotion that tears filled Lily's eyes. Burns and Allen relieved the blue mood with jokes that Lily did not always understand, but she laughed anyway. Sally Rand did her fan dance, and Lily was slightly shocked when, at the end, the fans were lowered, but would not let Chip know it.

There were so many acts that eventually Lily's focus blurred a little. She sat up, though, when Noël Coward sang "Mad About the Boy" liking it better than all the rest, even Lawrence Tibbett singing songs from the new opera *Emperor Jones*, or Eddie Cantor singing "Whoopee."

"You're tired, gal—I'll take you home," said Chip.

"No, sir! You go if you like."

"And leave you to the wolves—one in particular!"

Lily shrugged. The Vanities seemed to be coming to an end now. Andy came forward to thank everyone, and then to explain what was to happen next.

"Will all the people who see themselves impersonated here tonight, please find their impersonator, and bring him or her to the front of the proscenium," he called through the microphone.

A wild scramble of figures followed. Lily looked about apprehensively, but no Gamelda appeared and she sank back with relief.

"Well, no one's likely to claim me," said Chip, his laugh booming in her ear.

I wish they would, she thought.

"All right, people dear," Andy was calling now. "Starting at the end of that line, will you please tell us who you *really* are?"

Lily started to laugh, and kept on till her jaw and ribs felt stiff. Greta Garbo turned out to be Marion Davies, and Frankenstein Father Coughlin, and Rasputin John Gilbert, and Charlie Chaplin Irving Thalberg, and Amelia Earhart Katharine Hepburn, and Rudolph Valentino the Prince of Wales . . .

There were hundreds of others, and soon there was mass confusion, an uproar of shouting and laughter.

Lily caught sight of Andy grinning evilly before he nodded to the stagehands and the curtains closed him from sight.

From the other hall came sounds of a large band starting up. As if catapulted by a spring, Vitti was in front of her, his hands raised and beckoning.

Lily's laughter took another turn. He was hilarious, she thought, a goof—but the fact was she could hardly wait to start dancing with him.

"That's not fair, gal," Chip said as she jumped to her feet.

"Chip—there are hundreds of beautiful girls here tonight. I'm sure they'll adore dancing with you. See you later."

It was true, she thought. Chip Kenelm was, in his very own words, "a catch." She let Vitti hold her hand as they pushed their way to the dance floor set around the fountain.

"I'm a bit—oh, inebriated, Vitti," she said as she moved into his arms. "I'll probably trip."

His smile forgave her anything, everything. "Even when you trip a little," he said, holding her closer than before, "you will be the most beautiful dancer in the world."

She lodged her chin beside the gold buttons, and closed her eyes. Joel couldn't dance like this—but he had tried, for her. He had improved so quickly. He would have been good. She could even believe these were his arms that held her.

"I am so happy," Vitti said, looking serious under such encouragement. "Tomorrow, after you have long good sleep, we will go to a thé dansant at the Ritz-Ambrose. Tomorrow night we will go to the Starlight Roof, and the next to the Casino."

"I'm afraid of men," she whispered.

"*Mia cara*—not with me. Not until we are married would I touch you—and only gently, so gently then."

"I love someone—someone I can't have."

"You will forget, and love me. In June, we will have a wedding of great beauty. I will give you the paradise in Venice."

"The paradise?" She giggled soundlessly against him.

"What is called? Ah—honeymoon, yes. I will sing to you in the gondola, romantic songs."

She went on smiling to herself. Their dancing became more and more elaborate—they were an exhibition now—but she didn't care—she floated. She levitated, she spun . . .

She did not remember the rest of the evening clearly, only that the lighting got dimmer and dimmer, that there were dirtier and dirtier songs, that people disappeared into bedrooms and that she saw writhing bodies on beds, and that at one point the artist Diego Rivera was on a ladder, inviting everyone present to participate in a vast mural . . .

"He's a Commie, you know," someone said to her, and she shook her head.

"No, no—he's just a good person, a great artist."

"Lily Boeker's going to be a lush like her mother."

She had wheeled about. But there was no way to tell who had said it. She had wanted her daddy suddenly, and started to cry.

How had she got home? Chip? Vitti? The rest was blankness.

Chapter 8

"Oh, Maudie, my head! What time is it—what's that sweet smell . . . ?" Lily struggled up from a mound of crepe-de-chine pillows with the impression that she had been smothering in the rose arbor of her chalet . . .

Maudie's mouth suggested a prim smile. "It's noon, dear—and it's the roses. The whole suite is full of them. Beautiful dark-red ones, lovely and fresh. They must have come straight from the market." Maudie straightened the monogrammed sheets and satin bedcover, laid a light marabou shrug around Lily's shoulders.

Lily frowned. For an instant her heart raced with hope . . . "Who . . . ?" she murmured, her eyes wide on Maudie's face.

Maudie did not answer until the maid had laid a legged tray across Lily's knees and withdrawn. "Shouldn't you know, Miss Lily?" There was something almost arch in Maudie's tone.

Lily blinked. No—of course not . . . Joel couldn't have—people said roses were the most expensive flower you could buy . . .

"Not Chip!" she said, ready to groan, both at the idea and at the dull pounding of her skull.

Maudie poured coffee from the Georgian silver pot, her expression conveying a mixture of puzzlement and disapproval. "Is there not someone more obvious, dear?"

Lily stared. A blur of vague events pushed through her awareness. "Oh, Lord . . . I had so much champagne last night, Maudie, more than ever in my life . . ."

"Ah—well, that explains it, dear. Anyway, he's telephoned several times—and these came." Maudie took two deckle-edged envelopes from the pocket of her gray uniform. "I understand you will go with him to the thé dansant at the Ritz-Ambrose—that will be instead of . . ."

"Thé dansant . . . ?" Lily took the envelopes, held them gingerly. They seemed somehow ominous.

"Better drink your coffee, dear—it will clear your head."

Lily obeyed. After a few warming gulps, she slipped the butter knife through the tops of the envelopes, her fingers trembling with weakness, physical and mental. "*Mia cara*," she read, "you have made me so very happy . . . I have not been able to sleep, but walking around the city of yours like a wild man filled with passion—how can I wait for you to wake, so to see my beautiful girl, see you with my hungry eyes of love . . ."

Lily threw the letters across the bed. "Vitti . . ." she muttered. "That idiot . . . !"

"Idiot, dear?" Maudie stood back a little, as if better to appraise her mistress. "Have you not agreed to become Countess de Santi?"

Lily pushed at her hair. "Of course I haven't, Maudie. We were just having fun, he's handsome and kind of dashing—and we danced together like a dream . . ."

"Oh, dear," Maudie murmured. "Oh, dear, dear. The papers—they've been calling all morning. Whitey held them off, but the Count had already given out the news . . ."

"How dare he!" Lily sat bolt-upright, sending her favorite big cup with the gold flowers lurching across the tray.

"Well, dear, I think you must have promised more than you remember. He seems to think there's to be a wedding—in Rome, he said. A honeymoon in Venice . . ."

"How do you know all this, Maudie?"

Maudie pressed her lips, her eyes behind the enlarging lens of the glasses suddenly evasive.

"Maudie . . . ?"

"Well, Miss Lily—he was here. Whitey and I both spoke to him. He had telephoned Andy and Aunt Mirry, he said. We wanted to wake you, but you were so sound asleep . . ."

Lily gazed at Maudie in a new light. "What did Aunt Mirry say?" she asked in a softer tone.

"She is waiting to speak to you, of course. But I think she was pleased. She would like the idea of a count, dear, I'm sure."

Lily closed her eyes and sank back into the pillows. "This is *awful*, Maudie. How am I going to get out of it without a stupid scene? I mean, he's so ardent, so crazy!"

"Do you not care for him at all, dear?" Maudie set the cup straight, poured some more coffee. "Could you not be happy with him?"

Lily made a face without opening her eyes. "He's sweet, in a way. He makes me laugh—and he's a wonderful dancer . . . But I don't *know* him, Maudie. I only met him last night!"

"You loved someone else on sight, dear, remember—is it him still?" Maudie's tone was reluctant to such boldness.

Suddenly Lily could not speak. Tears rolled from under her lashes and down her cheeks. She would have to see him, she thought, have to—there *had* to be a way . . . !

"Why not just give this a try?" Maudie said, with a brief pat of Lily's hand. "Go to the thé dansant, see more of him, get to know him. Tell him that he must not rush you. He will have to understand that."

Lily's tear-filled eyes opened slowly. "Maudie . . . tell Whitey to find out the address of Mr. Maitland's boardinghouse—I don't care how she does it. And she's not to mention my name."

"Miss Lily . . . What about the . . . ?"

"And tell her to cancel everything I'm doing today. I'm seeing no one, talking to no one. Now, Maudie—have Ivy draw my bath."

Maudie stood quite still.

"Maudie—I mean it."

Maudie blinked, once. "Yes, Miss Lily." She moved quickly

off, her sturdy rubber-soled shoes making prints in the purple deep-pile carpet.

"Better watch out—they throw stones at cars like that round here," said the weary-looking woman who opened the door of the brownstone rooming house on Third Avenue. "What do you want?" connotations of possible charity lifting the dirge-like tone.

"I want to see Mr. Joel Maitland."

"Oh? Well, I'm sorry, he ain't in."

"He hasn't gone away, has he?"

The woman pushed strands of graying brown hair from her sagging features and stared hypnotically at Lily's jewels. "No— no, honey."

"I suppose he's at the hospital . . ."

"Not till later—he's gone looking for work." The woman tore her gaze from the jewels. "You got a job for him?" Her eyebrows rose shrewdly.

Lily looked over her shoulder at Thomas and the two body-guards in the car. "May I come in?" she asked the woman.

"Why, sure!" The woman held open the door and stepped back into the dim, food-smelling hall. "I'm Mrs. O'Hara," she said. "I run the place."

"How do you do. My name's Lily Boeker." How good it was, she thought, to say it with ease, out of the range of exploitation.

"Lily Boeker! *Herself!* Excuse me while I faint—I never thought *I'd* set eyes on you!"

"Please—you wouldn't tell anyone, would you?—this is a very private visit." Lily's eyes pleaded, without pride. "Joel would be terribly upset."

"I can't tell *no* one? Oh, dear, what a shame. Well, never mind. I wouldn't do nothing to hurt that boy. Would you care to wait in his room? He said he'd be back. But of course sometimes he goes hunting books in the secondhand shops."

"I'd like to wait, if I may."

Mrs. O'Hara wiped her palms on her sleeves, tugged at the bedraggled collar of her cotton dress and started up some stairs covered in linoleum worn almost through to the boards. "Mind them rods," she said, kicking one of them into place with a felt-slippered foot. "Can't afford to get nothing fixed no more. I get the fellas to help—Joel's handy for stuck windows and leaks. And if anyone's sick, of course." She turned to grin, showing dark-looking teeth. "We call him 'Doc' in the house. He don't like it, but don't say so. Too good-hearted."

Lily murmured appropriately. Her chest felt tight. Never in her life had she seen such shabbiness close to. There were big damp patches on the walls, strips of wallpaper hanging off.

"My husband used to keep the place up—but he got taken with pneumonia and passed to his rest. Three years ago this Thanksgiving. But I try to keep a clean house, and I don't give rotten food. Only one meal a day now, but keeps 'em alive. Here's the Doc's room."

"Thank you." Lily entered uncertainly. It was a room smaller than any bathroom or even pantry she had known. There had been no room as small even in her doll's house. And it was so bleak—a brass bed with rumpled covers, a lop-sided chair with horsehair sticking out of the cushions, an old table that held great mounds of books, another with one cup, one plate, one glass.

"Never leaves his washing up like the others, Miss Boeker, you see. Makes his bit of food—never leaves a crumb. Keeps his clothes the same—see the socks?"

Lily shook her head and smiled. "But some have holes."

"Yes—and when he gets time he darns 'em. Seen him doing it with darning eggs and wool his mother give him. Sticks his finger with the needle and cusses."

They looked at each other and smiled. "Sit down, honey, go on, sit down," Mrs. O'Hara said. Her weariness seemed gone. "So you know Joel . . ."

Lily saw that she was settling down for a lengthy exchange. "Yes . . ." she said, but stopped there.

Mrs. O'Hara lingered. "He don't talk much, you know. I never saw anyone study so long—hour after hour. One good thing in here's the lamp—brought that from his home. But it's sold now, the home. Of course you'd know that. It's terrible, isn't it, good, hard-working people losing everything?"

"Terrible." Lily edged forward in the chair as its stuffing pricked through her skirt.

Mrs. O'Hara looked at her thoughtfully, then wistfully, and finally sadly.

Yes, Lily longed to say, more than terrible. It would be so wonderful if he would let me help him, give him the money he needs and deserves. But he won't, you see . . .

"Would you like a cup of coffee, honey? Got some on the stove still hot."

"No, thanks, Mrs. O'Hara—I've just had breakfast."

Mrs. O'Hara gave her a last lingering look as if she might still be a dream in her afternoon catnap. "I often wonder what it must be like to be you," she said, "to live in them great houses and wear all them clothes and jewels and eat all that rich food. Not you, of course, but most they seem like snobs, them millionaires. Not caring about no one but themselves, just having a good time all the time. I ain't a bit sorry for the ones that jumped out of windows—they were crooks for all their brains and advantages, no better than gangsters!"

Lily was silent. The fingers of her right hand hovered nervously around a small ring on her left hand. The urge to take it off, to give it to the woman was so powerful that surely it couldn't be wrong . . .

"I suppose when you been poor all your life, you don't scare so easy. What you've never had you don't miss, my husband used to say. Still—I'd sure like to know better than what I've had!" Her laugh was mournful. "Just a few thousand bucks they'd never miss—like peanuts to 'em, like nickels—all the difference to us, all the difference."

Lily slid the ring slowly to the end of the finger. The double-ribbon effect of sapphires and diamonds was one of a trayful of occasional rings in her safe, one of the dozens left by a grandmother who never wanted rings, who preferred to go on cooking for her Wilbur but was never allowed in the kitchen after he was rich. Lily liked the ring, but wouldn't know it was gone . . .

"Well, miss, sorry I bent your ears. Don't get much excitement around here—not the good kind. So long, Miss Boeker—hope I see you again."

Lily slipped the ring into the palm of her right hand. She felt a feathery sensation of pleasure that always came with giving something to someone. Her hand moved forward . . .

The door closed.

Lily looked down at the ring and grimaced. She put it back on her finger impatiently. Where had she read the words "Neither fish, flesh, fowl nor beast"? That was her! Oh, Joel—hurry, hurry!

She rose from the uncomfortable chair restlessly and wandered about the small square room, looked wonderingly at the fraying curtains, the threadbare rug. A ragged, still damp bath towel was hung neatly over the back of the chair where he sat to study, and a small pot for making coffee had been washed and stood upside down to dry. She could practically see him here, moving about, coping doggedly with his meager lot. Love for him made her weak-kneed, desperate to see and touch him!

Time moved slowly on. Doors opened and closed, there were footsteps on the stairs and landing—but they passed. A smell of cooking seeped up into the room, curiously sour and sickening. The rumble from the El vibrated at intervals, monotonously.

Whitey would be biting her knuckle, thinking up excuses for her absence, coping with Vitti—it wasn't fair, but she couldn't help it. First things had to come first . . .

She looked at some of Joel's books, opened them, looked vaguely at the contents. The fine print, the technical terms, the foreign phrases, even the titles made her feel blind and dumb. How could he do this by *choice!* She looked at some notes—all indecipherable except for a word here and there.

But there was one, neat and clear as a child's. It was entitled "Budget," and it was a list of figures: "Board—$3.50. Fares—70 cents. Shirt—15 cents. Food—$1.50. Sundries—50 cents. Books—$3.00. Total $10.55." Across the bottom was written, "Owed: $13.00 to Mrs. O'Hara. $10 Uncle Fred."

She reached quickly into her lizard, leather-lined purse. In the inside pocket was a thin morocco-leather wallet with a gold edge. Inside it were several pristine green notes. She saw some $1000s, some $100s, some $50s. She drew out a $1000 note, looked for a place to put it where he would discover it later. Underneath a book called *The Brain from Ape to Man* by Tilney, with a card inside saying "property of Cornell University," seemed safe enough.

As she closed her purse, she heard footsteps and the door was opened in a rush. "Lily! I saw Thomas, the car—I couldn't believe it!"

"Joel . . . !" She looked at him, her relief and joy fading instantly. Although he seemed deeply shaken by the sight of her, he obviously wasn't pleased.

"Princess, you *shouldn't*—a place like this?"

He closed the door, threw off a worn hat, threadbare camel-hair coat. She went into his arms. "Hold me tight," she said. "Hug me with all your strength, just hug me."

He kissed her, held her, rocked her hard and close as if he did not want to let her go. "What on earth am I going to do with you?" he said. "If only I hadn't let Andy talk me into that debut —if only we'd never met . . . !"

She hung on to him, her eyes closed in ecstasy. But they had met, they had met, she thought. She looked up, her great azure eyes eloquent with the sum of her need, her confusion. "Oh, Joel, darling—it's no good without you—you were so right, I *am* lost . . ."

He looked at her with such kindness and compassion that her hope rose. "I've done everything I could, but none of it helped, Joel. My dancing isn't any use, after all, and Coggy says I can't even give my money away. I'm trapped with it, darling, no matter what I do. I've been a naïve dumbbell to think I could escape . . ."

"Poor sweetheart."

She reached up and pressed her hands to his face. "Oh, Joel— marry me. Please, please marry me. We won't use the money. You can take only what you need to accomplish your goals!"

He held her hands. "Princess . . ." His voice was constrained, unsteady. "I want to help you, I'd like to be in the position to love you—but it just isn't possible. . . . That's why I haven't answered your calls. I want you to rule me out, forget me . . ."

"No, no, no!" She kissed his face, threw her arms more tightly about him. "Don't say that—I never could, never . . . !"

There was a silence while he held her and Lily choked back threatening sobs. "Dearest," he said softly. "I don't want to hurt you or make you unhappy—that's the last thing I want to do. . . . But it's no use. When you're older, more experienced in life, you'll see that it could never have been right for you, for either of us . . ."

"But, Joel—it would be, it could be!"

"Sweetheart, listen—don't you see?—you're conditioned by your heritage and upbringing, it's ingrained in you—you'll never be able to throw it off for any length of time. And you won't even recognize it . . . !"

"I would, I'd learn—you'd teach me . . . !"

He stroked her hair softly, put his forehead to hers. "I couldn't surrender my identity, Lily, my very reason for existence—I'm just not a strong enough character to survive having everything handed to me, everything accomplished without effort . . ."

"But, darling—you'd still have to work! Money wouldn't guarantee your being a really good psychiatrist!"

"True." He leaned away, his hazel eyes, so keen and knowledgeable, seeming to her to lose some of their warmth. "I explained about that, princess—I must guard my incentive. Without it, the whole point would be missing. Don't ask me why. Perhaps someday everyone will have money, or money won't exist as such any more, so we can all forfeit it and strive for interior goals. Meanwhile . . ."

Lily drew slowly away from him. "I never thought *you* would be out only for yourself . . ." she murmured, feeling a stunned sense of betrayal.

"Not only, princess—mainly."

"But what about love—doesn't that mean anything to you?"

"Yes, of course it does—you know that. But for me, sweetheart, it comes second to exploration, to furthering understanding of the human mind itself—something that'll take all the years of my life. Think of it this way, if you were married to me, you'd hardly ever see me. I'd seldom be free to sit and talk or go anywhere with you. You'd be alone, lonely, left out. I, on the other hand, would have this excitement, this absorption."

"Then you don't *need* anyone?"

He touched her cheek. "Well, I do—but I'd never chain anyone to me because I needed them."

Lily's head lowered. She put her fists against his chest and tears fell onto her sparkling fingers. "I'm sure I wouldn't mind—I'd just look after you, help you, be a good wife . . ."

He closed her tighter in his arms, rocked her gently. "Let me explain another way," he said. "Today I found a job. I came home jubilant, all problems solved. I'd got a night shift in Child's, waiting on table. There were nearly a hundred applicants—but they took me. You know what it means to me that I can keep going, keep on—the whole world, in fact!"

"Child's?" Lily looked into his seamy, beloved face, blinked at her tears.

"It's a chain of restaurants, princess—very famous. You'll never see the inside of one, though, except for a lark, when you go slumming."

She tried to follow his reasoning. "You'd rather be a waiter, in a place like that, than . . . ?"

He released her, took her hands in his. "Oh, Lily, Lily," he said, the tenderness in his voice edged with finality. "Don't you see, this *has* to be goodbye . . ."

Her hands dropped slowly from his. She reached distractedly for the lizard purse on the table beside them, found a lace-bordered handkerchief, blew her nose, wiped her eyes. Loneliness, misery, engulfed her beyond further words.

"I'm sorry, dearest girl," Joel said. "You will understand, someday."

After a few moments, he put an arm around her shoulders and turned her towards the door. Taking her hand, he led her down the dingy stairs.

Out on the street a crowd of youngsters and hoodlums had gathered around the Rolls and Herman was about to disperse them. Instead, he quickly joined Thomas to lead Lily, one on each side, to the door of the car.

When Thomas started the engine and drove off, Lily turned to look back for a last glimpse of Joel, but at that instant a pebble hit the rear window, making a large, splintered crack. By the time she had recovered, both Joel and the brownstone were lost to view.

"I know it's sudden, Aunt Mirry, but you do approve of my being a countess, and Andy thinks it's wonderful. Besides . . ."

Lily watched herself in the mirror behind the escritoire as she spoke into the new gold telephone, a stranger wearing a shimmering satin negligee that matched her eyes, using her gestures to push at a light halo of hair, her voice to convey the excitement. ". . . he's so handsome, so in love, and we have such a marvelous time together—it seems pointless to waste time!"

"Well, dear—if that's how you feel, I agree. I'm certainly glad you've got over that . . ."

"You must come to New York and meet Vitti, Aunt Mirry—you'll adore him!"

"Well, I shall have to and if we're to arrange a wedding—it's terribly short notice, my dear—my calendar's crammed!"

"It always is. . . . But if it's too . . ."

"Oh no, no, no, dear girl—you must have a splendid wedding, splendid! After all, it is your first."

Lily smiled. "And it'll be my last, Aunt Mirry. I'm sure I can make Vitti happy—and he's so understanding of me, all my silliness . . ." Lily stopped. The rest was too intimate to share with her aunt.

"There'll be a great deal to do . . ." Aunt Mirry was not apt to pursue inferences over the telephone from Palm Beach. "It will take a great deal of organizing. . . . You'll need to see what's sailing, so you can synchronize the date with your honeymoon. Rome, you say . . ."

"And Venice . . ."

"Very good. Have you spoken to Coggy yet?"

Lily made a face in the mirror, and was reminded of herself as the thin, freckle-faced girl who ran to Aunt Mirry for rescue from Freddie. . . . "No—I was hoping you'd attend to that."

"Is he still annoyed with you?"

"No, Aunt Mirry—that's all been settled. But you're so much better at . . ."

"Yes, perhaps. But you'll have to learn, my dear. You're on your own now. I can only help to guide you—but I've given you good training, and set you an example."

"I know you have, Aunt Mirry. And now, with Vitti, I'm sure I can be more like you!"

"Well, thank you, dear girl. Now—let me see . . . Hold on while I talk to Mrs. Hamp."

Lily sat quite still, staring at her image. She had a feeling of floating, of being somewhere quite separate from the person she knew as herself . . .

"I can be there next week, on Thursday, dear. Make an appointment for me with Coggy for twelve, and tell him to save lunch. It might be best if you came along . . ."

"Must I . . . ?"

"Well—perhaps not. No—you just get on about your trousseau. . . . We must get Starenze busy on your wedding dress . . ."

"Oh, Aunt Mirry, how can I thank you!"

"By enjoying yourself now, to the full. It's about time. I'll say goodbye—the place is filling up with weekend guests . . ."

"Bye, Aunt Mirry—can't wait to see you!"

Lily hung up slowly. For a moment she stood looking intently at the huge baguette-cut diamond ring on the third finger of her left hand. It seemed to weigh the finger down. "Oh, how beautiful!" she had breathed when Vitti brought out the little box from Cartier's. "That's the most exquisite ring I've ever had!"

Andy had helped him choose it, he admitted modestly, so as to be sure that it would be worthy of her. "And, *mia carissima*, it is not so beautiful, not so exquisite as you—nothing in the world is that!"

His passion, his ardor were extraordinary to her. He seemed impervious to her laughter, her American reluctance to such excess. Of course, he did not see it as excess—to him it was the way the "grand" love was. And it was catching. She had never moved at such a pace, danced so much, done so many crazy, romantic things . . .

She could almost forget Joel. The dark, unendurable pain had diminished, had almost dissolved . . .

And yet—there was something she was not at ease with, a shadow . . .

"Too close, Vitti," she had said as they had danced the tango with such heavenly precision, to the sweet, seductive music of the Ritz-Ambrose thé dansant orchestra. Their bodies were pressed so tightly that she could feel the shape of him down to the knees, could feel the moisture of his cheek, smell the potent cologne he used, the pomade in his black curly hair.

"Sorry—I will be more correct." He had smiled lovingly, showing his amazingly white teeth, and loosened his hold. "You have nothing to fear. I respect you, my lovely girl. You are to be my wife."

She had thought it was a good time for confession. "I truly am inexperienced, Vitti," she said. "Do you believe that?"

"Why, natural! I honor you, I understand, I will be gentle . . ."

"People think I must be very sophisticated. I meet so many men, but if they want more than my money—if they . . . Well, I'd be too frightened—something terrible happened to me once . . ."

"Ssh." He had laid a finger on her lips, his dark eyes intense with adoration. "With your Vitti, you will forget all that has been bad. On the boat we will walk in the moonlight and dance —in Paris we will dance and see the sights—in Venezia we will sing with the gondoliers—in Roma my family will welcome you with the love—we will make the old palazzo beautiful, make it yours . . . Ah, so happy we will be!"

Somewhat reassured, she had relaxed in his arms, enjoyed their marvelously synchronized dancing.

Now, she shook back her hair, lifted her arms to the ceiling, twirled, the myriad-faceted chandelier above her spinning like sunlight in the huge, somber sitting room of her suite. "I am loved," she thought, "loved! I am to be the Countess Vittorio de Santi, a wife, needed, wanted . . . At last life is good, is real . . . !"

Coming quickly into the room to usher in another avalanche of long-stemmed red roses, Whitey broke into a satisfied grin.

Chapter 9

The S.S. *Aquitania* had been due to arrive in Manhattan on November 29, 1933, at eight in the morning, but was docking nearer to ten. The high winds that had slowed "The Ship Beautiful" (ruining her year's record of twenty-five knots) still blasted a wet chill over the crowds on the wharf.

In the looming heights of the immense ship, beyond the hundreds of peering faces and waving arms, Whitey looked down with binoculars, swept them slowly, carefully over the milling and waiting crowds below, then quickly returned to one of the suites Lily and the entourage had occupied, called "The Gainsborough."

Lily had backed closer to the fireplace mantel as the press crowded past Maudie, filling the luxuriously furnished sitting room with the smell of tobacco-permeated clothing and the instant crackle-and-hiss of flashbulbs.

"Not a sign, Boke," she whispered to her. "Unless I missed him somehow."

"Keep trying, Whitey—go down and look around, he wouldn't like all this . . ."

"That's why he won't be here at all, Boke—I'm sure of it."

"How could he *not*, Whitey—with a cable like that!"

"Because he can't help you, Boke. He simply can't. Don't you see . . . ?"

"All right, ladies and gentlemen," Maudie was announcing, "be quick, please. Miss Boeker is not at all well."

"We'll be good, Maudie." One of the reporters, pushing closer to the front, winked at the familiar stiff-backed little woman with a mixture of mockery and ingratiation. "Thanks for letting us see her."

The gray eyes behind the steel-rimmed spectacles remained expressionless. "No chewing-gum wrappers, no cigarette ashes or stubs on the floor, please," she said. She nodded to Thomas and the bodyguards, who closed the doors and lined up against them like three large statues in Boeker blue. Maudie took her place behind and to one side of Lily.

Lily looked into the shrewd, hard-bitten faces surrounding her, met their concentrated focus with a cautious smile. She felt the usual dread and resentment, the fear of their questions, the protest at having to answer them and not make mistakes, to try to win them. She had already made a careless slip with Reggie—describing her queasiness to him so that his eyebrows lifted and she was forced to say, "Oh, not *that!*"

(Aunt Mirry's voice rang in her ears with sudden, sharp warning. "Don't think aloud.")

Quickly, she lifted her chin, so that her head in the small sable hat surrounded by pale-lemon curls reflected regally in the mirror behind her. Unknowingly, with her almost ankle-length sable coat falling away to show the drape of the brown reversible satin-crepe dress that highlighted sharp hipbones and small full breasts uplifted by one of the new Parisian brassières, she was as poised as a star model. Winding slender, red-nailed, diamond-flashing fingers into her famous rope of pea-sized pearls (passed on by her mother on her twenty-first birthday), only a trace of weariness and insecurity in the soft, light tone, she said, "Good morning."

"Good morning, Countess de Santi," chorused the group.

"*Miss Boeker.*" She twisted the incomparable pearls so tautly that had they not recently been restrung by Cartier's in Paris they would have burst and scattered.

"Well, first off, Lily," called a female reporter in syrupy aggression, "who designed the stunning dress?"

"This?" Lily controlled a frown. "Vionnet of course." It seemed so obvious.

"And the perfume, Lily—is it the one created for you by Guérlain for your honeymoon, the one called Belle Lili?"

Pinkness outlined Lily's cheekbones. It had been stupid to wear the penetrating stuff—but they had given her so many huge bottles of it and she hated waste. "Yes, but I'd rather you didn't put that into your . . ."

"You're definitely dropping the title, Lily—right?" asked a man, gruffly overruling femininity.

"Yes, of course." Lily turned to him quickly. "I want that made clear."

"What about all the crests on your trunks and . . . ?"

"They'll be removed."

"But your marriage was a tremendous love match, wasn't it— and such a terrific event? Can't you forgive him, Lily?"

"Forgive him?" Lily paused a moment, not to consider her answer, but because the queasiness that had persisted since the revulsion to Vitti, stirred threateningly. She could no longer call it "seasickness." "Oh, I have," she said after a furtive swallow. "It was a ghastly shock, of course—even Aunt Mirry didn't suspect anything . . ." She drew in a breath. "What I mean is, you can't stay mad at Vitti."

"Is it true that your annulment cost you a million, Countess— and that you settled another on his . . . ?"

"These are not things I speak of. If you want figures, you must talk to Cogswell Brent, my lawyer, my trustee." Lily swiveled the ring she had chosen to replace her engagement ring, unaware that she drew attention to its spectacular diamond-and-emerald twin-squares design.

"Not a hint, Countess—Miss Boeker? Didn't you tell Reggie Blount . . . ?"

"No, I didn't—please, these are private matters. What I spend is my . . ." Again, she paused, cleared her frown. ("Select, my dear, highlight with care—but never antagonize.") "What I mean is," she added quickly, trying to meet all the cynical, vigilant eyes without flinching, "I didn't mind any of it—it was great fun restoring the palazzo in Venice—and you can't believe how happy the Alfa Romeo made him! You see, Vitti's really a very sweet person—so understandable when you know his story . . ."

Flashbulbs flared and smoked and Lily felt the gooseflesh of warning along her arms without now being able to stop.

"You see, he came from a tiny Italian village, very poor and remote. All the people loved beautiful Vitti with the soft dark eyes and the curly hair, and someone got the idea of sending him off to America to find a rich heiress. They took up a collection for his fare and he promised to come back with money for everyone and everything."

Pencils scratched furiously, but she couldn't stop to wonder what they wrote—it was true, and she wasn't telling *all* the facts. "He took the name of a rich family he drove racing cars for, and pretended their palazzo in Rome was his." Lily's gaze took on the softness that was generally described as "mysteriously feline."

"I liked that part, really—a lot of people benefited, and they were so pleased that I . . ."

"Then you'll remain friends?" a reporter asked abruptly, the cigarette in his mouth bobbing.

"Friends?" She wound the pearls through her flashing fingers and made her "lemon-eating" face.

There was a low hum of amusement.

"Really," she said, turning to face them in frank appeal, "be fair. Would *you* all want to talk about the intimate things in your lives, to people like *you!*"

The sound of their laughter made her smile—tentatively. "I suppose you'll print that, too," she said.

They lost no time in protest. "Lily—will you marry again?" someone asked rapidly.

"Good heavens—I doubt it. I'd never trust another foreigner—and American businessmen are too wrapped up in their work. And the man I want . . . I mean the *kind* of man I want, won't come near my money." She cast an uncertain look for Maudie.

Maudie moved forward a little, and the pace of the questions quickened.

"What will you do now, Countess—Lily . . . ? Go back to your dancing?"

"I doubt that—though I'll always dance for my own pleasure . . ."

"What about that prince on board? We were told it was a hot romance, and he didn't deny it to . . ."

"That's crazy! I danced with him *twice*. Most of the time I was indisposed . . ."

"Oh, yes . . . ?"

"I think that's enough for this morning," she said quickly, "if you don't mind . . ."

"Bravo!" called a voice from the doorway to a connecting suite. "Don't let the morons beat you down, sweet pea!"

Everyone turned to look at the tall, thin young man, his angular face twisted in mockery. He waved his long ebony cigarette holder. "Just saying bye-bye—we're all going on. See you at the party—no excuses." Blowing a kiss from long, manicured fingers, smiling snidely at the press, he withdrew, closed the door.

Lily suppressed a releasing giggle. She would prefer Andy's irreverence any day to Aunt Mirry's skill—if only *she* could cultivate that!

"Now you've come back from Europe," the tall reporter with the hat on the back of his head asked, "what thoughts have you got about your country, Miss Boeker—the Depression, the question of wages for Boeker employees?"

Maudie was suddenly in front of her. "All right, ladies and gentlemen." She shooed at them with bony hands that seemed older than her unwrinkled face. "The interview is over."

"Please—one last thing, honey," called the original questioner. "Would you say you were rather simply dressed for your arrival, suitable for a grim morning in grim times?"

"She certainly is," Maudie intervened. "Her blood has thinned from warmer climates, and she *needs* her furs."

Lily caught the woman's sickly smile and quickly switched her attention to the maid who brought her a brown crocodile purse and brown kid gloves. She let her do up all the pearl buttons, without raising her head.

When she did, the group was pushing towards the doors, shepherded by the uniformed trio.

When the door closed, Lily stood bleakly a moment. A silence fell. "I was the worst ever, Maudie, wasn't I?" She looked anxiously into the small, bespectacled face. "Truthfully?"

"None of it matters, dear. It all comes out in the wash." Maudie patted her arm. "And you'll feel better as soon as you're on land." She slipped a black coat over her gray dress, dismissed the maids with a nod and cast a final glance around the lavish, impersonal room, still thickly banked with flowers both fading and fresh. "I suppose the stewards will take them. Well, that's that."

"About Mr. Maitland, Maudie—did Whitey . . . ?"

"No, I didn't, Boke," said Whitey, coming in with a doleful expression that contrasted almost comically with the glow of her cheeks, her windswept bangs. "I spoke to the purser, too—nothing. Except a couple of last telegrams—one from Aunt Mirry saying come down to Palm Beach as soon as possible."

Lily lifted the deep cape collar of her coat high around her face, as if to hide, to somehow find shelter. "Oh, well . . ." She sighed.

"Now, Lil, don't forget," Thomas pronounced as she moved forward. "We're right behind you. Follow the plan exactly . . ."

"Yes, yes . . . All right, Thomas . . ."

"He's right, Miss Lily," Maudie urged. "We don't want any mishaps." She gave a firm, decisive nod.

Lily looked at her wistfully. For the first time in her life she thought of Maudie as a person to be envied.

"Miss Boeker, please—this is Palm Beach, Florida."

Whitey groaned inwardly and rubbed the back of her neck, which was stiff with writing letters and talking into this mouthpiece for almost three days on the subject of Boke's unavailability. "I'm sorry, Miss Boeker isn't taking calls," she said determinedly, and held her breath.

An all too familiar voice, supremely authoritative, rich with confident charm, broke through the operator's queries. "Miss White, this is Mrs. Court—I would like to speak to my niece!"

Whitey sat straighter, adjusted the bow of her blouse. "Mrs.

Court, I'm terribly sorry—but Boke . . . Lily is *still* in her gloom. It's much worse than last time . . ."

"But, my dear girl, surely you can rouse her! I've got something very important to talk to her about."

"That's just it, Mrs. Court—I *can't* rouse her. It's as though she were half dead . . ."

"What nonsense! The more she's allowed to retreat like this, the longer the unfortunate affair will affect her. I suggest you go to her right now. And do hurry, Miss White, I've got a dozen people waiting."

Whitey pressed the back of her thumb to her front teeth. Aunt Mirry gave her the chills. She had never recovered from that confrontation over the dress for the debut—looking back, she wondered how she had ever had the nerve to refuse to borrow one . . .

On the other hand, it was Boke she worked for. "I'm really sorry, Mrs. Court . . ."

"Miss White—I insist!"

Whitey nodded to herself. *Okay,* she thought—but at that instant the voice at the other end broke in again. "Just a minute, Miss White. I'm told the Earl of Cambrook has just arrived. I must go and welcome him. I'll call back later."

Whitey hung up. Well, she'd better have another look at Boke . . .

The main living room to Lily's suite was empty. A gold clock on a French commode ticked with sharp intensity. Whitey moved on to the double doors and without knocking went into the room beyond.

Far across, in a slant of winter sunlight between slightly opened drapes, Maudie was sitting working on what Whitey guessed was flower stitching on the sweater for Lily's old bear. Making hardly a rise under the white satin spread, Boke lay in the huge bed as still as someone dead.

"Ssh . . ." Maudie said as Whitey went briskly up to the bed and peered down at the wan face pressed deep into pillows.

Whitey felt awe mixed with her frustration. Boke's wet lashes fluttered, her mouth moved a little, her breath was light and even—how well she had perfected this escape! She wanted to shake her, tell her to snap out of it, force her to get on with life.

At the same time, she recognized that Boke's capacity for suffering was part of the wonder and fascination she felt for her, had felt ever since the day Lily, a "new girl," had arrived at school with two different Rolls carrying her possessions, one brown, one blue, with two maids and Maudie, and, despite her two real fur coats and real pearls, desperately lonely. How proud she'd felt to be chosen to defend and champion her against all the jealousy and cruelty! "You'll never guess who's my best friend this term," she had written to her family. "Little Princess Dry Goods herself! And she's so funny and—beautiful and extraordinary . . . !"

"Boke?" she said firmly now. "*Please* wake up—your Aunt Mirry *demands* to speak to you."

There was not the slightest response.

"I don't know what to do, Maudie," she said, shoving her hands through her bangs. "I'm going nuts!"

"There's nothing *to* do. She'll wake up when she's ready. She'll get hungry." Maudie gave one of her nods.

"Don't you think we should call one of the doctors?"

"I don't think they would know what to do, either, dear."

"If only Joel . . . *He* knows about things like this . . ."

"Best let that be." Maudie looked up, snapped a thread off between her teeth. "She'll like these," she said, holding up the sweater and a matching hat she had made, with two holes for the bear's ears.

"Honestly, Maudie. Don't you want to get out and get some fresh air—I sure do. I'm going to exercise in the gym, have a swim, go to the movies tonight with a boy I know . . ."

"I wouldn't do that, dear. Miss Lily might . . ."

"I'm not a prisoner, Maudie. And you shouldn't let yourself become one, either!"

Whitey was sorry the moment she'd said it. Maudie seemed suddenly smaller, as if she had shrunk within the grayness of her clothing. "Well, you know what I mean," she added.

"Maudie, Maudie . . . ?"

Lily's voice, faint and husky, made them both start.

Maudie put down her work and went quickly to her side. Whitey followed.

"Some toast, dear," Maudie said, "a nice cup of tea?"

"No, no . . . Nothing. Close the drapes, Maudie." She touched Maudie's hand, then sank back and turned over into the pillows.

"Boke, Boke—I want to talk to you!"

There was no movement, no sign of her having heard.

. . . Lily floated away from light and sound, from misery that filled all her being, all space. Her arms wound about the pillow in nameless yearning—for her father, her mother, for someone, anyone who would end the loneliness—but it was a sea of pain without a horizon . . .

She swam in it, back to some shore where dreams were not dreams . . . Bright, flickering images, feelings, fusing together . . .

"Fifty yards of finest Alençon lace appliquéd on gardenia satin, mademoiselle . . ." Soft as froth, rippling petals in the pink wind. Voices of sweet music on Nuit-de-Noël air, spinning wine-like off the ground. Magic awnings over tingling violins and love in doorways. Up over rooftops to tango the wide green Bois with Vitti and close-dancing dancers in dimness with white purposeful faces. Feathers, crepes, chiffons, brocades, billowing and twisting the Rue de la Paix in the stargazing Seine whispering the waving Notre Dame in glittering white . . .

"Boke! Open your eyes! Sit up—listen to me!"

. . . Slap-slap, slap-slap the gondolas and other boats —click, squeak against the wall, the cats under lamplight and silence in stone-blended squares of oblong houses. Red-ribboned hats over gondoliers' smiles and on the light-dotted liner on the canal small faces peering. Damp green and darkly glowing the palazzos of old moss stone and dark-deep velvets. Frayed gold, and thin noses in the great dark paintings, high above, dark eyes following, knowing her from another haze of time . . .

"I know you're awake, Boke—your eyelids are fluttering—stop holding out!"

"It's all yours, Vitti, for you—you're my husband. You must have everything that makes you happy. You must never think about money. Then I can forget it, too, you see . . ."

Lies. Like sinking—but rising because not caring, only wondering about no love and curious wanting at last to touch, be touched . . . what is it, Vitti—don't you love me, after all . . . ?

A secret . . . share the secret . . . only this way? Me kneel down, in front of you? A big mirror behind me . . . Just you loving yourself, not me at all? Oh, but your hands, like steel, Vitti, so hard, so rough, pushing me down, pushing me down . . .

Vile, oh vile, clamping me there, my face and only there of you . . . Oh, God help me . . . Joel, Joel, Joel, help, help, HELP . . . !

"That does it, Boke!"

Lily's eyes opened wide, dazed into Whitey's. She was still gasping, groaning. "What are you doing to me—why are you shaking me?" she murmured.

"It's me, Whitey—I'm sorry, Boke, but this is final."

"What? What are you saying, Whitey?" Lily struggled to a sitting position, leaned weakly back into the pillows. Her mouth was dry, her eyes burning, her senses wrapped in thick cotton.

"I'm not going to stand by while you do this to yourself, Boke —I'd rather join the unemployed!"

Lily wrapped her thin arms around herself and shivered.

Maudie was instantly there with a pink chiffon-and-lace bed jacket. "I'll get you a cup of tea, dear."

Lily nodded. Tears began to pour down her cheeks.

Maudie gave Whitey an angry glance as she passed, but Whitey, hands on hips, was oblivious.

"You'd leave me, Whitey?" Lily asked, her voice small and bleak.

"Yes, Boke, I would."

Lily searched the familiar face for signs of dissemblance; there were none. "You, too," she said forlornly.

"Boke, let's be honest—you're not really ill!"

Lily looked in wan envy at her firm, confident face. "You never feel curled up and dead in here, do you, Whitey . . . ?" She patted her chest. "You don't know why the blues were written, or why people put their heads in gas ovens, or . . ."

"Don't start that, Boke. It's not the point."

Lily nodded, sighed. "What do you want me to do, Whitey?"

"Get up, get Aunt Mirry off my neck, set things in motion again."

They looked at each other in silence. Lily recognized Whitey's finality with jolting panic.

"I'll make an effort, Whitey," she said. "I promise. You won't leave me if I try, will you?"

"Of course not."

Lily attempted a smile. "Thank you," she said.

Chapter 10

"Have you read this, dear?" Aunt Mirry, wearing a striped dress and her panama "working hat," smiled. She handed Lily a clipping from a newspaper. "I wish I had time to discuss it with you, but the builders have arrived. We're going to do alterations at night for the circus people—so no one is disturbed."

Lily nodded, smiled back. When her aunt had moved off with a retinue of overalled men, she withdrew her attention from the golfers on the last green of the palm-dotted golf course to scan the clipping.

"Titled guests of all ages and nationalities abound at Mrs. Court's this season," Tessa Webb had written in the Palm Beach *Trumpet,* "and Lily, 'pale and interesting' as the richest divorcée in America, is the queen bee of her aunt's 128-room hive, with not a moment to mourn her fake count. With, among others, no less than Aly Khan, the Bulgarian Prince Ogeven and Anthony Aylsden, Earl of Cambrook (England), three of the world's most irresistible men all under one roof, Lily has cast off all cares of the world to revel in their hot pursuit.

"Missing no function or activity in the nonstop round planned by her aunt and other leading members of Palm Beach society, she wears one more beautiful gown than the other, flirts with the art of a southern belle, plays tennis, golf, swims with girlish ardor and grace, and shows no trace of the mysterious "illness" which kept the press at bay in New York. There is a new spark to her personality, new bite.

"At this writing Anthony Aylsden, Earl of Cambrook, is very much in the lead in this arena. It is easy to understand. 'Tony' is tall, erect, lean, has vivid blue eyes that seem to undress a woman, thin sandy hair that kinks attractively (he'll go bald someday for sure, but who cares?) and a thin dashing line of mustache. But it's the naughty smile, the foxy twinkle that puts him in the irresistible class.

"Perhaps there will be big news for you soon—I will be the first to hear it and promise to pass it on to you as a TESSA WEBB SCOOP!"

Lily put the clipping into the pocket of her white linen shorts. Yes, Aunt Mirry *would* be pleased, she thought. She was completely illogical about Tony. The ruder he was, the more he derided moral codes, the more Aunt Mirry smiled. "He's incorrigible, of course—but so charming, so amusing—and the genuine article. I've met Lady Mavis, his mother the Dowager Countess, and the General knew his father during the war. Their home is one of England's finest, though it's run-down now—Aylsden wealth is a thing of the past, I'm sure."

It was comforting to know that Aunt Mirry had this chink in her wisdom. It had also been great relief to find that no confrontation had been necessary on the subject of her "gloom," as Whitey called it. Aunt Mirry simply didn't have time. There had been one brief, affectionate welcome on her arrival, one verbal bridge of Aunt Mirryisms.

"Don't be taken off-guard by Aly—his chief weapon is the *coup de foudre*. He counts on it. Of course, go to bed with him if it's useful. Don't take Oge seriously, he has a mistress and an arranged marriage to face.

"Forget Vitti—people as rich as we are don't explain, don't justify or rationalize. We're a law unto ourselves, you see. No, dear, boredom is our only enemy, not the press as you think, not world opinion.

"Of course, I myself am never bored, as you know. There's always some delightful challenge—some rare treasure which gives me great pleasure to find and acquire. And though I entertain so many of the world's most fascinating people, I'm not dependent on them. What I enjoy is the organizing. I'm a natural leader, a businesswoman, and I like making myself expert in whatever field of interest that happens to appeal to me. People respect money spent fearlessly, with flourish and knowledge, I assure you.

"Naturally, the General's a comfort. But I give him no more than I can afford of myself, and ask no more of him.

"However, I do see a great difference between you and me, dear. My childhood was rich, too, and I was adored. I've never been alone, lonely or on the have-not side of life.

"But nor in that sense have you, Lily my dear, have you? That's why you'll always have money. To those who *have*, shall be given—to those who have *not*, shall be taken away. This is more than a religious paradox—it's a law of life. You won't be happy until you accept it, wholeheartedly.

"Now—as you see, the house is swarming with servants, far too many, I admit—but it's only kindness to give them jobs, and I don't take advantage. Also, I give them a good home.

"Well, dear, I like the high thin eyebrows, the pale-blue eye shadow to match your eyes, a beguiling effect. You're beginning to mature and it suits your face, gives it more character. I must fly—but for heaven's sake, child, don't spend your time with Andy and that preposterous Howie—have a real vacation, let yourself go!"

Vacation. Lily shook her head. From what? But it was no use trying to think, to arrive at meanings or conclusions—not about anything. Twice, in the beginning, she had put in telephone calls to Joel in faint hope that he might advise her on how best to spend her time, if not her life—but he was not there. She'd meant to try again—but events had suddenly moved too fast.

She looked out to the green in time to see Tony wave his putter at her and grin. She couldn't help laughing to herself. He should never have told her the stakes of this match with Aly, but during that ridiculous hide-and-seek game in the jungle garden, all of them drunk from the round of parties, he had pushed her against the tree of stuffed parrots and whispered, "I'll win tomorrow, yes I will!"

"Win what?" she'd whispered, trying to squirm from his arms, which pinned her so hard to the trunk. She could hear people plunging about in the realistically dense undergrowth, screeching as they fell or touched a stuffed jungle creature.

"The bet with Aly. Whoever wins gives the other forty-eight hours, gets out of the way."

"Of what, Tony—oh, please, my *arms!*"

"To get you to bed, of course."

"Not a chance—not either of you." Laughing, gasping, she'd struggled to get free, but he'd begun running his hands over her, kissing her with such ferocity that she'd had to kick and bite— and the instant he'd lost his grip, she'd started running.

But they'd ended up plunging around in the pool among the crocodiles, giggling, hanging on to one another. She hadn't really been frightened of him, after all—but just in case, she'd locked the outer door to her suite before going to bed.

"It's the deciding putt," someone said beside her now. She kept a straight face with difficulty.

"God, that English bastard's attractive," said Penny Hammar, whose candy fortune did not fall as far short of Lily's as most, but whose face was a minor disaster of pitted skin and excess sun. "They say he can do it six times a night."

"What about Aly?" The Baroness de Brekvoort aimed black-pearl binoculars through the erect palms at a young man with dark, already receding hair. "It's quality, not quantity." She looked down at Penny, her limpid dark eyes challenging, her dark thin mouth disdainful.

"Well, dear—*you* would know. But I'd sure like to find out about Tony."

"He's a better golfer than the Ismaili," said Prince Oge, smiling. "Look, Lily—ah, that does it!"

Lily clapped with the rest of the group lounging in the cool dimness of the loggia.

But even before the two men had sauntered over to them,

there was a concerted movement of spectators towards the next event on Mirry's relentless calendar; clothes had to be changed once again, now for a lunch party at the Beach Club.

"Darling," said Penny to Lily, hovering with her eyes on Tony, "tell me what to wear—I'm getting giddy."

"Oh, anything light, casual—over that backless bathing suit, perhaps."

"Mmm. I've got a Patou sports dress that—"

"Fine. Don't wait for me." Lily cast her a quick smile.

Reluctantly, Penny moved on with the others, barely escaping (thought Lily) another of Tony's unsubtle barbs at her affected nasal "English."

As Tony and Aly came up, Miriam's house guests paused to observe, to smile at Lily and the two men with frank interest.

Her long thin legs tanned by Florida sun to a fine patina, her thin body in the white linen shorts and halter top, the nonchalant straightness of her shoulders, the slender face given its dimension of mystery by the huge tilted blue eyes, now with the brilliance of an underlit pool, she stood between the flanking men —one tall, thin, almost soldierly, the other dark, almost paunchy —like a feline goddess receiving homage from mortal males.

"Barge off," Tony murmured to Aly, his smile thinly innocent.

Aly's dark round eyes searched her face a moment. "Time will tell," he said. He brushed the back of her hand with soft lips and strolled away. Before he had gone far, the Baroness had slipped a hirsute, bangled arm through his.

Lily met Tony's impish grin with an innocent stare, but when he touched her arm, his blatant desire was like vibration.

"Do we have to go to this dreary lunch?" he asked as they stood momentarily alone.

"I do. But of course you don't."

"Christ. Well, all right. But you're sitting next to me. If one more American says, 'And where's your home, Earl?' Or 'I just adore England, all my ancestors came from there, you know'—I'll say something rude."

"You already have, Tony. Lots of things to lots of people." She tried not to grin.

"Not rude enough—they think I'm pulling their legs."

"I don't. I think you're insufferable and . . ."

He put his hand in the curve of her waist and gripped it. "Good God, a waist without a roll! Darling, darling—when are we going to do it? I've had a hard-on ever since last night."

"Tony! Honestly!" The idea that she was not appalled, not revolted, was like a gentle descent onto feathers, and an unexpected thrill struck low in her stomach. She pulled away, walked towards the interior of the house.

"Wait," he commanded. "Come back here."

She turned, curious, somewhat awed. Not since Freddie had anyone spoken to her like that. She arched her thin brows, lowered her chin, met his demanding gaze in exaggerated blankness.

"Come on." He snapped his fingers.

"I can't be late, Tony—it's in my honor." She went back to him, feigning impatience. "What is it?"

He put a hand on each of her thin hipbones. "Lily—do you want me to sleep with someone else?"

"I don't understand."

"It's simple, darling. You've kept me excited for days, ever since that first kiss—what do you expect me to do?"

She looked into the blue eyes. There was enough of a twinkle there to confuse her. "I don't know about—these things," she began.

"*Lily*. You've been doing it for years. Why not me?"

She drew back from his hands, her face stiff as a doll's. The thrill receded, there was disappointment, uneasiness.

"I've heard all the stories. Everyone knows what you had to do with the Count!"

The knowledgeable glint in his eyes, the way he touched his mustache and smiled, brought a wave of almost forgotten nausea.

"What's wrong, my sweet?" He took her hand, pulled her to him. "I thought you and I were . . ."

"It's not true, none of it's true," she said, looking up at him. "I'm . . . I've never . . ." Suddenly she shook off his hands. "Oh, believe what you like."

He grasped her hands back again. His sandy eyebrows drew high and peaked (the way Andy's did, she thought). "You've never had it? Is *that* what you're saying?"

"Tony—this isn't something you talk about in broad daylight on the way to lunch! Please—let me go."

He drew her close to his body, a slow grin creasing his tanned, lean-jawed face. The blue eyes gleamed, narrowed. "By God, you know—I think I believe you. It's too preposterous not to. Darling—let me come to your room tonight. We must talk—discuss this."

"No!"

"Just discuss, darling? I won't rape you, I swear."

She didn't answer. He let her go, stood smiling at her straight back as she moved off. Then nodding, smiling incredulously to himself, he followed.

In the early afternoon, the circus people began to arrive. Aunt Mirry put the workers in the servants' wing and the performers were put in guest suites. They were to give their identical New York performance for one night, and the rest of the time to holiday at Aunt Mirry's expense. A covered passageway had been completed while her other guests were at lunch. By the time they arrived back, an army of workers had almost finished erecting the vast tent. Four hundred tickets had been sold to local townspeople for the event, in aid of the Underprivileged Children of West Palm Beach.

Lily lay tense between pink lawn sheets. Whitey was in her special quarters near Mrs. Hamp, and Maudie had retired to hers next door. Mixed with occasional insect sounds, the sough of palm fronds in a light breeze from the sea, the far-off brush of waves to shore and a faint spasmodic cough from other suites, was the distant tap-tap of hammers, of muffled reverberations that would hardly penetrate even the lightest sleep.

Why hadn't she locked her door? she thought. Now that the mind-hazing round of activities (that had included the usual pool or dinner parties, with only one interval, to listen to "that man" give his Fireside Chat and to debate whether or not he was leading the nation to ruin, a reception for the Aga Khan and his Begum, gambling at Bradley's, a movie shown on Mrs. Kenelm's great lawn in the moonlight—luckily Chip was cruising the Indies—a late party where Cole Porter was induced to play and sing his songs, a later one where a game of nude Sardines—she kept her clothes on—ended in a free-for-all with the police called in—they stayed on for champagne) was wearing off, she wondered how she could have been so foolish.

She sat up, pressed the covers to her chin—was that the door opening now? Her light-blue satin nightgown, left over from her trousseau, seemed suddenly deliberately provocative, an invitation, in fact. Did she have time to slip into the matching robe of marabou and lace?

There was a thud, the sound of muffled swearing. She slid back down into the bed, the thumping of her heart loud against the pillows. Well—now she'd done it, she thought. He'd know the door could have been locked, and he knew, darn it, that she was not invulnerable. Still—he had said he wouldn't. . . .

Another strange thrill struck in the same place in the lower part of her stomach. Was it possible that this was the "desire" she'd heard and read so much about, the very idea of which had been sickening? She thought of the way he'd touched her all evening, ignoring her reserve, putting his hands on her breasts, moving them languorously down her back when they danced, running them up the insides of her thighs. When at any time she could have rejected him flatly, the feebleness of her protests had been a revelation. The nearest she could come to dignity was a lack of reaction. But he didn't seem to notice, or care.

Now there was the slight creak of boards deep under carpet, and finally, the bedroom door opening incautiously and a tall figure pushing through it and approaching her raised bed.

She pressed back against the pillow, forcing the lids down over her moon-reflecting eyes, feigning sleep as if it might protect her from him, deny participation in his being there.

"Lily?" He spoke softly but did not whisper. "Here I am."

Tony Aylsden, wearing pajamas and satin dressing gown, reached over to Lily's thin outline and pulled back the covers. "Delicious," he said. "And that perfume—mmm!" He moved into the bed beside her, stretched out close, touched her shoulder. "You're trembling," he said.

She tried to get a grip on herself, kept her eyes shut, but she could feel him laughing beside her.

"Come on, open your eyes," he said. "What are you afraid of?"

She opened her eyes. "I'm not afraid. You just shouldn't be here."

"You didn't tell me *not* to come, darling—did you?" He began stroking her softly, running his hands inside the low-cut top of her nightgown. When she pulled away, he turned her back with strong hands and eased the shoulder straps off, and began to knead her breasts, his breathing accelerating.

Flash pictures of Freddie went by in her mind, but somehow the fear was different. This was not terror, but a mixture of dread and excitement she lacked will enough to resist. A clean soap smell emanated from him, a heavy warmth like electricity to her own body.

"Lovely, lovely breasts," he said. "Oh, God—I can't stand much of this!"

"We were going to *talk*," she said.

"What about?"

"Tony—you're terrible! I thought we were going to discuss my . . ."

"Virginity?"

She could see his smile before he suddenly pulled the full length of her body close to him. "We will, my precious girl—afterwards. I'm not averse to pillow talk."

She felt swamped, her reason gone. It was useless to struggle, and her brief thought of screaming for Maudie was her last before Tony was kissing her with such aggressive abandon that the only sound she could make was a gasp.

"I'll be gentle, darling, don't worry. You're not the first—I know what to do."

Suddenly every nerve in her was relaxing, letting go in surrender—the whole world became a dimness of sensations, warmly frightening, thrillingly alarming, new as shock, tantalizing, pleasantly unpleasant.

"I can't last," he said, swiveling over on top of her.

A hard intrusion, an outrage, a betrayal. "Oh, I hate you, I hate you," she said, bursting into tears of fury, disappointment, disgust. "It's filthy, you're filthy!"

In the dimness she recognized chagrin in Tony's expression as he rolled away from her, but no apology.

"It's always rotten the first time," he said, patting her pale-blond mound of pubic hair. She tried to put on her nightgown, but he jerked it away from her. "Come close," he said, "let me hold you."

"No, thank you."

He leaned up on his elbow and foraged a large white handkerchief from his pocket and dabbed at her gently where the semen had spilled. "Poor darling—you girls have so much to contend with. It's a good thing I had the sense to withdraw—you might have got pregnant. Didn't you know that?"

"My information is limited," she said, allowing herself to be engulfed by his arms. "In other words, I'm an ignoramus."

He laughed, stroked her hair, rubbed her back with knowledgeable, comforting pressure, kissed her forehead, her nose. She felt her anger ebb and melt. "I like you this way," she said, sighing. "Oh, I do like you this way—it feels so good, so very good."

"It's extraordinary," he said. "The world thinks of you as a willful, spoiled brat, surfeited in male adulation—here you are a love-starved virgin!"

"That sounds awful. Worse than the other."

He laughed softly. "I agree. Poor little rich girl. If you're not careful, you'll live and die a cliché. You'd better marry me."

There was a silence.

After a while, he pressed her chin between his thumb and forefinger and turned her face up to his. "What do you say, old girl?"

She saw the irreverence in his eyes, the unconcealed mischief, but it charmed her now as it had done the moment she met him; it seemed almost a virtue, made other men seem plodding and spiritless. "Are you *that* sure?" she asked.

"Well, yes—and I'm not going to pussyfoot. I want your money. I want a bloody lot of it. Cambrook House is falling apart, Mother and I are living on credit, and the credit's running out. I've got astronomical gambling debts and bills and there are two women in England suing me for breach of promise."

"Tony!"

"Hear me out, darling. I'd like to reform. I'll soon be twenty-six. I've been doing it since I was thirteen, first with boys at the tutor's my father insisted on, and with every girl who'd do it with me, from then on. I'm oversexed, and I love it, but it's leading me by the nose. I want one woman to love, my debts paid, and a responsible position."

Before she spoke, he sat up, reached for a cigarette, lit it and lay on his side to wait for her reaction.

"And I'm the woman to love?"

He inhaled smoke, let it out slowly. "Yes. I was going to pursue you anyway. When Mother and I received the invitation from that indefatigable aunt of yours, it seemed like a signal from Lucifer."

"Not God?"

He grinned. "You're brighter than you look, my sweet." He kissed her lips softly.

"Your mustache scratches, you know," she murmured.

"So I've been told—but pleasantly, eh?"

"Eh. Kind of."

He kissed her again, harder. "Where was I?" he said, leaning back on his elbow. "Oh yes—Mother and I had a most interesting discussion. She said she could stomach an American if *enough* money came with her, that she treasures our home that much!"

"So it is only my money, really—isn't it, Tony? Tell me the truth—I *have* got feelings, you know."

"Oh, my darling!" He turned to stub out his cigarette, using a small gold whatnot dish in lieu of an ashtray and murmuring, "You must learn to smoke." Then he drew her back against him and covered them both with the soft, scented sheet. "The fact is, at first I thought I couldn't go through with it—I'd never met such extraordinary people, their voices, their maudlin sentimentality, their heavy humor, their vulgarity—I couldn't believe my eyes and ears when, my beautiful girl, you arrived."

"And?" Lily ran an exploratory palm over the sparse hair on his broad, flat chest and found it pleasant.

"Well, of course, you were God's gift. Even your accent was music after the rest of them—including your illustrious aunt with her pseudo-British, and I wanted you the minute I saw you. You do have, darling, the most delectable body, and your eyes gave me an instant erection."

"Tony—please! The way you talk—it's so *extreme.*"

"You want me to beat about the bush, eh? Well, I'll try, but I'm not your puritanical Yank."

She lay back, gazed into the vast pinkness of the ceiling with its glints of suspended Venetian glass. "I don't think so, Tony," she murmured. "There must be love."

"What do you know of that?"

"Something."

"Ah-ha. Well—I'll put my head on the block, then. I've fallen for you, Lily—madly, in fact."

"I don't believe you, Tony."

"That's because sex intervened. I'll make you love me, if you don't now."

She turned her head on the pillow to search his face. "I wonder . . ."

He kissed her with sudden urgent tenderness. "Yes," he said, "you will, you will!" His kisses grew more ardent, more demanding, spread from her mouth to her nipples, to her body, covered it.

She felt a response, vibrant, growing more powerful. How well he now seemed to know where to touch her, how to make every movement of their undulating closeness thrilling.

"That's it, darling," he said, "give it to me, move, writhe—I want every part of you, every part!"

Suddenly, again, he was entering. She heard herself groan with a mixture of pleasure and agony, of gain yet loss, of aggression yet surrender. Then, abruptly, it was over. Some final feeling was being denied her. Still, the deprivation didn't really matter—it was the promise—so . . . "Beautiful," she murmured aloud.

Tony grunted, spoke words she had only read in forbidden books, but with such abandon and force that she felt they were right. Then, like a sweet bell to her ears, he groaned, "Oh, I love you, I love you!" Suddenly he was still, the full weight of his body on hers.

His quick breathing made hers inaudible, but gradually they were lying in mutual tranquillity, still closely locked, yet in neutral areas of being.

"Yes, Tony," she said after a while.

"What?"

"Yes—I will marry you."

"It's what I'd hoped, of course—the best thing that could have happened," said Miriam Court. "He'll be expensive but worth it. You'll find Mavis formidable, but under the circumstances controllable. Now, let me see—the wedding could take place here. That would be suitably restrained for the times, and minimize the tedious dogma of church. You say a small wedding and reception—so I suggest no more than five hundred guests. I can't conceive of fewer without ill-feeling. You can have my yacht for the honeymoon."

Lily shrugged. "I'll put it to Tony. He wants to get home as soon as possible now."

Miriam raised her hand. "Time enough. The rest of your life. You must have one glorious, romantic interlude before facing the daily strains—so around the world, perhaps." She put down her pen. "You won't expect Tony to be faithful to you, dear, will you?"

Lily smiled at her aunt, finding her suddenly no longer awe-inspiring, in fact, from Tony's perspective, almost amusing. "I will, really," she answered. "It will be largely up to me."

Her aunt's immaculate head tilted. The rosy face was impassive.

"I know," Lily added. "You think he's incurable. But I'll have the whip hand, remember."

Aunt Mirry's eyebrows made two thick blond arcs. "That doesn't sound like you. Not that I don't heartily . . ."

"Yes, I'm sure you do approve!"

"You've had a lot to make you bitter, dear . . ."

"But I'm not bitter, Aunt Mirry. I'm beginning to wake up, to see life differently. I'm really quite happy."

"Ah. Good. Well—back to business. Let's talk about the date, the gowns, the trousseau, music, guest list. This will be an enchanting enterprise!"

Lily visualized the vast organization that would be launched on her behalf, the unlimited imagination without thought to cost. Yet only yesterday, the banker Malcolm White, one of Mirry's oldest friends, found guilty of swindling his depositors out of millions, had slashed his wrists in prison with the edge of a tin cup.

"Andy, of course, will be your best man. We'll have to hide

Howie among the guests. What I'd rather like to do is to trans-
form the ballroom into an English country garden—yes!"

After twenty more minutes of discussion, Lily rose. "Tony and
I are playing tennis, then going to the polo match. You make any
further arrangements you like, Aunt Mirry—it's your show."

"You're not interested?"

"Only in tying the knot."

"Oh, dear—you're like so many of the young today."

"Not quite." She gave her aunt a direct stare.

"I mean basically." Her aunt looked thoughtful. "Oh, one
more thing—shall we, dear, under the circumstances, ask Freddie
and your mother? To show we forgive and forget?"

Lily stretched her thin arms in the sleeveless Lanvin-bleu crepe
pajamas. "No. Only Mummy—if she's sober."

"Yes—well, I doubt that. But I'm very glad you're taking a
philosophical view."

"I'm not taking any view, Auntie. I'm just stating the case."

Her aunt's eyes followed her nonchalant exit with fascination.
"You'll make a top-hole Lady Aylsden, dear," she called in heavy
humor.

"I intend to," called Lily. She waved, smiled, passed from her
aunt's sight.

"What?" said Tony when she related the plans. "Spend weeks
or months at sea on her ruddy yacht! After six weeks in this dol-
lar Nirvana! Christ, I'd go off my nut. Not that I don't appreciate
the palatial aspects, the eighty in crew, the bacchanalian revels,
but . . ."

"We won't go, darling." Lily tapped his shoulder with her
racquet. "Simple."

"You're divine." He lowered his neat, wave-indented head,
spoke from the side of his thin mouth. "I get horribly seasick."
Involuntarily, Tony put his arm around her, high under her arm-
pit so that his hand fell loosely over her breast. "What I'd really
like, my sweet," he said, "is to get on with the harnessing straight
off."

"That's what I told Aunt Mirry."

"Ripping. If we could leap up the aisle by the end of the

month, we could catch the *Mauretania* on her next sailing—then go to the Ritz in London until we find a decent house."

"What about Cambrook?"

"Darling, you wouldn't want to live *there*. Not with Mother. At least not till it's renovated and staffed. We don't want you dying of chilblains, do we?"

"I suppose not—whatever they are." Something threatened—but it didn't matter—not if it was to do with money. Thank Vitti for that, at least. "A London house will be fun," she nodded.

"I'll cable old Guy Pickett. He'll see what's offering."

"Old Guy Pickett?" She smiled, and his hand closed tighter over her breast.

"My chum—one of them. Three of us chaps teamed up at Oxford. Inseparable—all that sort of thing. But now that the wine, women and song era's to die . . ."

"Not to die, darling, to be replaced—by something better?"

"Bravo! Quite right." He grinned and pinched her nipple.

Lily, Maudie, Whitey and Thomas stood together for a moment on the grand staircase of the *Mauretania*. "I want you all to know how grateful I am that you're with me," Lily said quickly. Tony found her relationship with the servants gauche, and from now on it would have to be circumspect, if not surreptitious; she had not liked the gleam of temper in his eyes when she persisted in it.

"I promise you," she added, "that nothing will be different in me—even if everything changes on the outside. And it will, of course. England's very different from America—Tony's told me many things about it that I never knew."

"Well, I knew them, dear," said Maudie. "All along."

They all looked at her.

"I was trained in the hierarchy of servants," she said, nodding.

"Well, I ain't gonna like it," said Thomas, "but except for Palm Beach, Lil needs guarding, and that's that."

"What about the rumor I hear that you want to marry Gladys?" Lily asked him. To her disgust, she had felt a kind of jealousy.

They all smiled at Thomas as he shifted his weight, jerked a shoulder in chagrin. "The maids give me a hard time," he said. "I can't shake 'em."

"Perhaps we'll have perky cockney ones," said Whitey.

"Enough of that," said Maudie.

"I can't wait to see England, Boke," said Whitey, who looked unusually chic in a navy velvet coat and hat she had accepted from Lily. "I remember everything I learned about its history. It's Westminister Abbey first stop for me."

"You didn't remember your spelling." Maudie almost smiled. "It's West*minster*, dear."

"Oops. We'll see where you came from, Maudie, won't we?"

"It wouldn't hold us—five rooms no bigger than the ship's bathrooms. A patch of garden. It's nothing to see."

Lily tugged at her dark-mink collar, her new rings, the immense solitaire diamond that all but concealed the platinum wedding band looking massive on the thin finger. "When we move into our London house," Lily said, "we must be very formal. The other servants will expect it. Maudie will tell you how to address me and what to do to fit in—so there won't be any embarrassment. Tony, Lord Aylsden, knows everyone up to the King and Queen, so we'll have to watch our protocol."

"At least it's all kosher this time," said Whitey. "And you look happy, Boke."

"I am—but scared." Lily looked into the brown eyes.

"That'll pass. You'll wow the British, including Lady Mavis."

"Yes?"

"We can always go home again," said Thomas. "You know that, Lil."

Lily shook her head at him. "Make that the last time you call me Lil, Thomas. I'd miss you."

Thomas looked away from her, turned his blue cap in his hand.

"Well, here comes my husband." Lily's eyes swept theirs with a last look. "All right? Everything understood?"

They all nodded. She gave them a last furtive smile as they moved on, and turned to watch Tony and his valet coming down the stairs. He looked marvelous to her in his navy pinstripe suit with the red carnation in the buttonhole, his face still tanned and his hair burnished by the Florida sun, the blue of his eyes intense by contrast. The way he looked at her as he ran lightly down the stairs made her think of his long, hard-stomached body and the fierce absorption of his lovemaking. It also made her laugh, for without doubt he would have some outrageous comment to make.

And, as well as that, she thought, letting her coat fall back to show the incomparable lines of Starenze's aquamarine crepe going-away dress, with its emphasis on her breasts, hipbones and natural waistline, she had for the first time in her life a feeling of power. Tony seemed incapable of leaving her alone. She could not bend over, lift her arms, pass before him in her slip or nightgown without being practically raped.

This was bound to ease off. He'd get used to her. Then they would settle down, get to know one another. Their love would get a chance to deepen.

She smiled up at him gaily. She hadn't thought of Joel now in two weeks except for that one terrifying moment as she walked with Andy up the flower-banked path in Aunt Mirry's breathtakingly beautiful "English country garden" towards the minister waiting under the great arbor of massed roses. Then, it was as though her brain had locked and left her in total blankness. She could not understand what she was doing there. Why, since she was wearing the lovely beige georgette wedding dress while hundreds of faces watched her expectantly, was this stranger walking beside her as if *he* were the bridegroom, not Joel?

Then Tony had pinched her arm a little, the music had swelled, and everything was fine again, as clear as the molten sunlight, the completely cloudless sky.

"Christ, you look beautiful!" Tony said, slipping his arm under her coat and around her waist as he led her towards their series of suites. "Burt informs me there's a 'surprise' Bon Voyage party, or I'd tear your clothes off. Also, we haven't fooled the press— they're all over the place like locusts."

Lily put her arm around his waist, kissed his chin. "I've never fooled them yet—but never mind, with you beside me I can handle 'em." She grinned smugly.

"Even the accusations of abandoning your own country at a time of crisis and taking your money elsewhere?" He grinned back.

"Sure. It's mine, isn't it? Grandpa Boeker didn't say *where* I had to spend it!"

He flicked her ear with the tip of his tongue. "That's my girl. Spoken like a true Aylsden."

Chapter 11

"So you know King Edward personally, then, Lady Aylsden?"

Lily smiled at the reporters who had come to the ship. Not only were they more polite here, but with Tony at her side she felt little of her usual anxiety. Pale-blue fox fur framing her face, diamonds shining bluely from the small fur hat, muff, ears, throat, wrists and fingers, she became increasingly expansive.

"Oh, I wouldn't say that exactly. I was only a child when he came to our Long Island house—but I think, you see, that's when he might have got his taste for American women."

"What Lady Aylsden means," said Tony quickly, digging his fingers into her arm, "is that *some* of us aren't prejudiced!" His grin was arch, his downward glance at her benign—but, suddenly businesslike, he added, "Well, thanks very much ladies and gentlemen—we must be off."

The reporters' pencils continued to scratch, bulbs flashed.

"One last question, Lord Aylsden," a young man in a mackintosh asked. "Will you live in London or at Cambrook Hall?"

"London, definitely. As soon as we find a house. Meanwhile—the Ritz."

"Oh, we'll visit Cambrook Hall, of course," Lily added informatively, "to fix it up." Her bright, inspired glance all round recaptured instant attention.

"You'll be restoring the Hall, Lady Aylsden?"

"Yes! Wouldn't it be a crime not to save that splendid old place. Tony's showed me pictures—it's so historic . . ."

"Good morning, thank you." Tony's voice snapped out with authority.

To Lily's surprise, hats were lifted, hands raised, repeated thanks repeated; in a few moments the reporters had moved away.

"Tony, why did you . . . ? Now what on earth did I say this time?"

Tony tapped his head. "What *didn't* you say!" He grabbed her to him, shook her, then broke into a grin. "Oh, well—who cares? It certainly doesn't worry *me!*" He kissed her, ran a thumbnail lightly over her bottom.

Lily started, but smiled. Turning to the waiting entourage, she held up her hand. "All right. We can go."

How small, old, quaint everything was, she thought, as they drove in hired Daimlers towards London. Already she loved Tony's little country. "You said it would be raining," she accused him.

"Well—the sun couldn't resist you, angel, any more than I can." He winked.

She was torn between moving closer to him and farther to avoid his hands under the fur rug. How happy they would be, she thought, if she could just keep him under control. Judging from their lovemaking in the trunk-and-flower-filled *Mauretania* suite, it would be far from easy, but she had to succeed—*this* marriage was going to last!

London was brilliant with spring sunlight, the buses a brighter red, the flower-strewn parks green and prettier than she had imagined—and the Ritz Hotel sparkled like an arcaded palace.

In the rosy Louis XVI interior with its circular foyer, winter garden and fountain, the welcoming attentions of Nikolaus and his staff messaged a familiarity with Tony that reminded her of a

past he claimed would "shock you to the roots." Well, she would
have to get used to this kind of thing.

She took his arm as they went upstairs under the staring gaze
of other staff and passing guests.

The main suites (the servants' rooms were on the other side of
the hall) were smaller than Lily had expected, but she liked the
marble fireplaces and big, cheerful fires, the large brass beds, the
beautiful views of Green Park sweeping away from the high
windows, and the little row of bells for summoning her own as
well as the hotel servants.

"Well," said Tony as the door closed on her pink-and-gold
suite, "that's a much better bed than we had on the ship . . ."

"Darling—everyone will be coming in and out . . ." She
pointed to the champagne on ice on a marble-topped stand.

"Let's drink a toast," she said. "Oh, look at all the lovely roses,
I wonder who they're from?"

He threw off the jacket of his light-gray flannel suit, moved towards her with an expression she was beginning to recognize too
well.

"Tony," she said quickly, "we mustn't waste a minute. We've
got the houses to see, and the men about the cars, and . . . well,
later we'll have to dress for the theater—it's the Noël Coward,
isn't it? I do love him, and we'll go to the Savoy after with your
musketeers . . ."

"Lock the door—first things first . . ."

Lily pushed at him very gently, kept a smile. She had already
learned to dread his unpleasantness when she had warded off or
denied him. "Darling, *please,*" she said. "They'll be wanting to
settle us in, to unpack . . ."

"You think more of your servants than me, old girl. Let them
get used to a bit of discretion." Tony ran his hands back across
the small crisp waves of his hair. "You'll drive me to drink." He
tapped the bulge in his trousers.

Lily wanted to laugh. She could not imagine what he felt, or
any reality to such a problem.

She took off her hat, her coat, looked at him in wistful apology, unaware of her slim voluptuousness in the Starenze-
designed "arrival outfit." Tony gazed at the outline of her nipples under the silk blouse, began to trace them with a finger . . .

There was a gentle triple tap on the doors. "Oh, come in, Maudie!" Lily called. She could not help the joy of reprieve. With luck, now, she thought, she could head him off until last thing tonight.

One by one, the staff came. Maudie and the maids went about hanging and ordering her clothes, lining up her shoes, arranging for pressing, setting out her cosmetics and perfumes on the big mirror vanity. They glanced uneasily at Tony, pacing down one end with a glass in his hand, and Lily knew they wondered why he didn't go to his own suite with Gorton in attendance.

Whitey came in with a pile of opened and unopened mail, the new Engagement Book, and, of course, the English checkbook by courtesy of Coggy's international arrangements. "Gosh, the bathrooms are cold, Boke," she said, "but, gee, they've got *hot towel rails!*"

"And you'll like the tea, I daresay," Maudie said, with a pert cock of her head. The maids smiled.

"Meanwhile, Whitey," Lily said, "join us in a glass of champagne provided by the hotel."

Whitey grinned, helped herself, toasted Lily. Tony was now talking with the gilt telephone on his lap, keeping his voice low, chuckling, bursting into short spasms of laughter, making inaudible comments out of the side of his mouth. Now and then he touched the thin line of his mustache, narrowed his eyes in gleeful appreciation.

Probably Ian or Guy, Lily thought. Above all, she would have to accept this old threesome—but it sent chills through her, as if she was about to confront clever enemies.

"Darling," she called out in sudden instinct, "darling—what was the name of that car you wanted—I want to tell Thomas."

Tony frowned at the interruption, but looked up sharply, eagerly.

"Oh—I'm sorry, Tony," she added, "I didn't see you were telephoning."

"That's all right, precious." Tony lifted the earpiece away so that the person at the other end would become part of the moment. "Railton, darling," he called, "Railton Sports Tourer."

She snapped her fingers. "That's right!" She nodded, turned back to Whitey, who gave her a puzzled look. "Now," she said, "what have we got in the mail? Not that I'm interested today unless it's fun!"

Whitey grinned. This was the Boke she was happy with. "Well, there are several charitable institutions who could do with some of your 'very kind and gracious assistance'—several people who have unique jewelry and collector's items, some real estate agents with properties 'suitable to your particular requirements'—a bunch of invitations that could fill the book!"

"Tony must have told people we would be at the Ritz—he's got so many friends!"

"But several of these are from Aunt Mirry's list, and yours—word travels fast with transcontinental air mail and transatlantic telephone."

"I suppose . . . We'll go over them later. Now I must change." She glanced at Tony. He had hung up, but made no move to leave. In fact, he was watching her over the top of an open magazine, his eyes crinkled at the corners, conveying both intimacy and ardor. He was right, she thought, they would simply have to get used to his presence—after all, she *was* married.

Still—as she allowed the maids to help her switch costumes, Gustaf to rearrange her hair, retouch her makeup, it did not seem natural to have him there, watching. She hoped he would not want to be with her all the time, that he would go off on all those interests of his the way Daddy had. Freddie had never given Beth a moment, always harassing her, always making demands. . . . But, of course, that was different . . .

Even so, they must not stay in this hotel too long. They must keep busy—boredom could come from too much time together, too much lovemaking in one confined atmosphere, too many excuses from her . . .

He would soon discover her pretending, the fact that she still didn't know what the actual feeling was that went with all that final grunting and groaning that meant so much to him—and, until she did know, found it best to match with her own, in case he should suddenly open his eyes, look at her as he had done once, and say, "What's wrong—Christ, you're not frigid, are you?"

The word had stood out, stark with threat. She had denied it to herself, only half knowing what it meant, instinctively feeling that it was an injustice, that it wouldn't be true if something—she wasn't sure quite what—were different.

"Let's have lunch," she called out to him, smiling prettily as the maid sprayed her with his favorite, Nuit-de-Noël perfume (Belle Lili, he said, reminded him of Flit, the fly killer).

He jumped up, slapped his hands together, reached for his jacket.

"Don't you want Gorton?" she called.

He shook his head. "My carnation's still fresh—I'll just wash in here." He headed toward Lily's big, tile-walled bathroom. The servants exchanged guarded looks, except for Maudie, who smoothed her dark dress primly. "Will that be all, milady?"

Lily gazed at her a moment, her eyes a soft pale-green in the park's reflected light. "No more 'Miss Lily'—or 'dear'? Aren't I the same?"

Maudie poked at the rims of her glasses, at her net. "Yes, milady," she said, "of course."

Lily bit her lip, knew she had been shown her own contradictions. She nodded dismissal, and the servants followed Maudie from the room.

Tony, his sandy waves damp, his hands and face smelling deliciously of her Morny's Fern soap, came to her at once, took her in his arms, careful not to disarrange her neat pale curls, her caplike sable hat, her earrings of pearls and diamonds, the six gleaming sables on her slim shoulders. "I told Ian and Guy what a lucky man I am. They're envious as hell."

Lily smiled, showing traces of dimples, the slight unevenness of teeth whiter than the pearls. "I hope they won't be disappointed."

"Not bloody likely, darling. Come on—let's eat."

The large, square restaurant was pleasant, again Louis XVI, with a blue sky and white cloud ceiling which, Tony said, was supposed to have taken two years to paint, quite good lusters and marbles. . . . "It's a bit like Aunt Mirry's Washington one," Lily whispered.

"I hope *we'll* have something cozier, old girl," Tony said when he was eating oysters, with what seemed to Lily incredible speed and zest. "I've had enough historic grandeur."

Lily speared her potted shrimp with delicate precision. "One must suit the background—I can't wait to see what's available."

"The one Bonky's selling in Grosvenor Square sounds good."

"You mean the Honorable Flanners Pond's—but only eight bedrooms . . ."

"And servants' quarters."

"But only five rooms for them."

Tony shrugged. "We don't want to be falling over servants."

"But we'll want to entertain, darling!" Lily's eyes shone into his, bright with visions.

He nudged her knee with his under the brilliant white cloth. "Anything you say. Just be sure you build the bed strong and wide."

"I want a small informal ballroom, a heated pool, a gaming room for you."

"A gaming room!" The height of his raised eyebrows gave his blue eyes a startled innocence.

She laughed. "All this gambling you talk about—I thought you could do it at home. I'd like to copy the *salle privée* in the Monte Carlo Casino—I've even got pictures of it for the architect."

"Where in the world did you get those?"

"Aunt Mirry had them—it was her suggestion."

He nodded. "Ah, she thinks that would keep me from Le Touquet and Deauville, et cetera."

"Does she? Well, *I* don't want to keep you from anything. You could have both."

"My love, my love—wait till I tell the chaps *this!*"

Lily thought suddenly of Joel—a disquieting sense of comment, as if he were watching her here in London with her handsome earl, flanked by quietly obsequious servants, subtly stared at by other distinguished but inevitably less wealthy diners, hearing this conversation. . . . Was this what he had meant? Had he been right—was this what she was really like, really wanted?

"Of course," Tony said, nodding his approval of the sample of Graves handed to him by the wine waiter, "you'll come with me, my darling. You'll adore the casinos. We must have a little plane to hop over to the Continent—perhaps a De Haviland Puss Moth, you could fit it out in Boeker blue."

She refocused his face. How attractive and appealing he was

when he was like this, pleased, excited. "Isn't it dangerous?" she asked, her eyes sparkling.

"Not with me, angel. I'm a fully qualified pilot—ask the King, he's the expert."

"You flew together?"

"When he was the Prince—before he got snared."

She laughed. "Mmm—this Dover sole is divine!"

"So's my mutton chop. What do you say, then?"

She saw the watchfulness of his eyes as he cut the meat, lifted it to his mouth.

"Darling," she said, touching him lovingly on the cheek, "if it makes you happy, if you think it will help our life to be gay and interesting—yes! Coggy might have a fit—but it's my money."

He laid down the fork, grabbed her hand, put it reverently to his lips. "You don't know the half of it," he said. "It'll be *bliss.*"

She had to laugh at the way he hissed the word, mocking its seriousness. Was he, in fact, ever serious, she wondered, except in his urge for sex (when it was dangerous to joke with him or even smile other than seductively)?

The maître d'hôtel bent to her suddenly. "About cars, Lady Aylsden," he said, "some men have arrived."

Lily nodded, smiled. "Ask them to wait, please."

"Yes, your ladyship."

"They're early," said Tony. "Anxious, no doubt."

"I'm finished, anyway, except for demitasse. I want to be hungry for my first English tea. You must choose a wonderful place for us to have it!"

"That's easy. We'll have it sent up. Blazing fire—tea for two, a bit of crumpet . . ."

"Oh, we won't be here—we'll be . . . uh—sightseeing!"

"Sightseeing!" Tony sighed. "Westminster Abbey, I suppose, and the Tower, and . . ."

"St. Paul's Cathedral, and the Houses of Parliament, and Big Ben . . ."

"Stop—you've got that nauseating American awe in your voice! And, darling—you've got *years* for that rot . . ."

"But I want to start today!"

He sighed distractedly, looked at his watch. Lily saw the restless twitch to his mouth. Why had she so suddenly needed to marry him? she wondered. And what did she really know of him? Why, for instance, had he been "sent down" from Oxford, what were the pranks he had played there with Ian and Guy (and ever since), and what was behind his irreverence for traditions and convention, when he so obviously believed the English superior?

She touched the gleaming linen napkin to her lips, smiled. Too late for all that, she thought. She had married in haste, but in leisure she would get to know and understand this husband of hers; and all would be well.

Hesitating while he scratched initials on the bill, she rose, accepted the sables laid on her shoulders. "Thank you," she said to the courteously smiling waiters. "Thank you. Very nice," she said to the maître d'hôtel, who looked at her in furtive adoration as he bustled beside her to the doors. "I hope your ladyship will enjoy her stay with us, enjoy England—such a pleasant time of year."

"I'm sure we will, thank you." Lily smiled, her blue eyes candid and friendly, acknowledging them as people.

"Don't lay it on so thick, old girl," Tony whispered as they walked to the elevator. "No need to ingratiate yourself."

"I never thought of such a thing, Tony."

"You're an earl's wife, a countess—not just a rich American trying to impress."

"Tony, *really!*"

For a moment, she stood still; stared at him; her eyes had an unfamiliar iciness. Tony blinked. "Hold on," he said, "just a word of wisdom, nothing personal."

Lily felt the flare inside her subside. "You don't have to worry about me, darling," she said. "I've always got on with servants— never any trouble at all."

"That was in America," he said, tilting his head, touching the side of his mustache. "We do have different standards here."

"I've been quite well trained, Tony. You should know that."

"By Aunt Mirry—well . . ." Tony smiled to himself.

Lily walked on. She felt injured, but strangely frightened of a quarrel. "You can order your Railton, if you like," she said. "Today!"

She flashed a smile at him over her shoulder. "It must be quite a car to make you look like that."

"It is, old girl, it is." He caught up with her, put his hand around her waist, slid it upwards and pressed her breast in the little lace-trimmed soft-satin bra. "We can drive out to Heston Airport in it to see the planes—that's where we'd keep the Puss Moth—it'll go a good ninety-five miles an hour!"

"But a Bugatti does more than that, something like a hundred and twenty-five."

Tony laughed. "What do you know about it, old thing!"

"You'd be surprised. Ask Thomas."

He opened his mouth, closed it.

"That's why I want him with us to choose."

"Your chauffeur!"

"Why, yes, even Daddy used to listen to him, and Daddy was a whiz."

Tony groaned.

An hour later, however, her heart racing at his sullen frown, Lily drew him into the discussion in the reception room of their suite. "Definitely the Sedanca de Ville Rolls in black with the smart ginger top—don't you think, Tony? And the smaller Daimler for just getting about, and the little yellow Mercedes-Benz for when we're alone and you're driving?"

Tony nodded reluctantly, shifted edgily in the gilded-cane chair.

"And is it the Railton, or a Bugatti?"

"The Bugatti isn't a sports car, my love," he informed her, his frown clearing, his tone indulgent. He straightened his carnation, gave his "foxy" twinkle.

"You're right. So—the Railton."

"You've made a great choice, Lil—milady," Thomas said sagely. "I'll take good care of 'em for you—don't worry."

Lily smiled at him. It made her feel less strange in this new world to see his big figure in Boeker blue, his familiar face.

"Can we have the Rolls immediately?" she asked the representative of that company as she signed the checks Whitey had typed.

"Give me an hour, your ladyship," said the small dapper man who seemed to Lily to be dressed for a wedding, even to the flower in his buttonhole. He slipped his books of illustrations and photographs into a leather attaché case, thanked her graciously, hurried off.

"Don't you like to take runs in the cars first, darling?" Tony asked. "Don't the motors mean anything to you?"

Lily sank back into the deep gold-brocade armchair, slipped off her shoes. "Not really. I go by the reputations. Why would they sell me anything but the best?"

He looked at her wonderingly, an eyebrow cocked. "Quite right, old girl," he said, nodding, "quite right."

"Phew . . . you know, I'm dizzy. Haven't got my land legs yet, I suppose." (Not to mention, she thought, that he had interrupted her sleep twice in the night and again in the morning!)

"We could take a rest, darling, a nice little nap?"

She sat up. "Oh, no—I'm fine . . . I'll be all right."

"Well, then what *are* we to do in the meantime?"

"We'll think of something," she said, slipping quickly back into her shoes. "We'll think of something . . ."

"You'd never know Bonky's old house, Lily," said Lady Penelope Drakehurst. "Knocking the two houses together was brilliant. And your Boeker-blue uniforms for the servants are too divine."

Lily walked from the high, oval-ceilinged dining room where she and Tony had just given a small dinner for forty, admiring the sleek dark hair of this moon-faced young woman who had once cut her wrists over Tony and still pursued him at every opportunity. Since Penelope was one of the "gay set" who laughed most derisively at the Boeker blue, she found it hard to meet her dark, patronizing gaze.

"Oh, thanks," she said. "It's a kind of tradition in our family."

The quick glitter of Penelope's eyes warned her that she had dropped another of her by now famous "Boekerisms," that it would travel the rounds of Tony's witty, outrageous friends, putting her at an even greater disadvantage in this incomprehensible society.

"Speaking of families," said the Honorable Fiona Cravid, coming up beside her, "could you and Tony come down to

Blairbourne this weekend? Mummy and Daddy would love to show you their gardens."

Lily turned. She had dressed in expectation of some dancing later, some gambling, a festive occasion. The spectacular effect of the new Hartnell, a lace-overlaid aquamarine satin dress with thirty yards of lace-appliquéd aquamarine tulle jutting from the knees, shoulder straps of square-cut aquamarine and diamante and a little bolero jacket of the same lace and tulle, complemented by aquamarine and diamond jewelry, made the oblivious self-confidence of the long-nosed, sandy-haired young woman in simple pink satin, with one strand of pearls, an irony. Although the "breach of promise" case had long since been dropped between Tony and the Viscount and Viscountess Cravid, and had, in any case, been a ploy to frighten Tony, Fiona still believed in her priority, her superior claim to be a countess. To get Tony alone and remind him of their old sexual rapport was her driving goal, and nowhere better than at Blairbourne House.

"Oh, Fiona, I'm so sorry," Lily said. "Tony and I are hopping over to Biarritz."

"What about the weekend after?" Fiona's gray eyes appraised Lily along the line of her nose.

"I believe it's Ascot—but you might telephone Miss White." She smiled radiantly.

If only Tony would drop these women from his past! Surely he had his hands full enough—there was the tall platinum blonde, one of Cochran's "young ladies" now, and the striking French model with the almond-shaped green eyes—to say nothing of almost any girl or woman who happened along when he was "feeling randy."

"Lovely dins, Lily," said Ian Flexner, following her to the huge, white "informal ballroom" where Tony insisted people had more "fun" than in the beautiful Adam Brothers' reception room with its graceful curved arches and delicately ribbed ceiling that, together with other slow restoration, had taken so long to complete that she had almost lost Tony to the casinos before they could get away from the hotel and move into the house.

"Thanks, Ian," she said. "I think we've finally got a really good chief chef." She took the arm of the tall, narrow-shouldered man with the bushy black mustache and bright black eyes.

"Is it true you're getting Tony a filly?" he asked.

Lily leaned away to see if he was carrying out planned intrigue; she could always tell by the slight twitch of his nostrils. "We've talked about it."

"Mmm. Nice."

"What's—mmm, nice?" said Guy Pickett, his good eye cocked at her under a fall of straight auburn hair that concealed his black patch. "Something to do with the filly, I bet."

"Now, look, you two—I won't be rushed."

"Seventeen thou's a good price for that horse, though, Lily," Ian said brightly. "A bargain."

"For who, Ian?"

"Why, you," said Guy. "Tony could recoup his losses, become solvent."

They both looked at her with bland smiles.

"And what would that mean for you two?"

"Ah," said Guy, putting his hands behind his stocky, rigid back. "We'd hope to have a small investment in the venture—small, modest."

"Sponsored by my friend the Earl, no doubt." Lily made a grim mouth.

The two men laughed appreciatively. "You're hard on the poor musketeers," said Ian.

"Tony's had enough, lost enough. My money watcher would say NO."

"But Tony without money, Lily? Think about it."

Lily looked from one to the other. "Put on the gramophone," she said. "Play my American records—they always love them."

"Yes, milady. And may I have the first dance?" Guy bowed with exaggerated stiffness.

"And I, the second?" said Ian.

"No need to prime the pump," said Lily. "And—don't encourage Tony with the chips tonight. Only one person pays—you know who."

They looked at her ruefully.

"Where's Roddie?" Lily heard Ian whisper to Guy as she walked on.

"And that awful name," she said, turning. "Couldn't you *please* drop it now that you're grown men!"

They exchanged startled glances, then burst into laughter. Lily knew the implications.

Shrugging, she went among the assortment of guests to play her role. At least in this regard she had been granted "a certain gauche charm" (by one writer of social gossip for a glossy magazine), "a kind of barging knowledgeability, that confidence without par of such wealth" (by another). Also, her parties, a society columnist had said, "were uniquely noteworthy." He wrote of the "lavish food and wines, the orchestras brought in from nightclubs along with cabarets and famous performers, the dancing on a perfectly constructed dance floor under heavenly lighting, the dazzling miniature casino with imported croupiers (that the stakes were genuine could only be assumed!), the heated, perfumed, mosaic-tile swimming pool where an evening might end in ecstatic athleticism in the well-equipped gym followed by a rubdown by skilled masseurs, a 'black velvet' pick-me-up (champagne and Guinness), scrambled-eggs-and-caviar breakfast and steaming pots of French coffee to fortify one for the 'poisonous' dawn air out in Grosvenor Square."

As this particular evening progressed, she wondered again why Tony was tolerated by such prominent members of the English social scene. She could understand that film directors, playwrights and theatrical people, artists, designers, ambassadors, diplomats, celebrities in general might put up with him, but some of his companions bordered royalty itself, and together their titles couldn't be counted.

Was it because his outrageousness amused them? "Tony is the epitome of adolescent amorality," the Duke of Moorsham had whispered to her once, his shirtfront creaking out of place with laughter as someone recounted one of Tony's "pranks"—which ranged from sheer schoolboy trickery to the gleefully malicious.

It did not seem the whole answer. Perhaps it was also his combination of cunning and largesse, fused with charm, his uninhibited pursuit of women and the "main chance," that kept them intrigued, fascinated, in some cases seemingly spellbound, as with Geoffrey Chetsmanford ("the dancing lord").

Why else, she wondered, thinking back for an instant, would that big, distinguished man have invited Sari Gerowska, a party girl famous for swimming nude, to the same weekend at Minor-

dene? He had, of course, been sure of "fireworks" of some sort or
another, and he hadn't been disappointed. What he hadn't bar-
gained for was Tony's ridiculous prank that followed the mass
convergence of bare swimmers in the dark, tree-shadowed pool.

Tony had disappeared—but that wasn't unusual. Left alone to
wander, Lily had not, as usual, found compensating attention
from the seemingly endless supply of candidates for her body,
money or preferably both, but kept an eye on Tony and his
"henchmen" (her name for Ian and Guy, whom Tony always
managed to get invited as well) and Sari. Sari, who had survived
a sexual bout with Tony both in the pool and in one of the vast
mansion's hundreds of rooms, was also missing.

What on earth, she had wondered, were they doing out there
on the great semicircular driveway in the dark, with only occasional barks of protesting dogs to break the stillness? She could
see nothing but the black shapes of cars, like glinting beasts.

Suddenly there had been the quiet sound of motors, the soft
crunch of gravel—four of the black shapes were moving off.

She had peered from behind a Jacobean column, holding her
wide floral chiffon pajamas from floating into sight.

. . . Footsteps crunched faintly. Car doors were gently
slammed, motors started up—and four more shapes moved
away . . .

Should she go out there, try to stop whatever it was that he
was up to?

"Ah, Lily!" someone said behind her. "Are you all right, my
dear?"

She had turned quickly, smiling with innocent surprise. "Oh,
Lady Chetsmanford."

"Violet, please." The handsome, black-haired woman, in a
dowdy black lace dress and a careless assortment of old jewelry,
smiled in vague appeal. "I'm afraid I've quite lost track of what's
going on. Chetty *is* so careless whom he invites. Last weekend he
actually had Black Shirts infiltrating our ranks. . . . Oh, I do
hope you aren't too shocked—the English aren't all like *this*, you
know."

"No . . . Oh, but they're a lot of fun." (What else could she
have said?)

"You're so beautiful, my dear, and charming. I do wish Tony

took better care of you. I loved dancing, you see . . . Chetty . . . Well, I was so *young* . . ." She moved her large shoulders upward, spread her hands. "Things get away from one . . ."

"You were very kind to have us—I've never seen such a beautiful Jacobean house, or such inspired landscaping. I could just walk for hours out there."

Her hostess had blinked with interest. "Do visit me again," she had said. "Are you keen on horses? Hunting?"

Lily shook her head sorrowfully. "I'm just no use—something made me afraid when I was a child."

"Pity. But come anyhow. I should very much like to talk to you. I spent several months traveling in America—extraordinary people. But *you* don't say things like 'pleased to meet you' or 'glad to know you'—most disconcerting, don't you think?"

Lily had laughed appreciatively.

"I mean, my dear—*why* are they pleased or glad? One could be the most ghastly bore—or evil!"

"It is funny. I never thought of it before." Lily felt some of the strain of the humiliating weekend lift.

"Well, I'm off to bed. The rest is up to Chetty. Are you leaving tonight or in the morning, my dear?"

"Well . . . I'd like to get Tony back." She had stopped, met the woman's gaze awkwardly.

"I know precisely what you mean. I *am* sorry . . . Not that *I* can talk." She smiled with sudden charm, put out her hand. "Well, in case you do leave, my dear, goodbye."

"Goodbye, and many, many thanks!"

Violet Chetsmanford had visibly withdrawn from such effusion, nodded, gone on up the huge, ancestor-lined staircase in stolid dignity.

Just as Lily had been about to resume her vigilance, Chetty and a man called "Major Angus" had come up to her, swept her off forcefully to a game they called "Truth or Consequences" in a tremendously somber, candlelit library. Some of the other participants, sitting in a ring of leather chairs and couches, had already removed various items of clothing. They all looked at her strangely when she told them the truth frightened her, that she would rather not join in.

After that, there had been other claims and she had given up on Tony's activities.

It was not until the next morning that she discovered what he and his cohorts had been doing. In the night, mysteriously, inexplicably, everyone's car had vanished. Chauffeurs ran about conferring. Guests walked in and out, out and in the great front doors, angry, puzzled, hovered on the steps in helpless confusion.

Eventually the police had arrived.

"Tony," Lily had whispered to him, "you should be shot!"

"For Christ's sake don't say anything, darling," he had whispered. But he and Ian and Guy and Sari had become so bent over with laughter that first Chetty and then all the frustrated guests standing about with their servants and baggage had begun to catch on. The anger had turned to relief, to good-humored swearing and much reluctant laughter.

Later, the press had arrived, and there was an effort to hush up the prank, but it came out in one daily paper as "People in high places kick up their heels at Minordene weekend—Earl of Cambrook and friends remove guests' cars in the night. 'Harmless fun,' said Lord Chetsmanford. 'We're all schoolboys at heart.' "

. . . "Darling," Tony was whispering now, in his own home, grasping her elbow, "I've had a request for my rude film later—would you mind dreadfully if I showed it? Much later, of course, just a few of us?"

"Tony—must you? It's so filthy, so *revolting* . . ."

"You could go to bed, old thing? I'd say you had one of your headaches."

"That's just what Penelope and Fiona want. They'll get into a fight. Oh, darling, we can't have any more scandal!"

"Nothing like that, I assure you." Tony nipped her chin between finger and thumb. "I'll come to your room afterwards . . ."

"*Oh*, no. Last time after that film you wanted to tie me to the bed while you and Ian and Guy . . ."

"Ssh. We were drunk, darling! I'll be good, this time I promise —just straightforward." His blue eyes held an ardent plea.

What was she to do? She couldn't bear another of his ugly moods. All eyes were on them now—he could suddenly say something cutting about her accent, her Boeker Emporium background, cause a silence, a scene—or he might refuse to speak to her for the rest of the evening. And in any case, he would show the film because that was what he *wanted* to do.

She shrugged wistfully. "I'd hoped this would be a nice, gracious party for once. The servants have worked so long and hard in the kitchens, everything was so carefully planned. You don't seem to appreciate . . ."

"Lily—what else are the servants supposed to do—that's what we pay them for, isn't it?"

"*I* pay them!" Lily's eyes, ice-blue, flashed to his. "And Whitey tells me you've slipped her another sheaf of bills for over two thousand pounds!"

"Why, darling—you astound me. That's nothing, mere expenses!" Tony looked baffled, hurt.

"You've had two substantial settlements to take care of those, Tony. You should have plenty of money of your own now. Why haven't you?"

Tony looked behind him, to the left, to the right. "Old girl, this is hardly the time or place for a financial conference."

"You've lost it again! You told me you'd won the last time."

"I did, my darling, I did—but, well, to tell you the truth—I went over again when you thought I was down at Mater's. I'm sorry—it was rotten luck, rotten."

Lily stood and looked at him. No, it was not the time or place, but she felt an overwhelming desire to hit him, to tear the pale-green carnation from his buttonhole and stamp on it, to rip off his immaculate Savile Row Tails, to shriek out to the whole room her frustration and outrage.

"Lily?" he said. "Darling?" He took her hands, drew her to him, looked into her eyes for the room to see what a loving husband he really was.

"I'm just about finished with you, Anthony Aylsden," she said, her voice trembling. "This time I mean it."

He smiled gaily. "All right, darling. Let's call the whole thing off!" He began to hum the popular tune. "Come on, let's start the dancing, put some life into the proceedings!" He grasped her and whirled her towards the polished hardwood floor. "Turn down the lights!" he called out to footmen hovering by the doors.

The guests broke into applause as the wall lights and chandeliers dimmed, as a rosy suffusion fell across the floor, followed by pale purple, sapphire blue, emerald green, light green, golden orange, and back to the deep soft rose. They got up from chairs and couches, wandered from the fireplace over which hung the portrait of Lily and Tony painted by Hothstile, and joined Tony and Lily to the sounds of "I've Got My Love to Keep Me Warm," coming from the big mahogany cabinet.

"Believe me, old dear," Tony whispered against Lily's rigid cheek, "I do love you. You'll see—it'll all be different when Lady Lily comes romping in at the Derby. You watch—that Boeker blue will be right out front the full course. Desmond says she's in fine fettle, can't possibly lose!"

"You'll put it all back on the tables. Coggy says no more, not another thousand."

"I *am* your husband, darling. Surely it's up to you."

"Within reason. He doesn't consider three million pounds that. And nor do I."

"Come off it, angel—you don't know the meaning of money. You don't count it or know what things cost."

"That's not true. I live within my means—means laid out by Coggy. If he says I'm going beyond them, then I'd stop and cut down my spending."

He leaned away, curled an eyebrow. "That's hilarious. You *are* developing a sense of humor."

Suddenly Ian was tapping Tony's shoulder. "Come on, Roddie, give a chap a chance."

Tony's eye corners crinkled. "My pleasure, Flex, old boy. She's all yours." He released Lily, bowed, winked furtively.

Now what were they up to? Lily wondered.

In the next moment Penelope was sliding from her partner's arms, winding quickly between the dancers to Tony. Lily saw them move together, press close and hard the lower halves of their bodies. It was early for Penelope, she thought. Sooner than usual, she would gradually drape herself on him, hoist her skirt as if by accident to show that she wore nothing underneath; "Penny's compulsion," it was referred to in Tony's circle.

Yes . . . They were a splendid-looking lot in their beautifully cut evening clothes, gowns from famous couturiers, jewel heirlooms. Writing to Aunt Mirry, she had expressed her constant disillusionment that almost no one of this international set roving between the two continents was what he or she seemed. Tony kept setting her straight, or she herself would discover that a particularly commanding marquis was "a raving queen," the jolly, open-faced Lady Jelling was a "roaring Les," the most heralded deb this season, Mary Hartbell, was actually the illegitimate child of Lord Vursmere, the Duke of Moorsham, so correct and formal, kept a Chinese girl, and Lieutenant General Foxworth, paternal and wise, gave whipping parties for women in black boots and corsets.

"My dear," Aunt Mirry had written back, "humanity was ever thus—you must wipe the dew from your eyes. Can't you meet Tony on his own ground, beat him at his own game? If you don't, you'll wake up one day to find your fortune gone and yourself in the cold. Brace up, Lily dear—remember who you are. Don't let your grandpa down! Best love, Aunt Mirry. P.S. Reggie is doing a fine job of defending you in the press for what they call your 'uninhibited splurging on your foreigner husband while the country that made you still struggles to get back on its feet.' Nonsense, of course. There's also a lot of to-do about taxes. They seem to think there's something sinister in Coggy's ability to pay no more than is absolutely necessary. As J. P. Morgan said—'if Congress insists on making stupid mistakes and passing foolish tax laws, millionaires should not be condemned if they take advantage of them.' And, of course, you know how I feel about spending—it's the sound and logical way of distributing wealth."

Guy took over from the footman who wound the gramophone. He put on Fred Astaire singing "Cheek to Cheek," and the dancers resumed—hardly any of them, Lily thought, kept really good rhythm, really knew how to dance.

She felt a deep, plunging loneliness.

"Lord, here's Bonky," said Ian. "Shall I save you?"

Lily turned quickly, took the hand of the Honorable Flanners Pond. "Hello, enjoying yourself?" she said, smiling fondly.

"Hello. Rather. Spiffing party. You certainly know how to lay things on, Lily!"

"Thanks, Bonky." She looked at him gratefully. She was fond of this blond buck-toothed Englishman who had admired her with helpless lack of concealment since the time they had met over the transfer of the house. She only wished he would tighten his limp hold, keep the beat.

"Lily, the way you've done these two houses is pure genius. You could make a fortune as a decorator." He gazed into her eyes adoringly.

"You know, I actually dreamed the ceiling picture—dark blue sky—dense flocks of white birds flying across it, a sudden break of intense light and the birds lighted up . . ."

"Did you, by Jove? Then had it put into effect. Good girl." He bounced happily on his toes, jerking her with him about the floor.

Lily's face looked softer, younger. She got so little genuine encouragement for her efforts. "You're not sorry you sold your home, are you, Bonky?" she asked.

"Good heavens, no. Except when you invite us, I don't stir from Surrey. They say I *look* like a horse—do you think so?"

Lily had to laugh. Tony called him "horse face" (also a "drear"—his ultimate veto).

"I think it's a compliment," she said. "Horses have nicer faces than people. And I wish *we* had lovely fur all over us! Bare flesh is so . . . bare!"

He leaned back, surveying her with delight. "I couldn't agree more. Oh, Lily, Lily." He sighed deeply, tightened his grip on her, fell into a heavy silence.

Lily stirred in his hold, remembering when he had been extricated from her on the dance floor at Ciro's with a sudden clip on the jaw from Tony which had sent him backwards into oblivion. It had been three days before the newspapers dropped the subject, and his wife (a stern, bespectacled woman who seemed to loathe him) had barely spoken to him since.

Fortunately, the record ended—but the moment a new tune was put on, this time "Small Hotel," Bonky grabbed her back. "One more, while I've got you, *please?*"

Lily looked apprehensively for Tony. As much as he did as he pleased, Lily was HIS property. He might share her with the musketeers—but that was different . . .

To her relief, he was nowhere in sight. Some couples had drifted back to couches and chairs in the distant shadows. Some seemed to have left altogether—but Lily knew they could be found only too easily; weren't guest rooms meant to be used!

. . . And then, suddenly, she saw him. Jammed into a corner of a deep-cushioned couch, one of a matching pair in a high-vaulted alcove, he seemed almost alone, until she made out recognizable legs, a dark-red dress.

"Bonky?" she said.

He looked up, dazed with emotion. "Yes, Lily?"

"Will you do me a favor—go along with a kind of joke?"

"Anything, old girl."

"Wait here."

She moved around the edges of the shuffling, swaying dancers to the gramophone cabinet. "What do you want, ducks?" Guy asked, his back even more rigid as the effect of alcohol accumulated.

"Something snaky. Let me see." She riffled through the numbered and titled stacks. "Ah!" She put on her old favorite "Mood Indigo," returned to Bonky.

"Come on, Bonky." She led him to the middle of the floor. "Just go along with whatever I do," she said, smiling at him sweetly.

"Anything, old girl!"

She drew him close, pressed her cheek to his, closed her eyes and began to do a slow "snake hips," her hips undulating in the way she had seen Negro dancers when she had gone with Andy and his friends to Harlem nightclubs.

But it was so easy, so much fun that her hips swung wider and wider to the sensuous wail of the saxophone, the slow, rhythmic beat. "You ain't been blue," moaned the husky singer, "no, no, no . . . You ain't been blue, till you've had that Mood Indigo . . ."

Bonky moved with her like a puppet on a sagging string, his knees bending at the wrong time, his shoulders and hips rotating in limp opposition to hers, to the rhythm.

"That's right," whispered Lily, as other dancers began to stop, to gradually clap in time to the wide-arc movements of her hips. Her arms, slender and white as the wide bolero sleeves fell away, made sharp, bizarre angles.

"Here comes Tony," Guy came up and whispered. "Watch out, old dear."

Lily smiled, raised outspread fingers, undulated her shoulders, moved her neck from side to side, then spread out her arms and began to rotate her hips to the drumbeats, coming up at the end of each swing with a subtle upward thrust of her pelvis.

"Didn't know she had it in her," she heard someone say.

At that, her knees bent deeper, her hips swung even wider until it seemed they must go out of joint, and the upward thrusts became more of a large "bump." She couldn't remember ever having enjoyed dancing so much—it was all her pent-up desire for movement since her childhood.

"Ravishing, Lily!" someone called out. The watchers drew closer, surrounded her, imbibing the sensual message of her breasts, her hips, her entire slim, curved body, her moist open mouth, pale banner of flung-back hair loosed from curls.

"Christ! What the bloody hell do you think you're doing!"

Lily felt herself jerked upright. Her teeth cracked together. In the next instant, Bonky was somehow flat out on the floor. "You stupid little whore!"

Lily's eyes opened wide; dilated with shock, they had never seemed huger, bluer, more brilliant.

"I say, Tony—that's not cricket!" said a tall red-headed man, moving forward protectively. Guy and Ian were holding Bonky's head. They looked up at Tony in confusion.

Tony's collar jutted from his chin, his shirtfront gaped, his hair stood on end. In his eyes was a look Lily had never seen before, flinty, vicious.

"Come on, darling," Penelope Drakehurst was saying, smoothing her hair, replacing a shoulder strap, snapping back together a garter and stocking and pulling down her dress. "Don't be a dog in the manger."

"Are you all right, Bonky?" Lily bent down, and Bonky opened his eyes sleepily into hers.

"I see an angel . . ." He smiled dreamily.

"Get him a brandy," Guy said to Ian.

No one seemed to notice that the gramophone record scratched on and on, finally wound down.

"I think it's time to go," someone said.

"No, no," said Tony, quickly putting himself in order, smiling in wistful charm all round—"don't go, anyone. Sorry about this.

Sorry, darling." He kissed Lily, looking abject. "I'm such a jealous bastard."

"Are we or aren't we going to see the rude film?" Fiona asked.

He gave her an irritated but conspiratorial look above Lily's head. "We're going to do whatever we want to do—the evening's young, positively unborn!"

The atmosphere relaxed. Bonky recovered. Someone put on another American record. A few people indicated they were leaving, thanked Lily for the divine time and her divine dancing, but those who stayed gathered close to Tony as if awaiting further instruction.

"Do you want me to stay—is there anything I can do, Lily?" Bonky asked through his stiffening jaw.

"Oh, Bonky dear—how can I apologize?"

He took her hand, held it to his lips, swayed a little. "*You* never have to do that," he said. "Never. Whatever I can do, anytime."

She kissed his cheek, took his arm, led him through the big black-and-white marble hall to the white Georgian doorway, where the English butler, Trowbridge, looking drawn and weary, gave him his hat, coat and stick.

"Cheerio, Lily," Bonky said, "take care of yourself." He went out into the stilled square.

"You may go to bed, Trowbridge," Lily said, "so may the others."

"Yes, milady." He avoided her eyes. (Maudie told her that Trowbridge only withstood his hatred for Tony because he was sorry for her.) "Thank you, milady."

"And thank you, Trowbridge." Lily smiled at him, then turned and went slowly up the big divided staircase, along the silent rose-carpeted hall to her snack kitchen (copied from the one in the Fifth Avenue mansion). She drank a tall glassful of the freshly squeezed orange juice that was always left for her, ate a large slice of devil's food cake, then went on to bed.

Sometime in the near-dawn, she was awakened by hands slowly kneading her breasts. "You're a very naughty girl dancing like that, darling," Tony was whispering. "Do it for me now, do it for me now?"

Lily pulled away with a jerk, turned over and kicked his shins as hard as she could. "Get away," she said, "get away from me! I hate you, hate you, hate you!"

"Oh, Christ," he muttered, sliding from the other side of the big white satin canopied bed. "You really are a bore! If it weren't for all that damned money, you could stuff it."

Hoisting up the bottoms of his silk, initialed pajamas, tying the silk girdle with a jerk, he strode barefoot to the door, closed it behind him with a loud slam.

"My dear Lily," Aunt Mirry wrote, "if I could come over at this time, I would—but Will's not well and I'm entertaining the Maharani at the Mountain Lodge next week. What I really must urge is that you do nothing rash—divorce is a tedious business in England. I strongly suggest that you mark time and be patient. First of all, Tony isn't going to let you go without a fight—he may reform in order to hang on to you, or at least try. Secondly, you might find that you could go your separate ways without hostility. *This could be very convenient.* After all, you don't want to rush from one marriage to another. And in this case, you would find the degree of tolerance for whatever you do exceeds that of severing a marriage. Do let me know. Love, Aunt Mirry. P.S. What did you think of the Abdication? We heard his speech on the radio here—very moving. Well, *his* roving days are done! P.P.S. By the way, that picture of you taken in the Royal Enclosure at Ascot, looking so splendid in that great flowery hat, and Tony so grand and handsome in his top hat and racing clothes, was printed alongside the picture of the Boeker Emporium employees on strike for what they call 'a fair wage.' They simply don't understand that you have nothing to do with the Emporium affairs any more. I've asked Reggie to do a piece on it. It's a good thing you aren't here just now."

Now—for three months, Lily had been following Aunt Mirry's advice. She had also talked to Violet Chetsmanford—after all, Violet had suffered Chetty—and two days alone with her almost convinced her of Aunt Mirry's good sense. If Violet had survived for all these years, perhaps she could, too.

She had started her independent life by going about with Bonky. They had seen several shows (Lily had seen Tony's platinum-blond girl friend in Cochran's Revue, dripping with feathers and mascara) and the ballet at Covent Garden, had had supper at the Savoy Grill and the Kit Kat, and the Café de Paris. Thomas had also driven them through Shakespeare country and they had punted along the Thames and stopped for tea at a riverside hotel near Maidenhead.

Lily began to feel closer to England, to its ordinary people— but, of course, there was always the difficulty of really seeing them because they were always looking at her first; somehow she was always recognized, somehow the press always seemed to know where she would be—there was a barrier, a kind of veil between them.

She found that Bonky was a gentle man who enjoyed the chance to air his views to someone who would listen. He was fearful of another war, and they often talked of what would happen if Hitler could not be stopped. "Dear old England," Bonky said, "so vulnerable. Nothing to protect us but grit and character."

Bonky did not believe she should stay with Tony. He thought she was entirely wasted. "Suppose you should have a child," he said. "He could use you terribly, old dear."

Lily herself was having doubts. It didn't seem the kind of life she would ever want. Bonky wished he were free to marry her, but they both knew that wasn't the answer. More and more she longed to throw over "good sense" and see the last of Tony.

He was completely incorrigible, even at a distance. She and Whitey, going over the accounts together to see what he was now spending, found out that he had ordered seventeen suits, a dozen pairs of handmade shoes, karakul-collared overcoats, mink-lined coats, innumerable hats of all styles, cuff links of jade, ebony, gold, diamond, ruby and pearl, countless ascots, ties, scarves, dressing gowns, smoking jackets, riding clothes, silk shirts. He had also ordered a Bugatti, which, they found, he had then sold to raise cash.

"Give me some *cash*, for Christ's sake, Lily," he had demanded, striding into her bedroom one morning. "I can't move an inch except on credit."

Lily had swallowed a strawberry, whole. "It's not my affair," she said. "Coggy says no more—that's that."

"I only need one good win to get everything straightened out."

"Sorry."

She and Whitey had then discovered that he was selling paintings off the wall. (Apparently his mother had gone through the same experience, and when he went to Cambrook someone always watched his every move.)

Lily wrote him a last check for two thousand pounds. "That's it," she said.

"That's chicken feed," he said. "You spend that on a dress."

"If we were happy, Tony, it would be another matter."

"Let's try again?"

"No, thanks."

Soon after, Bonky had retired from circulation while his wife at last divorced him. Lily was often alone in the big Grosvenor Square house, not knowing exactly how to proceed, longing for love, for closeness with a man, but afraid of more unhappiness.

"Come to Le Touquet this weekend, Lily," Tony said one day. "For old times' sake."

She had thought: Why not? She had nothing better to do.

Ian and Guy went, too. They flew over in the Puss Moth, and Lily could not help feeling that some plot was brewing. At the casino, she decided to keep out of their way, to try her own luck this time instead of watching.

She went from one to another of the big green-baize tables in the great baroque room with its low-hung lights, trying every game from chemin de fer to roulette. (Everyone in the room watched her, as if she held the answer to all the mysteries of money itself, marveling at her beauty in the long-sleeved, backless forest-green velvet dress with the deep low neck where flashing emeralds emphasized the whiteness of her flesh, the lightness of her hair, the feline glint of her great eyes.) Was Tony playing his last two thousand pounds? she wondered. Well —it was up to him. If the purpose of bringing her along was to supply him with more chips if he lost, then he and his musketeers were wrong. Glancing at the guard she had brought, she put her diamond-edged green satin purse on the edge of the table and sat down.

"Careful, Roddie," Ian whispered, leaning down to Tony. "Don't count on anything."

Tony frowned, shook his head, indicated it was no time to

stop, that good money after bad was now his only expedient.

Guy adjusted his patch, lifted the hair from his good eye, focused on the play.

As cards were dealt from the sabot one by fateful one, and the banker decided whether or not to stand or draw, Tony's points fell inevitably too low or too high. Drawing his last francs from his wallet, he cast a grim glance toward Lily, now playing roulette and watching the wheel spin with excited absorption.

Tony played out his last francs, stood up, beckoned the two men to one side. "The luck's bound to turn. Either of you two got anything? I'll get it back to you somehow, you know that."

Ian and Guy indicated empty pockets, their usual state of affairs since his drop in cash flow. He nodded. "Wait for me."

His face reflected the green of the table as he bent to Lily. "Darling," he whispered, "just five hundred till Monday. I can get hold of something when I get back."

"No," said Lily, her smile remote.

"Please, darling." He put his mouth closer to her ear. "Everything will be different after this, everything. I'm going to start all over again!"

Heads lifted, faces peered at them in fascinated attention.

Looking up into his miserable face, the creased forehead, the abject pleading eyes, Lily had a sudden illumination: Never mind Aunt Mirry. She would divorce this dreadful man the moment they got back. She and Whitey and the others would go on a lovely long cruise, open new horizons, see the world! Just like that, the answer had come!

"I've got an idea," she said, her fair eyebrows rising above sparkling eyes.

"Yes?" His face brightened.

"Why not put up the Puss Moth? We could always go home by boat."

The shift to rage in his stare was electric. He leaned to her ear. All Lily caught of his hoarse whisper was something profane, something to do with the vulgar source of her wealth.

Lily quickly placed some chips on the red 26—the number of her years.

"*Rien ne va plus!*" called the croupier, and the wheel began its smooth, portentous spin.

Held by fascination beyond his control, Tony paused, his gaze stark, watched with anticipation.

The ivory ball clicked steadily on its circular journey over the alternated black and red numbers, the circle of faces hovered expectantly like pale grim masks.

The wheel slowed, the ball jerked, rattled, came to a stop.

"*Vingt-six. Rouge.*"

Lily felt a glow. Laughter bubbled up in her. As she raked in her winnings—never in her life had she felt such a thrill of achievement!

"Christ." Tony jammed his hands in his pockets and walked away.

Chapter 12

Sir Patrick Hutchin, well known to be a favorite physician of the Royal Household, set down his cup. "Now, I must really be off, Lady Aylsden. If I can be of any further service to you, please let me know. I shall be happy to look after you and see that all goes well with the birth. Don't hesitate to ring me at any time."

The portly man with the neat silver hair took her hand, touched it with his lips and, leaving a faint scent of disinfectant soap behind, left.

Despite a day crammed with appointments, least of which was another visit to the firm of solicitors she had hired (through Coggy's recommendation), Lily sat on awhile, in the lime-green and gold sitting room of her bedroom suite, frowning, her lips tight.

There was that little red-headed maid Thomas took out. Rumors were that Thomas had put her in a similar fix, and that they had gone to some woman above a chemist shop in some dingy part of the city. But I can't ask them, she thought. Perhaps Maudie could, though, in a diplomatic way.

She got up, rang the bell for her.

"Maudie," she said when the familiar figure stood before her questioningly, "I'm going to tell you the truth about my nausea—I'm pregnant." She tightened the belt of her negligee as if to ward off reprimand.

"Oh, I know that, milady. We all know that."

"All?"

"The servants. The entire staff. They don't know whether to be pleased or sorry—they're very fond of you, Miss Lily."

"Oh." Lily paused, ran a finger along the mink trimming, down the straight line of her nose, across the forehead on which were the faint tracings of new lines. "Maudie—you've got to help me. You've got to find out how I can have it taken away."

"Adopted!" Maudie's face started to turn pink. Her hands locked tightly against her chest.

Lily shook her head. "No, Maudie, not adopted—*aborted*. How can I have a baby now?"

"Oh, Miss Lily, no—no, no! I wouldn't be a party to anything like that. I've heard some terrible stories—and it would get out and make a big scandal in all the papers, and you'd get black-mailed, and . . ."

"All right, all right! Honestly—you sound like a Victorian novel!" Lily folded her arms and began to pace. "Never mind, then, Maudie—I'll ask them myself. What about that nice-looking parlormaid who had it done—or that wine butler? . . . I hear these things, you know. They talk to me, tell me their lives."

"I'm aware of that, Miss Lily—milady. But it would be a very dangerous thing to get so intimate. It only takes one traitor, and there's trouble. Besides that . . ."

"I could die."

Maudie's lips tightened. Lily felt the uneasiness of her disapproval, the chill approach of defeat.

"Send Whitey to me," she said. "And, Maudie, have the coffee taken away and ask them please not to send croissants in any more—I've turned against them. I'd rather have . . . uh . . . a pineapple in the mornings."

"A pineapple."

"Yes—sliced, with lemon and sugar, and cream."

"Yes, Miss Lily, of course."

"Maudie?"

"Yes, milady."

"You never call me 'dear' any more?"

Maudie paused at the door. "I didn't realize—I'm sorry, dear." She closed the door.

When Whitey came in, Lily asked her to sit down and forget about duties. "I want to talk to you," she said.

Whitey could not resist a look at her watch. Her office was humming with activity and her assistant was away with a cold. Not only that, but there was trouble with the plumbing that had to be seen to, a disaster with the main stove and a quarrel brewing beween the assistant and chief chef. She folded her arms. "Okay, Boke. What's cooking?" She blew bangs from her brow, opened her brown eyes with dutiful alertness.

Lily looked away, suddenly overwhelmed in bleakness. She loved Whitey, but somehow she was like a rubber cushion that rose to its original shape the moment you took your weight off it; there was no way to leave an impression.

"Well—you probably know I'm that way. Getting a divorce and pregnant. Isn't that ripping!"

"But, Boke, you can still get the divorce. Nobody would care if a woman in your position had a child by a discarded husband. People would understand. You'd just explain to the press, the way you do, you know?"

Lily looked at her blankly. "What about the child? Heir to a name, part of a heritage, never knowing its father . . ."

"But why wouldn't it know its father? You could share its custody just the same!" Whitey grinned with inspiration.

"But that's later, Whitey! Right now I'm facing months of looking like an elephant, by myself!"

Whitey's grin hovered.

"Besides, Whitey—even if I could face that, Tony's not going to let me go. He's capable of anything—it's the access to my money he's been praying for!"

Whitey's grin retreated altogether. She sat staring at the face of her friend. The young schoolgirl who had fascinated her with her golden aura of wealth was merging into this matron with

problems that got in the way of the fascination she still wanted
to feel. "But how can he possibly stop you, Boke, and how can
he possibly get money from you if you don't let him have it? Just
phone Coggy! Get Aunt Mirry into action . . . !"

"Talking about me?" Tony came in without knocking. He had
never looked more attractive, more spruce; a beautifully cut suit
of a brown-and-blue mixture was set off by a cream silk shirt and
silk tie of two shades of blue. His perfect red carnation, de-
livered to him dewy-fresh each morning, complemented the
healthy tone of his skin, his "sky-blue" eyes, the glints in his
crisp sandy hair and mustache.

The two women looked startled, confounded. Both of them
knew he had not come home until dawn, drunk, shouting insults
like "that Yankee peddler's grandchild"—"that nasal-voiced American peasant"—and others more obscene.

"Well, little mother," he said, with his most charming, most
appealing smile, "how are we feeling?" He moved quickly to her
and planted a tender kiss on her forehead.

Lily sat as if struck.

"Isn't it wonderful news, Whitey?" he said. "You'll be unusually
busy, no doubt—for some time to come."

Whitey looked puzzled.

"Oh," he said, "I've telephoned all the papers personally.
There should be an avalanche of reporters. I've told them I'm
willing to give interviews with or without my wife, according to
her state of health. I told them that we are both overjoyed, that at
last the Aylsden name may be carried on—and, of course, even if
we have a girl, nothing could make us happier."

Lily sucked in her lips, dug the fingernails into her palms. A
scream was rising from her toes.

"And, oh yes, I've naturally informed Mater, and she hopes
we'll have the child at Cambrook Hall according to our old tradition, in the first Earl of Cambrook's bed, and that we will come
to visit her soon—if not, she will come here for a lengthy stay.
Also, old girl, I've rung your solicitor and told him the facts and
that the case is withdrawn."

"You haven't the right to do *that*, Tony."

"But I've done it. They were most sympathetic and sent their
congratulations. Your Mr. Kingsley-Bates seemed much relieved.

I once did him a favor—only a small thing—but I publicly denied indiscretion with his wife and saved him from the embarrassment of scandal. Actually, I was only twenty and all that happened was a bit of up-your-skirt in the back of the punt on the river at Oxford, routine stuff, *but* witnessed." He grinned with reminiscent amusement. "We chaps laughed to split our sides."

He looked from one to the other of them, then slapped his pockets. "Well—I'm off to see Lord Stymon about buying that gelding—I may switch from casinos to racing. You'd like that, wouldn't you, Lily—our jockey in Boeker blue?"

He winked at Whitey. "I've notified Gorton—so you can collaborate about interviews. I'll be back for lunch. Free thereafter."

At the door he paused. "By the way, I'll join you and the others in the box for Ivor's play tonight. And the Duke's supper party afterwards."

"*You* weren't invited—I'm going with Prince Oge."

"Under the present circumstances! I'm shocked, my dear. No, little mother—you must have your husband about you now."

Lily stared, her face a blank.

"And, oh yes." He touched his mustache, raised his forefinger. "I refuse point-blank to live on credit one more day. Cash, please, Countess. Something useful this time. I'll pick it up when I get back."

He closed the door with a sharp click.

Whitey and Lily sat in frowning silence.

Lying in bed, as she so often did in the progressing stages of her pregnancy, Lily looked more beautiful every day. Luminous shadow seemingly enlarged her eyes. Her hair, drawn up on top of her head to keep it out of the way and from adding to her general irritation, revealed a milk-white complexion where stray lemon-pale wisps delicately glinted against rosily flushed cheekbones.

Set off by one or the other of her exquisitely handmade silk, satin or fine-wool bed jackets, trimmed in antique lace, threaded ribbons, embroidery or pastel shades of marabou, she leaned into mounds of voile, lace and satin pillows mourning her lot, conducting listless interviews, complying with Whitey's various requests for money or decisions, demanding Maudie to sit by her and read from P. G. Wodehouse novels, Edgar Wallace mysteries, or toying with certain of the jewels she had brought to her, imbibing their beauty and workmanship as if it were her only remaining reality.

Sometimes she chose maternity dresses from designs brought to her from couturiers and had them made up. Three oil paintings by masters, bought simply because art dealers had pointed out their availability, leaned against chairs where she could see them and commune with them like silent friends.

"You *must* get out more often, milady," Maudie kept insisting, and all of them, Whitey, the maids, Thomas, thought she should see some of the friends who telephoned.

Lily's compromise was to order Thomas (who insisted on a guard as well) to drive her with Whitey to various shops. She could find nothing worth buying in the famous Harrods, and more to avoid going home empty-handed than because she was enraptured, took several bolts of rather interesting floral silk from Liberty's. She was disillusioned. Always the great department stores seemed to beckon with promise; the truth was they had nothing she wanted. But Whitey had enjoyed herself, and sent some English china home to her parents. ("I could have given you better than that to send, Whitey," she had said, but Whitey spent her own money and was strangely stubborn.)

Tony sometimes barged into her room with Ian and Guy to tell her some latest bit of gossip about various members of "the set" which he thought she would find so amusing that any hostility in their relationship must naturally succumb. When Lily only stared at him in apathy, he would exchange glances with the other two, confirming her American humorlessness, and depart.

Only once did he arouse her to animation. When he gleefully pulled back the covers to show them her swelling breasts and stomach, she shot her hand across his face, leaving red strips on his jaw. He looked as if he would hit her back, but didn't. His thoughts were only too plain—she might still lose the child.

Her only goal now was to endure him, somehow, until the baby arrived. Then, they would all go back to America.

Meanwhile, out in the square, from the railed gardens, reporters watched the house. Whatever she did was recorded. Pictures were taken of her stepping expressionlessly from her Rolls to enter the solicitor's office or merely down her front steps that vied on front pages with those of Neville Chamberlain shuttling back and forth to meetings with Hitler.

In the later months of the pregnancy, Lily developed a growing interest in collecting. She bought an assortment of ancient clocks that traced the development of timekeeping, some curious chairs and other furniture dating back to the fourteenth century, rare carpets and tapestries, great quantities of antique glasses, odds and ends of unique mirrors, scent bottles, porcelain, earthenware plates, candelabra and bronze figures.

Wandering about the house, she would try to decide where to place them, but couldn't make up her mind. How beautiful the great rooms were, though, she would think, noting the hang of the brocade and velvet draperies, the subdued harmony of mellowed woods and time-softened paintings, the subtle glitter of mirror and crystal, gilt and satin, the richness of velvet and pile. Wasted on Tony, of course, but oh such grace and splendor—she could not help but be pleased with it, even for herself.

Coinciding with governmental announcements of new hope of peace, with the filling in of trenches in the parks and the setting aside of air-raid precautions, one day Lily felt a sharp kick in her stomach. It awakened her to frenzied awareness of the fact of life inside her. Up to now she had thought of nothing but the discomfort, inconvenience, disadvantage. Now, suddenly, she visualized a small person who would be part of her, close to her, her own!

Galvanized, she set about creating the environment for this new life. The top floor of the house was transformed into several rooms of glowing blues, ivory and gold. Walls were covered in pure soft leather, pastel silks, white fur. Kitchens and bathrooms, formerly for the staff, were enlarged, made clinically pristine with gleaming white walls, floors and equipment. A vast layette was ordered, an avalanche of toys. Two nannies were chosen from hundreds of applicants for their impeccable references. A special night watchman and guard were hired.

A longing to talk, a pervading and intensified loneliness, now led her to the servants' quarters. Maudie advised against this.

She said that Lily should grow out of this tendency, that she demeaned herself.

"But I've nothing to lose," Lily said.

She chatted with the maids and footmen, the cooks and scullery maids, and the potent cooking smells, the bustle, the earthy observations encouraged by her ease with them, brought her a sense of warmth and comfort.

They gave her cups of strong tea and asked her about life in America, and were spellbound by her accounts of her childhood, clicked their tongues over her mother's drinking, her father's death, Vitti (which made her smile—beside Tony, he now seemed rather innocent and sweet).

When the kicking became a permanent state, Lily began to lie awake all night filled with terror. Her need to share the responsibility of the child with someone who cared (other than paid help) became sharp and desperate.

One morning she telephoned Tony's mother at Cambrook Hall.

"My dear," the Dowager Countess said, "I should be delighted if you came to see me. It's also about time you saw what we've been able to accomplish here. I gather your social life has kept you in the city."

Lily smiled with relief, with new excitement. "Not exactly," she said. "I've been very quiet, except for getting the nursery ready."

"Oh. Tony hasn't been keeping me informed. Is he there?"

"Not at the moment. I think he's on the Continent somewhere, or racing Lady Lily. I don't keep track."

"I know, I know. He always was mercurial."

Lily warmed. Perhaps she had been wrong about Mavis. Perhaps she had wanted too much acknowledgment and gratitude. After all, it had not been a hardship to help out, but a pleasure.

"Thomas will drive me down," she said. "I'll bring Maudie and a maid."

"If you like—but you'll find us a good deal more civilized than on your last visit. I've even been able to find passable staff. Come in time for tea."

"Stop a minute, Thomas—let me look!"

Cambrook Hall, as Lily remembered it from the strained beginning as Tony's new American wife, had seemed less impressive than sad. The great pile of ancient stone and brick, originally Elizabethan but added to in later styles by successive earls, had chilled her with its ghostly splendor, its stone-mullioned windows brooded like watchful eyes over a vast network of gardens and parklands almost obscured by tall grass and weeds.

"Nothing a few hundred thousand can't cure," Tony had said, with a sly grin at her stricken expression.

But when she had seen the inside, she couldn't believe it; room after room had been closed off, the archaic plumbing had all but given out, there were leaks in roofs, doors and windows, stonework was crumbling, gilt and paint peeling. Since there was no one to cut sufficient firewood, the Dowager Countess kept only essential fireplaces working and between the stone-walled rooms in which they burned swept damp icy drafts from which there was no escape. Lily had shivered and trembled, her teeth chattering throughout three unbearable days and nights. Holding her blue fingers to the fire, pressing her feet to the quickly cooling hot-water bottles in the huge canopied bed she shared with Tony, had been her only reprieve—neither Tony nor Mavis seemed to notice. They spoke snidely of the central heating in America, how unhealthy it was, and how when they were there they had nearly suffocated.

Worst of all had been the echoing emptiness of its immense, high-ceilinged chambers, the many great drawing rooms opening one into another, the tapestry-hung halls and long paneled gallery of silent peering ancestors, the huge solemn library, many of its shelves empty from sales of treasured volumes, grand staircases creaking with history at every step, and never a servant to be seen, to give the place life and livingness.

She had been right, as it happened. It had cost her a great deal more than Tony had dared to say. "How kind, how very kind" was all that Mavis had written about the checks that had flowed into restoration work.

But as she saw it now, Lily was filled with wonder and her old feathery feeling of pleasure. Aunt Mirry was right, England's historical houses must be preserved, "in spite of them, for *all* of us."

"Drive on," she said.

"Your maids and Miss Maude arrived with the other chauffeur, milady," a new butler told her. "They are unpacking your things in his lordship's old quarters in the east wing. Lady Aylsden is waiting for you in the new library." He took her white flannel coat.

"Thank you." Lily looked quickly around as she followed the butler. The atmosphere was entirely different now. Everything sparkled with new giltwork and paint, and the first thing she noticed as she walked into the least overwhelming of the great rooms was the freshness and light of the restored ceiling with its intricate molding, of wall friezes, woodwork, carpets, upholstery, even the busts and statuary. She only wished there were flowers in the big vases to provide warm color, but a blazing fire compensated.

"Hello, Lily, my dear." A short woman with drab graying hair cut short, a bony, prominent nose, greeted her from a large, deep-cushioned leather couch. "I hope the journey down wasn't too tedious."

Lily decided on a quick handshake rather than the kiss she'd intended. "Not at all, Mavis—it was wonderful to see the countryside and breathe some fresh air. And how beautiful the house looks!" She sat down beside her.

"It does look fair—much to do yet. One realizes what the estate managers contended with. Sugar?"

"Yes—three, please. I seem to crave sweet . . ."

"Interesting. It was salt with me—kippers."

Lily laughed, but Mavis waited for her to stop, watched her with narrow-set, gray-lashed eyes of a much paler blue than Tony's. Lily could not help thinking again how profoundly colorless this woman was. The dun tweed suit she wore must have been made in another age—more of a man's than a woman's style, the skirt baggy at the back, the big deep pockets of the jacket hanging in the perpetual shape of heavy objects carried in them over the years. Her stockings were brown cotton, her shoes oxfords covered in dried mud. Her hands, with only a gold wedding band, were thickened by work, the nails blunt, cracked.

"Is Boy making you unhappy, child?" she asked.

Lily blinked. "Well." Her blue eyes sought a deeper communication. "Yes—"

"I should be very surprised if he weren't. He's the image of his great-grandfather, the fourth Earl. He practically ruined the family, too. The rest of the line have been as upright as pillars."

Lily restrained another laugh. "What did his wife do about *him?*"

"Wives, my dear. He went through three. Wore them out. One, of course, died of smallpox, but she'd have succumbed in any case. They endured him. There was no alternative then—this place was a small town, a world unto itself. Women didn't get away. But then you don't want to, either, really, do you?"

"I *had* started divorce proceedings." There, it was said.

There was a silence. Lily heard dogs bark, horses neigh, the soft crackle of the fire.

Mavis finished her tea in short gulps. "Yes—so Boy told me. But he *is* pleased about the child, you know. I don't think he's unredeemable." She smiled thinly.

Looking at her weathered, autocratic face, Lily saw a blend of rigidity and indulgence that gave her sudden insight into Tony's private anarchy.

"And naturally if it's a boy and saves our line, then we'll all be grateful."

"And if it's a girl, Mavis?"

"Well, we hope you'll name her Deirdre after my dead child." She looked at the quietly ticking old clock under a portrait of Tony's father as a young man riding out to hounds in Cambrook's green hills. "I'm sure you'd like to rest," she said, "and I still have many chores these days. Shall we meet for a sherry before dinner? Don't dress up, if you don't mind—I shall only wear my old black."

Lily rose, feeling stiff, cumbersome, not looking forward to the big cold rooms.

As if reading her thoughts, Mavis added, "There's plenty of hot water now, if you'll just tell Jenkins when you want it, and fires in the rooms."

Lily thanked her.

"I'm glad you've come, my dear," Mavis said, with a brisk nod. "Very glad, indeed. You're about to bear an Aylsden heir—you must know our family history. You're part of a great heritage, Lily."

"Yes . . ." Lily felt her gaze become vague, her hopes of this visit recede in proportion to the possessiveness and pride in this woman's words and expression. She felt as if Aylsdens of all ages and costume, from the fourteenth century to the present, were massing around her like a small army, squeezing the breath from her body.

"You'll want to see pictures of Boy as a child. . . . And, oh yes, the christening robe you'll use, handed down from century to century."

"Marvelous." Lily managed a weak smile.

Thank God, she thought as she went from the room and up the second of the grand staircases, that Maudie was up there, that Thomas was somewhere in the vast stone reaches of these halls.

"Oh—good morning, milady. We were not told you were coming back." The butler in Boeker blue hid his surprise with a quick cough.

"A sudden decision, Trowbridge," Lily said.

He attempted not to look behind him into the house, but Lily had a distinct premonition of something untoward. "Is Miss White up?" she asked, giving him her coat.

"Yes, milady."

"Where is she?"

He spoke with reluctance. "I believe she's in the gold-and-white drawing room, milady."

Lily looked into his furtive eyes. "What's going on, Trowbridge?"

His sallow face relaxed its mask. "Milady," he said in a low tone, "there's been one long carrying-on since you left—gaming till dawn, strange guests in all the rooms and the staff run off its feet."

"I might have guessed. And what of his lordship?"

Trowbridge lifted one eyebrow, one shoulder. "Sorry, milady."

"Well—I'll try and restore order, but I haven't got much mobility."

She put her palms on her stomach.

Trowbridge frowned. "You'd be better off somewhere else, milady. There's been a lot of bottles opened."

"I'll not be put out of my own house, Trowbridge. Just alert the staff—I'll count on their support."

"Of course, milady!"

Lily went to find Whitey. With some maids and footmen, she was dolefully surveying Lily's priceless Louis XIV carpet.

"Boke!" she said, forgoing surprise at her reappearance. "They've burned holes all over it—how could they be such clods! And look at all the drink stains!"

Lily felt a dizzying fury. "Why in here? And who are they? Surely not people we *know!*"

The servants looked at her in gentle sympathy.

"Some were, some weren't—Tony and his two pals have brought them from the casinos, the racetracks, show business and off the street. There was nothing we could do—he said it was a grand blowout before becoming a father."

Lily sat down in a winged tapestry armchair. Her knees were weak, her heart racing.

"They've broken two of those lovely four-foot vases among other things."

"Don't tell me any more, Whitey!" Lily's face was stern and white.

The servants, exchanging looks among themselves, moved away. Whitey came and stooped beside her. "Boke—you okay?"

"You should never have talked me into staying, Whitey—I don't care what happens now, it's the end. I'm going to have him locked out."

Whitey's hair bounced at the vigor of her headshake. "You can't do anything yet, you've *got* to wait till the baby's born, Boke—for your own sake!" She took one of Lily's hands and pressed it.

Lily looked into the earnest brown eyes. "I'm all right now," she said, starting to rise. "Tell the staff they're to wake all visitors and tell them it's time to leave. I'll take care of the host. I want the house empty in an hour."

"Boke—I've never seen you like this."

"I've never felt like this."

Whitey stood up, moved quickly off.

"By the way, Whitey," Lily called, "which room is Tony in?"

"Yours, Boke. Brace yourself."

Lily walked firmly up the big divided staircase. Except for snoring, occasional grunts, the bedroom doors, closed or ajar, gave no clue to what lay within.

At the end of the first landing, her door stood wide open.

Maudie came up behind her like a small apparition in the dimness, but Lily waved her away. As she neared the door there came a potent, stifling smell of alcohol and cigarette smoke. For a moment she battled nausea.

Straightening her shoulders, she pushed into the darkened room, waited for her eyes to adjust.

On the great bed, under the square, modern canopy, one dark shape hurled itself over and groaned, and then another. "Go away," a man called huskily.

Lily knew that voice—it was not Tony's.

In abrupt decision, she turned on the ceiling light. The chandelier sent a stream of conical rays over what seemed to be six bodies flung over each other like sacks of flour. A face rose from the general heap, then another.

"Christ, Lily—you!"

Tony's bare shoulders emerged. He yawned loudly, scrubbed at his upstanding hair, rubbed hard at his beard-shadowed jaw. "What do you want?" he asked.

Ian Flexner unwound himself from a blond female, whose age was not yet discernible, and covered his pale, hair-dotted chest with his arms. "I say—sorry, Lily." His mustache twitched to one side, then the other.

A plump-faced brunette shook the hair from her face and prodded Guy Pickett, who quickly rearranged the strands of his hair over a bald spot and adjusted his patch. "Good God," he said. "What time is it? What are we doing here?"

Another female seemed to emerge from behind Tony. She had matted platinum-blond hair, mascara and red lipstick smudges over most of her face.

Lily didn't recognize any of the women. "I want you all out of my bedroom, out of the house—now, at once," she said. "Including Anthony Aylsden, Earl of Cambrook."

"Don't be stupid, Lily—forget it, chaps." Tony lay back with a groan. "For some reason I'm badly hung over," he said to the others. There was muffled and pained laughter.

"I mean it," said Lily. "Or I shall get the police."

"The police—for your own darling husband!" Tony laughed hoarsely.

"It's my house, and what's going on here is quite enough to . . ."

Tony shot up. A look of inspiration cleared his forehead. "Chaps—do you hear that?"

Guy and Ian looked at him uncertainly over the tops of the women's heads.

"Why don't we ask her to join us? You should see her now—makes me horny to think about it."

"Not Lily," said Guy.

"Stow it, Roddie," said Ian.

"Oh, come on, it'll be more fun than anything we've done."

Ian and Guy watched him in furtive intrigue.

"Ladies—would you mind hopping it," Tony said quickly, clicking his thumb and middle finger.

The three assorted females looked at each other, shrugged and reluctantly extricated their bodies from the mangled bedclothes. Slowly, searching out strewn clothes and covering themselves, they started away with uneasy backward glances.

Lily backed away. The implication outdid nightmares; she could not take it in sufficiently to scream.

With a sudden grab, Tony had her arms, his hand over her mouth, and Ian and Guy had her legs. Carrying her, struggling, to the bed, they got her clothes off . . .

"Our pregnant countess," said Guy. "I say!"

"Isn't that delicious?" said Tony. "Look at those big tits, that belly . . ." He started to run his tongue over her. "I'll go first," he said. "I can't hang on."

"What about the child—won't it . . . ?" Ian stuttered, his face red.

"If copulation ever hurt a baby," Tony said, "the race would be extinct. Quick, keep a hand over her mouth, hold open her legs!"

Lily felt the forced entry like the burn of white-hot metal. She writhed frantically, desperately, tried to scream . . .

Suddenly the hand on her mouth slipped from its hold—Ian, busy watching, was forgetting. . . . With one mighty effort, Lily screamed.

The door flew open—Maudie rushed in.

Chapter 13

On the tenth of July 1938, Lily gave premature birth to a baby girl. Brought on by violent shock, mental and physical, Lily was both unconscious and hemorrhaging. Only the most advanced methods of modern medicine held any hope for her survival.

Sir Patrick Hutchin called in three other consultants, one of them physician to the King. No effort was spared on her behalf; she had the largest available room, round-the-clock nursing, and Maudie and Whitey slept at the hospital just in case she should awaken. Andy, who had been in Paris, had flown to London and barely left her door.

The press waited with less patience, hovering like human flies around the hospital with cameras and note pads, and even the most prominent journalists waited at their telephones for word—one way or the other. What they wrote in the meantime was uniquely kind. For once, in England, in her own country and the rest of the world, Lily Boeker was temporarily forgiven her money. Everyone now loved this vulnerable young countess, wanted her to live and know the universal joy of motherhood, something no amount of money could buy.

Tony was not allowed near her. It was not clear to the outside world why. He seemed so inconsolably upset, so desperately anxious to see his little daughter, so hurt when his mother was permitted to do so; obviously he had been very, very naughty and some scandal was most likely in the offing. Meanwhile, he told of the dreadful worry of her collapse in her bedroom in his very arms, of how he had found himself crying for her pain.

Maudie walked past him without acknowledgment when he tried to speak to her at the hospital doors.

He shook his head in bafflement for the benefit of the watching reporters. It was just as great a mystery to him as to them, his sad shrugs conveyed. Sticking by him in his adversity were his two great friends, who seemed equally grief-stricken, equally prohibited.

Luckily, the child, though small, with hair and fingernails not quite finished, was in good health and growing stronger each day. No infant ever had more care and attention. Soon she would be recognizable as a baby with dark-blond hair and identifiable features, and be given a name.

But at present, Lily was a still, white-faced form and, in the white bed, looking so nearly dead as to keep the tense-faced medical men in constant attendance. Their bulletins to the press were terse, noncommittal. Even to Miriam Dundell Hower Court, many cables were brief, without encouragement.

But at long last, Lily's blue-veined eyelids fluttered, and one thin white hand changed position. Faces bent quickly over her.

"Her pulse is picking up."

Lily opened her eyes. The faces floated in a white mist. She was too weak to puzzle about them.

It seemed the moment to tell her. "You've had a lovely little baby girl, my dear," Pat Hutchin said. "She was a bit early, but none the worse."

Lily stared at him, her tired, dark-circled eyes seeming overlarge in her thin white face. She could not connect what he said with anything she knew. "I don't understand," she murmured.

He explained. "You've been through a big ordeal, Lily—shock

and loss of blood—but it's true, believe me. As soon as you're up to it, we'll bring her in for you to see for yourself."

"But honestly, it can't be mine"—she smiled—"I'm not even married."

"You are, dear. And you're going to be well now, and remember, and be glad." He patted her hands, nodded to the nurses.

Lily turned her face deep into the pillow, closed her eyes.

"Earl says he couldn't please her! Lily is unhappy girl who never wants what she can have, says rejected husband."

With hundreds of similar headlines and newspaper accounts to support his case, and a statement from the Dowager Countess that she would undertake to bring up Lady Deirdre at Cambrook under "normal, healthy conditions for a child," Tony managed to confuse the custody issue—but not for long.

Lily's counsel was able to divulge the truth of her experience as Tony's wife in a private hearing. She was granted full custody of the child except for two months each year, when the father would be allowed to have her at Cambrook, on the condition that either the Dowager Countess or other suitable guardianship could be provided to Lily's satisfaction. In the meantime, until a decree nisi was granted, Lily was to have custody, and the father visiting rights on arrangement.

With the gradual return of her strength came fanatical joy in her baby. Nothing else mattered now. Two nannies did not satisfy her fierce protectiveness. Three were only just enough to see that her treasure was guarded minute by minute of every day and night. To supplement the night watchman's vigilance an alarm system was installed in the nursery complex that could awaken the whole household if anyone tampered with a window, and the windows themselves heavily barred. Lily, remembering the Lindbergh case, had every tradesman and visitor appraised by a plainclothes detective before allowing entry.

She refused all social life, and her greatest sadness was that she had been too ill to breast-feed the angelic little thing, but as often as she could, she held it in her arms for its bottle. The small pink face, the fair, downy head, the large blue eyes looking steadily into hers, filled her with bliss. She laughed when it kicked its tiny feet in happy jerks, and felt loss when the nanny on duty took "Deedee" from her to bring up the "bubble." "That's not for you to do, milady," she had been told, yet Lily yearned to be the one to bring that look of relief to the tiny infant, its face contorted with discomfort.

Maudie and Whitey, with less to do, joined in Lily's single-minded interest, and most of the household was now concentrated on "her little ladyship," whom everyone considered was the best, the quietest, the happiest baby they had ever known.

Resting, brushing her hair, reading her mysteries, waiting for her times with the baby, Lily felt renewed zest for living. As soon as her darling was old enough for the journey, she would take her home—no one had said she couldn't do that, just as long as she brought her back to Tony for the two months.

Tony might even let his rights go—after all, he wasn't really interested in the child itself. It would probably be a nuisance, cramp his style. He would be trying to find another source of supply now that no further settlements were in sight. That she was to be responsible for Deedee's education, that Coggy had already set up a watertight trust fund for Deedee's future, was of little personal use to him.

Making plans, comforted and half transported away from this country which she could only regret not knowing better, she felt no vindictiveness.

Her eyes soft with dreams of a new life with little Deedee, she could hardly wait to make the booking, to be on her way across the Atlantic.

"I'm fearfully sorry, milady—I don't know how to tell you this."

"I'll tell her, my dear." Maudie patted the arm of the weeping woman in starched white uniform, and moved toward Lily, who had just come in the front door, dressed in a short-jacketed black silk suit with a small side-crushed pink hat and tall-cuffed pink gloves, her face pink, too, from the August sun and her smile as sparkling as her diamond earrings, clip pins, new Cartier bracelet.

"What's going on?" she asked Maudie at once, her smile fading.

"Miss Lily—dear," Maudie's gray eyes shone faintly, wet behind the glasses. "It's the baby—she's gone."

"Gone!" Lily put a tentative hand to her heart. "What do you mean—gone?"

"She's not in her little bed—not anywhere. We've all been searching."

Behind her now, in the quiet, lofty hall with its standing statues and slender pillars, other servants came uncertainly towards her, their faces solemn.

"No one has any idea how it happened, Miss Lily—Whitey wasn't here."

"Why?"

"You gave her the day off, Miss Lily. She went out with that young guardsman."

Lily looked dazed. "I don't understand—the watchman, the alarm system—all you people . . ." Like a diminished light, the pink had drained from her face.

"Miss Lily—I'm sure the police will find her—it's probably some simple thing."

With a small faint moan, Lily crumpled into Maudie's arms.

"Telephone Sir Hutchin!" said Maudie to Trowbridge as the servants converged.

But Lily was already opening her eyes. "I'm all right," she said, "just a bit faint." She drew up, put her face in her hands a moment, swayed. Then, suddenly, she looked up. "It has to be someone in this house," she said, darting a quick look into all the surrounding faces. "Someone has let his lordship take her, haven't they? You know they have!"

"Miss Lily—please . . ."

"I know—you're all my friends, but someone has taken a bribe —or has a soft spot for Lord Aylsden!"

The servants looked from one to the other, stunned.

"I'm very sorry you should think that, milady," a short stocky footman said. "We've been loyal to you."

Lily's blue eyes riveted his. "Yes, Locke—but it only takes one traitor, just one. He was here, wasn't he!"

"Well, his lordship did come for some of his clothes—and he took his friends up to see the baby—just for a minute."

"And I saw them, milady." Mrs. Bolton, a heavyset, gray-

haired woman with glasses, moved forward promptly, her thick
white oxford shoes squeaking on the marble floor. "I was in the
pink room with herself—I never let the little lady out of my sight.
I had just finished changing and dressing her—she'd had her bottle, and—"

"Mrs. Bolton—a baby doesn't vanish into thin air!" Lily
brushed past her, threw her hat, purse and gloves onto a chest,
started up the stairs, her long slim legs taking them two at a
time.

Lily only half looked now—into the pink-marble bathroom, the
laundry room, the picture-gallery kitchen, the nannies' quarters,
where the off-duty women, who would normally be resting at
this time, started up at sight of her with strained faces.

She shook her head at them, at the watchman who came from
his small sitting room to ask if there was news, and rushed back
downstairs.

"All right," she said. "I want everyone in the Grecian Room at
once!"

"Kitchen help, too, milady?"

"Everyone."

"Don't upset them *too* much, dear," Maudie whispered, "you
could lose your staff."

"Maudie," she said, "my baby's been kidnapped!"

Maudie pressed her freckle-spotted hands. Her netted red hair
moved closer to the tops of her spectacles. "The plainclothes detective telephoned the police, dear," she insisted. "They'll be on
the job in no time. Would it be better if the questions come from
them?"

"Oh, yes—the whole *world* will know! There'll be six-inch
headlines and chaos. No, I'm not waiting." She moved on, her
shoulders straight, her black silk skirt swishing against her
seamed flesh-colored silk stockings.

The servants assembled slowly, forming a blue-and-white-
uniformed rank against the backdrop of formal opulence. This
room, kept for their most formal entertaining, had had little use.
Tony had walked through it when it was finished, deeply
amused. "No one could say you wouldn't rush in where angels
fear to tread, my pet."

Lily had not been sure what he meant. One had to have a

room that met standards of culture; where else could they have received royalty or heads of state, no matter that it was infrequent?

She realized that at this moment she meant to use the grandeur she had achieved to awe the guilty person, bring him or her to confession.

"All right," she pronounced, standing in front of the tall, columned fireplace on either side of which stood marble busts of the first Earl of Cambrook and his bonneted Countess, "I'm going to ask you once again—which one of you helped Lord Aylsden to take the baby?"

There was no movement, no sound except the deeply muffled hum of traffic out in Grosvenor Square. Faces that had represented friendship and support were frozen in disappointment, in pity, in resentment.

"Just one person is responsible for this terrible thing," she continued. "Not the rest of you . . . Unless, of course, it's a plot." She paused, frowning, this thought taking shape. Perhaps it had all been planned . . .

"Lily—milady!" Thomas pushed his way through from the door, his boots making a loud squeak as he crossed to her. "The police are here. And Whitey's back . . ."

Lily looked at him irritably. The police would spoil everything, she thought. They would overrun the house, organize everyone, take over. Meantime, Tony could be on his way out of the country with her poor helpless little baby!

"Lil," said Thomas in a low whisper, "I got a hunch."

"Yes?" Her irritation was replaced by sharp interest.

"That Mrs. Bolton, you know. She once worked for the Dowager Countess—when his nibs was a boy, remember? Suppose she trusted him and left him alone with the kid, then didn't dare get him in trouble?"

"Go on . . ."

"Why don't I just take a quick run out to Cambrook Hall and case the joint? He *might've* took her there."

"Yes, Thomas, yes! Do it—quickly! Just say you're going to park the car!"

Thomas's face lifted. With a meaningful nod, he hurried away, already putting on his peaked cap.

Lily faced the waiting servants. "You can all go," she said. "The police are here—they'll probably question you."

In baffled silence, they filed past her towards the big double doors. "I'm sorry," she called after them.

Some of them turned. One or two nodded, conveying understanding.

"Boke—oh, Boke—I heard! It's on the wireless, all over the place. Is there anything I can do before I help Linda with the telephone calls?"

"No, Whitey. Just see that the police are shown to the Ivory Room—it's a good place to talk."

Whitey ripped off her small white hat, shook free her dark hair. "Whatever happens, Boke—don't panic. No one's going to hurt Deedee while she's worth money!"

Lily gazed at her as if through a fog. "Money?"

"Of course, Boke—what else!" Whitey shrugged regretfully, and hurried from the room.

Lily stood transfixed. "Of course," she murmured. It was suddenly clear. She had projected a different worth on her child. For a few minutes, she had quite forgotten Deedee's value in terms of cash.

As she walked steadily towards her confrontation with the British police, Lily felt the darkest of her horror lift.

Early that evening, she sat in stiff expectation, barely registering the headlines of papers brought to her by Whitey, where news of the baby's disappearance took up more space than Hitler or Chamberlain combined. When Whitey announced a telephone call—"From Thomas, Boke. What in the world does he want?"—she leaped to her feet, her heart jumping so hard she could hardly breathe.

"Lil?" Thomas's voice was strangely tenor. "She's here—she's okay! It was just as I said."

"Oh, Thomas—oh, Thomas, my dear friend! Get her. Bring her back!"

There was an instant of silence. "Lil—it ain't that easy. They ain't giving her up without a fight. The old gal wants to keep her, says she won't let you take her off to America. You'll win, Lil, but it could take awhile. Your best bet's the Earl."

Lily leaned so heavily against the little Louis XIV chair that it threatened to crack. "Oh, God . . ." she moaned softly.

"Lil—listen, Lil—he's given me the word. He don't want to write it down on paper, see. But if you make a million-pound settlement on him, he says he'll oil up the old gal and get the kid back. Says it's a promise."

Hysteria rose chokingly to her throat, erupted in wild amusement. In the midst of anguish, she could visualize Tony, his eyebrows raised high over his vivid blue eyes, somehow as blandly innocent as Deedee's, his forehead creased with the inspiration, and his smile almost startled by the wonder of his own astuteness. She could even see his two-man chorus rubbing their hands, and his mother in the background, righteousness in her cause of saving an Aylsden from the Barbarians.

"Thomas," she said, shaking her head, smiling, crying, "tell him all right. Tell him to bring her to me immediately, and I'll make all the necessary arrangements tomorrow. Call me back."

"Okay, Lil." Thomas hung up.

Lily, her hands wringing, her eyes still filled with tears, spoke to the small group of waiting detectives. "It's all right," she said, "my baby has been found! She's with her father and the Dowager Countess at Cambrook—safe and sound! I'm sorry I panicked. I apologize for wasting your time. Thank you, thank you very, very much . . ." After they had gone, Lily went to tell Whitey, Maudie, the servants that the child was found. She apologized humbly. She said nothing to Mrs. Bolton. All she wanted now was her baby.

By early May of 1939, Lily had managed to wind up her legal affairs, to arrange for the closing of the London house and to secure passage for herself and her entourage on the homeward-bound *Mauretania*. She took with her a minimal staff—an English nanny, Mrs. Fiske, guard Barney Cogan, for Deedee two guards, Maudie, Whitey, two maids (one from the North of England with her eye on Thomas) and Thomas. Her baggage count had risen, of course, with her European acquisitions and those for Deedee. There were over sixty pieces; this, despite extreme economy and ruthless disposal. (Many of her female servants had benefited from this, and Lily was told that they sold the dresses she gave them, which they were unlikely to wear themselves, for prices sometimes in excess of their yearly salaries. Lily was pleased.)

Now, as they drew up to the pier at Southampton, Lily felt nostalgia and excitement at the sight of the red-topped black funnels. It was a lovely, graceful ship and she was glad to be having the same suites as on her last crossing, plus one more for the baby, and the one Andy had taken for himself and Howie.

Reporters were everywhere, and it puzzled her how so many knew she was sailing, and about her settlement on Tony. Perhaps Tony himself had told them. He had suddenly become so reasonable and charming at the end that she felt the old attraction stir, had decided, after all, that he needed the last public word.

Deedee, now almost ten months old, was stolid, good-natured and looked more like her Boeker grandmother than an Aylsden. Energetic, undaunted by new faces or changes of routine, she was equally affectionate with nanny, maid, chauffeur, streams of smiling strangers or her ardent, kissing-and-hugging mother. Lily sometimes had qualms about this lack of selectivity. Wistfully, she longed to go off with her alone somewhere, be with her all the time, so that the dear blue-eyed creature would depend only on her, look only to *her* for love.

Gazing at her now, her lower half swathed in soft white wool lace, her rosebud face emerging from a white crepe-de-chine bonnet, her shoulders straining away from Mrs. Fiske's navy serge coat to look at the crowds, the traffic, the big liner, Lily made a new resolve to learn how to do all the chores of looking after her (surely they could not be so specialized and mysterious as the nannies made out)—she would make a new beginning with her on this journey home . . .

But life was so unexpected, she thought later. She had pictured a quiet crossing, hours spent with the baby, reading, talking and laughing with Andy and Howie, perhaps a dance or two, a good sleep, dreams of Joel—a pleasant bridge between her past and her future.

But as it happened, over three thousand people had surged aboard, and the passenger list for First Class had revealed so many familiar names of the international set, celebrities and acquaintances from Palm Beach, New York, London, Paris and Long Island, that she could not put faces to them; at twenty-seven she had already met, talked to or spent time with more people than she could remember, and they spun in her mind as types rather than individuals.

Her first inclination after dining once in the ship's-width Louis XVI restaurant, with its great center dome, its pilasters, columns, balconies and big circular tables of magnificently dressed diners, all either knowing her or looking at her as if to know her, had been to retreat to her rooms for the rest of the journey.

But at Le Havre, a gentle, friendly man who came aboard stopped on his way to his suite along the corridor to lean down and speak to Deedee. "Hello, there, Cocky—how are you?"

The baby had gazed at him with large blue eyes, given him a placid smile.

"We're off to our sunshine," Mrs. Fiske said.

"Great day for it!" He had turned, seen Lily and grinned with shy pleasure. "Lily Boeker, isn't it? I've seen your picture so many times."

"And—haven't I seen yours?" Her eyes widened. A faint dimple appeared.

He laughed and put out his hand. "George Ware."

"Oh, of course!" Lily felt like a schoolgirl. Wait till she told Whitey! Down the corridor, the guards hovered with the subtlety of rhinos.

"Well—got to get settled in. See you later, perhaps."

She nodded, thinking that she had never seen a more open, candid sweetness in a man's face, not a trace of conceit, of ego, of that pseudo-modesty of most famous film stars, particularly male. And he was considered not only the handsomest man in the whole industry, but the most popular Hollywood actor in the world!

"He likes children," said Mrs. Fiske, her mouth tugging with pleasure as they walked on. "Quite an ordinary nice sort of man. I must write to my sister—she'll want an autograph. Not that I'd think of asking for it."

Lily nodded. Strolling on to the raised terrace, she wondered if she had ever actually liked anyone so much instantly, on sight. It helped old wounds, made the world seem a better place.

That night, she reversed his telephoned invitation to dine with him and asked him to join her table. He looked quietly magnificent in his dinner jacket, his dark wavy hair glistening under the strong lights, his smiling, even-featured face and tall slim figure, but seemed oblivious of it, moving with easygoing, unselfconscious grace, gazing at other people with such interest that they could not openly stare at him.

Andy had been delighted when Lily told him. "We've met many times, sweet pea! He's an absolute *dear!*"

Howie, whose pallid face and stringy yellow hair convinced Lily he was ill, gave him a scathing glance. "No hope there, sweetie."

"Droll," said Andy, peaking an eyebrow at him.

They made up a party of ten at the big round table. There were two other friends of Andy's ("downright pansies," Tony would have called them), Princess di Frado, a broad-chested, heavily jeweled woman with short black curls, noted for her extravagant parties for celebrities, Hobey Grasse with thick tortoise-shell glasses, whose new musical, *Hey, Nonny, No!* was to open shortly in New York, and a flying couple who had recently broken a world air record, who smiled a lot but had little to say.

Lily and George, sitting next to each other, riveted the attention of the room as if a blazing light hung directly over them. And afterwards, when the group moved on to the ballroom, no person in the room was fully occupied with any conversation or dance step as George took Lily to the dance floor.

Lily's new Mainbocher was a cascade of soft black lace frills over pink chiffon. It rippled over her slim body in provocative shadows as she moved, hinting at what was underneath. Her much-written-about diamond and black-pearl jewelry seemed almost overweight on her small ears, her thin white wrists and hands. Her eyes took up the myriad lights of the candlelit room and shone with pale, incandescent beauty.

"You're so *very* lovely," said George Ware as they danced to "Thanks for the Memory," played by the Al Giddings orchestra, famous for their shipboard style of music called "The Subtle Ally of Romance." "And what's more," he added, smiling down at her, "I like you. I sort of knew I would, the moment I saw you."

"That's funny—that's what I felt." She shook back her light shining hair, gazed up at him. "It's just so good to really like someone. Does that sound stupid?"

His grip around her tightened. He put his cheek against hers. "It's music to my ears, Lily. Hollywood's full of phonies, full of beautiful girls . . ."

"My life's full of phonies, too. I never know when people are sincere, just can't seem to tell. With you . . . well . . ."

They danced without speaking. Lily felt a strange quiet happiness. His grip kept tightening and he, too, was smiling . . .

"George," she said suddenly, "I think every single person in this room is staring at us. Perhaps we'd better kind of . . ."

He looked up, startled—then his smile broadened. "I get you. I see you're in the same pickle I am—only more so."

Hand in hand they returned to the table.

After that night, they were together every day, starting with breakfast. They walked, played deck tennis and quoits, swam in the pool, exercised in the gym, bet on the wooden-horse races, sunbathed, danced till the late hours.

George was lighthearted, easy to be with. He spoke honestly of his life, himself. He told her that when he worked he concentrated so hard that he was a lost cause to others. When he wasn't working, he liked to be with old friends, children, animals, to swim at Malibu beach; his tastes were prosaic, elementary. He had been born in a remote part of Western Australia, had never seen a town until he was twelve. But he had liked to sing and dance, and when he was fourteen, had entered a competition in Queensland for a role in a big musical. He had won, and the next thing he knew he was plunged into the sophistication of the city and show business.

It wasn't easy—there had been times when, with no money, no roof, no work in the offing, he had slept out or sung and played a ukulele to raise a night's lodgings.

Then, suddenly, he had been picked as an extra in a local film, seen by a Hollywood scout and finally sent to Hollywood with a seven-year contract. He'd said goodbye to his family and sailed. The contract had had loopholes—what it meant, in fact, was that if a small part came along, he would be tested for it, stand a chance of being used.

The contract ran out before this happened. He half starved, pawned his suits to stay alive, and when he was lucky became one of thousands of extras in large crowd scenes. Vainly, he knocked on doors, wrote letters, tried to trick himself into interviews and the attention of producers.

On one occasion he had crashed his car outside the studio, breaking an arm, in the hope of talking to Jules Silverfeldt.

It hadn't worked—his phone had remained silent. Then, without warning, a bit part came his way from Central Casting. They wanted someone "tall, dignified and handsome" to escort a star to the microphone at a preview. He fitted, and he was widely observed. A part in the star's next picture followed. It was the beginning. Now he rated thousands of dollars per picture, called the tune on scripts and lived in a Spanish house—Moorish with a swimming pool.

It made him laugh. "The world's a mad joke. Half the time I'm lonely. My only friend for years was a chap called Pogo. He did the laundry, cooked, took care of mail. I'd take out some beautiful starlet or star, leave them at the door and go home to Pogo."

"What happened to him?" Lily wanted to know.

"I bought him a small cottage on Malibu beach and settled some money on him. He paints and putters about—poor old Pogo. He had such huge ambitions. He was going to be the great character actor of Hollywood. But it happens to thousands."

He told her that Hollywood was a deathtrap, a killer of values and ideals—but there were some good sides to it: the grandeur of the California country itself, the Spanish architecture that gave it an exotic quality, the wonderful climate and the beach life. He wondered if Lily liked to swim . . .

She confessed that she was not much good at any sport, but she liked tennis—and swimming.

"Come out!" he said excitedly. "See for yourself. I promise you a good time!"

"Would you let me watch you work?"

"Of course—but you'll be bored. I'm ugly and noncommunicative, and there's less glamour than people suppose. Lots of repetition, terrific heat under the lights."

"But so *interesting!*"

He smiled. "So it's yes—you will!"

She had put her arms around his neck and by the rails of the quiet upper deck, knowing she was being watched by the guards, in the shifting shadows of a cloud-trailing moon, with phosphorus cresting the black-jelly waves behind him, she kissed him.

"You never know," she said.

The lovely time, the sweet gaiety ended abruptly with the stark, towering skyline of Manhattan. Even the ship's paper should have warned Lily, with its reprinted "Lily and Filly run for cover. The U.S. good enough as war clouds loom in Europe." —"What price titles! Boeker employees weep for poor Countess and toil harder so she can fork out more millions for English Earl."

"Pay no attention, sweet pea," Andy had prompted as they watched the geometric mass single itself out into buildings, some of them new to Lily. "You can't expect violins and rosebuds. Besides—look out there. Does that look like poverty? Don't let them kid you."

"He's right," agreed George, pressing her arm reassuringly. "There's more building going on, more luxury, more progress than ever before. For all its problems, America's the richest, most powerful country in the world today!"

"God Bless America," someone sang.

There was laughter. Everyone leaning there, her friends of the voyage, added comments of support, of encouragement. She nodded, was grateful, not convinced.

"Can I help?" George asked. "I could face them with you . . ."

"Oh, heavens no! We'd be locked in for life!"

He laughed. "Goodo—I'll stay clear."

Unfortunately, it was not that simple. Not only were they captured together as they came up the central staircase with Mrs. Fiske and the baby, and Maudie and Whitey coming up in the rear, talking and smiling in animated closeness, but because George's most recent picture, *When You Went Away*, was a record box-office hit, he was in almost as much demand as Lily—the two together constituted the scoop of all time.

It did not matter how often or how candidly George spoke of

their shipboard friendship as having no other connotations, the newsmen were aggressively unimpressed.

They were pursued, cornered, and in the main lounge of the great ship unwittingly provided pictures for immortality in a quick goodbye kiss on the cheek.

"But this is completely ridiculous," Lily told those of the reporters and columnists she knew or remembered. "I haven't even got my decree nisi yet and I met George on board. We had a nice time—a nice crossing. Now we go our separate ways." She had smiled at the baby in loving concentration, emphasizing where her main interest lay.

"Sure—sure . . . But we heard different, Countess," said a cigar-smoking newsman pushing his hat to the back of his head. "We heard George Ware proposed and that he plans to . . ."

"Make four major pictures in a row," said George. "And I hope Lady Aylsden will visit me on the set someday!" He had winked at Lily, patted the baby's cheek, pushed on through the crowd, over to the gangplank.

As the reporters surged closer, Lily felt a moment of terror. In her black straw hat with velvet-dotted nose veil, black dress with puffed sleeves and pleated skirt, her paleness and fragility were emphasized by the brilliance of her eyes, red lipstick, icy-blueness of diamonds. Her thin hands grasped her soft black antelope purse, crushing it as if it were silk. "Please," she said, "let us pass. I'll talk to you one by one at the Ritz-Ambrose tomorrow. I promise."

"How many rooms have you taken this time?"

"We understand you've got sixty-five pieces of baggage and seventeen boxes of European art objects and paintings in the hold, and . . ."

"One moment, please! Hold it . . . !" Lily felt her elbow gripped hard. A voice whispered, "Say no more—read this from your aunt!" A large white envelope was thrust into her hands.

The newsmen and newswomen gathered closer. Lily looked at the man who had appeared beside her as if from the air, feeling instant, unreasonable dislike. Frowning, she looked at the envelope. It was Aunt Mirry's bold, definite writing. She slit it open. Her lashes formed dark arcs on her pale cheeks as she read:

"Dearest Lily, this is to introduce Lacey Depew. He is the

most powerful public relations man in the country today and I
have paid his very stiff fee to protect you from the bitter antago-
nism and press attack facing you on arrival. His job will be to
steer you back into the acceptance and affection of your fellow
countrymen. I suggest that you do and say exactly what he tells
you, and let him handle every situation which arises. I know you
won't like this, but you've had enough to bear in your young life,
and I can't stand by and see you persecuted through misunder-
standing. We intended to meet the ship, but the General's back
is bad again and I've got a houseful of Washington friends here.
Call me as soon as you can—at least we can talk. Your loving,
Aunt Mirry."

Lily looked up slowly. Lacey Depew had a short, squat,
plump face that seemed to slant sidewise at the mouth. His
white hair was cut so short it rose from his head in brilliantined
clumps, and his hazel eyes glinted cynicism. "Okay?"

"Well—okay . . ." She felt slightly giddy at the abruptness of
the situation.

"Okay. Look," he whispered hoarsely, "play up this romance.
This man's a good American citizen, believes in our democratic
system. You're through with European men and Europe. You
never *invested* over there, always *here*, and now you're going to
settle down where you belong. You were homesick, and so
on. . . . And whatever you do, don't mention the medical
hombre! He simply don't exist. Get it?"

Lily felt blood moving into her face. Mistakes, foolishness,
carelessness were one thing, outright lies another.

"Come on, Lily—what's the lowdown?" someone called.

Lacey Depew moved slightly to her rear.

"I . . ." Lily's blue gaze swept the assemblage in one last
nervous appeal. "Well," she said, her voice unnaturally soft and
low, "we shall have to see, won't we? I certainly don't want anything more to do with . . . Europeans."

Chapter 14

"It won't be long now, Boke," Whitey said as the Santa Fe Chief left the desert behind and started into California. She lifted Deedee to see the snowcapped mountains, the orange and lemon groves stretching greenly into the far distance.

A corner of her satin-lined afghan tucked securely into her mouth, a finger resting against her nose, the baby stared out of the observation car at the rear of the train in placid interest.

"It hasn't bothered her," Lily said, "three nights, three days of rattling across three thousand miles on wheels."

"Nothing does," said Whitey. "Lady Deirdre Aylsden is a tough kid."

Lily smiled. "Who do you think she's like now?"

"If you really want to know, Boke—the Dowager Countess. I think she'll ride to hounds before she walks!"

Lily laughed, nodded ruefully, felt a faint twinge of projected fear at the idea.

"Phew!" she breathed presently. "I'll need lighter clothes than this." She looked down at her Chanel mint-green pongee suit with the huge white buttons and piqué shoulder flower. "I wonder who's good out here?"

"George will probably know," Whitey said, with indifference to her own pink cotton dress already three years old and white off-the-face panama she had had since school. "Too bad he can't meet you."

"He's got his work," Lily said, feeling pride at this fact, so new to her experience.

The flickering palm trees, the brilliance of the sky, the unbroken hum of wheels against steel were dazing. Lily thought of Joel, their talks, so brief and sterile, reducing her to a persistent client seeking advice and getting it, his kindness so detached that the problem seemed unworthy of his time. But her gloom had been the shortest yet—George had intervened . . .

What a wonderful two weeks they had had, dancing at the Casino in the Park to Tommy Dorsey, touring the World's Fair, nightclubbing at El Morocco and the Stork Club, mixing with what these days they called "café society" (George was so good at handling the crowds, often he was the one they looked at, surrounded, asking for autographs—such a relief!), and they'd gone to parties and ridden round the park in a hansom cab and gone to parties . . . She'd felt like part of the world, into real life . . .

And there was never any strain between them. They seemed to have known each other forever. When he smiled and held out his hand for hers, her hand was already halfway to his. Altogether, he had a kind of tranquil grace that soothed, comforted . . .

"I'll take my lamb now, milady," Mrs. Fiske was saying, taking the child from Whitey.

Lily smiled lovingly into the unblinking blue eyes of her baby as she looked back from the shoulder of her governess, but Deedee's happy gurgle and kicking was for Mrs. Fiske.

In the big crowd at the Los Angeles station, Lily saw many people vaguely remembered from her twenty-first birthday, and George's observation that titled and famous Europeans were beginning to infiltrate California in anticipation of war seemed confirmed by faces she recognized. Only a few autograph books were visible, but after all, she was not a movie celebrity.

As Lily and her entourage assembled with baggage and por-
ters, Thomas, wearing his summer-weight Boeker-blue uniform,
appeared with a wide grin. "I made it, Lil—just a day ahead of
you! She took it like a breeze—not a scratch on her!"

"Good, Thomas!" Lily smiled, almost wanting to kiss the familiar face that always seemed in need of a shave.

"Herman's with me and I got another guy here to help. We'll
get you there, Lil."

Lily kept smiling, her pearly, uneven teeth glinting in the
strong sunlight. Cameras, like so many square black eyes, focused her every move, flashed, spat, flashed again. Lacey Depew
pushed up to her side. "Remember—no private thoughts—just
how tickled you are to be in L.A., how eager to see the great studios and how pictures are made—stuff like that. Okay?"

"Okay."

It was suddenly so much easier. How right Aunt Mirry had
been, what agony she had saved her—even if Lacey Depew *was*
the pain in the neck Whitey had called him.

She talked to the reporters without trouble, her sunlit hair
blowing from her white silk turban in the hot breeze, her square-
shouldered white crepe dress fluttering from her slim legs, her
face pale and mysterious in large dark glasses.

"Take off the glasses, Countess," someone called. "We want
the orbs!"

"I can't see a thing in this haze," she said, laughing, showing
how her eyes watered at the unaccustomed glare.

There were quick flashes. She waved to everyone. As the
crowd went with them to the car she smiled, looked on lovingly
as Mrs. Fiske allowed pictures to be taken of Deedee, who
frowned crossly into the glare, struggled to be put down.

Gradually, the curiosity was appeased. The entourage was allowed to move on to the light-blue Rolls that replaced the old
chocolate one, and the green Cadillac behind it. A few last
flashes and Lily was inside.

"You're okay, Lily," a hatless young man in rolled-up shirt
sleeves called, waving his notebook. "Keep us in the know."

She raised her hand to him, to the crowd in general, her rings
casting pale-blue fire into the outer brilliance. "I will," she
called, smiling.

Lacey Depew squeezed onto one of the small seats, took off his straw hat, mopped his perspiring face. "Eureka," he said. "Now for the next round."

His presence in such close quarters reduced some of Lily's gratitude. She wondered how long she would have to listen to his nasal wisdom, look into his shrewd eyes, smell his soggy cigar. "What are your plans, Lacey?" she asked as Thomas drove off into the fast-paced traffic, followed by the second car.

"Why, yours of course, Lily, what else? We got a lot to accomplish yet. Now, this house—you might think it's kinda poky—but we gotta cut down the ostentation—know what I mean?"

Lily's blank stare made Lacey Depew's shoulders shift, his mouth tug further sidewise. "You gotta prove you don't have to live in a palace or castle, that you can be a regular, everyday kind of American gal," he added.

"Oh." Lily thought about this. "Well, I hope it isn't too poky," she said. "I want to brighten up my life, do a lot of entertaining out here."

Lacey grunted, folded his arms, went into temporary retreat.

Lily's gaze now concentrated on the colorful scenery beyond the city, the palm-tree-lined streets, the sweet little Spanish-Moorish-style stucco bungalows coolly surrounded in deep, lush vines, cypress, orange and lemon trees. They passed wide boulevards and smart, recently established shops, and soon, almost abruptly, came to the mauve-gray rise of mountains, of gouged-out canyons sprinkled with larger houses that had red-tiled roofs, shadowy arches, spacious patios, gardens of bright golden poppies and semitropical flowers. Finally, they were climbing a red-clay road that flattened and broadened as it rose, spread itself into a verdant plateau of total isolation . . .

Lily peered with interest through the reddish dust on the car window as Thomas turned sharply left, then right—and suddenly there was a tall stone wall with a towering black-oak gate. Two young Filipinos opened it and bowed as Lily passed through.

"The staff was left here when Kurt Von Mohen, uh—passed away. I took 'em on for you."

Lily nodded. Aunt Mirry had known the famous director who shot himself because he was bankrupt; she had heard of some of his parties here.

Thomas rounded a long bush-edged drive, and Lily saw an elongated stucco structure with tiled roofs glowing redly against the vivid blue of sky. Further on, a series of shallow steps passed upward through vine-grown archways to massive Spanish oak doors. On the far side she could now see a triple-tiered patio, more lawn, sloping into the distance and bordered with stone steps leading to a huge glittering swimming pool. . . . Beyond that, several tennis courts, gardens, groves, an orchard . . .

"It reminds me of Palm Beach," Lily said. "Like some of the lesser houses."

Lacey, behind her back, gazed heavenward.

It was cool, almost cold in the big polished-tile hall. As they wandered through some of the main rooms, Lily got the overall impression of heaviness and gloom, of massive dark furniture, moss-green and maroon plushes, time-darkened brocades and tapestries, dim walls hung with weaponry, embroidered banners, funereal paintings with eyes that seemed to follow intruders into their orange-and-wax-smelling sanctum.

"Von Mohen had sinister taste," Lily said, with a slight shiver. "He imported the grimmest of European culture. However—it seems adequate. At least for the moment."

Although she talked to him on the telephone, it was nearly two weeks before Lily actually saw George. First he had been on location on Catalina Island off the Los Angeles coast, where he had been hit on the shoulder by a falling beam in a boat scene. Then when he had recovered he had had to redo the scene.

When she had finally seen him, he had driven straight to the house in ragged ducks and shirt, his face so darkly bearded and tanned, his teeth so white when he smiled, that she hardly recognized him. Standing back shyly, in her bright coral dinner dress with the cape sleeves and plunging neckline, she found it difficult to kiss him, even on the cheek.

He smiled apologetically. "I couldn't wait to see you, Lily, not even to shave. . . . I won't stay long."

She tried not to show her disappointment. "You'll at least have dinner, won't you?"

"I can't eat, actually—we've all had dysentery. But I will risk a drink."

From in front of the vast stone fireplace in which Lily had ordered a fire (California evenings were unexpectedly chilly) George beamed at her, rubbed his hands with delight, as the Filipino boy in the white starched jacket brought in chilled martinis on a heavy silver tray. "You remembered!"

Standing beside him in the fire's glow, she smiled at him, a sleeve falling away from her slender white arm to show her alternated trio of emerald and diamond bracelets as she lifted her drink in toast. "Of course. To New York!"

"To us." He touched her glass gently with his. "Do you like the house?" he asked. "Can you be happy in it, dear?"

"Well, it's kind of depressing—but the staff all like it, and Deedee's thriving—about to walk!"

"No! I want to see little Cocky—I hope she'll remember me."

"She wouldn't at the moment."

They laughed.

"George—when am I going to sit on a set and watch you work? I've been looking forward to it so much!"

"In about a week, dear. When I start my next picture. I'll arrange a tour of the studio, and we'll go sightseeing, driving to the mountains and canyons and neighboring valleys, and, of course, swimming . . ." His eyes brightened with anticipation. "I can hardly wait to get you on the beach!"

"Oh, but, George—in the *meantime*. What do I do with myself?" She sank distractedly into a huge roped-back couch of somber green plush. "I'm so mixed up out here—all day the phone goes with people who say they know me or I know them, asking me to every kind of party, dinner, previews, premieres, or for money because they're on the brink of starvation or bankruptcy or want to back a picture—and they lurk at the gates and hide in the bushes to watch everything I do—and I've had two threats on my life . . ."

George reached quickly for her hand. "My poor girl—how I wish I could protect you . . . !"

Lily sat still, suddenly bleak. "You could . . ." She gave him a tentative smile.

George was quiet. The gentleness of his expression was incongruous on the roughly bearded face. "Look, dear," he said after a moment, "we've had a couple of wonderful weeks—you aren't even free yet. . . . Let's not rush, let's get to know each other really well, see what time brings . . ." He pressed her hand, smiled tenderly.

Lily felt warmth rise to her cheeks. "Of *course*—I was thinking of that myself!" Her eyes widened with disingenuous excitement. "Actually I'm thinking of building a house, something spectacular and very modern, on a cliff or mountain overlooking the ocean . . . !"

"That's bonzer—it'll keep you busy and interested." He glanced quickly at a clock. "I'll have to get going . . ." He put down his glass, rose, extended his hand.

Lily got reluctantly to her feet, returned his light kiss, accepted his concern for his makeup getting on her "exquisite" dress.

She watched him run down the series of steps and archways, jump into an old-model Buick roadster, wave, race off into the palm-spiked, hill-shadowed darkness. A cough, the glowing ends of cigarettes under some nearby palms, reminded her of the guards watching.

Turning inside, she felt the sharp ache of loneliness, of futility. She knew that building a house had been offered to him as sly inducement, a nervous habit of power, to get what she wanted in the only way she was sure of—or had been. With George, it had no effect—and even sex did not seem a substitute hold as it had with others.

Standing in the vast gloomy hall, hearing somewhere the ponderous tick of a clock, a radio and the faint flowing voice of Kate Smith singing her "When the Moon Comes Over the Mountain" for Camel cigarettes, she closed her eyes, almost faint with a sense of disorientation. Opening them dazedly, she started involuntarily up the wide, wrought-iron-railed staircase towards Deedee's nursery—then remembered she had already kissed her good night, that she would be sound asleep. Mrs. Fiske would be distant and accusing if she awakened the "wee thing."

Whitey . . . She had gone out with some young man she had known in New England and looked up.

Maudie . . . Writing her letters home.

Lily started towards her room, then stopped. Maudie was aging, growing homesick for the land she had seen again, more than hinting that she would like to retire, to go back and settle in a country cottage near her relatives.

It would be a wrong time, a dangerous time to interrupt her.

Suddenly, against the restless pressure in her nerves, she walked to a tasseled rope and pulled it. A bell clattered and echoed in a distant part of the house. Filipino boys in white coats came running, maids came to the stairs, Thomas appeared, jacket over his arms, food still rotating in his jaws.

"I want to change into a formal gown, Rita," she told one of the maids. "Call Maudie. And, Thomas, can you find your way to Princess di Frado's in Beverly Hills?"

"Why, sure, Lil—it's up on Della Canyon Drive—Lacey Depew pointed it out when I drove him to the station—the day he went back East, remember?"

"I'll want you to take me there, Thomas, in fifteen minutes."

"Alone, Lil?"

"Alone, Thomas."

They eyed each other a moment, then Thomas nodded. "I'll get the Rolls and call Herman."

"There's only one thing to do when you're robbed," came Aunt Mirry's firm tone from Washington, "buy double the amount. There's a man out there called Grekler who knows his business. If he can't find you some good pigeon-blood rubies, I'll be very surprised."

Sitting in a low floral chair on the terraced patio with newspapers strewn about her, Lily smiled. Already she felt better. "What about the horrible publicity?" she asked.

"A disaster, but you're insured—forget it. Get yourself engaged to George, even if you break it off later."

"Oh, Aunt Mirry, if it were only that easy. He's just so terribly busy."

"Ah, well—I'll get Lacey to patch things up. Why don't you come here? The place is swarming with ambitious young men who could use some help." She gave one of her rare, low-key laughs, and Lily found herself laughing in response.

"They're swarming here, too," she said. "Every size, shape and color!"

When she hung up, her mood was gay, determined. At last,

she was going to spend the entire day with George, watch him work, swim with him afterwards at Malibu, then have a "quiet, simple dinner" at his house. Progress would be made.

Sipping her coffee, eating figs from the garden, she listened to the chattering of birds in the trees, the motors of lawn mowers, the soft hiss of sprinklers (so many to fight the dry earth here!), the occasional splash from the pool as Whitey took her early-morning dip, the dovelike sounds of Deedee talking to herself as she alternately walked and fell in her playpen.

How good life could be, how right.

The way she had behaved last night would never be repeated. She had come to the end of the long line of parties set in motion by Fraddie's that first night, each one seeming more grotesque than the other. Never again would she dance like that, be carried away by such an insane urge to escape herself through wild, abandoned movements, through intoxication of drink and rhythm and stupid, indiscriminate flirtations . . .

. . . Good God, hadn't the police arrived at some point . . . ? All she could remember was doing some kind of a barefoot jungle dance with Lupe Delmar, the Mexican star, who was wrapped in gold lamé from head to foot, except for a chestful of pearls and a feather headdress—someone beating a drum— everyone, the whole party joining in—a crescendo of sound, loud and wailing, a great climax of mystical vibration . . .

. . . And then voices saying, "Lily, Lily, put on your dress— run . . ."

"The cops, darling! Hide—it'll be in all the papers . . . !"

"It's all right, Lil . . . I'll take the Countess home . . ."

Thomas . . . Thank heavens . . .

The last thing she would have noticed was that the pigeon- blood rubies Tony had "given" her (charged to her account) were missing from her throat. Nor could she imagine how she had got grass stains all over her gunmetal Paquin moire, or how the white-ermine shoulder bands were broken . . .

Anyway, it was all behind her now. How very right George was to keep his working and private life apart, to guard himself against the false values of fame, to shun the social life of the film colony! He was an extraordinary man, and she was very lucky— or would be . . .

"Come on, me darling," said Mrs. Fiske, reaching for Deedee. "Time for bathie."

"Oh, can't she stay, Mrs. Fiske?" Lily got up and held out her arms, but the sturdy, fair-haired child was already reaching hers to Mrs. Fiske.

"I'm sorry, milady—it's just that we're so much together."

Lily nodded. "I know . . . It's my fault. I must do more with her . . ."

"You will, milady, I'm sure, when she's older and talking."

"Yes . . ." Lily watched them go, waved, but Deedee seemed unaware of her. Married to George, it would be different, she thought, they'd make a family.

She dropped off her terry-cloth robe and went down to join Whitey, her white bathing suit showing that a real California tan was yet to be achieved.

"They've probably got binoculars trained on you, Boke," Whitey called. "From those trees."

Lily shrugged. "Never mind—Garbo has the same problem. How's the romance?"

Whitey squeezed water from her seal-flat hair, pulled the lobe of an ear to let out water. In her black suit, she had the compact figure of a professional swimmer; her skin was a burnished mahogany. "He's rushing me—wants to get married."

Lily paused at the end of the diving board. "What does this man of yours do?"

"He works out at Douglas Aircraft. He says they're turning out planes by the hundred and doing research. Not only for the airline travel, but war!"

"War?" Lily frowned. "We won't get invaded, will we?"

"He says we never could stay isolationist with this Berlin-Moscow treaty if anything happened to France and Britain."

Lily gazed down into the clear, glinting water, as if it were a crystal for the future. "I couldn't take Deedee back."

"You won't be able to anyway, Boke, if England's at war."

"No. I wonder what will happen to Tony."

"He'll probably get some job at the War Office."

Lily smiled. "You can't tell—he certainly knew how to fly!"

"And drive a car!"

They laughed reminiscently. Lily completed her dive.

When she emerged from her swim to dry off, Maudie was waiting.

"I'd like to take this opportunity of a word with you, Miss Lily," she said.

"Yes, Maudie?"

Maudie automatically helped to rub her back, to put her robe about her shoulders. "It's about my going home," she said. "Dear, if England goes to war I'd never forgive myself for not being there. So if you can arrange it, I'd like to go back as soon as possible."

"Maudie!" Lily felt the color drain from her face. She had not seen Maudie's expression so blankly set since the time she had first asked her to stay. "You'd leave me, leave Deedee, after all these years—just like that?"

"It *is* my homeland, Miss Lily." There was something like outrage in the gray eyes.

Lily let her hair fall to dry it. "I'll have to think about it, Maudie. I don't know how it could be done . . ."

"I'll go steerage, Miss Lily, on any boat sailing."

"That's not important, Maudie—when you retire, I'll see that you're very comfortable for the rest of your life. But it's too soon. . . . I need you, Maudie. I—I . . ." Suddenly there were tears in her eyes. She reached out to her.

But Maudie stood back, warding her off. "I *have* to go," she said. "It's *now* that I must go, Miss Lily."

Lily stared into the bespectacled gaze, the taut, etched face that was like looking into a mirror at her own image. Thoughts of Beth rushed through her mind, of Daddy lying twisted on the ground, of all the come and go of her life that seemed to have no human center of gravity . . .

Her head lowered in guilty acknowledgment of Maudie's rights. "I'll look into it, Maudie," she said. "If it's at all possible—if *we* don't get involved—I'll get you back."

"That's all I can ask, of course. Thank you, Miss Lily—and bless you."

Lily could not afford to look up.

Sitting quietly in the far shadow of the enormous set where

George was working on a frenzied musical with a cast of thousands called *Fiesta Grande,* Lily's mind wandered.

More and more, she was feeling the strain of his noncommitment. Even the movie magazines and gossip writers had either given up their guessing game or plumped for a secretly accomplished marriage. Aunt Mirry was all for her giving up and returning East.

Still—as far as she could tell, George did love her. In a way, it was painfully simple. He had told the truth when he said there was very little left over from his work—and these days this was his survival. One director told her that George was the only star on the payroll at MKR who would outlast the rigid economies now necessary. George never "fluffed," could be counted on to do his scenes in one take. George always understood his role, was word-perfect, punctual and, above all, humble. Now that the war had cut down the European market, George would also outshine the greatest geniuses in the business.

She admired this in him, and understood that when he did, briefly, relax, he wanted to spend most of his time on the beach, or, at the most, entertaining his old friends, a motley group of extras, out-of-work actors, people who had given him a helping hand in the past, or quiet people like his faithful ex-secretary, Pogo, with whom he felt comfortable and at home in his modest, isolated bungalow with its single tennis court and just-adequate pool. His idea of a marvelous time was a barbecue picnic, music on the victrola or radio or piano, in old clothes, everybody fending for himself and not a servant in sight, having given the one cook-houseboy the evening off. Long since forgotten were the festive times on the boat and in New York.

When she went with him to the beach, the chances were that he would doze off beside her, and she would be left sitting there, hour after hour, until the moisture had left her skin and her hair stood about her now darkly tanned face stiff as straw.

But he did like to have her there, and when he woke up he would smile at her, stroke her, gaze adoringly into her eyes. Often he would kiss her with his constrained passion, and she thought he was about to say it, say the words.

Once, sitting close together outside their cabana after a moonlight swim, he had reached into the pocket of his white ducks and brought out a small leather box.

"I've got something for you," he said, grinning. "I hope you'll wear it. It'd make me so happy to see you wearing it."

At last, she had thought—this is it! She had taken it with a quiet, expectant smile, opened the box.

It had been an ankle chain. A fine gold chain with a heart-shaped padlock.

Somehow, she had controlled her reaction. She had put the chain on her slender tanned ankle and George had closed the lock, his fingers trembling slightly.

How vibrant and handsome he looked out there now, as the street-festival scene rose to a great climax with George raised high on the men's shoulders while he circled a red bandanna jubilantly above his head . . . ! What a dear he really was! And he had never looked at another woman since he had known her . . .

But something must happen soon—it was 1941! Poor little England had been bombed for months. Tony, who had been in the RAF for over a year, had not been heard of recently. Deedee was calling George "Jerjee" and singling him out for attention, the decree nisi had been granted and her house high in the Santa Monica mountains was nearing completion.

Lily snapped open her platinum cigarette case, took a cigarette from the neat white line, remembered that smoking was not allowed on the set and put it back. Her glance roved the great arc lights hovering giddyingly over the realistic Mexican town, drawing down around a black-haired girl in an off-shoulder blouse, frilled cotton skirt and bare feet who was preparing to dance.

The clappers smacked, someone called "Take nine!" and the musicians began to play the song expected to be an all-time hit, "Fiesta, Fiesta!"—a slow rumba with a crescendoing tempo.

Lily sat forward a little, her shoulders and feet moving to the hard, rhythmical beat. Oh, if only she could be out there, doing something herself, instead of just sitting watching . . . !

"Hello, darling, that winds up my stuff for now," said George, suddenly appearing, kissing her cheek. "Getting bored?"

"Not bored—a bit envious, perhaps." She returned the grip of his hand.

"Of Lupe! She'd give her eyeteeth to be you, dear! Any girl would. Come and have some coffee."

"Wouldn't you be proud of me, George, though?"

He looked down at her as they sauntered toward the bungalow dressing room hand in hand. "I would not," he said emphatically. "I'm proud of you as you are."

"Doing absolutely nothing?"

"Yup. Exactly."

Lily shrugged.

Sitting in low-slung canvas chairs in the unlit room, with the venetian blinds sending the late sun upwards, a softly whirring fan dispensing mingled scents of cosmetics and fruit, George and Lily sipped their coffee.

"I don't think you ought to wait for me tonight, Lily," George said. "The way things are going, there'll be a lot of retakes of the big scenes. I thought I'd have a word with Pogo afterwards—he's got problems of some kind."

"I see—well, I'll go on. I'll run up to the house. I've got some more ideas."

George smiled at her indulgently. "Those poor guys—you'll have them in straitjackets."

"Darling," said Lily suddenly, "there's something I want to say." She put down her cup, crossed her legs and straightened the long, jaunty scarf of her square-shouldered yellow dress.

His eyebrows rose. "I've done something wrong, dear?"

She smiled. "No—but you might not like this."

"Oh?" His amiable expression became exaggeratedly solemn.

"George—I've never done anything like this before, but I'm getting jumpy, not sleeping, sort of permanently restless."

He frowned in quick sympathy. "Is it me—seeing too much of me? God knows, I'm a dull . . ."

"George! That's just the trouble—it's not seeing you *enough!*"

"My work—it's getting you down . . ."

"Will you *listen!* What I'm trying to say is . . ." She stopped, looked at him fearfully a moment, then plunged. "Do you or don't you want to marry me?"

His jaw dropped, his eyes widened—then suddenly he smiled

with embarrassed, rueful understanding. "Oh, Lily—what can I say—that I'm not worthy, that I'm not sure I can make you happy . . . ?"

Lily's eyes grew large and wistful. "That means you *don't* want to . . ."

"Oh, no, no, no!" George lowered his head. "It only means that it's such a big decision, dear. You see, with me it's a forever thing, like my parents had, final . . ."

Lily saw, with sudden illumination, that it was now, or perhaps never . . .

"At least be engaged," she said quickly. "Nothing formal—and then either one of us could change and the other understand. . . . See?"

He looked up at her slowly. The dimple that was famous to his fans appeared at the side of his mouth. He reached for her in wry uncertainty. "I don't hold with a woman proposing to a man," he said, "but maybe I have to have my mind made up for me." He ran a strand of her hair between his fingers reverently. "Besides—who could resist beautiful Lily . . . ?"

Chapter 15

As the war spread to world involvement, George entertained or
served meals in the Hollywood Canteen. He hoped to be accepted into one of the services and go overseas, but, in the meantime, he gave unstintingly of his time and money in every way
possible, on one occasion donating his entire salary of $115,000
from *He Was Her Man* to the Red Cross.

Lily, left more and more to her own devices, donated huge
sums to almost every war cause. She ignored Coggy's warnings
and loaned the American government her house in London, gave
them money necessary for its upkeep.

The criticism that her new mountainside home had initiated
died away in the confusion of her generosity. Her huge parties
were overlooked (she had slipped back into the habit of giving
them), and her seemingly significant absorption in tennis with
the famous pro Sonny Somerville was muted, put aside for less
traumatic times.

Lily wished there was someone she could talk to about

George. His protracted evasion of actual marriage was a growing frustration. She even thought of putting aside her pride and seeking out Joel for advice, but Aunt Mirry told her that he was heading up some psychological survey on the part mind played in war casualties. Her problem would seem so trivial. Yet there was something puzzling about George's halfheartedness, something she felt that Joel would understand . . .

On the other hand, there might not be anything meaningful at all in his lack of eagerness. They did have lovely times together—and sex of a sort.

That it was somewhat ineffectual on his side could mean that he would have preferred a more moral approach, to have waited until it was legal. But apparently men had this conflict—women who were interested in lovemaking, either before or after marriage, tended to be classed with whores. Yet—if they weren't interested, they would have to pretend they were in order not to hurt the man's pride or, worse, to be called "frigid"!

Well, no doubt it would all work itself out soon . . .

She rang for Maudie and Netty, changed from the neatly fitting blue-gray uniform she had had designed for her canteen work, into her wide-legged sharkskin shorts, short-sleeved blouse, anklets and sneakers.

"The tennis instructor is waiting," a footman told Maudie from the door.

Lily nodded. She did not need Gustaf to push her high-rolled hair under a Mexican bandanna, and she brushed Maudie's white handkerchief aside . . .

"I'm on my way, Benson," she called.

She ran lightly down the steep, backless stone steps that joined the gigantic tiered levels of the house like a broad zigzag spine. The uncluttered sweep of the glass-walled or completely open rooms, with their giant plants and whole trees, wall-length murals, huge, height-staggered modern paintings, gleaming redwood floors scattered with brilliant-colored rugs, gave her their usual pleasure as she passed. No house had ever sat so satisfyingly on her artistic senses, not only in its bare, rugged grandeur, but in its cool unconfining atmosphere in which the sound of gently splashing water of indoor fountains, the tinkling of vast glass and celluloid mobiles was a sensuous and soothing background music.

"Yes, dear," Aunt Mirry had said when she and the General paid a brief visit, and Lily was able to give them the Moorish suite that extended so far out over the mountainside that it seemed to hang on air above a glittering Pacific, "it's very nice, very nice. You've done well." (She suggested "many" more blossoming trees and a waterfall to extend from the top to the bottom level, spilling downward to an artificially constructed lake; this, she would stock with fish, and she knew just the man to design it for her.)

Sonny Somerville did not see her as she approached the four red-clay courts, surrounded by tall, vine-massed wire netting. Of medium height, his short red hair and ruddy face glinting with sweat, his muscles hard and rippling in his bare forearms and legs, he hit the ball with rhythmic ferocity and accuracy, occasionally swearing to himself.

She called out as she closed the gate behind her and he stopped abruptly, his face breaking into a wide, welcoming grin. "Hello, baby," he called.

"Hello, Tarzan!" she called back. "How much handicap do I get today?"

"Hey, none of that—you're getting good, honeybunch. Another few months and you'll be ready for Forest Hills!"

While George now visited hospitals and army camps in scores of cities across the nation (his picture in the papers looking handsomer than ever in officer's uniform, smiling his warm smile at hundreds of unfortunate soldiers), Lily tried to fill her life with more meaningful activities.

Strangely enough, although her donations were appreciated, her personal work was not. It was the same old story; it not only annoyed the other women, from housewife to top star, that she should hand out food or dance with doughboys, but they seemed to resent her very presence, the very principle of her "descent from the heights to the hoi polloi," as it was put in one particularly nasty write-up.

Lily felt the sting, and her smile became strained, unsure, her eyes darting and evasive. She decided to give up all physical endeavor other than scratching her signature on large checks. Immediately, she was reinstated as a monarch one could throw bricks at but not depose.

But oh how she missed shuffling about the dance floor with the boys to "I'll Be Seeing You," "Dearly Beloved," "Take It Easy," "Swinging on a Star," played on a Solovox or sung on radio, all seeming so heartrendingly sweet and poignant under threat of war, and each soldier she danced with, no matter how rough-and-ready, unattractive or clumsy, seeming dear, rating affection . . .

Now—with foreign travel out of the question, her home perfected in every detail—she'd even put in the waterfall and lake, though not the fish—and no one the slightest bit interested in her dancing any more, there seemed little to occupy her.

Only Deedee, always bored indoors, with the distances so great between houses that playmates had to be imported (usually the children of directors or stars), presented the semblance of a demand on her resources or time.

Smoking more and more cigarettes, Lily wandered the house and its gardens, the mountains, the beach, gazed out over the boat-dotted ocean and tried to get some inspiration. She had already bought Deedee a pony for trekking (Mavis had written that she was training up a horse for the time Deedee would come to Cambrook) and shown children's movies in the movie theater. Deedee had an extremely short attention span. Her only nonphysical interest at the moment was her doll's house, and she would sit still by it for a while, putting her dolls in, taking them out, arranging and rearranging the miniature furniture.

It was this that one day fused in Lily's thoughts like a light. She, too, had loved her doll's house, an enormous one compared to Deedee's. Why not an architecturally scaled big one, a castle, made of genuinely duplicated materials, furniture and fittings!

Deedee did not, of course, grasp the significance of such a project, but Lily felt an obsessive excitement mounting in her, dousing out her boredom like water on hot ashes. She summoned available architects, builders, furniture makers, jewelers. They were asked to take on the challenge of working in miniature. Some demurred, but others accepted with growing enthusiasm.

Deedee's second sitting room was allocated to the venture,

cleared of all furniture, and the work begun. Lily barely slept for the ideas that coursed through her head. Although it was known locally as the "great showplace of Hollywood," the mountainside house now seemed a dull structure compared to the Lilliputian artistry required for the ten-foot-square castle. Every day presented problems, demanded utmost ingenuity—what to use for floors, for lights and a lighting system, for the tall windows, the beds, the kitchen and bathroom equipment.

The humming activity riveted Deedee for about an hour or so each day, then she would revert to her normal preference for the outdoors.

Lily would stay on, conferring with a retired studio engineer called Dan O'Connors who was almost as obsessed as she was with the constructional challenges. He devised a way of constructing each room separately. Its interior would be shaped, painted and decorated according to Lily's decorative scheme, and the shell put together. Then artisans of all kinds would be consulted and given the task of putting her ideas for furniture and fittings into effect.

Minute light bulbs were devised, many of Lily's jewels cut up for the tiny and perfect chandeliers. Floors were made of marble, ivory, ebony and jade; Persian carpets specially woven; pillars might be of rose quartz, mother-of-pearl, black glass, gold. The high-ceilinged reception rooms, ballroom and banqueting halls were embellished with tiny copies of famous statuary, famous grand and spiral staircases from palaces of Europe; hangings were cut from rare velvets and brocades and hung with precise correctness at the handsome windows, some made of stained glass in faithful imitation of those in well-known cathedrals or medieval castles.

Boudoirs had canopied beds with proper mattresses and covers of gold cloth, satin, velvet or ermine. Every piece of furniture in all the twenty-five rooms was a faithful replica of some famous antique; the drawers worked, the cupboards opened, the tiny chess set on one rare-marble table could actually have been used by people as small as the minute figures that comprised the inhabitants, a king, a queen, two princesses, a prince and various retainers, all in sumptuous or appropriate clothing.

The castle had a functioning water system, a moat, a drawbridge, and swans made of real swan feathers floated on a real-water lake, and when the whole structure was lit up to its fullest, the brilliant glittering beauty and art was overpowering. . . . Lily could not call a halt to the possibilities; the castle had become an addiction and many members of the film industry who had taken a hand in the creation found it a fascinating escape and pastime.

Elsewhere in the land, there was sharp criticism of her extravagance. The headway made by Lacey Depew began to crumble and long articles appeared condemning her self-indulgence. Lily was not quite sure how she could amend it, and in any case, George, when he was there, seemed to welcome her absorption.

Eventually, "The Dollhouse Affair" (Reggie Blount's term) was logically terminated. With the gradual depletion of male staff and the difficulty in finding replacements, together with Whitey's sudden departure to see her gravely ill mother, Lily found herself living a strange new life, trying to instruct elderly or untrained servants to deal with the requirements of the household (Japanese were interned, of course) and grounds, to cope with her mail and the telephone, to keep up with the myriad details of food buying, finance and entertaining. Often, these days, George would end up in the kitchen with her after a dinner party, actually helping Maudie (who had, of course, not been able to travel home) to wash dishes. It was that, or not entertain at all.

Then, too, Thomas chose this time to announce that he wanted to marry Netty and retire. The betrayal (so soon after Roosevelt's sudden death, which had a surprisingly depressing effect on her) put Lily to bed for three days, but when Mrs. Fiske declared she was unable to cope with "the little miss" any more and would she please hire someone else, Lily was forced from her bed for inescapable confrontations.

She asked Thomas if he could not wait until the war ended—after all, Italy had surrendered, it surely wouldn't go on so very much longer.

"When I'm married and we're all settled back into normal life again, Thomas," she told him, going to sit with him on the servants' patio, "and I can find someone to replace you, I'll set you up in a good house back East or wherever you like."

"To be honest, Lil," he said, rubbing his black-grained chin, "I've got a tidy sum laid by. Netty and me might settle in her territory in the North of England—I kinda liked England."

"I'll have to take Deedee back, Thomas, the minute it's safe to travel—you could come then."

Thomas eyed her so knowledgeably that Lily was forced to look away. Her hands were trembling.

"Well," he said after a moment, "I don't want to let you down—I'll talk it over with Netty. I suppose we could stay here— only I ain't sure she'd like it. She wants a home of her own, and I do too—I been in service since I was nineteen years old and that's too long. Besides, Lil—I don't like this climate and all the phonies you run with. . . . If only you and Mr. Ware . . ."

"Thomas! That is not your business!"

He looked at her shrewdly, ran a hand over the spot on his head worn thin by his cap, tugged at the collar of his white shirt. Suddenly he grinned. "You're right at that," he said. He snapped his fingers. "Dead right."

She saw instantly the point he was making. "I'm sorry, Thomas," she said quickly, "my nerves aren't very good at the moment . . ."

Her soft gaze, her sudden smile took effect. His shoulders relaxed. "I always forget my place. I didn't mean nothing."

"Thank you, Thomas. I appreciate your loyalty. I always have."

It was the most she had ever said to him, and she ran off quickly up the rock-indented steps back to the house, her tanned legs still as slim as when he had first been put in charge as her driver.

She would give Thomas and Netty a wedding, she thought, a really tremendous celebration, all the servants of her friends from all the neighboring houses invited, two or three orchestras, a teasure hunt and gifts hidden for everyone—oh, she could already think of a dozen things to make it a moment in time . . . !

But—Netty, the dark, stocky little maid with the good-humored face, had not wanted such an occasion. *She* would be embarrassed, she said, even if Thomas wouldn't—they were too old for that sort of thing, and would prefer to slip off somewhere, tie the knot and have a week's quiet, maybe in some nice small hotel where they wouldn't have to drive or do anything for themselves.

Disconsolately, Lily had offered to pay at least for that. She had wandered about, unable to take an interest in anything the ensuing days offered. George was away, in Texas, or was it Nevada . . . ?

Then one evening, resignedly attending a dinner party in honor of Celeste Chrystie, whose recent picture had helped MKR over a rough financial stretch, and finding herself picking at lobster thermidor next to the new star's director, a miracle occurred. Suddenly, drastically, Lily's life was lifted out of its cul-de-sac of purpose and given bright new hope.

"You know," said Saul Neuberger, a short heavyset man, totally bald, deeply tanned, with a guttural voice that was at the same time kindly and paternal, "you've got a beautiful, photogenic face, Lily. Too bad to waste it. You ever think of making a test?"

Lily turned her blue gaze fully to his. She had worn a backless aquamarine Paquin, long matching earrings, her hair swept back long and shining behind her ears. With her tan, the effect was startling. "No one's ever asked me," she said.

Saul Neuberger had shaken his head. "People are so dumb. They see money—they think, no talent."

Lily's fork hovered. So did her breath.

"Now me," he said, "I got it here," he tapped his bald head, "and here," he tapped the side of his nose. "You take a face and shape like yours, give a little training, get the right lighting and camerawork—and who knows? Maybe another Garbo, another Shearer, another Colbert."

"Really? One wouldn't need to have had acting experience?"

He chuckled. "It sure as hell helps—but you know and I know, there are other ways. Like influence. Some girls sleep with the right guy, others gotta a name in legit. Girls with pretty faces and potential, we call starlets, put them on long-term contracts and groom them, see how they do . . ."

"Where would I fit in?" Lily tried to smile casually, but it did not convince.

"Interested, eh?" Saul Neuberger's eyes narrowed on her face.

"Well, the way I figure it, depending how you test, we'd put you in a small part, just to give you confidence. Then, if that looked good, we'd start the build . . ."

"How do you mean—the build?" Lily did not remember the lobster until it was taken away. ("Yes, I'm finished," she murmured to the waiter, "thank you.")

Saul Neuberger popped the last lump of lobster into his wide mouth, wiped his hands on the damask napkin. "Bigger parts, studio publicity, how you were discovered, MKR's hopes for you, photographs of you working, the serious actress . . . Stuff like that."

"But would anyone else take me seriously?"

Saul Neuberger patted his tuxedo lapels. "You bet they would. Once we get behind you. The public believes what we tell 'em."

"But suppose it isn't true—that I'm . . ."

He leaned towards her, his voice lowering. "If that's the way it worked, we'd scrap the test. No one'd ever know. We're not gonna risk our necks, put a fortune behind someone who hasn't got what it takes. Don't you see?"

Lily nodded slowly. "So if you did take me on, it would mean that I had genuinely potential talent?"

"Check. And if you want an honest opinion of one who doesn't need to look for talent—who turns away hundreds of hopefuls a month—you're gonna have it, star quality."

They both leaned back as lemon soufflé was placed in front of them.

"What makes you think that?" Lily asked, forking some soufflé with delicate precision.

"What gives me my hunches?" The heavy-shouldered man leaned over his plate to catch a trembling forkful in his mouth. "Is that what you're asking?"

Lily gave him a quick, self-accusatory smile. "I'm sorry . . ."

He broke into a broad grin. "That's okay. But you want to ask MKR about Neuberger's hunches. Without them, they'd have no great names, no great movies, no studio!"

Lily looked properly respectful. "I have heard George say that," she said.

"Ah—speaking of that one. Now there's a guy who's gotta get a new leading lady he don't overshadow. All that twinkle, all that masculine charm, the gals look washed out, like housewives on a day off. Now, with *your* glamour . . ."

"Oh, no . . . !" Lily sat back. "That's going *too* far."

"Is it? So that's what you're telling me? That I don't know my business? That I don't know what I'm talking about?"

"Saul—I didn't mean . . ."

"Look, Lily—what kind of a monkey do you think I am? If I didn't think it was possible—I didn't say *sure*, I said *possible*— why the hell do you think I'd say it?"

"But, how could *I* . . . ?"

"Let me finish." Saul Neuberger put down his napkin. His big face grew solemn. "If, I'm saying IF, you got what I think you got, you could not only match up to your hero, but you'd have every leading man in the business vying for you. What I see is a new romantic duo, like Garbo and Gilbert, Colbert and Gable— so on."

Lily was silent. The man on her other side asked her a question about George, another about Palm Beach. When she had finished a short conversation, Saul Neuberger was still looking at her, waiting to continue. Her heart was beginning a speed-up of excitement she found it difficult not to convey.

"So—want to give it a try, Lily?"

There was another short pause, while Lily felt her whole life might be in the balance.

"It'd only be a test, honey. Nothing lost. Maybe another experience for the richest girl in the world." His smile was sly, persuasive.

"It *would* be an opportunity. . . . I can't tell you how much I'd like to be doing something constructive with my time. If I thought I could really do it . . ."

"Say no more. Seven A.M. Monday on the lot. I'll leave word at the gate what you're to do and where to report. Meanwhile, I'll send you over a script."

A thrill ran down Lily's spine and tingled somewhere in her toes. To be ordered, to be told, to have an assignment! "All right, Saul," she said. "I'll be there."

He nodded, pleasure jerking back his scalp, smoothing his face. Lily could hardly hear what anyone said to her for the rest of the evening; it was all so inconsequential. How in the world had she ever come this far on such aimless trivia . . . !

The makeup took the longest—but it gave her extra time to go over and over again in her mind the lines of her sample scene, an excerpt from *The Unholy One,* a light romance that had been a hit for Ida Nolan. "Here I am, Ronny—I was hoping you'd take me to lunch. I want to have a serious talk with you . . ."

"Keep your mouth still, please, dear," said the makeup man. "My, what a pleasure to work on a real face."

Lily's wide-open eyes, the lids and lashes already emphasized with shadow and mascara applied with ultimate skill, looked questioningly upwards.

"I mean, no nose to modify, no bags or lines to hide, clean, classic planes, beautiful skin . . . Of course, they'll eventually want you to cap those front teeth . . .

"Don't look startled. They make them so you can pop them on before takes. Most of the stars have them. Easier than making pegs. George has the best dents in the business, of course. All his own. What a surprise he'll get!"

Lily's fair eyebrows were held high, as if to help with the elaborate proceedings. (And it would be so much better for him, she thought, not having her on his conscience, taken up with something absorbing of her own at last.)

"There. Perfect. I don't see how you can fail, Miss Boeker. Now, Olga will take you along to Wardrobe."

At exactly seven A.M. (having got up at five, just the way George did, and been driven to the studio by Thomas), Lily was led to the set in Studio 5, a completely furnished "office" with a large businesslike desk. The young bit player who was going to feed her her lines was not yet there, but all the technicians were setting up their lights and cameras, and they smiled down on her in a friendly, comradely way which helped to calm her, to lessen her trembling.

The Continuity girl came in and took a chair and smiled at her. "You look lovely, Miss Boeker," she said, nodding towards Lily's simple black suit with the white stand-up collar, the tiny black-and-white feathered hat they had pressed in behind her smooth pageboy hairstyle. She opened her large notebook, checked her over for clothes details.

("You never have time to talk to me at home, Ronny—so I thought we would meet in town, and that perhaps you'd listen to me, all the way through. . . . Yes, it is important, darling. To me, it's as crucial as one of your big deals is to you. . . . No, it can't wait. . . . All right, Ronny—but I think you'll be very sorry. . . . Tell Mr. Big-Wig from wherever or whatever, that it was him or me, and that you chose him." Well, she seemed to remember all right—if only she could be sure not to forget at the moment . . . !)

"Hi, Miss Boeker!"

Lily turned to see a blond young man in a gray business suit, very handsome, yet somehow just missing in stature. "I'm your Ronny," he said, grinning.

She shook hands with him, and he stood beside her while they each tried to find something further to say.

"Ah—thanks for being so punctual, Miss Boeker."

Suddenly a wiry man with tightly kinked iron-gray hair was beside them, looking as if he had just come from a game of golf, played in a beret instead of a cap. "Guess we're all set."

Lily looked at him uncertainly.

"Oh, excuse me—my name's Sy Gregory. I'm directing you."

"How do you do. But isn't Saul . . . ?"

"Saul? He's working with Celeste on the new one—did you want him for something?"

"Oh, no . . . No . . ." How stupid of her, she thought, to have expected Saul himself to bother with so small a task.

"I don't want you to worry about a thing now. . . . May I call you Lily?"

"Of course . . ."

"All right, Lily—you know the scene. Shall we run through it once?"

"Well . . ."

"Okay—if you know your lines, there's no need. Just stand over there, dear."

Lily moved to the spot to which he pointed. A makeup girl came up to her and pressed a large flat puff against her pancake makeup, flicked away some stray hairs. The huge arc lights were turned onto her, to the set.

"Jimmy . . ." Sy Gregory nodded to "Ronny" and the young man quickly took his place behind the desk. The cameras drew in. Lily felt herself surrounded and trapped by huge snakes of cables, by moving wheels, by a barrage of almost unbearable heat and brilliance.

"Wow!" someone said, from high up on a crane.

"Okay. Now, dear—you're in a highly emotional state, you want to tell this business-obsessed husband of yours that you're extremely unhappy, to try and get his attention so that if there's a chance, you can straighten things out before it's too late. You've put on your best clothes to look smart, hoping he'll remember that you're as attractive as all the women he meets in business. . . . All right?"

Lily nodded. For a moment, as the young man with the clappers ran in front of her and shouted, "SST5—Take one!" and there was that sharp "clack" she had heard so many times while watching George, she thought she would simply sink to the ground in a faint. Her heartbeat was so hard that it seemed to take over her body.

She wanted to speak, but no words would come, none at all.

"That's all right, dear—just relax. We're all friends here. We love you. We're all pulling for you—you're going to be just great . . ."

They started all over again, but all she did this time was to say, "Ronny . . . There's something . . ." Then her throat went too dry for more.

"Give her a glass of water," Sy Gregory called out.

"You're fine," said a man in shirt sleeves, handing her the glass. "Everyone's nervous to begin with." He grinned at her, and Lily smelled his sweat like a reminder of real life. "Thanks," she said and, smiling, felt the ice break a little.

She resumed her position and nodded, and once again the young man with the clappers jumped in front of the scene.

This time, she went all the way through without a mistake. Her relief made her giddy, she kept smiling, saying "Phew . . . !"

"Great, Lily—terrific, dear. Now—someone take some stills, and we're all through."

"Is that it?" asked Lily, feeling bolder, more talkative.

"That's all, darling. We'll be getting in touch with you."

"Will Saul . . . ?"

"Sure, dear, sure. Saul sees everything. We'll all be in the projection room like one big happy family." Sy Gregory patted her, hugged her, handed her over to the makeup girl, who in turn handed her over to Netty, who had come along to be of help.

Within another hour, Lily was home. For the rest of the day, she was at a complete loss—the letdown, the waiting was more than she could withstand, and from what she had read, they could keep you waiting days, even weeks for word . . .

But at five o'clock Benson came in to say that MKR was calling, "a Mr. Saul Neuberger, milady."

She ran, almost tripping in her abandoned haste . . .

"Yes . . . ?" she said, and closed her eyes.

"Darling—just like I said. Star quality. You look like a million and you come over just great. Of course, we'll have plenty of work to do—you need to loosen up, to gain savvy . . ."

"Oh . . . ?"

"Don't *worry*. We got acting coaches, speech coaches, singing coaches—you name it. You'll have to come over to the Studios and go over all the things you know how to do already—we'll draw up a contract, work out a plan . . ."

"A contract?"

"Why, sure, honey. Afraid to be committed?"

"Oh, heavens no! I'm just so thrilled—I can hardly believe this is actually happening to me . . ."

"Well, it is. And when that boy of yours comes back, we'll have to celebrate in a big way—we'll have us a shindig that'll make headlines."

Lily laughed. What a new experience to *want* to be in the papers!

"Can you be in my office at ten A.M. tomorrow, Lily?"

So quick, she thought—they must actually be enthusiastic!

"Yes—yes, I certainly can, Saul."

"Take care, girlie. So long."

After she had hung up, Lily wrapped her arms about herself and squeezed them with her fingers till they hurt. Was she dreaming, or was this the happiest moment of her life?

When George called, a few days later, Lily could hardly wait to tell him her news, but he was in such a hurry that she did not have a chance. "Dear," he said, "I'll be back tonight. I want to be with you alone—can you arrange it? Let me cook you something at La Habra?"

"There's a party of us going to the marathon dancing—you'd like that . . ."

"This is important to me, sweetheart—do you mind?"

"Of course not." Lily felt a melting sensation, a kind of release, as if her years of uncertainty and waiting were about to end.

"Goodo, dear. Get Thomas to bring you over at eight o'clock —I'll have showered by then. Goodbye for now, dear."

Lily dressed simply that evening, the way George liked her to, with just a minimum of jewelry, a white bandeau holding back her hair, the casual, pajama-style trousers and square-shouldered "pea jacket," which she herself had designed for just such an occasion, and a long, pure-white polo coat (in case it got cold) that had a masculine severity.

He whistled when he saw her, and blinked exaggeratedly. "You dazzle me, Lily," he said, and took her in his arms with unusual fervor. "I must be the luckiest man in this state!"

She returned his kiss, surprised at its passion. "My . . . !" she breathed. But he relinquished her quickly, to get on with his chores. "I thought we'd cook steaks outside, have avocado salad, corn on the cob . . ."

"Hey," she said, following him to the simple kitchen, which never seemed worthy of him in its dated, even shabby equipment, "not too much of anything—I've got to keep thin."

"You!" He laughed, as if she had told a very funny joke. "Champagne?" he said, his tall figure in frayed white ducks and shirt stooping to a cabinet of bottles.

"Oh, yes—always." She felt rising excitement.

"Have a look at the fire, will you, pet?"

Lily spread her hands. "What should I look for?"

"See if it's getting a glow . . ."

"Oh."

George smiled indulgently. "You'll learn," he said mysteriously.

But it was not until they were settled in deck chairs with their champagne, watching the huge sun begin to dip behind the lemon trees, that George spoke what was so obviously on his mind.

"Dear," he said, his expression boyish and tender, "Pogo's been with me on this tour, and we had a chance for some long talks, the way we used to . . ."

"Before me." Lily smiled.

"Before you. Up to then, I left it pretty much to him to fend off the fair sex—God knows, it wasn't easy. The image I've created seems what every woman wants—*badly*." He shook his head.

"What did Pogo do?" Lily had never heard about this, and her curiosity was acute.

"Coped." George shrugged. "He can be quite formidable, you know—that white face and supercilious expression . . ." George chuckled. "I tell him he looks exactly like a camel with black hair going bald . . ."

Lily giggled softly. "That's right—exactly!"

"Anyway—Pogo knew you were different. None of your Hollywood tinsel. A lady. A beautiful, glamorous girl, but dignified, sweet, sincere, not looking for publicity, for a show. . . . Oh, yes, he knew this was the first *real* woman interest in my life."

"And—he approved?"

"Pogo doesn't approve or disapprove. He just . . . Well, I'll put it honestly, dear—I know you'll understand. . . . Pogo has more than affection for me."

Lily met his significant gaze. "I see . . ." A light came into her eyes. "We have that in common."

"Ah . . ." George reached for her hand, lifted it to his cheek. "You do understand." He kept her hand in his, sat up a little. "So now let me come to the point."

Lily's lashes lifted high. She held her glass carefully, in case her grip should loosen.

"Pogo pointed out, and rightly, that I've been a blind, egotistical bastard—that I deserve to lose you. . . . But, worse, that I'm an impostor."

"An impostor, darling—in what way?"

"He said that I'm playing at being a man—that I can't go through with it!"

"But how *cruel!* Did you fire him?"

George shook his head. His expression was the most solemn Lily had seen. "You don't fire Pogo. He just is, or isn't—if you know what I mean."

Lily looked as befuddled as she felt.

George's solemnity lifted. "Well, never mind all that—I only wanted to explain that I've suddenly recognized what's been going on, and I want to make up for it—quickly. I want you to marry me, dear. Tomorrow, if possible. Before I start on *The True, True Story* for Saul . . ." He pressed her hand so tightly that Lily almost winced.

"George! Tomorrow! Oh, I'd love to, but it's so . . . I mean, I thought we'd have such a . . ."

"No, dear, no—that's just what I don't want—one of those ghastly affairs like an MKR crowd scene, cameramen tripping over the guests. No—only a justice of the peace, and a couple of witnesses, here in Los Angeles. After the picture, we can sneak off somewhere for a honeymoon, somewhere no one will know or recognize us."

Lily put down her glass and sat back. "Oh, dear," she murmured.

"What is it, sweetheart—Aunt Mirry? Perhaps we *could* wait an extra few days, if she wanted to fly out and be with us . . ."

Lily could not answer, somehow could hardly bring herself to tell him.

George released her hand a moment to refill their glasses and cast a glance at the fire, the glow of which was beginning to deepen in the dimming light. "I know," he said, "I know. It's not your way, you can't think in these terms. . . . You'd like to have the full splash, wouldn't you, the creative exorbitance!"

Lily pressed her lips a moment. Suddenly she leaned towards him, her gaze pleading. "It's not that at all, George, nothing to do with it—you see, I had something to tell you, too . . ."

"Oh, yes?" A frown made two short furrows in his wide, smooth brow, a well-known expression to his fans.

"George—while you were gone I made a test . . ."

"A test?"

"A film test, darling. For Saul. You see, I sat next to him at dinner and *he* suggested it. And so I did it—and it went all right, and they've given me a contract to build me up, train me, maybe someday to be a really good actress!"

George sat very still. To Lily it did not seem possible that anyone so tanned could look white. Her heart lurched with some unnamable fear. "You're not pleased . . ." She pressed her hand slowly to her mouth.

"Pleased?" George's eyes seemed to have lost their depth, their warmth. "I'm shocked, Lily. Shocked, and disappointed."

"But why, darling—does it make such a difference? I thought it would bring us closer together. It won't make any change in getting married—I don't start my first part until next month . . ."

"They've actually given you a part?" The warmth had gone from his voice as well.

"Yes, darling . . . And the publicity campaign has already started. They take my picture doing all kinds of things, you know—for the movie mags and papers . . ."

"And you'd lend yourself to all that, get into this cheap Hollywood racket, allow them to exploit you, your name!"

"Oh, George, you've got it all wrong. They aren't going to exploit me—and they're actually going to change my name, so that I won't be associated with my . . ."

"Oh, my God—Lily." George drew in a hard breath. "I've always known you were naïve, by force of circumstance—and it was endearing—at least to me. But this!" He folded his bare, tanned arms. "How much did they get out of you."

Lily felt heat wave up through her face as if the sun had suddenly returned full force. "I don't see what that has to do with it . . ."

George sat up, bounced his right fist against his left palm. "I knew it. The bastard. He got this brain wave looking at you, not only your name for surefire publicity value, but your cash!"

"But Coggy looked into it, George! Coggy said once these strikes and monopoly trials were over and the industry got back some of its European markets, there'd be a big boom, and that it was a sound investment idea for Boeker money . . ."

George sank back, clasped his head in his hands.

"And my test *was* all right, darling," Lily said. "Even Sy Gregory said so. Everyone seemed pleased . . ."

"I bet they did. Licking their chops!"

"Oh, George, that isn't fair!"

George raised his head slowly to look into her earnest face, her protesting gaze. "Lily, I don't like to say this—but you, dear, have been *had*. Even if there was film in the camera, which it's quite possible there wasn't, they'd have still told you 'fine, fine, fine, full of potential'—don't you see, even if you were so lousy they groaned in the projection room . . . !"

"George, that's not like you—to be so . . . well, spiteful. As if you *want* me to have done badly!"

"Nonsense, dear. I just want you to face the truth. If you don't believe me that it's a put-up job, I'll call someone I know who would tell me straight. Do you want me to, right now? You can listen in."

Lily's chin rose. "Why can't you believe that I might at least have a chance, that it's at least possible I could do something well? For instance, Saul says I'll have to work hard, but that I photograph well, and that when I've had plenty of coaching . . . !" Lily felt her voice rise, the hysteria of not believing her own words vying with the need to convince him.

"Of course you'd photograph well—you're a beautiful girl, dear, with a foolproof face. But for one thing, there's your voice —much as *I* like its softness, it's just so upper-class-rich-and-*refeened* no coach on earth could do anything with it!"

Lily looked at him in total dismay, fell into stunned silence.

"I'm sorry," he said, "but, dear—I do *know* this business. My advice to you, for your own sake, is to cut out quick, before you become a laughingstock, the butt of every joke ever invented about the rich—to say nothing of the anger of the profession. If there's one thing sacred in the arts, Lily, it's that you *can't* buy yourself into it, you have to earn it, one way or the other."

Lily stared at her hands, not knowing what to say, to do, to feel. To fight him further seemed only to increase her own doubt. "I've got a *contract*, George," she said finally, lamely.

George nodded vigorously. "I don't doubt it! They've got to give you *something* to show for the money. And mark my words

—it'll test Coggy's wits to the limit to get you out of it. You won't get away before that check is cleared—and spent!"

George poured the last of the champagne, downed his in one distracted gulp. "I'll be honest with you, dear girl," he said, as if getting the words out before they could retreat, "it's up to you, of course—but if you go on with this, it would change everything." Almost shuddering, he got up quickly to poke at the fire, to fork one of the steaks and place it over the coals.

Lily stared at the familiar, appealing profile silhouetted against the evening light, at the broad yet lean back, suddenly no one she knew, remote. "You don't really love me at all," she found herself saying quietly. "You never have . . ."

His shoulders shifted uneasily. "Things aren't black and white, dear," he said, "you must know that. But at least one thing's sure —your money didn't come into it."

"No . . ." She touched her engagement ring absently, thinking it was the only one given to her that she had not eventually paid for herself. She watched the flame seize the meat, the sparks fly upward as if to join the pale stars. There was the sound of night insects, of birds finally settling . . .

"I'm not hungry, George," she said suddenly. "I really couldn't eat—anything. I'd just like to go home . . ."

George turned quickly. "But you'll have to . . . I mean, it's early—we should talk . . ."

Lily shook her head, picked up her cigarette holder, scarf and compact, slipped her arms into the white coat that had been lying on the back of the chair. Strangely, she felt no threat of tears. It was as if this scene had already happened a long, long time ago.

"It seems such a waste . . ." George cast a regretful glance at the steaks, sizzling now, sending out a charred, appetizing aroma.

"Perhaps you could call Pogo," Lily said softly, without malice.

He stood stock-still, his gaze riveted to hers.

"Goodbye, George," she said. She put out her hand.

Involuntarily, he took it in a formal clasp.

Throwing her scarf lightly over the top of her head, before he could say more, Lily moved quickly off to the shadowed drive.

Chapter 16

"You must believe me," Lily said, as she received the newsmen in the S.S. *Normandie*. "We're still extremely fond of one another—but our interests were too far apart for marriage—and, well, you know, life moves on."

Lily could see out of the corner of her eye that she had given them their headline.

She spread her hands, practically pleading with the shrewd, watchful group, some of whom she had never seen before. "I'm taking my child to see her father—that's all. She hasn't seen him since she was a baby. He was taken prisoner, and has had a *terrible* time. Yes, Deedee is seven now—looks like an Aylsden, doesn't she?"

Lily pushed at the big gathered sleeves of her ankle-length mink, and looked for Maudie. Maudie stood at the back of the crowd like a small gray-black statue. "The Countess thanks you," she said automatically. "Thank you, ladies and gentlemen."

"Thank goodness we're going back to civilization!" said Maudie
as she closed the door.

"Why, Maudie!" said Lily. She and Whitey exchanged an
amused glance.

Still, thought Lily, Maudie could be right. She herself was dis-
enchanted with America. Now that the war was over, whatever
it was that seemed noble and worthwhile in the American character seemed already to have vanished. There were massive
strikes for higher wages "to make up for the loss in take-home
pay caused by the return of peace," and President Truman's ter-
mination of the Lend-Lease, which seemed so harsh to other na-
tions, particularly Britain, was hailed as showing that the United
States would no longer be played for "suckers" by the rest of the
world.

On the other hand, she wished that it hadn't been necessary to
go back to Europe just yet. . . . But—the fast trip to Palm Beach
and the round of parties and activities at Aunt Mirry's had only
made her lonelier. The endlessly trivial chatter of house guests,
even old friends, like Baroness de Brekvoort (looking stiff-faced
and surprised from an experimental face lift that had gone
wrong), Prince Oge, Nina Glendower and many others, increased her feeling of emptiness and despair. Although Mirry's
advice to buy a house near her, and decorate it to occupy her
mind, might have been the answer, the incentive was lacking;
her heart was still with the cliffside house she had left behind.

And now there was the guilt for holding on to Whitey, exploit-
ing her old loyalty; Whitey did not *want* to go to Europe again.
Whitey wanted to go home, she wanted to be free to start a life
on her own. "I feel secondhand all the way down in my bones,"
she had pleaded. "I don't *want* your clothes, Boke. I don't *want*
your gifts. I'm losing my perspective, my sense of proportion. Let
me go, before it's too late!"

"Give me another six months," Lily had said. "Just this
difficult time with Deedee. I'll try to find someone in London to
take over your duties. I really will."

Meeting the familiar blue eyes, Whitey had shown the conflict
of gratitude and fondness, and growing frustration. She had
sighed, smiled grimly. "Okay, Boke—another six months."

Lily's relief was laced with new resolve: she would double

Whitey's salary, give her more cash to spend, more free time—and she would bring her more into her social life so that she could meet someone who could take care of her in the way she had become accustomed to—Whitey had admitted herself that her home had looked unbelievably tiny and shabby, the townspeople had seemed narrow-minded, smugly ignorant of the rest of the world and she would go stir-crazy living there again.

Another regret nagged at her, too, as she prepared to sail away from him again—Joel. He had sounded kind, if hurried, on the telephone. "No," he had said, "I'm not married, had to put it off for various reasons." He hadn't been able to see her, but she couldn't help feeling that his feelings for her were still alive, that if she could have lingered in New York longer, been patient, kept control of herself, they would eventually have got together again. She could only hope that when she got back, his marriage would still be "in abeyance." If it was, it would be proof that *she* was the cause.

There remained the question of Maudie. "I shall soon be sixty, Miss Lily—you said you would let me go when we got back to London. I'd like very much to retire as soon as possible."

Lily, aware only of the absence of her "dear," had placed a cigarette in her jade holder, lit it calmly and murmured that she would "go into it." She had recurrent nightmares ever since that Maudie was no longer with her.

To top off the uneasy journey, they hit stormy weather and Lily was so seasick that she could not so much as glance at the seesawing gray horizon without gushing nausea, and finally took to bed until they arrived in Southampton.

Now, the reporters asked if she had known of Tony's long imprisonment in the Stalag camp in Germany, and she told them yes, the Dowager Countess had kept her informed.

They asked her about the life in Hollywood. Were the big studios fascinating to her? What had it been like mingling with all the big stars and directors, being with such a popular actor, and wouldn't she miss all that glamour here in battle-scarred England?

Those were subjects for another time, she told them, and promised interviews. "Now, please, my little girl is getting impatient."

They took pictures of Deedee, whose dark-blue expressionless eyes watched from under the blue straw hat with elastic chin-band, blond, blue-bowed braids jutting from each side of her fair squarish face. "When do I see my grandmother and father?" she said to Mrs. Fiske.

"Wave, darling," Lily said. "Smile."

"Soon, my lamb," said Mrs. Fiske, setting straight the shoulders of the child's blue reefer.

Lily kept smiling. At last the assorted men and women filed away. With her entourage of Maudie, Thomas, Netty, Ruby, Mrs. Fiske and Deedee, Gustaf and Whitey, Lily disembarked, waited at the curb for the black Rolls and Daimler to be brought up.

"They've been kept okay, Lil," said Thomas, moving out to take charge.

Lily was grateful for the way he had rationalized his continued service by designating himself her general manager, and for the way Netty had taken over as head housekeeper; it reduced some of the apprehension of returning here.

"Raining as usual," said Whitey.

"How dismal it all looks—you think you can imagine what it must have been like, but you can't. . . . Poor little England."

Maudie cast her a quick glance of restrained accusation.

"Duck, Lily," Whitey whispered urgently. "That sweat-bee Russian prince!"

Lily dipped her black velvet brim, raised her mink collar, and before Thomas could assist, plunged into the Rolls. "Thanks," she breathed as Whitey moved in beside her.

"Holy smoke—*now* it's that car salesman, Victor Cammrose!"

Lily dipped her brim again as a large man in a navy pin-striped suit ran up to the Rolls, thick dark hair falling over one green eye, grinning, panting. "Ah, just caught you!" Victor Cammrose peered through the rolled-down window, his old school tie dangling inward. "You didn't tell me where I could reach you, Countess Aylsden."

Lily could not help smiling. She raised her head and looked at him. He had been unshakable since arrival. He had an introduction from Ian Flexner, whom he had known in the war. He'd like very much to interest her in a Bentley. Probably yet another cadger, but his appeal was difficult to deny. "The Ritz," she said, "for a few days."

"Ah." His big, craggy face cleared. "Be in touch." He raised a forefinger, stood back, patted the pocket from which protruded a pipe bowl.

"He'll never let go till you've bought something, Boke!"

"Never mind. It must be hard going after four years in the trenches—that's what he said, isn't it?"

"The navy."

Lily shrugged. Looking anxiously to Thomas, she signaled that she wanted Deedee in with her, but the little girl was already climbing in beside him. Thomas spread his hands.

"Her wish is his command," said Whitey.

Lily sat back again, the gloom of the countryside as they drove to London permeating her like a chill. But when the Ritz loomed into view unchanged, she felt something of her old enchantment. How welcoming the recognition of the staff! A bundle of letters and messages waited, and this time she had been given the corner suite that looked out on both Piccadilly and Green Park.

Whitey took charge of the mail, and as she did so, Lily suddenly saw her in the context of time-passed. The intervening years had only made her jaw firmer, set the lines of her grin, mapped her frownless disposition. With her hair still worn in the same girlish bangs, her casual indifference to chic, she was immutably herself; always would be, even with gray hair and, eventually, wrinkles, she thought. Dear old Whitey . . .

"You're looking *very* well, milady," Nikolus said, accompanying her to the door of her suite.

Lily thanked him, but was not convinced; servants were kinder than mirrors. She knew very well that she had changed, that a certain radiance had gone from her face (if not her eyes, thank goodness), that maturity was altering it in subtle yet definite ways, for better or worse she was not sure—in fact, she had lost any valid focus of herself, physically or mentally.

"Boke—this will interest you." Whitey came in, already settled to her duties.

"Yes?" Lily allowed the maids to take her mink, her hat, shook out the curls of her long bob.

"Sonny Somerville wants you to call him the moment you get here—he's playing a match at Wimbledon!"

Sonny had lost quickly, decisively, totally unexpectedly, and it was a toss-up whether his serve or his timing had been worse. After the cup had been presented to the winner, an obvious air of anticlimax hung over the huge, slowly rising crowds, as if they had been cheated of what they came for.

Saying goodbye to the Royal party, Lily got into the Bentley Sedanca Coupe Vic had persuaded her to buy, and Thomas drove her home. She did not chat with him, but sat back, sunk in foreboding. She was to join Sonny tonight at the players' traditional ball at the Grosvenor Hotel . . .

Oh, God—if only she could get out of it, plead one of her migraine glooms! But it would only make matters worse—a confrontation was inevitable. She had looked down on him for trying to pay his own way, had been impatient with his fumbling over too large accounts, had been bored by confinement to *his* financial limits. And in her heart she knew that she *had* been unable to respect him because he would not let her pay, that she *had* undermined the very core of his self-esteem, his self-confidence by overruling him . . .

She pressed a perfumed Egyptian cigarette into her diamond-initialed ivory holder—Bonky's present on her thirty-fifth birthday—and lit it with the small enamel lighter Sonny had given her for the same occasion. Never in her life, she thought, had she so well understood the need for a drink! Thank heavens the house was moderately full this week, that Reggie Blount was there to fence with in her own terms . . .

But it was so obviously time to move on. There was something ghostly about the place without Tony's irreverent presence, something defunct that could not be revived. The same applied to her life here; despite the steady flow of invitations to lunches, dinners, balls, parties of all kinds, she felt what George would call "miscast" in London, in England altogether. She was always conscious of the ridicule that simmered just below the surface of press reports and interviews, particularly the ones that "told it straight," leaving the readers to form their own image of her, which was, of course, subliminally conveyed by the clever wording.

Well, the moment Deedee came back this time, she would go to the French Riviera, where she had been headed before.

Lily stirred in her leather seat, frowned. How strange to feel almost afraid of one's own child. The older Deedee became, the more remote and self-possessed she seemed. There was not only an absence of love in her level glance, but even affection.

Lily's lips pressed, remembering how the little girl, trim and erect in her beautifully fitting riding clothes, had stood rigidly to her kiss, keeping her cheek averted and quickly drawing away from her embrace. "I want to stay here, Mother," she had said. "I can't leave my horse."

Tony, a soberer, heavier man these days, with deep lines across his forehead and a smile made grim by indescribable experience, cast a quick look at his mother.

"She's very happy with us, Lily," Mavis had said, with heavy emphasis. (She looked no older, Lily had thought, and surely it was the same tweed suit she was wearing!)

"I'm glad of that," Lily had answered. "But it's long past time for her return—naturally, I want her with me."

"But I don't want to be with you, Mother," Deedee had said quickly, and walking to her horse had leaned her forehead against the chestnut's smooth, glinting nose. The horse had nuzzled her, and Lily's emotions were torn down the middle with understanding on one side, hurt and disappointment on the other.

"I'll see that you have a horse, darling," she had said. "We'll buy a house in the country and have stables . . ."

"I only want Rob Roy. And I want to be with my father and Gran."

"Your father isn't here that often, dear," Lily had started to say.

"The thing is, Lily—I'm getting married," Tony said. "We're going to live here and try to raise an heir or two." There was a ghost of his old twinkle.

"I see."

"Fiona's my friend," said Deedee. "We go hunting!"

"Fiona!" Lily could not help the involuntary exclamation.

"Sorry," said Tony. "What can you do with a determined woman?" He raised an eyebrow, tried one of his old smiles.

Lily took a breath. "Well, I hope you'll be very happy. But I'm not giving up my child."

"Of course not, dear," the Dowager Countess put in. "We would never ask *that.*"

"Just let her finish out the summer, eh?" Tony said, moving over to pat the flank of the horse. "We'll straighten things out by then." He had winked at Deedee, who winked back.

Lily had given in. They had followed her to the Rolls—a small, closed corporation waving her goodbye—all Lily could think of was that Deedee had not even smiled at her.

Sonny had been consolation for a while, although not so much as Vic . . .

Dear Vic, so patient and understanding, so wonderfully solid and reliable. Sometimes she wished she could sleep with him, make him happy—he'd be so grateful, so faithful and loyal! Perhaps, despite the fact that he was essentially a drifter and sponger, *he* was the right man for her, the one that would fit most logically with her ways, her life . . .

The ball was as she had expected—much jubilation (for the winner, of course!) and what George Robey the comedian would have called "badinage." Sonny, in an ill-fitting dinner jacket, trousers made slightly too short by muscular calves, was alternately morose and gay. "Come on, baby, let's show 'em I'm not licked!"

Off they'd dance into the huge throng of tennis enthusiasts looking variously better, worse or strange in their formal attire—and their wives, sisters, girl friends. After a few minutes of vigorous dancing that fell a long way short of his tennis skill, of singing into her ear, "So in love, so in love, so in love with you am I," to the big thumping orchestra that drowned out the melody, he would suddenly grasp her hand and waist in a vise and say, "Oh, God, I've made a shambles of it, baby, a shambles!"

Lily tried not to think of her clamped-up gown, their faltering steps, the eyes that were on them, to keep smiling, reassuring and saying over and over again that he had done no such thing, that someone had to lose, it was just bad luck and he should know better than to take it badly . . .

"It's you I'm thinking of—I've let you down."

"Don't be silly—I'm not let down, I'm proud of you."

After a while, she had suggested they go home, but he wanted to hear the speeches. His face got ruddier, his brown eyes redder, his red hair damper, his grip heavier. Where, oh where, thought Lily, was the high-spirited young man with whom she had joked and played in Hollywood, felt so blithely young, such secret attraction!

"Let's sit," she said suddenly, disentangling herself from his lurching hold and making for the big table of people of importance to tennis. Oh, how she yearned to leave—but she could not quite bring herself to abandon him.

At long last, the laborious evening was over and Thomas had deposited them in Grosvenor Square. Lights were on throughout the house, and Lily was almost relieved to see that Reggie Blount was making use of it to entertain a large gathering of his international friends. To his delight, she joined them for an hour or so, their gossip a relief from Sonny's soggy emotions.

Although Reggie had aged, grown so corpulent that he could barely see over his great stomach and had several new chins, Lily found his American wit, his comments on President Truman, the Marshall aid plan, and other news from home, stimulating.

"By the way," he said when she was on her way upstairs, "you've had a great champion back home in George Ware—he took all the blame . . ."

"There was none." She smiled. "Good night, Reggie. Have anything you want—don't forget the gaming room, the pool, enjoy yourself." Lily went the rounds of several formally dressed people in the room, saying a few words, nodding good night.

In the big dim room, she lay in the same enormous bed she had so often been forced to share with Tony, waited in rigid anticipation for the furtive knock. "Yes," she called when it came, and saw Sonny's stocky figure move towards her in uneven steps. Oh, God, she thought, he's still drunk—it would be that much worse.

And she was right. After frantic wet kisses all over her body that somehow missed her every point of response, he lay beside her in muttering torpor. "Christ, I love you, baby, oh Christ, how much I love you . . . If only you knew, if only I could get it through to you!"

"You do, Sonny, you do! I believe you, honestly." She wound her arms about him, cradled his head, feeling his tears against her bare breasts. "Don't worry so, take it easy. You'll win *next* year!"

"Sure—but what good would it do me? You don't respect me. You never will. You *can't*."

"Oh, come on." Lily stifled the intense boredom that was creeping through her like a slow poison.

"It's the truth, baby. And to think that way back then I used to be sorry for you! I thought you were a good kid, unspoiled, lonely, wanting real fun and life—and, what a laugh, that *I* could help you, give it to you."

"Sonny—it's no use going back . . ."

He sat up suddenly, leaned on an elbow looking at her. In the faint light from tiny rose lamps at the far end of the room, his eyes glowed speculatively. "All the things that are said about the very rich—they're so goddamned true. You're just not like ordinary people. You *feel* superior, like some kind of special breed. And everyone around you with less money has to feel put down, strange, uneasy. It gets to everyone no matter how hard they try to insulate themselves. Even rich people with less than you try to match up, dropping names, showing off who they know and where they've been and how much they own—if they're naturally modest, they strain, go out of character . . ."

"Sonny—that may be true but it isn't fair to . . ."

"Of course, *you* can't see it!" There was triumph in his expression. "That's the whole point. You're on the top of the pyramid!"

Lily lay back, a flat sense of depression silencing her.

"You'll *never* see it!" Warming to his point, Sonny reached quickly for a cigarette, lit it and, after a deep drag, continued: "Take the way you feel about me. Look how crazy it is! Because I won't let you play God with your presents and goodies, you're forced to contend with a lower standard, my standard—which, by the way, my friend, is damned high, relatively speaking!"

He sighed. "But you wouldn't know about that, either. But it's put you off me, as if I had lowered myself in some way, as if *I* were less by *having* less!"

He paused, gripped her shoulder, shook her slightly. "I could kill you. It's crept into me like a disease. I *feel* inferior now. I'll never be the same—even if I never see you again, you've totally *demoralized* me . . . you've destroyed me."

"Oh, Sonny, please—that's too much . . . I don't understand myself at all—I wish I knew the answer."

Sonny was silent. Lily saw the glow of his cigarette dwindle as he smoked, finally diminish. "Oh, fuck," he said, stabbing it out in an ashtray by the bed. "Forget it, skip it. Go to sleep, my gilded Lily." He patted her, stroked her hair, pulled the covers up to her chin, rolled over to the far side of the bed.

Lily lay for a long time, staring into the dim heights of the room, where her imagination played out old scenes with Joel, with Aunt Mirry and Coggy—her father's face with the sightless eyes turned to hers in a last message, Maudie in her starched white uniform, young, then, saying, "You must develop your own good values, Miss Lily, stick to them—it's not what you look like or own that counts, it's what you think and feel inside that make people love you" . . .

. . . There must be a self somewhere in all of it, a self of some shape she could recognize, see as a person, act in accordance with . . . Not just this blurred, unreachable image, this shifting confusion of values, thoughts, feelings . . .

. . . She must have fallen off to sleep. She was aware of Sonny getting back into bed, twisting, turning, groaning . . .

"Ssh," she murmured. "It's all right, everything's all right, dear. You'll get over all this . . ."

She awakened suddenly, abruptly, her senses somehow alerted —yet there was no sound in the house, in the room. A faint haze of light surrounded and brightened the thick white draperies. She glanced at the little gold clock on the night table—only five.

Turning, she looked at Sonny . . . How strange he seemed. Frowning, she bent closer, stared down at his face . . .

It had a strange, set look, the eyes wide, the mouth open. His arms were flung wide and his naked body seemed profoundly still.

"Sonny?" She shook him slightly, watched his chest for movement. There was none, and his body felt cold, stiff . . .

She drew away, swamping fear nearly stopping her heart-beat . . .

"Oh, my God," she said. "Oh, my God!"

She got up, put on her floral nightgown and robe and went quickly out into the quiet hall—then in the only direction her mind would take her.

"There's only one thing to do," Reggie Blount said, struggling into his brocade dressing gown. "Get him back into his own bed."

"Her mourning attire was starkly simple (we wonder who de-signed it), and never has Lily Boeker de Santi Aylsden looked more ethereally beautiful! Lifting her heavy veil to dab at occa-sional tears, the delicately boned face with those immense, aqua-marine eyes had the iridescence of a stained-glass saint's. Her statement that she and the runner-up at Wimbledon were only 'close friends' was belied by her obvious grief. We have it on pretty good authority that he hoped to marry her in the near fu-ture; certainly they have been inseparable these last months, the ex-countess never missing one of Somerville's matches. Reggie Blount, whose gossip column 'To Put it Bluntly' is the most widely read in the United States, has intimated that Sonny was intensely jealous of another man in Lily's life, and that he had been depressed before the match that lost him the cup everyone expected him to win. This combination, Blount comments, un-doubtedly led to the taking of his life by an overdose of sleeping tablets in Lily's house in Grosvenor Square (where he had been a house guest for some time) after the celebration ball."

Whitey finished reading. Gathering up the sheafs of cuttings she had made, she placed them in one of the huge tapestry scrapbooks. "I'll enter these, Boke, unless you'd rather I didn't."

Lily moved her head against the big satin and ecru-lace pil-low. "What's it matter? Might as well keep the gory tale intact."

"Okay—can Reggie come in now?"

Lily sighed, nodded, reached for her holder and a cigarette.

"You're looking much better, dear," said Reggie as he crossed the big room to her bed, looking freshly shaved and elegant in morning coat and striped trousers, a flower in his lapel. "I'm off to the Matthews-Bailey wedding at St. Margaret's."

"Mmm . . . I think I was invited to that."

"You were. But no one will expect you. Now, Lily, I've got some strong advice to offer—backed up, I must add, by your aunt. We feel you should leave for the Continent, possibly Paris, at once. Andy's there, Penny Hammar, the Duke of Moorsham and several other of your friends—and she herself will be over for the collections—apparently the new 'New Look' interests her, particularly *Dior*."

"Will she? How wonderful! Oh, I want to see her so badly!"

"Then go." Reggie nodded with satisfaction.

Her eyes brightened a little. "I'll take Vic . . ."

"Take who you like—but get away from this cloud. Give it time to blow over. Send for your yacht, bring it over to Nice and do a Mediterranean cruise—Mirry's been complaining about it being lying idle. It wouldn't take long to spruce it and the crew up—Mirry would see to that. And—if you'll invite me, I might accept to join you in Cannes, where I'll be with my friends the Count and Countess de Rocquambert. I think things will be sparking up again this year—everyone's tired of grimness and austerity."

Lily leaned into her pillow, put her arms behind her head. Her eyes were soft now, shining with daydreams.

"Settled then?" asked Reggie, looking at his watch.

"I might buy a house in Paris . . ."

"Good idea."

"Or Cannes—everyone says it's so beautiful, so gay . . ."

"Do both. Well, dear—I must leave you. Oh, and if I were you, I wouldn't say anything to the press. Just fold your tents and quietly slip away."

Lily broke into a grin. "That'll be the day! But we can try."

"Oh—one more thing," Reggie said at the door. "I wouldn't disrupt Lady Deedee. You can always send someone to bring her to you later—or slip back, if she misses you."

"Yes . . ." Lily decided not to make the obvious comment.

When Reggie had gone, she rang the bell for the maid. "Please ask Mr. Cammrose to come in, if he's here."

"I believe he is, madam."

Vic was there in a few moments, with his pleased, eager, at-your-service smile. "You wanted to see me?"

"Yes, Vic—come and sit down. Do you want coffee, tea, a drink, champagne?"

"Nothing, Lily, just to look at you."

She smiled. He seemed so big sitting in the little lime satin boudoir chair, like an enormous, tousled teddy bear in a suit. She particularly liked the way his eyebrows descended on their outward arcs, giving him a permanently anticipatory, somehow tender expression—and the greenness of his eyes was a note of interest, saved him from a rather homespun masculinity.

"How would you like to come to Paris with me?" she said.

"Why—I'd love it, Lily, of course! Do you mean it?"

"Reggie thinks I should vamoose, take a powder."

He laughed. "I agree." He clapped his big, rough-nailed hands together, looked at her expectantly.

"You must have some clothes, Vic, some decent shirts—a few things . . ."

"Yes? I certainly need them! Haven't had a new suit since before the war, to be honest."

"I know. Darling, speak to Whitey, tell her I said you should have a thousand pounds for your pocket. That way you can take care of tips and so on."

Vic's seamy face was a map of pleasure. "Would you mind if I gave my old mum fifty quid of it?" he asked. "She's having a rough go and I haven't been in a position to—"

"You never mentioned that, Vic." Lily felt the beginning of her old "feathery feeling." "What's wrong with her?"

"Well, she's on her own, for a start. Old house, damp, cold. Arthritis. That sort of thing."

"She ought to have the house seen to, or move."

"Of course—if I had the necessary."

"What's that?"

"In round figures?"

Lily shifted impatiently.

"Five thou—six?"

"That's about twenty-five thousand dollars! That's enough for a house?"

"Yes, Lily—her kind of house. Plenty!"

"Well, she must have it. You can't enjoy yourself in France, with her suffering—nor could I."

"I admit it wouldn't be easy. I'm fond of the old girl."

"I'll give you the money, Vic—get the house, but at once, and someone to look after her, live with her. I'd like to leave within the week."

Vic was open-mouthed, silenced. "How can I thank you?" he said finally.

Lily sat up, pushed back her shoulder-length hair, unaware that her lace bed jacket fell away to expose her round white breasts almost to the nipples.

His eyes half closed. "Whatever you want of me, darling Lily," he said.

She put out her hand; he took it, holding it as if it were a white jeweled bird in his big hands.

"We'll have a lovely time," she said. "Now—if you don't mind, I want to get up and dressed—I've got a million things to do."

"He's so sweet," she murmured to herself when he had gone. What exquisite relief after Sonny—and surely she couldn't feel guilty about his suicide *forever*. "What's done's done," Reggie had said. She couldn't bring him back, and she couldn't have changed herself. It had to be forgotten.

After an exodus by night ferry, Paris, despite a lingering grimness, was exciting, somehow as new to Lily as if she had never seen it before. She decided to rent Oge's great house on the Ile St. Louis, which he seldom used but kept staffed, and which had thirty-six magnificently furnished rooms, thereby freeing her for enjoying the city with Vic.

As they ran the gamut of opera, theater, races, receptions, dinner parties, fabulous restaurants, all manner of nightclubs down to the very shadiest, Lily found Vic a perfect companion. He was always good-humored, amenable, keenly interested, and Lily felt at peace with him. That he was, perhaps, a blotter, soaking up as much as she would give him, was irrelevant. She loved buying him everything he wanted or admired. He seldom protested, but when he did, such as with the exquisite ruby cuff links, she told him gaily that Grandpa Boeker would be only too pleased—why else had he given her his money than to enjoy it, to spread it around! What else, anyhow, was money for! You couldn't take it with you, and none of us knew just how long we'd be in circulation.

"Wear it with joy," she would say, flipping her checks like a deck of cards. "Use it in good health." Smiling, she used the accent of her Germanic ancestor.

Victor Cammrose became the epitome of the well-dressed man-about-town; any trace of his old "heartiness" was submerged in elegance, the opulence of his appearance. Lily gave him a Fiat sports coupe he happened to pause beside in a showroom, a small bookshelf of first editions which he had eyed with longing (a good education lay buried in his prewar years), a famous black-pearl tiepin, a collection of unique pipes (his favorite gift).

They settled into a quietly contented routine, strolled in the Bois, the Tuileries gardens, along the Seine (left the Rolls to follow), waited for the long fresh loaves of bread to come in at dawn near Sacré Coeur on the hill of Montmartre, sipped Pernod and coffee and watched passersby in the sidewalk cafés of Champs Élysées, stood in awe under the Arc de Triomphe by the tomb of the Unknown Soldier, gazed over all of Paris from the top of the Eiffel Tower, imbibed art at the Louvre and, just a short ride from the city, the great palace at Versailles . . .

There were only two snags: Vic could not tango (oh, how Vitti could!) or dance with any imagination—and Vic, try as he might, as a lover, was fervent, but uninspired. He seemed to know what he was doing, but the truth was that Lily had resigned herself to a peculiar mixture of self-arousal and self-induced climax.

"I'll learn," he said, one night, as they twisted, writhed, bounced, pumped in the fifteen-square-foot sable-covered bed (Oge's prize possession). "I promise you."

"It's your timing, my darling," Lily said. "Couldn't you read something—order some books."

Vic, so tender, thoughtful, dear, was not a good student, apparently. Coming eagerly towards her from the gold and black-marble bathroom, his hair-matted body damp from his bath, smelling of a new, exotic perfume they had picked out at Galeries Lafayette, he had gone straight for her clitoris, bitten, sucked as if attacking a meal. She had felt nothing but discomfort, the need to free herself quickly before destruction.

"It's not quite right," she said, and regretted it at once—for his penis descended like a shot bird and shriveled to nothing between his legs.

She tried to help him, but it was useless. An hour later, aroused as ever by her slim body, with the light, thick pubic hair, the large, pale-pink nipples, which lay naked and patient beside him, Vic tried again. This time she had reverted to her old technique. Having furtively massaged herself, she was prepared, responsive, and when, as usual, he plunged to his climax too soon, she reached her hand in between them and helped herself to join him—luckily, he never knew the difference.

As the days wore on, though, she felt increasingly fond of him, increasingly maternal, increasingly unaroused. Fortunately, at that time, Aunt Mirry arrived. Vic was far too much part of her life now, and too valuable as an escort to risk losing, and when Aunt Mirry met him, she was discreetly approving.

"Is this serious?" she asked.

"I'm not sure," Lily said truthfully.

Vic, the General (how very old and grizzly he looked, his heavy eyebrows like those of an ancient ferret!), Whitey, Penny Hammar, Zincy (Baroness de Brekvoort), Andy and Howie (both paunchier and looser-jowled) went together to the various fashion houses. Aunt Mirry, looking ever more splendid as she aged (reminding Lily of pictures of the younger Queen Mary) was visibly moved by the drastic change in designs, in the lavish use of materials after the stringency of the war years and enthusiastically ordered many outfits modeled by the cadaverous-looking mannequins. Lily felt a new excitement in clothes; she would have to discard almost everything she had, she thought, and start over—but what fun!

With Vic's encouragement, she ordered a suit in fine, ivory-colored wool with a peplum and gored skirt that came to the lower part of the calf, a dinner dress of paper-thin black taffeta with a "fishtail" cascading down the back and a deep, plunging neckline, a day dress in heavy navy-blue silk with long sleeves, "sweetheart" neckline, pushed-up three-quarter sleeves, a deep-red evening gown of velvet-dotted satin with an off-the-shoulders top, and a nice little green broadcloth dress with a high white collar, high waist and one hip-deep pleat up the front. It was all she had use for, and even now Maudie grumbled at so many trunkloads to move about.

Fittings were a bore, but synchronizing appointments with Aunt Mirry was often a way to catch her for private conversation.

"I've never done this," Aunt Mirry sighed as the women in black with pins in their mouths bent earnestly to their task, "and I'll never do it again. The trouble is, Starenze's beginning to creak and I must replace him. How do you think the General looks? He's not well. I don't know if he'll last. Did I tell you I've willed the New York house to the Jonesburgh Museum? I'm delighted to think of the enlightenment my glass and Far Eastern treasures will provide for generations to follow. You really should take your collecting more seriously, dear!"

"I've got some marvelous clocks—I'll go on with those someday, when I'm more settled. And my doll's house—I loved that, hated to leave it. I thought Deedee might like it."

"You'll have to think about her schooling." Aunt Mirry turned her thickening body one way and the other, frowning speculatively, then nodding. "They know what they're doing, at least. This will be a good background for my Marie Antoinette diamonds—I hope you're keeping your jewels cleaned, dear—you mustn't let them get that dusty look."

"Yes . . . She might be tutored at Cambrook, or go to an English boarding school."

"You've given up, my dear. And so you should. It shows remarkable common sense. The child will benefit, and so will you."

"You really think so?"

Aunt Mirry's dark-blue eyes met hers in stern directness. "Why else would I say it?"

"She *is* very happy there—and Tony's become a good father, I think. If they have other children, it will be a good family life . . ."

"Exactly."

Lily smiled at her aunt. How wonderful it was to see her again, to feel this sense of belonging—if Aunt Mirry wasn't a mother, at least she was family!

"I hope you and Vic will come with us to the night race at Longchamps, dear—I've taken a box on the grandstand so we can see the Corps de Ballet and the Imperial Russian Ballet perform —and I believe there'll be nine orchestras playing at different points around the racecourse. You could wear that pearl-encrusted white satin, and that headpiece with the osprey—it's that sort of occasion."

"We'd love to, Aunt Mirry!"

Aunt Mirry allowed the heavily embroidered blue brocade with the heavy panels to be lifted off her. Lily was amazed at her true stoutness, so rigidly corseted in under the peach satin-and-lace slip.

"I've invited Prince and Princess Dompagni Cordovuso—she was Ohio soap money, a dark-haired beauty you might like—and Countess di Frado."

"Fraddie!"

"Of course—you knew her in California. And an American, Dan K. Weble—he's in line as the next ambassador in London, and Mary-Lou his wife, very southern—General Lundeman, friend of Will's, the Marquesa de Anselmos, widow, owns countless homes, charming, exotic, redhead, and Baron Pierre de Clavières, probably the most sought-after man in Europe, or the world for that matter."

"For what?" Lily asked, giggling as she slipped her arms back into her maroon dress and lifted her hair for the fitter to reclasp her pearl necklace.

"Not his money—it's his wife's!" Aunt Mirry's mouth gave a smile-like twitch. "Something more valuable—I don't suppose these girls speak English—well, even if they do—"

"I'm agog."

"Well, dear, it's said that he outdoes Aly."

"You mean—in the hay?"

"Don't use that coarse expression—yes, in bed. He's not even very good-looking, but women fall all over themselves to sleep with him—and he does. They say no one ever refuses him, either —he can have any woman he wants!" She lifted her gray, winged brows.

"My God, I'll stear clear of him, Aunt Mirry! That sort of thing makes me ill. How can women be like that!"

"I don't understand myself. Apparently he has some kind of technique that never fails—but what it is, I'm not clear. I once asked Aly, but he said it was 'a trade secret.' *He's* so amusing!"

Lily put on her side-pointed white hat and long white gloves. "Vic may not be an adept, but at least he's sincere and faithful. I'm beginning to think I'm very lucky."

Aunt Mirry's sable cape was placed on her shoulders. "You could do worse," she said. "But you could do better."

Lily shrugged. They hooked their purses over their arms, left the salon and went across the tree-shaded courtyard to their respective Rollses.

Strolling around with the women of Paris society showing off the season's star numbers of famous couturiers under the Longchamps floodlights, Lily was even more pleased with Vic. Not only did he look as handsome and impressive as any man there, in white tie and tails, but he seemed more genuinely a "gentleman" than any of these hand-kissing foreigners, some of them with dirty necks under their potent colognes.

Later, as she sat beside him in Aunt Mirry's box and noted the intent stare of the famous Baron, who was ignoring the lovely red-headed woman with him, she wondered if she might not just marry Vic, settle down with him. After all, what was doing "better"—did Aunt Mirry mean richer, with an exotic title like this balding little Prince Dompagni Cordovuso the American girl was married to? If so—she was bananas (a passé expression, perhaps, but apt).

She squeezed Vic's hand, and he shifted closer, his sloped eyebrows lifting tenderly, his green eyes glinting with love.

"You are long in Paris, madame?" asked the Baron.

"Not long," she answered, barely turning, keeping her eyes on the race just begun.

"I will be honored if you and Monsieur Cammrose would come to my château in Molle for Sunday. Your aunt and uncle are coming, and we will be about forty only. I would like to give you *le tour de la proprieté*. My gardens are *très jolies* at this time."

"How kind. I don't think we can—but I'll ask my secretary to telephone you." Lily avoided his deep-set brown eyes, so bent on

meeting hers. He was a type of man she abhorred, his classical
nose with the round, flared nostrils, his extremely high brow and
dead-straight black hair brushed stiffly back, emanating a
supercilious self-importance. Whatever this famous "technique"
was, she thought, he could have it and good luck!

"Thank you. I shall hope very much it is yes."

Lily squeezed Vic's hand harder and gave her attention to the
race.

". . . It's Courageux! By a nose!" the General said, rising in his
excitement, waving his thick, small hands.

"That's your horse, Countess," said the Princess, "isn't it?"

"Why, yes!" Lily leaned back toward her, thinking that here
was a girl she would like as a friend. "I picked him with my eyes
closed!"

The dark-eyed American girl, whose name was Terry (erst-
while a Seever of Ohio), grinned, looking more like an Italian
princess, with her sun-ingrained complexion, dark, neatly rolled
hair and starkly simple black Vionnet gown, than did her Italian
husband, who could easily have been an American barber except
for his superb manners and linguistic ability. "How lucky can
you get?" she said. "Mine came next to last."

Lily laughed. "By the way," she found herself saying, "I'm
bringing my yacht over to Nice, making up a party—nothing formal—just wandering here and there—perhaps you could join us?"

Terry's eyes widened. "*That* sounds like fun. Let's keep in
touch—the address is just Villa Dompagni, Rome."

Lily nodded, smiled, turned back to Vic. "So you've decided,"
he whispered.

"It seems so." They smiled at each other.

"Pierrot's got his eyes on you," Terry whispered when they
moved on for langoustes and champagne. "Watch out—they say
no woman's ever refused him."

Lily frowned. "Pierrot?"

"Baron de Clavières—that's what they call him." Terry lowered her voice. "He's had all of us, darling, barring you and
Mirry. Isn't it a riot? They say he sandpapers his fingertips to
make them sensitive—worth testing, I assure you!"

"Really?" Lily felt a slight disappointment in her new friend.

"The trouble is—once you've got a taste for it—well . . ." She lifted a gleaming shoulder, a smooth palm. The wink of her blue-white diamond ring seemed part of her innuendo.

Nuts, Lily thought, and quickly changed the subject.

The following Sunday, however, she could not refuse Aunt Mirry's near-command to join them at Molle, and Vic shared Mirry's sharp interest in the château that had been built in the reign of Louis XIII, had a ninety-acre park, gardens, forest and superb hunting territory.

"You can learn a great deal from these old French châteaux, dear," Aunt Mirry said. "There's nothing like them anywhere in the world. One can't buy them, and it's very difficult to gain entrée."

Lily had given in, and a fleet of cars set off for the village, through delicious countryside, faintly hazed in gold, about forty kilometers distant. The moment the vast, imposing stone-and-brick façade had come into view, her personal aversion to its owner was replaced by appreciation for the sheer beauty of the mellow, history-laden structure.

The first shock, after a brief tour of many sumptuous, treasure-filled rooms, was that the tall black-haired woman with the faintly mustached upper lip who had greeted them in perfect English, with a grimly restrained smile, was not the Baron's mother, but the wife. ("*Quelle formidable femme!*" whispered Aunt Mirry.) The second was that the woman was rising above intense fury with the gathering, which consisted of at least five exceptionally beautiful women many years younger than herself.

"It's *her* ancestral home," Aunt Mirry reported, after a chat with the lady, "and, apparently, she *was* once a beauty."

"He's a *stinker*," Lily whispered back.

"But she's still wild about him—you can tell."

Lily put her arm through Vic's. He looked wonderfully safe and sane in his English tweed jacket, with his pipe, his steady attentiveness. Nor was he dull or a fool; he read to her, taught her to appreciate the classics, shared his good education with her—a real man compared to all this . . . decadence.

She had to admit, though, that the lunch was superb, haute cuisine at its most sublime. "I could get very fat on this kind of cooking," she said to Vic.

"Why not get some of these recipes, Lily?" Vic suggested. He nodded encouragingly, conspiratorially.

"He's quite right, madame—we have a treasure house of them, going back to Versailles—the most famous French recipes in existence." Pierre de Clavières, at her elbow, touched it lightly. "Accompany me, please. I will show you."

Lily's hesitation was ingrained reluctance to blunt rudeness. "Well . . . thank you."

"We will meet the group at the western edge of the gardens, Monsieur Cammrose."

"Capital." Kissing Lily's cheek lightly, Vic strode after the large cluster of people moving off into the vast grounds.

"This way, please. Are you interested in wine, Countess? We also have famous vineyards and cellars."

"Not too much. I don't drink a great deal—champagne's my favorite."

"Ah, no developed palate."

Lily did not like the glance he gave her. She did not like his beautifully fitting crash-linen suit and dark, formal tie; she found him curiously repellent. He's a cruel man, she thought. Cruel to that wife, cruel to women.

"Before we go into the recipe safe—let me just show you the room, the actual room where Louis XIII stayed when he came to hunt in this part of the country."

Lily could think of no polite, not too devious way to refuse.

The room they entered was enormous, with gleaming parquet floors, walls hung with seventeenth-century tapisseries, and dominated by an immense velvet-canopied bed over which hung a somber oil painting of the king in question.

"Here," said Pierre de Clavières, stretching out his hand, "let me show you the actual pillows, with his crest still on them."

Lily moved reluctantly forward. "Is it always this dark in here?" she asked.

"It is to preserve the tapestries, and tissues—light is the destroyer of ancient fabrics, madame. Come—it is easy enough to see. Very unique, very *intéressant*, yes?"

His smile was assured, without seduction. Surely, he would not be this obvious?

He reached for her hand, drew her up beside him. "Look—a lace handkerchief he used, still here, a nightcap."

Suddenly, yet smoothly, his hands were on her waist, gripping it tightly. "You're enchanting—such *belle, belle* eyes," he said calmly. "I should like so much to make love to you."

Lily moved from his hold. "Thank you," she said briskly.

He smiled, raised his palms. "It's up to you. I dare you, though, to lie down with me, for a few moments!"

"What incredible conceit!"

He smiled gently. "Not curious? *Pas un petit peu?*" He followed her, put his arms around her from the back and pressed his lips softly against her ear. "It is very nice, very, very nice—I promise."

She pulled away. "Monsieur de Clavières," she said, "you did not exactly invent sex."

He shrugged, drew in a sigh. "There is sex, as you say, and sex."

"Oh, yes, I've heard of your *skills!*"

"I could see you had. Learned in the Middle East, *chère* Lily, with great care. There's an art as well, and most men, don't you agree, are hardly *artistes?*"

He caught up with her by the door and barred her way. "No one will be worried."

"Except your wife."

"She accepts. If I had some of her money, I would not be here —she knows that."

"She loves you!"

"But, of course. I am very good to *her*, too."

"Let's go," Lily said. "You're wasting your time."

"As you say." He turned to the door, reached for the handle, then turned back again and pulled her against him so quickly that she had no time to resist. She felt the soft pressure of his hands move slowly up and down her back, and suddenly, without warning, as his mouth found hers in unhurried pressure, she felt a deep sharp stab of excitement, starting between her thighs and rising hard into the pit of her stomach. She heard herself gasp.

"My darling," he said, his breath quickening, "*chérie, chérie*—

you have such a beautiful body—it should know itself, it should know to be loved in every way . . ."

She tried to push him away, to gain control, but in some mysteriously gathering force, she was wanting—not *him*—but what he offered, wanting it badly, her nipples hardening under the green silk of her dress, her eyes closing, her mouth opening . . .

. . . A heavy bell clanged suddenly, reverberating dully through the thick doors . . .

"*Merde, alors!*" He sighed; released her, shook his head as if emerging from water. "Forgive me, my little *chérie*—but she does this when she is *agitée* . . ."

Drawing a deep breath, Lily looked at him in bafflement, chagrin. "Thank goodness she did. It must be the power of suggestion, all the things I've heard—"

He smoothed back his straight hair, reminding Lily suddenly of Freddie (was there some buried response from that near-rape?—how unfathomable sexual processes could be!). "Perhaps."

"To be truthful, I'm not even attracted to you."

"But you are attracted to my attraction to you—yes? Through me you love your own body—I will *show* you."

That this was not a question filled her with icy anger. "These things are far from my mind, I assure you."

"Call me at my Paris apartment. But soon—as I travel *bientôt* to Cannes, where there is much activity." He gave her a last smile, doleful, apologetic. "So very many women without this happiness. Is not true?"

"I wouldn't know," said Lily, feeling an unfamiliar dishonesty; confidences of women friends, as far back as she could remember, supported his claim. Why shouldn't she admit it? "It's a Victorian brainwash," Penny Hammar had said. "No nice woman is supposed to like it, and when she does, there are no men who know what to do about it!" Still, there was something repulsive about this mechanical, specialized approach.

"You *will* know, later." He lifted her hand, turned it over, brushed her palm with his lips. "Now—we shall find a few recipes, no—for decorum?"

She was able to muster a smile. The intensity of her dislike had strangely abated. In fact, following him through the huge, painting-lined halls, she found him subtly, disturbingly appealing. But of course she would neither call him nor ever see him again, if she could help it!

Chapter 17

"Aren't you bored with me, darling? I certainly am." Lily leaned back in the cushion-padded wicker armchair and put her feet up on its matching stool. In this light, her eyes took up the color of the sea, intensifying it with strange brilliance.

Vic looked at her slim legs, extended from her white short-shorts, gleaming with rich tan under the powerful Mediterranean sun. "You'd like to be rid of me," he said.

"No, Vic, no!" Lily adjusted her striped head scarf, stretched her bare arms, lifting her breasts high and outlining them as clearly under the white cotton shirt as if they were bare. "I'm thinking of you. I'm not being fair, or kind. In fact, I wonder how and why you stand it."

Vic looked into the bowl of his pipe. In his white slacks and navy Basque shirt, his face deeply tanned, his thick hair bleached here and there to lighter brown, he looked more hand-some but less sure of himself than ever before. "I keep hoping it's a passing phase, that you'll tire of him and come back."

Lily half closed her eyes and felt the gentle, rhythmic hum of *Sea Lily's* diesel-engine motors like the touch of Pierre's hands passing through her senses. "You should have more pride, Vic— you should turn on me, despise me!"

"I never could. Impossible."

"Do you think we could have been happy?"

"We get along so well, Lily. I think I understand you—or thought I did."

"I'm still very fond of you, darling—it's so mixed up. And guilty. Shouldn't you be getting on with something, establishing yourself in some way?"

Vic nodded. "Yes. But what? Back to selling cars? Even then I didn't know where to head—the war caught me before I'd got my bearings, then after, I never found them, Dad died—I took anything."

"And then you met me?" Lily felt a chill through the heat. "Let me start you up in some business, anything!"

"You're casting me off, then?"

"Vic—don't be silly. I'd keep you by me forever, just to know you were around. I'm trying to save you from what I seem to do to everyone."

He looked at her, his eyebrows rising in the center—the wistful, tender, surrendered expression that wrenched her heart.

"You might need me," he said simply.

"Oh, God."

They sat in silence.

Lily reached for her dark glasses. "Well, don't say I didn't try —come on, let's get a cocktail before lunch."

He leaped up, helped her from the chair, followed her like a man reprieved from doom.

Everywhere on the 320-foot Boeker-blue-painted yacht, people who were awake were rising from chairs, tables, wandering away from deck games towards the bar. As yet, there was little sign of animation, and Lily knew that it would not return until restored by alcohol—after all, very few hours had passed since they went to bed. How they all managed to *look* so attractive was a source of wonder to her—but she had chosen her group with an eye for vivid and colorful personalities, for glamour and chic as well as complementary characters. They were all peo-

ple who knew how to make use of facilities on board, the
hairdressers, the valets, the maids, the masseurs, the gymnasium
and perfumed swimming pool, the dispensary and twenty-four-
hour food service to keep fortified against the nights. (Aunt
Mirry had done a superb job of it—even the crew of fifty were
reuniformed, every detail of equipment made shipshape.)

Seeing that Pierrot had not yet appeared, Lily was grateful
for the ennui that postponed small talk that grew daily smaller,
more incestuously snide, as they roamed the coast in search of
diversion. Thank heavens, she thought, Cannes was next. Without
having seen it, just by Pierrot's description she knew she would
like it—and if she and Pierrot could slip away while the others
did their rounds of casino, restaurants, beaches, shopping and
nightclubs, she could try to find a house that Pierrot liked, where
they could live when the cruise was over . . .

"Vic," she said suddenly, "order a shaker of pink gins—see
that everyone's amused—I'll be back in a minute."

He looked at her quizzically, nodded dutifully.

Lily took off her scarf, shook out her freshly washed and
waved hair and scanned her face quickly in her big gold compact as she ran quickly up the blue-and-gold spiral staircase to
the bridge deck and her private apartment.

In the big bedroom, Pierrot was still asleep, his arms thrown
upwards behind his head, his mouth clamped tight, his blue-
veined lids as still as if he were dead. She sat on the edge of the
big gondola-shaped bed which carried out the room's Venetian
motif and stroked back the strands of black straight hair with
light, careful fingers. Then she placed an equally light and careful kiss on the frown between his eyes. He did not stir.

Poor darling, she thought, he was utterly exhausted, and all on
her behalf. Her insatiability had proved greater than any in his
previous experience, and his way of lovemaking, the mysterious
technique which had turned out to be no more complicated than
an almost supernatural ability to abstain, to give pleasure without reaching his own climax, had been taxed beyond his
strength. Finally, in order to reduce the gap between their
scores, he had allowed himself one of his cautiously rationed
climaxes.

Suddenly his eyes were open, staring at her from their deep

setting under his thin straight brows, coolly remote. "Leave me alone," he said. "I wish not to be disturbed."

"It's lunchtime."

"I want nothing."

"You should have *something!*" At the blank dislike in his eyes, she stopped, her heart accelerating.

"You have new lines under your eyes," he said. "You're not a girl any more."

"I know that—I don't pretend to be, do I?"

"You expect so much. There are three younger women on board, more beautiful."

Lily was still.

He gave a sudden restless stir. "I'm bored with you, Lily. I'm used to my variety, not just one."

"Darling, it hasn't been just one. I'm not blind or deaf."

"Well. They tell me with their eyes—what can I do?"

"Have I complained?"

"You don't dare. Tonight, I bring another in with us."

"Pierrot!"

There was a faint smile on his mouth, but his eyes were watchful. "When will you give the commitment, Lily, when? Unless I am free of this wife, there is no point in servicing you."

"Servicing!" Lily put a hand slowly over her mouth. "Oh, my God!"

"What else do you call it?" He gazed solemnly at her rings, brought into prominence on her hand. "Do you want pretty words? From the beginning, it was this—did you think I fell in love with you, someone your age, when I can have any woman I want!"

"I'm tired of hearing that, of your prowess."

"But you can't deny it!"

She drew in a breath, was silent.

"Come, *mon petit chou*, let's be honest. I enjoy, yes, caressing your charming body—you have delicious boobs."

"Don't use that revolting word!"

"I have learned it from *les Américaines*, my dear."

"Even so."

"So you have *gentil* breasts, *charmant derrière*, nice little twat, a good grip . . ."

Lily drew in a hard breath of rage sharpened with desire. She started to undo her shirt, to lean over him, her breath hard and rasping.

Smiling, he lifted his inert hands and touched her breasts, lifted them slowly out of the small silk brassière, took one nipple slowly into his mouth, gently sucked . . .

"Oh, oh, oh!" It was wrung from her, like a cry, against her will, against everything her mind intended.

He slid one hand slowly between her legs, pressed gently—then, as she began to writhe, he took both his mouth and hand away.

"A commitment," he said, "a commitment, *mignon!*"

"Later—later—"

"Now."

She moved toward him, pressing her breast back to his mouth. "All right, all right."

"Five hundred thousand dollars?"

"Yes—yes—I"

"When?"

"Right now, after . . ."

"Promise?"

"You'll stay with me? You'll keep loving me?"

"But of course."

The frown cleared from his brow. He drew her to him . . .

. . . An hour later, he appeared in the smoking room on the poop deck wearing linen trousers, navy-and-white-striped fisherman's vest, a small red scarf at his throat, a white beret on his head. He smelled of cologne, looked rested, unusually good-humored. "Lily will be down later," he told people taking their liqueurs in the heat-immune dimness. "She's having a little afternoon siesta."

"Sure," whispered Princess Dompagni Cordovuso to the handsome blond skier from Norway. "The lucky so-and-so."

"Perhaps I can learn his tricks," said the skier, "if you show me."

"I doubt it—but nothing to lose."

They laughed softly, got up, strolled from the room.

"About Maudie, Boke. Please listen, she's terribly low, poor old thing . . ."

Lily sighed, drew her gaze back from the shimmering, boat-dotted Mediterranean coast, a sea so brilliantly blue it made her eyes water, and slipped her slim, red-toenailed feet into cork-platformed beach shoes. Pulling her awning-like beach robe around her shoulders, she sank onto a large reclining chair on a balcony of the rambling white villa with its sun-baked terraces and vines, its great cool rooms and tile floors (often confused in her mind with others in Palm Beach, California . . .). "Yes, I must talk to her."

"She wants to go home, Boke, you *know* it."

"Well, I'm sure we'll all be going back soon—I must see my baby."

Whitey cast her a puzzled glance.

"Now Thomas and Netty want to go back—everyone's abandoning me!"

"That's not true, Boke. But things don't go on forever—they change."

"Yes." Lily could barely keep tears from her eyes. "Never mind," she said brusquely, and suddenly jumping up again, went quickly into the bedroom, where a new French maid, who knew nothing of her but what she had learned in Cannes, waited to help her dress for dinner. She saw Whitey hover a moment, then walk off along the balcony to her own quarters.

"*Où est le Baron*, Claudine?" she asked.

"Ah, madame, he takes a small rest. He is—'ow you say?—not to be disturbed." The dark-eyed little woman smiled—too sympathetically, thought Lily, but she smiled back.

"*Merci.*"

. . . Downstairs they could be assembling, she thought, all the lovely, scandalous, chattering *haut monde* she had gathered up. When she and Pierrot were ready to travel on, many of its members would join them again for more and farther ports, for more sun-glazed afternoons and starlit nights of softly swishing waves and warm salt breezes, of golden dawns, golden sunsets, of sense-drowning marimba, swing, jazz, sweet-throated crooners, of out-of-season, rare and exotic foods, too delicious to describe, so often too much, not wanted, of the finest, subtlest wines chosen by Pierrot himself, too freely flowing, tasted by dulled mouths, sated taste buds, of clothes endlessly changed, one beautiful dress or costume after another, all colors, shapes and fabrics, of jewels that canceled themselves out in general abundance, lost their surprise in custom and overuse, in the relative age, beauty or lack of it, of the breasts, necks, wrists, ears and hands of wearers, of one body or another leading to one bed or another, one weary face or another to confront on the pillow at noon . . .

"You'll run out of time, *chérie,*" Pierrot had said, eyeing her cruelly. "You too will cross that border from which there is no return. You will use your creams and lotions heavier, and someday you will have your little cuts and stitches—and still, time will undo them again—like Alida's, who has had six lifts to her face and cannot have more because no skin is left . . ."

"No, Pierrot, no! Not yet—don't rush me *there* . . . !"

He had smiled, given her the cynical look only Frenchmen achieved, reached for the telephone, spoken softly, seductively to some invisible new amour . . .

"Ask Mademoiselle Maude to come here, please, Claudine," she said.

"Yes, madame . . ."

Lily looked up into the pale dry face. The freckles had faded and where the pink band used to be on the bridge of her nose, there was now a deep line into which the spectacles were grooved. The red hair was almost entirely gray and the thin mouth almost invisible. "Maudie."

"Yes, dear?"

"Tell me what to wear tonight?" Lily opened her eyes to their widest. (This much she could still count on—no matter what aspects of her beauty may have been lost, her eyes were still a power!)

"I'm afraid I've lost track . . ."

"Cocktails and dinner here for twenty—then the casino, dancing, fireworks display, nightclub."

Maudie wiped the steam from her glasses and moved off, her white shoes making the same squelching noise on the tiles as they had as far back as Lily could remember. Did she feel beholden to wear them, Lily wondered, and that dull silk black dress with the plain collar?

"I'm not so good at these present fashions, dear," she said, returning, "but I thought the ice blue with the low back, or the pale green with the little mirrors?"

"The mirrors don't show when I sit, Maudie, and the blue is last season's . . . !"

Maudie nodded, waited.

"All right, nobody's seen it. I'll wear the blue. Tell Claudine."

"Yes, Miss Lily." She turned to go.

"Maudie—sit with me a minute. Talk to me. You don't know how much I miss your advice!"

Maudie's face reddened. "I have none these days, Miss Lily."

Lily met her uneasy gaze. "I've let you down."

"Not me, Miss Lily." Maudie turned away. "I'll see to the dress . . ."

Lily sat long in the richly perfumed bath, too lethargic to leave it.

The maid came in. "The chef says dinner cannot be late—there are the soufflés, madame."

Lily nodded.

When she was dressed, she studied herself apathetically. Her shoulder blades and hipbones were too sharp, her arms too thin, her cheeks too hollow. Her eyes dominated her face—and if it were not for the becoming frame of light, shining hair worn in a roll on top and behind her ears, it might be said that Lily Boeker was losing her bloom—that any day now, in fact, it could be lost.

The aquamarine pendant necklace helped, though, as did the large aquamarine and diamond rings and bracelets. White fox fur, for later, she thought, as the maid squeezed the cut-glass atomizer of fleur-de-rocaille all about her shoulders.

"*Très, très belle, madame!*" she said, standing back.

"Magnificent," said Gustaf, nodding to the young man who would soon take his place when he left to open his own salon.

Lily looked at them both in the mirror. "Are my pills in my sack, Claudine?" she asked, sighing.

"*Mais oui,* in the little silver box, madame."

"Thanks."

She moved from the room, paused in the wide, palm-potted

hall, then walked softly to a door along from her own. It was not locked, or even quite closed—she pushed it open, went into the dimness.

"Pierrot?" she called softly.

There was no answer, only movement, a rustle, hard breathing . . .

"Pierrot—you can't still be sleeping, it's dinnertime!"

Moving closer to the bed, she saw a pale face rise up, the flash of eye whites, the sound of profanity muttered in rapid French. Rage rose in her, choked her throat like tight fingers. "For God's sake, Pierrot, not again, not *another!*"

Reason told her to retreat, to escape the issue, but she could no more have acted on it than taken off on wings—she snapped on a lamp.

Whom had she expected to find? she wondered. Terry? The Marquesa? Penny? Penelope? Lalla, the auburn-haired model? Maria Costaine, the singer with the huge breasts?

The girl whose face she saw was a shock. "Nini!"

The girl hid her face in her mass of curly dark hair, exposing the thin, telltale neck of her youth.

"Pierrot—Nini's not yet fifteen! How could you?"

Pierrot swiveled his bare legs to the side of the bed, pushed back his hair, fumbled for a cigarette. "*Chérie*—it is her mother's request."

"Paola? She wouldn't."

"It's not his fault," the girl said quickly, covering her thin body with sheets and satin covers. "I'm a virgin, you see—Mama and I thought it was an opportunity."

Lily felt an urge to abrupt renunciation—but Pierrot put out his hand. "It makes no difference, *chérie,* does it? I have not gone from you, I keep my promise, yes?"

Lily stood for a moment, staring at him, at the girl. No logic would move her, no ferocity of effort. Only the memory of last night had any power—seven climaxes—they had counted them—and yet still wanting more . . .

"Please get dressed quickly," she said, "people are waiting."

Nini gaped at her wonderingly, but Pierrot nodded. "Fifteen minutes, *ma petite,*" he said, his hand extending automatically toward the girl.

The months drifted past. They drove to Monte Carlo for the Monaco Grand Prix, watched the winning car reach the finishing line, congratulated the driver as he came up to the grandstand after his "lap of honor," to receive his wreath. They wandered La Croisette, swam from the beach in the Palm Beach Casino pool, played tennis at the Carlton, or on one of Lily's three courts. They gambled in the various rooms of the casino, lunched and dined there and at restaurants along the coast, they danced to American, French and English orchestras, to marimba, to Argentinian music.

Vic had become a despairing spectator whose pockets she supplied, whose thoughts she avoided.

Lily got even thinner. Her cheeks sank further in. She sat longer and longer staring out over the shimmering hills, her expression indecipherable in black glasses, her cigarette holders, her glass, seldom empty. Everyone knew she took tranquilizers sent to her from America, and she didn't care—as long as it helped her to endure, to keep Pierrot from deserting.

Whitey brought her news of the outer world, of what the press had to say. Whitey took snapshots of everything and showed her how they all looked as they went about—always entering one print into the bulging scrapbooks. She was the one to tell Lily that Tony had had twin boys, that the horse she had given him had come in first at Epsom Downs, that the Dowager Countess had had a small stroke, that Penny Hammar had married an Indian prince of uncountable wealth, that various servants had left and been replaced, that maintenance men and estate managers were needed in one or another of the houses, that this scheme or that to get money from her had been squelched.

"What does Aunt Mirry have to say?" Lily pointed to a long letter lying unread on the table beside her glass of gin.

Whitey took it up, read, then shook her head. "She's reviewing her will. Wants to know if it's all right to leave you the Palm Beach house. Uncle Willie is slowing up—they've had to put off several receptions. Andy had another flop and is in the doldrums. She saw an article about Joel's work in psychoanalysis, and she says Beth has deteriorated. Freddie's made a killing on the stock exchange and bought the Rounstrath Hotel in Newport. She's going to have another face lift, just a few tucks taken up—so she'll be incommunicado for three weeks as usual. She wonders who's to replace Thomas and Maudie, and are you all right and seeing the right doctors for your tummy?"

Lily felt the tightening of her rib cage, the tremors underneath, the nausea . . . "Don't talk about it," she said, "it gets worse. What's on today? I forget."

"Pierrot's asked sixty people to lunch on the terrace—but they must all be gone by three because you're going to that tennis and pool party at Elsie Dorcliffe's."

Lily nodded. "Who's the luncheon in honor of?" she asked suddenly.

Whitey's eyebrows stayed up, hidden under her bangs. "That Bolivian heiress—"

"Ah, yes—so I'm faced with deposition."

"Boke—you asked her originally—I've had a helluva time scraping together staff. You don't realize things aren't back to normal."

"I'll cable Joel." Lily sat up, put down her glass. "He'll tell me what to do."

Whitey shifted her beach-pajamaed legs, shoved a hand through her bangs. "Boke—oh, Boke . . . Look—you can't *force* a father out of Joel. You've *got* to let the poor guy go . . . !"

"I have, Whitey, I have—I only want his advice . . ."

"That's what you always say!"

"Find out where he is, Whitey, so we can send it." Lily's gaze broke from Whitey's, traveled to some point on the horizon.

Whitey was silent. "Well," she said presently, "I'll do my best, but I don't know where to start looking for him."

"You'll manage, you'll find him." Lily's sudden quick smile softened the peremptory tone. "I mean, you've always been able to, once you put your mind to it, haven't you?"

Whitey's slow nod was enigmatic.

Half an hour later, Lily moved slowly down the wide tile stairway with its Caucasian battle scene rug that people said should not be walked on but hung, wondering how she had ever found the zest to furnish this house, how long ago it already seemed!

In the long, wide room that opened out onto the vast main terrace, a roomful of beautiful, interesting, festively dressed people looked over at her as she wandered in, looking exquisite yet

somehow isolated as she greeted or was greeted by these guests
in her own house. She looked into their tanned, brilliantly alive
faces, tried to think of things to say, while her dazed, green-blue
eyes searched everywhere for Pierrot.

"Lily," said Vic at her elbow, "are you all right? You're as
white as your dress!"

She nodded, glad of his supporting hand.

"Darling—he's over there, with the Bolivian guest of honor. I
understand he's seating her at the head of his table, despite protocol."

"And where am *I* to be put?"

"Next to me, with the people from the ballet company."

"I see." Lily gave a sound like a low laugh. Her beautifully
shaped mouth tugged unbecomingly. "So I'm to be *publicly* put
down?"

"Lily." His grip tightened. "Wake up! Do something! Please!"

She lifted her gaze to him. It was vague, somnolent. "What?"
she said.

"Take charge! The servants are confused and miserable—*no
one* wants to see you destroyed!"

She stood still, feeling strangely alien, unable to think. "I can't
live without him, Vic," she said.

Vic released her elbow. "Then, darling, no one can help."

"No. Thank God I've still got more to offer than the Bolivian
—she's younger, but she's not in my league, for all her tin."

"Lily, Lily, Lily!"

"Come on, Vic—none of it matters as long as my bid's highest."

Lily walked forward, her legs slightly unsteady—she had taken
both the gin and Miltown, but the tide of gloom moved on in
her, too deep and heavy to shift.

Vic caught at her arm as she swayed. "Don't go out," he said
as the guests at Pierrot's nod moved in a straggling body towards
the tables set out under gaily striped and fringed umbrellas on
the brilliant, mosaic-graveled terrace. "I'll say you're not well—
lie down, darling."

"Boke, Boke!"

Suddenly Whitey was there, intercepting. "A cable, Boke," she
said. "I think you'd better read it!"

Vic held Lily's elbow while she took the yellow envelope, focused her gaze. "Beth dying," she read out, "asks for you. Better fly back immediately. Love, Aunt Mirry."

It took a few moments for the words to penetrate. Lily fluttered her long, darkened eyelashes, tried to clear her focus and her mind. "My mother . . ." she murmured, looking from one to the other of them. "My mother?"

"Yes, darling," Vic said.

"Shall I arrange a flight?" Whitey asked, her voice steady, low. "I'll come with you. Maudie can take charge here."

Lily nodded slowly. Then suddenly her eyes were wide, filled with horror. "Yes, oh yes, Whitey—quickly, as soon as possible!" She clutched their arms, pushed at her hair. "My mother!"

Vic and Whitey exchanged the barest of glances, a furtive relief.

Even the wildness of Lily's dash in her first air crossing had not been fast enough. Beth's eyelids had fluttered slightly at the sound of her voice, then the ruined face had relaxed into a mask, closing her out forever.

In the following days, people streamed from all parts of the country to the funeral of Beth Boeker Osborne. The Long Island mansion filled up with the cousins Lily didn't know she had, distant relatives she had barely heard of, friends who all seemed more familiar with her mother than she herself had ever been.

Caught without a wardrobe, Lily left the question of her mourning clothes to Aunt Mirry, who brought old Starenze with her from Palm Beach. He brought his younger assistants and they made Lily an abundant supply of becoming black dresses, coats, veils and scarves. Appropriate shoes were sent in lots for approval, as were hats and gloves, and Lily, whenever she emerged, looked thinner, paler, lighter haired and eyed than ever, and, in some inexplicable way, more beautiful.

A temporarily softened press wanted to know why Victor Cammrose had come with her. What part did he play in her life, and what about the French baron? Did she plan to marry either, and would she stay on in America or return to Europe? Brief as her answers were, they were the material for many long reports and articles by "experts" on her character and life, which was

now so rich with incident to titillate or enrage readers old and
new that it was often condensed or carried over to back pages
like serials. Only Hilda Housman (now the leading journalist on
the social scene) asked, "And where, one wonders, is the young
Lady Deirdre, heiress-apparent to the Boeker money, of whom
nothing is seen and less heard?"

Lily took to wearing her dark glasses even in the dim bedroom
where she retreated as often as she could, and when Andy arrived, looking anxious and calling her "sweet pea," she broke
into sobs that lasted for nearly two hours.

After this, she became strangely quiet in herself, strangely formal and calm. It was as if she had come to the end of the road
which was her youth, a road that wound itself up behind her
and could not be retraced. Now was an emptiness, a vacuum,
and ahead, many roads, out of which one would have to be
chosen, but not yet. . . .

On three occasions, she had been able to speak to Joel. He was
so sympathetic that she had asked him, quickly, to come to the
funeral, to be with her this once—there was no one else in the
world, she told him, she needed more at this time. He said he
would try, but had not called back. When she called him, the
second time, he had had people with him. On an impulse she
had called him again, late at night. He had already gone to bed
and was dazed with first sleep. "Oh, Lily, dear girl," he had
pleaded. "I'm reeling with overwork. The best I can do is give
you the name of a fine psychoanalyst I know who I'm sure could
help you. . . !"

"Goodbye, darling," she had said softly, and hung up.

The next-best thing was Vic. She was so grateful to him, for
him. He asked nothing and was always there. She provided him
with mourning clothes, and asked him if he might not like to
start a private plane passenger service, she would provide the
planes to get him started—he thought it was a good idea, and
said he would think about it—meanwhile, he was too worried
about her to be concerned with his future.

As they all started out for the funeral service, Thomas cast a
sideways gaze at the old chocolate Rolls, visible in one of the garages they passed. Lily caught his eye in the mirror, but the
emotion she felt did not bring tears—she seemed to have done

with them. Thomas looked so old. Lily saw that the hair visible under the back of his hat was gray-white.

Somewhere in the vague sea of familiar "mourners" she saw Freddie staring at her, sullen, curious, like a figure in an old, threatening dream.

"I thought you'd like to know," Aunt Mirry whispered, breaking the spell as she lifted her heavy black veil, "that Chip Kenelm's still coming. He was on a business trip and the plane was grounded—an exhaust caught on fire."

Lily nodded. It was no time for past enmities and aversions— Chip could even have mellowed. People said he had never married because of her, but she didn't believe it; more likely, he hadn't had time, the way his business mushroomed. She couldn't help a vague annoyance, though, to find him on one side of her during the burial service. What was Aunt Mirry up to?

The question was lost in the final horror of ". . . ashes to ashes, dust to dust . . ." For a moment, her knees buckled, but Chip held one elbow, Vic the other, and she somehow endured the last vanishing traces of her mother's mortal life.

"You were magnificent, gal," Chip said, bending to her as they walked away followed by the large crowd of black-appareled mourners.

Over the top of her veiled head, Vic gave him a sharp, questioning appraisal.

Chapter 18

"Now that you're Mrs. Harvey Kenelm the Third," Chip said, as they danced at the Stork Club to "Some Enchanted Evening," "you're going to stay that way, hear? None of these decadent affairs. And I warn you, if you ever try to divorce me, I'll fight you in every court in the nation!"

Leaning her head against his shoulder, Lily could not see or be seen by him, one advantage to his ever-increasing size. "Don't worry," she said, wishing he would vary his steps, "I'm well and truly harnessed."

His big, smoothly tanned face (in the absence of sun he used a sun lamp) showed no responding smile. He nodded his neatly-thatched brown head and studied their images in the mirrored walls, she in her dark-green taffeta with the rainbow tulle underskirts and green-roses bodice, wearing the emerald drop earrings (his wedding gift to her), her beautiful back exposed to the waist, her long light hair floating from her bare shoulders, and he, in immaculate white tie and tails, a good head taller than any other man in the room—yes, unquestionably the most impressive couple present.

He always smelled of Lifebuoy soap, Lily thought, having visions of him emerging from showers, his hulking body pink-red all over, slapping himself, puffing and grunting with exertion and exhilaration. "Ah," he'd say, "ah," as if reborn. And wrapping his hips in a towel, his next step was to the scotch, more grunts of satisfaction. Satisfied that his teeth were brushed, that he had gargled a sufficient number of mouthfuls, cleansed his eyes, ears and nose, shaved, tweezed his nose and eyebrow hairs, pared his nails (on fingers and toes), he'd be ready to relate to her, whether for conversation or lovemaking. It did no good to interrupt the process—once in momentum, it gathered a strangely formidable force, and there was no question that she was intimidated. His bullish aggression suggested an incipient tyranny.

If she had noticed this before, she thought, would it have stopped her marrying him? Probably not. By the time the decision was made America had gone to war in Korea, and Europe seemed unreal. Loneliness, bad memories of her moral disintegration—the stream of proposals from weird to naïve that had come by mail, telephone or in person from young and old men who told her they would really love her in return for sharing her wealth—added to her self-confusion.

When Vic had gone back to England to try out his plane service, it had left a far larger gap in her life than she had been prepared for . . .

Flying back to Cannes, she had found a fancy-dress party in full swing, every room in the house taken up and the largest food and wine bill with which she had ever been confronted. Pierrot, his jaw smashed by some jealous husband, weeping and clutching, crawling on his knees to her, had left her sickened, even more horrified with what she had lent herself to.

Finally, there had been the last moments with Maudie. Even now it brought tears. Waving goodbye to her as Thomas drove away from the little beamed cottage with its surrounding garden and old trees, seeing her familiar, bespectacled face dwindle into the distance, she had had to clutch at the seat for security; nothing would ever be safe again, she had thought, biting her lips to keep from telling Thomas to turn back . . .

Prior to this, she had been able to parry the pressure of Aunt Mirry's campaign, of others who had backed her, Chip himself, and even the press, who were all saying, in essence, that her patriotism was mandatory, her European connections unsavory, and that the Kenelm family represented the true solidarity, true "blue blood" wealth with which she should align herself.

One night she had awakened from a nightmare—in it Chip had decided against her, had found a younger, more beautiful, more responsive woman. "You've lost your chance, gal," he'd said, "and don't blame me for what happens to you from here on!"

Sinister implications. Intimations of disaster and doom. Where was she headed? Not long from now she'd be forty—"No woman is glamorous after forty," Claire Boothe Luce had written. From then on, it would be only her money—there could be no other reason for anyone to want her—she had no particular attributes. There was nothing to love—even her own beloved little girl couldn't find any advantage in being with her.

"Mother," she had said when Tony had brought her to the phone, "I *couldn't* leave my little brothers, my daddy, my grandma, my darling horses. Besides, I have to be in horse shows!"

"She's taken all kinds of ribbons, Lily," Tony had interjected. "We're very proud of her—Fiona's put her in her old school in Sussex, and she's doing very well, very well."

How stuffy, upper-class British he now sounded! None of his old irreverence, his "naughty" humor—or perhaps it had gone out of date.

"Deedee—Deedee! Don't you want to see your own mummy? Don't you miss me at all? I miss you so much, I think of you all the time and wish you were here with me!"

"What would we be *doing*, Mother?"

"Well—lots of things. Seeing places. You could ride here."

"But not *my* horses!"

"Perhaps. Yes, we could bring them over!"

"Oh, no, Mother, that would be cruel to them. Besides, I have Timmy and Foxie, my darling dogs, and Wumple, my ginger cat, and Sarah, my donkey! And there's my second cousins Adrian and Veronica, and my school—I've got a topping green uniform, and I play half-wing on the hockey team, and lacrosse, and—"

"Oh, darling—did you know I'm marrying again, a very nice man? I do so want you to be at the wedding!"

"But I don't know him, Mother!" The quick, sure English accent had traveled the Atlantic high and clear. "I wouldn't know what to say. But I do hope you'll have a nice time and be very happy."

"Deedee—suppose I say you *must* come. After all, I have my rights. I don't *have* to leave you there."

"Oh, Mother—you wouldn't do *that*."

There had been a moment of silence, then Tony's voice again. "She seems a bit upset, Lily. Perhaps we'd better ring off?"

"But, Tony!"

"Yes?"

"Oh, nothing. Send me some pictures—take care of her."

"Of course! We all love her dearly! Anything else?"

"No . . . Goodbye."

"Goodbye, Lily—bless you."

Lily had hung up, thinking: The English say "bless you," when they couldn't care less!

What would she do if she *didn't* marry Chip!

Oh, God! She had picked up the telephone and called him, got him out of deep sleep. "I'll marry you, Chip," she said. "It's okay, I've decided."

"Well—that's good news, gal. About time, too! Not doing yourself much good hanging 'round loose. When do you want to tie the knot?"

"Anytime."

"I suppose you'll want a big wedding."

"I'd rather not—couldn't we get a justice of the peace, do it quietly?"

"Well—I'd as soon not be too quiet. After all, we're a pretty newsworthy pair."

"Whatever you like, then."

"Where will we live?"

"I thought you'd want to open the Newport house?"

"Impossible. You forget there's a war—you wouldn't be able to staff a quarter of that old pile. I say we live in your houses—I'll keep the Ninetieth Street apartment—then we can build somewhere later."

"All right."

"I'll phone the papers in the morning. Why not meet me at the Ritz-Ambrose for a celebration dinner? I'm cooking up this huge new project through the day—something you'll be very interested in. By the way, what do you want as a wedding present?"

Lily had closed her eyes. "I haven't the faintest idea."

"Well—think about it. Something very special."

When she hung up, she was shivering, her teeth locked with tension. Reaching for the bell, she remembered it was still late at night—that she didn't know what she was ringing *for*.

She reached instead for a Miltown, lay back. It was only then that she realized that neither of them had mentioned love.

"You're mighty quiet, Lily-filly," Chip said now, gripping her back, his heavy hand clammily possessive. "Come on—let's do our stuff."

Lily gritted her teeth—this meant a bracing up, a muster of alertness to a sudden spatter of old fox-trot steps combined with a tap-like shuffle which seemed to have earned him the name of "great dancer" at college. With it went a fixed smile, open mouth and hard breathing.

Never mind, she thought, these were little foibles—the least she could accept in a situation of permanence. Perhaps, in time, they would even become endearing. And God knows what her own foibles might be—some, he told her: "You frown, Lily." "You bite your lips." "You don't *listen* to me."

He also complained that she made far too many excuses not to sleep with him, and had compiled a list, "headache, too tired, haven't had my bath, people will hear, too much to eat or drink," et cetera, et cetera, which he showed his friends, and over which they all laughed in sympathy and recognition.

On the whole, he told her, she was a better wife than he expected. She did a "good job" of running the home, entertaining his business friends, stringing along with his sailing, golf, hunting and other outdoor activities. He did not expect her to take part in his endless business talks with men, to try and understand his huge-scale transactions, from buying and selling of stocks and shares, to launching new products, floating new companies. He showed intense irritation with her unquestioning faith in Coggy, in the fact that she took no interest whatever in what was done with her money. Nor was he impressed by the fact that her principal had never been touched, that her income was ever-increasing, that no world event had yet endangered her fortune. He laughingly rejected Aunt Mirry's claim that Coggy was "a genius of finance, for whom there is no substitute and will be no replacement." Any "sharp manipulator" could have done what he did, Chip said, and added that he would like to have had a fraction of his opportunity—Lily would not only be the richest girl circa her own time, but in the times ahead, when America had a growing plethora of millionaires who would one day outstrip her; she would be as rich as the Begum Aga Khan, the richest princess of India.

How would he do it? Lily asked, but got only a smile in answer; a categorizing of her intellect to which she became resigned.

Marriage to Chip was not without its compensations; Lily felt she was coming close to a normal world, to social acceptance without awe, rancor or ulterior motive. The press left her alone, and there were many days when she could join other married women for golf and lunch at Long Island Sound's famous Brevoorte Club. Although the wealth of the women she played with was generally on a lower scale, they were far less uncomfortable or unnatural with her than she was used to and sometimes shared their confidences with her. (It seemed that many of their husbands were as obtuse on the finer points of womankind as Chip, and some of her frustrations, particularly with his perfunctory insensitive lovemaking, were submerged in mutual laughter.)

"Considering how colossally rich she is," one woman had told a lurking reporter, "she's a perfectly nice sensible human being. I don't believe half I've read now. I think you guys have twisted things around to make sensational stories. What's more, she's given generously to almost every local cause, and there's no end to the personal, impulsive gifts she makes. You only have to breathe a hard-luck story to Lily, and her hand's reaching for a piece of jewelry she's wearing, or the checkbook."

There was not much rebuttal to this: not only had Lily endowed another college, given hugely to the war effort, started a college-scholarship plan for underprivileged teen-agers, supplied funds for an orphanage (always one of her favorite charities), but she had underwritten a camp for slum children in upstate New York comprising two hundred acres. Since TV had swept the country, people saw her in person for the first time and were taken aback by the simple dignity of her bearing, her low-key good manners and voice. They turned from the blow-by-blow McCarthy "witchhunt" for Communists in key places, to catch firsthand glimpses of Lily Boeker arriving with her tycoon husband at the Metropolitan Opera House in sable, chinchilla, mink or ermine, ablaze with jewels, looking fragile and radiantly beautiful, and scarcely remembered their resentment or envy. When, at the first night of Ethel Merman in *Call Me Madam* and *South Pacific* she had refused to go in until the houselights were lowered to avoid being stared at by the entire audience, they were sympathetic. The lead article in a morning paper suggested strongly that it was time to give Lily Boeker de Santi Aylsden Kenelm her chief human right—privacy. "Why, in any case, single her out for such obsessive attention when there were other wealthy and glamorous women, many younger, whose peregrinations could provide more current diversion."

Strangely enough, Chip's gleaming brow had etched with dismay when he read this: "Good publicity's meat and drink for business! If they start leaving us out of the news, be sure to inform them yourself!" He thumped his fist on the breakfast table, causing his red setter hunting dog, Rooster, to growl. "With this new company forming, I want our names up front."

"Why mine, dear?" Lily asked, casting Rooster an anxious glance. (Sometimes she thought her wedding present to Chip of this $10,000 setter had been a big mistake. It had taken an instant dislike to him, and the more he commanded it to do his bidding, the greater its antagonism.)

"Because, gal," he had answered, "the combination of our names is political dynamite. I'll have no trouble raising the kind of interest I need—"

"It must be a huge project, Chip—more coffee, croissant, brioche?"

"I wish you'd forget that European nonsense now. I'm an American and I like an American breakfast. And speaking of that

—let's have less of these fancy French dishes when we're not entertaining—I've never really gone for them. There's nothing beats a good steak, corn on the cob, old-fashioned strawberry shortcake."

"All right, all right, dear." Lily had known her first acute oppression, her first intimation of unbearable boredom. "Tell me about the project."

"Well—it's a bit premature. I shouldn't involve you at this point."

"Come on, Chip—I'm your wife." Lily had pushed at her hair, pressed her hand to her throat, flashed a vague, apprehensive glance at the far-off Sound, glittering under the cloud-hazed sun. Could she live the rest of her life without Europe, without the culture, the sophistication, the conversation, which, even at its most vacuous or dissolute, had subtlety, an edge of wit, an enchantment with its own rhythms and nuances? And to go there with Chip would kill its charm . . .

"Are you listening—you never do, gal!"

She had opened her eyes, wide and attentive, on his solid face, put her hands under her chin, leaned towards him.

"That's more like it." He folded and rolled his newspaper, smacked his large hands, rubbed them together. "Well—I'm going to build the largest single marina in the country. I'm going to sell my seat on the exchange, draw out of two companies, shed some stock and put it all in this."

"It sounds intriguing—but . . . well, is it worth so much sacrifice?"

"Good question, Lily-filly. The answer is, yes. I'm going to build it to include the old house, and buy up two others and turn them into hotels."

"Will the residents stand for that?"

"I won't tell 'em, until it's official. Then they'll get such good money for those huge, outmoded heaps they'll leap at the chance. I've got the greatest designers in the country lined up. We'll make a harbor that surpasses anything in the world!"

Her eyes brightened in slow excitement. "Could be marvelous!"

"It will be! Talk about your fortune—this will make it look like small potatoes!" He had spread his big forearms, tanned and muscular below his rolled-up blue shirt sleeves, shaken them at her belligerently.

"Have you thought Coggy might be interested—I mean, if it's a really good thing?"

"What do you mean *if!* Naa. He's an old-timer—he wouldn't give it the time of day."

"If *I* asked him, he would. It is *my* money."

"Sure—and if he said no, you'd say no—you'd never go against the genius!"

Lily gave a sidewise smile. "I've never had reason to—there's always a first time."

Chip had looked at her skeptically. "Go ahead." He had shrugged his immense shoulders. "I'd give you a damn great kiss if you swung it, I'll tell you." He grinned admiringly, the way he had at her twenty-first birthday party, when he'd said, "You've got good gams, great orbs, you know I'm crazy about you!"

Well, even if this marriage wasn't all it could be—was anybody's? she thought. It might yet ripen to *some* kind of bond and it was better than being alone.

"I'll talk to him," she said. "You give me all the dope, the figures—he'll want to go over everything with a flea comb. So will his partner, though Aunt Mirry says he's not as astute."

"Attagirl!" He had come around the table, given her shoulders a squeeze that took her breath, a kiss that moistened most of one side of her face. "We'll call it the Lily-Harvey Marina!" He had laughed heartily at his wit.

"What do you say we call it a night soon, Chip?" Lily said as they walked back to the table and the photographer took yet another picture.

"On our anniversary! Anyway, it would clean the place out if our party left!"

She had to agree. How selfish she had grown! But as she looked at the faces of their friends, a deep ennui weighted her lids, her smile. At first, Chip's friends, many of them extremely masculine outdoors men, who seemed to find him a "great sport," and their confident, smiling wives, had seemed a welcome change, refreshing after the kind of people with whom she had so far managed to spend her life. They seemed to be "doers," as opposed to "idle rich," to lead constructive, purposeful lives and to stick pretty much to their vows.

It had been the worst disillusionment yet to find the men had mistresses, the wives slept with their friends' husbands, had affairs with their chauffeurs, golf or tennis pros, sons' friends or anyone else willing and available. Within the first few weeks of marriage, she had had to deal with predatory husbands finding excuses to drop in.

In fact, she had talked Chip into spending time in the Fifth Avenue and Palm Beach houses (Beth had managed to leave her, not Freddie, the Venetian-styled house there) to get away from them—but it hadn't helped: wherever they were, the same kind of society gravitated and the story repeated itself.

To escape the numbing effect of this and despite Coggy's stern warning not to deplete her living allowance while so much money was tied up for Chip's venture, she had thrown herself into remodeling the Long Island house, which had about it the unmistakable stamp of its day.

Because of the difficulty in obtaining good permanent staff, Lily did over the servants' quarters, made fewer but larger rooms, created more light by adding windows, doors and balconies, and totally redecorated them in cheerful light colors. Then she completely modernized with dramatic splendor the glass of the huge sunroom, so that it could be a kind of indoor beach with artificial sun when the weather was gloomy, ruthlessly modernized the rest of the rooms, decorated them in "diamond-fire" blue and "ice-white," used the immense carpet she had had in storage since London, and to relieve the stark lightness added large cushions in pastel floral patterns, great white vases of multicolored flowers, and a big portrait of herself done by Vaughan Yates (famous for his portraits of royalty) in a purple velvet dress with a vivid cerise satin stole around white shoulders, hair like pale sunlight, eyes that reflected the light walls in startling rainbow flashes that were the artist's interpretation of her diamonds.

With all these changes, and many others, Chip was delighted. They signified a successful man's affluence, the brilliance of this merger of two fortunes. "The rich have to stay with their own kind," he told a reporter. "Otherwise they're always looking down on others who are looking up, and it's damned uncomfortable. This way we meet each other on the same ground, as equals."

Since the ennui had only been diverted but not overcome by all this activity, Lily inaugurated an ambitious garden project; she had opened the Long Island gardens. Magnificently kept all these years by Hellsman, the famous landscape gardener (who had also designed many of Aunt Mirry's gardens), and a team of now quite elderly men who knew their business better than any of the young men, who were not at present available, they had become an instant success. For three days every week in the appropriate seasons, anyone who was interested could join a guided tour, stroll in the 1500-acre estate, free of charge, between the hours of noon and four, and see the breathtaking display gardens of Italy, India, Persia, Japan, Hawaii, France, England, China and various parts of America. As well as correctness of detail, soil native to particular plants had been imported and every condition required to make them thrive provided.

The tour, which took nearly two hours, brought thousands of visitors, from local townspeople to horticultural experts from all over the country. Lily felt a guilty satisfaction, for none of it had been her own inspiration, but Beth's and Dick's, in those "champagne years" when their love and their wealth had no foreseeable limit . . .

. . . "Okay, gal . . ." Chip was tapping her on the shoulder. "We're all going back to the apartment for a nightcap."

Lily closed her eyes. "That's just *fine,*" she said, through her teeth. But Chip didn't notice, for as they rose, the orchestra played "Lily, Lily, Lily," as they had when she and the group of thirty had arrived. With Chip's hand on her arm, she paused, turned, smiled, blew the leader a kiss—he was someone she had known since her debut, since the days of "boîte-hopping" with Andy. It made her feel very old.

When the party filtered on out of the big, dimly lighted rooms, the music wove into "Good Night, Sweetheart." Lily did not look back. Joel was beside her, leading her from the ballroom of the Ritz-Ambrose . . . Life seemed to have got nowhere.

"Boke," Whitey said when Lily had finally opened her eyes

after more than three weeks of her "indisposition" (described by Chip as "female trouble," and Whitey as "galloping apathy"), "there's something I've got to talk to you about."

"Now, Whitey?" Lily wrapped her arms around her chest, yawned deeply. The vivid blue of her eyes seemed all that was alive in her thin, wan face.

"It has to be, Boke—for your sake."

Whitey's cheerful expression was absent as she approached Lily's prized half-tester bedstead with its tall back canopy and absence of front posts.

"You look so matronly in that brown suit, Whitey."

"I'm no chicken, Boke, remember—besides, it was a bargain."

"I'll never understand you, Whitey."

"Boke, listen." Whitey drew up a gilded-cane elbow chair. "I've been doing a spring cleaning of your papers—"

"You haven't touched anything of Chip's?" Lily's eyes messaged woe. "He gets murderous!"

"I'm coming to that—you see, Boke, there were several small files missing. I was going back over all the stuff you've given out for the past couple of years—and, incidentally, I didn't know you'd sent my family another check!"

"I thought they ought to pay off the mortgage once and for all."

"Thanks, Boke." Whitey's brown eyes were warm and fond. "I hope you realize how grateful I am, we all are, always have been."

"Shut up, Whitey." Lily shook her head. What she wanted was sleep and more sleep. The more she slept, the more she wanted to sleep. The weakness in her body was progressive—she could hardly lift her hands, had no desire to . . .

"To get back, Boke. What I think I've discovered is damned scary."

"Yes?" Lily yawned so long and hard that tears ran from her eyes.

"I mean it, Boke. I hate to say this, but I think Chip's in some kind of financial mishmash. When I went looking for your files in his study I saw a batch of letters in his filing cabinet that look like big trouble."

Lily felt a faint animation. "How? He's always dealing in complex mergers. And, Whitey, you shouldn't have read them!"

"To be honest, your name caught my eye. When I read on, I found that it was something to do with there being no such thing as the Marina project, and that your name had been fixed to a lot of false documents. It looks as if he's been juggling things around so that he could float a huge loan from the bank."

"That's ridiculous—he doesn't need to do a thing like that. He could just have asked me for the money. You must have misunderstood, Whitey." Lily yawned again.

Whitey pressed her thumb against her front teeth.

"He must have needed you not to know his position. There has to be a reason. Sy Roff's threatening to expose him."

Lily sat up a little, frowned, bit her lip. Her heart gave a sudden, uneasy lurch. "You sure of that? He's the most feared attorney in America . . ."

"I wouldn't come to you, Boke, if I didn't think this was serious. I think you should talk to Coggy."

"Go behind Chip's back! He'd kill me."

"So he would if you confronted him, Boke!"

They looked at each other in silence. The fabulous old clocks Lily had been collecting before her latest gloom had set in ticked about them like a chorus of woodpeckers, chimed occasionally, thinly, sweetly . . .

"I could say nothing," Lily said.

"Could you?"

There was another silence.

"Do you want to see the letter for yourself, Boke?"

Lily shook her head. "No. I don't understand the first thing about finances. Besides, I'd feel sneaky."

"No wonder he wouldn't let anyone in there!"

Lily shivered, sat further up, made an effort to focus her mind. "I suppose I could talk to Coggy. But what would I say?"

"Ask him if everything's all right, if his partner's satisfied. Just chat with him."

"But I never do that—he'd ask me outright what I wanted."

"Well—what's the answer?"

Lily put a hand over her mouth, lowered her head. In her heart for some reason there was really no doubt of Whitey's discovery. For several months now, she had found Chip less and less likable, less and less trustworthy. She had accidentally learned of the long-time mistress he had continued to keep after he was married, that he had long since lost the affection of his younger brother in Tasmania, his older sister who bred horses in Ireland, because of unscrupulous handling of family funds, that his expansiveness was a front, his high-flying schemes built on uninhibited greed, and that Aunt Mirry's belief in him, like that of many others, had been based on the younger Chip, before lust for money had carried him away.

"Oh, Whitey," she said finally, "for better or worse, they said. I can't be the one."

Whitey's hard expression softened. "Shall I do it, Boke?"

"No. That would only put you in a bad light. Let's leave it."

"What about your money?"

Lily shrugged. "It's only that, Whitey."

"It could be a tremendous loss."

"So. I wouldn't mind being poor."

Whitey broke into a grin. "You haven't the faintest idea what that is—you'd be scared out of your wits if you did."

"Maybe—but Coggy wouldn't let me find out. It's only the disappointment—I couldn't touch Chip after this."

"I'm sorry about that, but—"

"You knew it all along."

"You make me sound smugger than I am. Let's say I never trusted him any further than I could throw him."

"Why on earth?"

"His eyes. Something about his eyes, they never really look at you—and he came on too strong, Boke." Whitey rose. "Well—we'll just have to see what happens. I wish you'd get up, get some air. It's nice and crisp out—we could make a snowman. On the other hand, I've got the Christmas list to work on. How about staff gifts this year? They're mounting up something fierce."

"Everyone must have something decent, something worthwhile."

"Okay—if you say so. By the way, Boke—those emerald earrings Chip gave you as a wedding present? Not paid for. Just saw the bill from Winston's and a note to himself saying 'put with Lily's bills.' Apparently he counted on you not noticing or questioning."

"I wouldn't have, either. Oh, Whitey!"

"I know, Boke."

After a moment, she moved quietly to the door, and Lily sank into her pillows.

"Oh, another thing, Boke. I'd start keeping the dog by you at night," Whitey said at the door. "That prowler was seen again last night. The guard's been doubled, and I don't suppose there's anything to worry about—but just in case. I hope you've let Miss Dimpkin put all your odds and ends in the safe—you don't want *another* robbery like the last one." She went out.

Lily tried to sink back into her twilight nothingness but the depth of lethargy had passed. What now, she thought, what now?

The day wore on. Maids brought food. Maudie's well-meaning replacement fussed without Maudie's efficiency, her large, bosomy figure and protruding dark eyes never inducing the same comfort.

In the late afternoon, Whitey came back with the evening papers. Her eyes were eloquent as she handed them to Lily, patted up her great nest of pillows, switched on lamps.

Lily looked at the first headline, her heart pounding under the lacy georgette bed jacket. "HARVEY KENELM III," it said in huge bold type, "ARRESTED ON CHARGE OF GRAND LARCENY."

"A lawyer telephoned, Boke, to see if you would stand bail for twenty thousand dollars."

"Naturally," she said. "Tell him to contact Coggy."

"Coggy called, too. He would like you to come to his office first thing in the morning."

Lily nodded. "Whitey," she said, avoiding her eyes, "hand me the Miltowns from the drawer."

"I wish you wouldn't, Boke."

The words fell with the same monotonous effect as the ticking clocks.

The gist of newspaper comment was summed up in a morning paper: "More trouble for Lily Boeker as third spouse is charged with embezzlement in vast network of fraud involving friends and family alike, making him our richest girl's most expensive mate so far. Where will she turn now, poor thing? Some people have all the luck—they *don't* inherit $200,000,000!"

Chip had come home. It had been strange; birds sang, sprinklers worked on the freshly seeded lawns, servants went about their appointed rounds, and Lily, back in bed after a brief spurt of activity and press interviews, made no mention of the scandal enthralling the nation.

Taciturn, humiliated, Chip seldom spoke, spent most of his time at his desk figuring, figuring, figuring, until the study was covered with balled-up paper and he fell asleep at his desk, head on hands.

Lily had tried to follow Coggy's explanations, what she read in the paper, heard on TV and radio, but the exact way in which Chip had juggled funds, stolen bonds, played one of his "holding companies" against the other using every fine point of legal transaction to stave off collapse, was beyond her grasp. "The man was just as brilliant a financier as he bragged he was," Coggy said, "but on the wrong side of the fence." Of course, he reminded Lily that he had been wary of the Marina project all along. "After all, *you* didn't need to take chances." His partner had offered to resign, but Coggy had told him that the best way to learn was a mistake like this. He implied that the same held true for Lily.

Charged a second time, Chip's bail was raised to $100,000, again paid by Lily. Tonight, once more, he was home—somewhere in the house, avoiding her sad, questioning eyes.

Lying in bed, Lily listened to the night insects, watched the stars come out, gazed at the sliver of moon riding deeper and deeper into obscuring cloud. Depression was like lead in her body, in her senses. Yet she was jumpy, strained, aware how easily the prowler could have found the balcony of her french windows. Suddenly the lights went on.

"Nothing to worry about, Boke," Whitey said, coming in with the latest batch of the novels on regular order. "They now think he's a friend of that new maid's—they're going to arrest him. Look what I've got here—D. H. Lawrence, a new Hemingway, Faulkner's collected stories, Joyce Cary's *The Horse's Mouth*, Or-

well's *1984*, Frances Parkinson Keyes, Sandburg's poems—these
should keep you going."

"Oh, Whitey, I can't *read*. My mind's a merry-go-round."

"Then watch your TV. You like Groucho Marx and Arthur
Godfrey."

"I hate Arthur Godfrey!" Lily stubbed out a cigarette, put another in the holder that matched her pale-green pajamas, lit it,
sighed, frowned, shifted her feather-jacketed shoulders.

"Okay—so there's *Dragnet*—you love that."

"Tonight! Whitey, your head needs examining."

"Mmm." Whitey nodded. "Well, try Jack Benny's show on
your radio." She put the books on the empty side of the huge
bed. "Tomorrow," she said, "we've got to go over some pretty
big problems."

"Oh, no, Whitey—not more!"

Whitey folded her arms. Still youthful-looking, despite two or
three sharp lines shooting outward from the corners of her wide-
apart eyes, a gray hair here and there in her bangs, she had,
lately, a curious new ripeness—this was the only word Lily
could think of—that made her seem more confident, even radiant.
Yet there was a growing impatience to her work.

"Boke—you've got to come to grips with changing conditions.
So far I've been able to keep housekeepers, all the houses, a skel-
eton staff, older head gardeners, chauffeurs, managers—but you
haven't got a clue how much all this entails. Even with Brooke
and Gruber, the stuff piles up for decisions and action. You've
been promising ever since we came back that you'd try to slow
down, cut back, gradually organize and replace me."

Lily felt the last words like a sharp pain in the chest. "Then
you still want to leave me."

"Boke—don't take it *personally*. You know, after all these
years, I won't let you down while you need me."

"*Is* there someone in your life, Whitey? Why won't you level
with me?"

Whitey met the sad, appealing gaze a moment, then shook her
head. "Of course there's someone," she said, shrugging, "but that
isn't the point."

"Some reason you can't marry him?"

Whitey looked suddenly inaccessible, as only she could do, a breezy grin canceling the connotation of drama. "Less said, the better—okay, Boke?"

Lily sighed. "Well—if you insist on closing me out."

"What about tomorrow morning, Boke—you've got nothing in the book—a real down-to-business session?"

Lily shook her head, drew in smoke, exhaled it slowly through tightly flared nostrils. "Don't you think I'm harassed enough, with all that's going on? My nerves are stretched like wires. I'm afraid, scared out of my wits."

"Of Chip, or the prowler?"

"Both, if you want to know the truth. I wouldn't put it past Chip to go berserk. Look how he beat Rooster—even if Rooster did snap at him. You hear of these things all the time. Everything's bottled up inside him . . ."

"He wouldn't hurt *you*, Boke. Besides, from what I've seen of him, he's a broken man—he even told Gruber he was looking forward to prison!"

Lily shuddered violently. "Well—there's the awful feeling that this man is creeping about the moment it's dark . . ."

"I told you—forget him. He'd have to be plumb crazy to try and rob you a second time in three months!"

Lily could not feel convinced. "You'll sleep in the next room, won't you, Whitey—just in case?"

"Sure. Boke—you're the best-protected lady in America tonight!"

"Oh, Whitey—this isn't the time for corn."

"Sorry, Boke." Whitey glanced at one of the ticking clocks. "Well—your dinner will be here in a minute, and I'd better get mine. Try to relax and get a good night's sleep, old flower, won't you?"

Lily nodded, felt pacified, warmed by the old girlhood endearment. "I'll try, old bean." She smiled.

Soon the maids came in to prepare her for dinner, and the footmen rolled in a table of silver tureens. "Tell Chef I can't promise to eat much of this," she said.

They all smiled understandingly. "It's very light," one of the footmen volunteered, "a little consommé, sole Colbert, green salad, a few strawberries." He lifted a carafe of white wine. "And the wine man chose this light Montrachet."

"I'd rather have had champagne, but never mind."

"Yes, madam."

The footmen in Boeker blue withdrew without looking at one another.

"I don't need you, thanks." Lily waved the maids away. When they had gone, she gazed listlessly at the food. It *looked* so appetizing, and the vase of heavy-headed red roses looked so pretty beside it.

After a few mouthfuls of each dish, she pushed them away and sat back to sip the wine. It made her think of Pierrot—how he had known wines, the quality of every grape, vineyard, year. Intensely, humorlessly, sampling a mouthful, considering it at great length, he would order a particular bottle as if the fate of their lives depended on his judgment, his choice.

She twirled the delicate trumpet-twist wineglass with its Jacobite engraving, wondering where she had got these—perhaps a wedding present from one of her marriages?

Or had she found them somewhere and shipped them back?

She slipped deeper into the pillows, her brow lined with pervading despair, pervading fear.

The maids knocked, came in—the footmen withdrew the table, the room was darkened, the doors gently closed. She tried to sleep, woke with a start, tried again, gave up. The clocks ticked each second of the interminable hours.

Lily smoked one cigarette, then another, watching the glow as if it were a point of life in death. What would she do, she wondered, if a prowler did appear? First, perhaps, there would be some small sound, then a shadow falling across the filmy curtains.

She heard her heart thump rapidly against the pillows.

What would Joel say? That she was transferring her inner fears to an outer symbol? In his new book, *Troubled Humanity*, he had described how neurotic people did this, substituted hatred of the government for hatred of a wife or husband, racial discrimination for self-rejection, and so on. She hadn't understood it too well, but she got the idea, particularly the part about being "accident-prone" as a way to hurt oneself, and the "death wish" that made people abuse their health and put themselves in dangerous situations.

She had read a short story once, where the girl knew a rapist was coming towards her house in the dark, warnings were out and she was told to stay indoors—but, at the end, the girl had looked outside into the fog, the light shining behind her, and then stepped out into it—and waited . . .

The pace of her heart quickened even more, was small thunder in her ears. She could not bear to lie there another moment.

Sitting up, she slipped out of bed, moved quietly towards the curtains, pulled the drawstring across the tall, triple french windows, stood to one side peering past the balcony into the darkness beyond . . .

The massive outlines of trees, the smaller ones of bushes had a static ghostliness and the huge dome of the sports house had a totally unfamiliar loom that gave the entire landscape as far as the sea an altered perspective, as if seen through black, distorting glass . . .

She drew back, enthralled by her own fear, knowing she could probably dissolve it by turning on a light, yet somehow unable to, or unwilling.

Instead, she trembled with anticipation so intense, so certain that it was only a matter of minutes till a figure moved along the connecting balconies from one room to another to match her expectation, that she turned quickly back into the room to find some kind of defensive weapon.

Faint light from the windows slanted across a bronze figurine of a stretching girl that stood on a small French Empire side table. Almost as if she had already been aware of its deadly potential, she picked it up, went back to the window, stood just behind the curtain with it half raised in her hand . . .

If someone had come in through the bedroom door just then, she thought, they would decide she had gone mad.

But this held no deterrent to the dread certainty mounting in her that she must be prepared, that her survival was dependent on her alertness.

. . . Suddenly there was a slight crunching sound, a scrape, a rustle . . .

She barely stifled a scream. In that flash instant, she knew she had not expected anyone at all, that it had been a form of hysteria. The reality shot bolts of panic through her body, into her hands . . .

And now, like the play-out of a dream sequence, a figure of a man, surefooted, silent except for the faint rasp of breathing, moved steadily into her vision, moved nearer and nearer . . .

He'd been here before, to this very room, in just this way, she thought—he'd got past the guards!

He paused, half turned, seemed to be listening, to be scanning and assessing his position . . .

Waiting no longer, she moved to the higher ledge of the doorway, brought the figurine down on the dark shape of his head . . . His groan was mournful, brief.

Lily stood for a moment, frozen with shock—then she stepped down to the balcony level, stooped lower to see whether she was still in danger, the figurine poised for another necessary blow.

A muffled scream burst through her lips. She bent, touched the smooth face. Blood ran onto her hand, the man's head fell heavily to one side.

She went, in strange numbness, to switch on the lights, to call Whitey on their interconnecting phone. "Come quickly, Whitey," she said, "I think I've killed Chip!"

Whitey was there in a few moments, still tying the cord of her blue wool robe. Lily tried to explain what had happened as they bent together over the inert sprawled body.

"But the prowler was only a small man," Whitey said dazedly, "young and thin."

"No one told me that."

"And the balcony made you higher."

Lily nodded. "What can we do! Oh, Whitey, will you call Joel for me?"

Whitey stood up. "Joel? Why Joel?" Her expression was stiff, vaguely hostile.

"He'd help me—he'd work something out. He would, Whitey, I know he would!"

"Well—then *you* must do it, Boke!"

"No—he might be angry. He'd listen to you."

Whitey shook her head. Her face was as pale as Lily's. "All right. You sit down—get hold of yourself, Boke."

Lily obeyed, listening like a forlorn and hopeful child as Whitey explained to Joel, who had obviously been awakened, why they wanted him to come, immediately.

"Well," she said, hanging up, "he'll be here as soon as possible. He'll tell the guards he's the doctor you've sent for because you're not well. I'll go down and wait for him."

Lily nodded.

Within an hour he was there, having driven with his MD's privilege of speed. Lily had not seen him for so long that she could not take her eyes from his face—still so wonderful, she thought, stern, strong in a way no other man in her life had been —his brown hair had receded, grayed a little, and he now wore horn-rimmed glasses, but he was the same, kind under his brusqueness, competent, quick-minded. "He's dead all right," he said after carefully examining Chip, more to Whitey than to her.

"Oh, Joel—this is the end of me," Lily said. She looked up at him, knowing how pitiful and despicable she must now seem.

"Tell me exactly what happened," he said, "everything you thought and did leading up to the blow." He drew up a chair beside her, put his hand over hers. Whitey brought up a chair on her other side.

Lily told them the whole story, her low voice faltering, broken occasionally by a sob she couldn't contain.

"If it weren't for your husband's present circumstances, Lily," Joel said, "the case could be clear as crystal. You were obviously wrought up over this prowler—a mistake anyone could accept."

"But," said Whitey, "now the vultures would have a field day. Holy smoke, you could even go to jail while they wrangled!"

"Exactly," said Joel. He rubbed his brow, his face and chin. Suddenly he looked at Whitey. "There's a way," he said. He turned to Lily. "Do you mind if Pamela and I have a private word?"

Lily shook her head, her huge eyes dilated, their blueness dimmed. While Joel and Whitey were out of the room, she sat very still, her face peculiarly drawn, a color that barely contrasted with the green of her satin feather-trimmed pajamas. Her fingers, free of all but the bluish-green stone of her engagement and wedding rings, twisted slowly against her lap.

"All right, Lily," Joel said as he and Whitey came back in, returned to their seats beside her, "here's how we'll handle it."

Lily blinked, looked from one to the other, then back to Joel's face. A sudden thought occurred to her, but she had no time to form it.

"Now, listen carefully. Okay—you were nervous as hell about the prowler, about this noise you heard—you got up and went to Pamela and asked her to stay with you. Then Pamela saw the figure, picked up the statue and struck. An act of protection—right?"

Lily stared, her mind befuddled. She watched Joel get up, wipe the figurine with his handkerchief, hand it to Whitey, who grasped it and brought it down through the air as if striking, then carried it to the balcony and laid it down.

"Pamela called me because she didn't know what to do and was afraid the police would misunderstand—also, she wasn't sure Chip was dead, you see. She uses the excuse that you aren't well. . . . I get here, see that Chip is dead, and we decide it's best to call the police. Pamela will see it through, Lily—and she will be exonerated."

There was a silence. Lily was too stunned to break it.

"All right, Boke?" Whitey said softly, touching her shoulder.

"I don't understand . . ." She shook her head, pressed her face into her hands.

"It's a parting gift, Boke."

"In return, Lily—you'll let Pamela go."

Lily looked up. They were both waiting to meet her eyes. Their hands were locked.

Chapter 19

"Darling, there's nothing to worry about. Good Lord, I haven't seen the woman in five years, you know that! I'm just going to meet the boat, that's all. I do owe her that much, you must admit!"

Victor Cammrose looked at his watch. "I've got to hurry, dear. See you tonight—yes, of course I promise!"

He smiled as he hung up the phone. He had not told Angie the whole truth. There seemed no point in it; his excitement was only the normal anticipation of seeing someone who had meant so much and been so generous—why lay it open to dissection?

"I'm away," he said to the manager of his Cammrose Air Charter Service. "Tell Ethel to take a clear message on that SPG booking—I'll be here in the morning."

"Roger."

Vic drove the Fiat Lily had given him (still in good repair) to Waterloo, parked it and caught the boat train to Southampton. Her letter had said she had too much luggage to fly, that she was bringing several of her staff and planning to be a long time away from "home" ("wherever *that* was," she had added). Her object in coming to London was to get Deedee and take her along on the world cruise. She would explain more about *that* when she saw him—she pleaded with him to meet her. She had missed him dreadfully and had so much to tell. "I've been very, *very* ill," she ended, "so be prepared for a shock."

He read the letter twice, put it back in his tweed jacket pocket, got out his pipe. He supposed the inevitable press would be there, and that his presence would be interpreted as a resumption of their affair—perhaps on a more serious basis . . .

She had been marvelously reticent and controlled about Chip —probably loath to compound the general condemnation . . .

He sat back, tried to relax, but there was a residual spell about his relationship with Lily. It was as if she had lifted him so far out of the prosaic world that he had never quite got back into it —despite doing moderately well with the start she had given him, despite his love for Angie, his relief that he had been able to become a normal married man—a family man, with luck.

The old tenderness, the old protectiveness lingered, too—the publicity had wrenched his heart, the horror of what she had been through; even though it had been the secretary who had dealt the deathblow, the newspapers hadn't let go of it for months. Here in England they still spoke of it, though nearly three years had passed—and Chip Kenelm's court trial, which would have led to certain imprisonment, probably for life, still held international fascination, lending itself to reams of journalistic and media coverage.

Poor darling, Lily. Such a sitting duck for the worst in humanity—yet was there any answer? Once he had had the temerity to think *he* could be, that he loved her deeply and genuinely enough to make her happy. But as a fallacy, it now seemed pitiful. (Her formidable aunt had known that from the start . . .)

He shifted uneasily against the plush seat. It behooved him, he thought, to keep his head! Flicking open the *Times* he had brought, he drew on his pipe and concentrated on the latest developments in the proposed summit meeting of the United States, the United Kingdom, France and the U.S.S.R.

When the gangways came down on the *Queen Mary*, Vic saw

that he had guessed right. He even recognized some of the newsmen and cameramen from the past in the group that surged aboard. Nor was he alone in meeting her! He recognized several of her old companions from London, Paris, Cannes, Long Island —how they got about these days with jet travel opened up!

Finally—Lily herself. She didn't wave, smile radiantly as she had done when he knew her, but lifted her gloved hand, gave him a wistful, dignified nod that somehow singled him out of the milling crowd, and when she came up to him, kissed him fondly on each cheek and took his arm.

He was instantly appalled. Where was her lovely slim but rounded figure? She seemed almost wispy in the pale-blue velvet that matched her eyes—reminding him with unexpected force how compellingly childlike yet somnolently feline they were with their subtle shifts of blue-green light. Although she was still amazingly beautiful, he thought, with that small, straight nose, classic bone molding, there were little lines of bitter humor beside her mouth, an overall diminishment of youth that cosmetics did not conceal.

"I'm thrilled and delighted to be in England again," she told the reporters, posing willingly and pleasantly for the photographers. "As you may know, I've been under the weather for some time—that's why I'm going on this cruise. I hope to stop off in India and see my old friend Penny Hammar, now the Maharani of Tailapur, and to visit parts of the world I've always been interested in.

"No—no heartthrobs at the moment, only a desire to feel well and enjoy life again. No—I wouldn't dream of marrying again. I shall try to live in such a way that you fellows will have nothing to write about."

There was a round of appreciative laughter.

One reporter asked her about her daughter, and she explained that she had done what seemed in the best interests of the child —now that Deedee was a young lady, it was time to show her the world and how many other of its inhabitants lived, so that she would get a broader perspective. The world had changed so much, hadn't it—and it was almost necessary now, didn't they think, to equip oneself—after all, horses weren't everything.

More laughter.

About houses—where did she plan to live after the cruise?

"You ask me to project into a future I can't imagine," she said reflectively. "I know I don't really want to live in America again. It's funny—but I guess I did get Europeanized without knowing it. Of course, I shall go back for visits later—when some of the cobwebs have blown away—"

She paused, blinked slightly, aware of excess, but continued.

"I'll always want to see my relatives, my friends, and to be of use to my country in any way I can. I've donated the New York mansion to the city as a museum, because Wilbur Boeker collected a great many unique treasures which can be shared, particularly with young people who will never see their like . . ."

Lily looked thoughtful now, and both the news representatives and those who had come to meet her were still.

"I'll want to go back to the palazzo in Venice," she mused. "The one I bought on my honeymoon with Vitti—Vittorio de Santi—my first husband, you remember. As for Pacifica, my house in Los Angeles—I don't know. It is so very beautiful . . .

"Still—I can do better. I learned a lot building that place—you do, you know, as you go on. I'd like to try my hand at something really unique and utterly beautiful—someone has said that the Isle of Picco would make a fabulous setting, with its view of Vesuvius. I'll probably look into that. Well—I hope that's enough —I'd like to get on—friends waiting—so on and so forth!"

There was a quick, friendly response.

"My God, she looks as if she's been through the wringer!" a woman reporter whispered.

"Right. But with that kind of money you survive."

Smiles were exchanged.

"How do you like her plans?"

"Oh, *modest*. I wish she'd subsidize my fortnight in Brighton— do you think she would?"

"Ask. And while you're about it, put in a word for my overdraft."

"Actually—she's improved. More humor. Tougher."

"Agreed."

Vic shook his head. At what price? he thought. And how would any of them fare on such a griddle?

At long last they were in the Rolls.

"This is looking old-fashioned," Lily observed, sitting back with a sigh. "I'd let you rake up a new one if I was staying that long."

"Where's Thomas?" Vic said, indicating the new faces of her menage.

"Semi-retired—managing Long Island. They've got a son in their old age." She gave a subdued smile.

"Whitey?"

Lily turned quickly, to look out the window. "Nowadays we have Tilde Brooke, who takes twice as long to do half as much, Elmer Gruber, who's having early senility, that dear girl there just out of college, Arline Stewardt, two new maids whose names I keep forgetting, René, Gustaf's successor, Armand, who massages like a dream, and Fanny Dimpkin—my mother substitute."

"So many, Lily." He ignored the jab at herself.

"Well—I don't go into beauty salons, shops or hairdressers."

He smiled reminiscently at her logic. "Nor do you."

"Darling, you were sweet to meet me. I was so afraid you wouldn't, that you would have crossed me off by now." Lily put her arm through his, pressed it warmly.

"I'd never do that." He pressed her arm in return, smiled with affection, with vulnerability—untouched by time. "But I thought you'd forgotten me long ago."

She shook her head. "Never. I think of you as my only real friend."

"Really! What about all the people . . ."

"No one. People in my life come—and go. Whenever I think I've made some genuine friendship, it usually works out that they're impressed with the money, not truly relating to me as a person. Whitey was the nearest to a friend I'd ever had—and Joel was the only man I've ever really loved."

He pressed her arm harder. "You still believe that?"

She turned the lapis-lazuli eyes to his. "Do you think it was you?" Her voice was a soft whisper. "All the time?"

He shook his head. "I'm not that much of a fool."

She sighed. "Oh, Vic, what can I do to feel . . . *Valid. Real. Lovable.* Even *likable.* I can't see myself for looking."

Vic studied her thin, ringed fingers with the lovely almond-shaped nails, the softness of the hand that had never done hard work of any kind. "I don't know now, any more than I did then, Lily."

She nodded. "Well—that's better than some of the lectures and sermons I've been getting. I think I'll just follow Aunt Mirry's advice—as usual."

"What's that?" he asked, with sharp curiosity.

"Enjoy, enjoy, enjoy. Spend, spend, spend—employ, employ, employ. Make my money a happy, happy thing. She's always maintained that this is the finest function I can perform, the most valuable use of my inheritance."

Vic nodded slowly. "She could be right. Certainly hoarding it isn't going to help anyone, or being miserable."

"I guess not."

"You sound more American now, Lily."

"Do I? Oh, dear! Well, I suppose it'll wear off. Vic, will you come on the cruise with me?"

Her abrupt question was not supported with a glance, as if she could not bear to hear a rejection. "We'd be gone about three months," she said. "Everything you need, naturally . . ." She let the implication hang.

"I'm married, Lily," he said, as if even as he spoke, the fact dwindled in attraction to him, in importance. He realized that Lily was looking at him. There were tears in her eyes. "What's she like, Vic?"

Vic shrugged, his eyebrows rose in the center in wry contemplation. "How does a man describe a woman he married half-heartedly . . . ? She's not as tall as you, brownish blond, a bit heavy just now, but dieting. She's an assistant buyer in a chain of underwear shops. Efficient. Bright. Comes from a working-class family."

"Would three months make all that much difference, then?" Lily said meaningfully, still gazing into his eyes.

"Oh, Lily!"

"Vic—you'd have had a glorious experience, something to remember all your life! To tell your children!"

"Sorceress . . ."

"You'll come!" Lily's eyes brightened with childlike hope, but tears still hovering.

"I'll . . . Well, I'll think about it, Lily. There's not only Angie, there's Cammrose Air Charter Service, my business, thanks to you . . ."

Lily drew in a deep breath, released his arm, reached for her cigarettes and long, thin mother-of-pearl holder. "We'll have lunch at the Ritz, darling. I'll write you a check to get you started. We sail two weeks from today—but if you like you could hop over to Paris with me in the meantime while I get some clothes. If everyone comes there'll be twelve or fifteen in my party, including Deedee."

"Oh, Lily, what you're doing to me!" Vic's guilt vied obviously, unmistakably with mounting excitement.

She smiled, lowered her lashes, drew on her cigarette.

Lily could not believe her eyes or ears when she confronted Deedee. Tony, now portly, florid, balding, had come with her, acting so much the personification of protective father that Lily had smiled with the same amusement she had felt for his irreverence.

But it was a serious matter, he told her, his very mustache twitching with righteousness.

"But I *am* her mother," Lily answered. "Something you have all conveniently forgotten."

"A convenience for you, too, my dear, from what I read."

Tony's thin smile was that of a vicar for a moral stray.

Lily had poured tea unsteadily from her George IV silver teapot.

"I hope you've been equally observant of your own record," she said. "Does Deedee know of it?"

"That was a very long time ago, Lily. There was a war— remember?" His eyes had a glint of accusation, of contempt. "One learns, comes to terms. I cannot think how you would expect us to expose Deedee to *this* arrangement. Have you lost all sense of proportion?"

"Have *you?* Surely if I wasn't sure this would be a broadening and educational experience, as well as great fun, I wouldn't ask her."

"Have *I* nothing to say, Mother?"

They had both turned to look at the young girl sitting in the brocade armchair holding a thin white-and-gold teacup in her broad, weathered hands.

"Why, of course, darling," Lily said quickly, "of course!" She smiled hopefully.

Tony sat back, looked at her with complacent anticipation.

"Well, first of all, Mother, let's face facts—I'd be a complete fish out of water. I'm not interested, not the least tiny bit interested in gadding about in exotic places, doing feeble things to idle the time away. I despise the kind of people you mix with. Daddy knows that—he used to know some pretty ghastly types himself."

Tony cleared his throat, set his cup down with exaggerated calm.

Deedee took several gulps of the tea and a large bite of cake, which she seemed to swallow without chewing. She had grown taller than Lily, had larger feet, a heavier, more compact body with a thicker waist. Whatever breasts she had were tightly constrained and diffused in contour by a rough, bulky sweater, which she wore with a brown thick tweed skirt. Her straight planted legs in thick-thread nylons were sturdy and muscled and ended in brown oxfords. Her short, dark-blond hair showed contempt of all fashion by an almost pudding-bowl cut held on one side by bobby pins, and she wore not one pearl or ornament that could denote that she was in line to be the richest girl in the world. Her only claim to distinction was the flawless, high-colored complexion of perfect health.

"Not only that, Mother," she went on in a high clipped tone that seemed to Lily to caricature British affectation, "but I loathe clothes. Fiona insisted on my dressing up today, or I'd be in my riding things. The only time I put on a skirt or dress is for church or the odd hunt ball. In fact, I'm refusing point-blank to come out or any of that rot. I intend to spend my life with horses, to breed them, show them, ride them—and the only people who interest me in the slightest are others who do the same thing."

She gave Lily a sudden wise smile. "Fess up, Mater—I'd be rather an embarrassment, don't you think?"

Lily felt her heart sink as if on lead weights. "That isn't the point, darling," she said. "I just seem to have been cheated of my own little girl."

"Oh, I say—that's a bit thick. Isn't it, Daddy?"

They looked at each other as if sharing a philosophy far beyond Lily's grasp. A furtive shiver of guilt went through her. "I've always wanted to have you by me," she said, but her voice rang spuriously in her own ears.

"Your fight to do so hasn't been spectacular, my dear Lily," Tony said. "Mind you—we're all grateful for the do-re-mi, trust fund and so forth."

"Yes, Mother—that's been super."

Lily clasped her ringed hands about one slender calf (below which glinted the thin ankle chain with a tiny heart padlock given to her by George) and gazed wistfully, longingly at the sturdy, confident girl. "I had so hoped to buy you a lot of lovely things to wear in Paris, to do something pretty with your hair, to show you some of the world's great beauty—there are even two young men I thought you would have fun with . . ."

"Oh, young men are dead bores—I'm not ready for all that romantic twaddle!"

"Young Lady Deirdre prefers her horses," Tony said, which brought a flung serviette to his head.

"You should have gone to finishing school as I wanted you to," Lily mused, her hands beginning to twist.

"Mother—they wouldn't let you bring your horse!" Deedee explained as if to a child.

Lily looked from one to the other. A silence fell.

"So you don't think of me at all," Lily said finally, eyeing her daughter in painful resignation.

"Oh, Mother—of course I do. Only a few weeks ago they opened a new Boeker Emporium in Blattesford near us! I felt like going in and telling them who I *am*, hmm, hmm." She made a pompous face for her father. "Don't be glum," she added, in remorseful awareness, "perhaps I could come and stay here with you when you get back?"

"We'll see," said Tony quickly, starting to rise. "First, we must do a bit of growing up." He cast a conspiratorial glance at Lily as a final capper to his case.

"I wonder if that can be achieved in stables," she said.

"Oh, we're not as steeped in manure as you think, old dear." Tony's smile was a thin band of darkening teeth.

Lily stood beside him, bone-slender and supremely elegant in her long-sleeved mauve crepe, a twist of pearls and amethysts at her throat. "Miss Dimpkin will send you my itinerary," she said, "just in case. By the way, give my best to the Dowager Countess."

"She's slowed up, I'm afraid. Forgets who you are, gets you mixed up with other females in her life."

"Don't worry, Mother—she gets me mixed up with the horses. The other day she called me Daisy, the name of my new pony!"

Lily nodded. "And Fiona?"

Tony avoided her eyes. "Quite fit, thank you."

"Come on, Daddy—I've got chores to do!"

"Yes." Tony put out his hand. "I'm glad that's cleared up. Keep in touch."

Lily shook his hand, and at the last minute, by the doors of the vast, splendid room which had recently been described in *Gracious Living*, Deedee remembered her etiquette, turned back and put out her hand. "Thanks for the tea, Mother. Bon Voyage and all that."

Lily drew her closer, reached up and kissed the smooth young cheek. "Goodbye, my darling." Her blue eyes filled. "Write to me."

"I'm hopeless at letters, Mother—but I'll try." She plunged out the door, her face suddenly pink.

"Cheer up, old nag," she heard Tony say as they strode off across the hall, his arm about her. "You'll sour the milk!"

A sound of a laugh, the hall doors opened—the hall doors closed.

Chapter 20

When they finally allowed the orchestra and singer to stop, Lily's guests moved out from the big main lounge of the *Astrilania* to the wide, ship's-length deck Lily had taken for the journey. The gleaming white 20,000-ton ship rode gently at anchor on the dark sea, and they strolled to the rails to stare at the Gateway to India steps (built by George V of England!) looming out of the moonlit sky.

"Bombay looks rather jolly," said Richard Cromway, the gray-haired English character actor. "I can't wait to ride an elephant. Such a relief after camels."

A murmurous agreement rippled along the row of people in evening clothes. "Lily says we're to be royally entertained by Her Highness the Maharani of Tailapur, alias the Candy Kid," said Christopher Zill, a handsome young man with a chiseled profile, sandy hair and sideburns. "With ragas and dancing girls yet!"

"Not to mention the guru Penny's got for Lily," said Terry Dompagni Cordovuso.

Her husband, the Prince, grunted in restrained cynicism. "Apparently he's transformed her life!"

"Sure!" said Buddy Russell, whose face had been described by a Hollywood film critic as a "poor man's Errol Flynn." "And Lily will fill his begging bowl, too!"

"And why not?" said Victor Cammrose, knocking his pipe on the rail and relighting it. "If it helps."

"Wouldst that it could," said Reggie Blount, giving an enormous yawn. "Well, if we're to be up and at it again at the ghastly hour of seven, I'm folding my tent."

"Do we or don't we sail somewhere again tomorrow?" said Richard Cromway. "I seem to have sightseer's glut—or perhaps it's the heat."

"Don't try to figure it out, darling," said Paola, Marquesa de Anselmos, taking the pins out of her big red bun and letting the thick mass of glinting hair fall to her waist. "Just follow old lady Gruber's orders."

"That man does a fantastic job," said Buddy. "Think how many things could go wrong."

"Give it time, Buddy boy," said Reggie. "We're only halfway—what about the Suez trouble—the voyage back?"

The Prince groaned, laid his palm to his balding head. "It is beyond the mind! Why are we here?"

"Because it's the chance of a lifetime," said Buddy. "Gee—how often do you get a chance to see the world all expenses paid!" He glanced left and right in earnest reprimand. "You guys have no gratitude!"

"Speak for yourself, chum," said Terry, smoothing her small high bosom and nudging Paola.

"Sì—we are not *all* in Lily's largesse, darling."

"If you're not," said Reggie curtly, "then you've got a lot of unpaid-for goods in your possession."

"*Touché*," said Vic.

"Gifts not asked for, darling," said Paola.

"But accepted. Everything your greedy little hands reached for."

"Well, sì, but that's very cruel, Reggie—what can one do?" The tall, statuesque woman creased her low brow, shrugged. "Lily is a—how you say?—a compulsive giver."

"That's right," said Christopher Zill quickly, as he lit a cigarette with an onyx-and-gold lighter, amethyst cuff links glinting at his wrists. "There's nothing a person can say!"

"How about 'no, thank you'?" said Reggie. Suddenly, ambiguously, he laughed. "Well, good night all. Remember, seven A.M. Sharp."

"Oh, I say, chaps," said the Honorable Flanners Pond, emerging from the doors and coming towards them. "Message from Lily. She says there's chicken sandwiches and champagne on ice in the Crow's Nest bar, but please excuse her."

"Something the matter?" asked Vic, straightening, alert.

"Not as far as I know," said Bonky.

"Just pegged out. Understandable, don't you think?"

"Entirely," said Richard Cromway, his mobile face creating an expression which made some laugh, others fall into uncomfortable silence.

"I wonder where the boys are," said Terry, arching her long neck, peering at a shadowy line of chairs.

"Gone to bed—hours ago. Exhausted, they said."

Buddy grinned.

"Poor bastards," said Richard, "they've never recovered from that party."

"Well, hello there, everyone!" said Charley Wister, coming down from the boat deck with Nini de Anselmos (now in her twenties and reported by gossips to be a nymphomaniac, thanks to one Baron Pierre de Clavières). "Dancing finished?" The thin elderly man in hornrims buttoned his dinner jacket, wiped his mouth with the back of his hand.

"Dancing! We're just going to bed!" said Terry.

"Oh, no!" said Nini. "You can do *that* when you're ninety!" She caught hold of Vic's arm. "Is that not so!"

"That's just my age!" he said, disengaging himself.

"Come, darling," her mother said. "It's another big push tomorrow." She held out her hand.

"Chris?" said Nini, ignoring her, taking off her shoes and whirling her thin figure in a dance of invitation.

"Uh-uh. I'm going to have a sandwich, bubbly, and hit the hay."

"Buddy?" She threw back her long black hair, snapped her fingers in the air.

"Ditto, cookie."

"You're all big bores, the biggest in the world. I don't know how Lily find you, ask you, want you—I would change the whole of you for one big Italian *contadino* with a large . . ."

"Nini!" Her mother grabbed her arm. "Come!"

Nini shook her off, grabbed Charley Wister. "Let's go swimming, darling, without our clothes?"

He looked at her helplessly, followed her at a half run.

With handshakes, rueful waves, the last of the party dispersed.

In her large white-walled suite amidships, Lily stepped from her halter-top chalk-white jersey dress, handed her jewels to the maid, took off her white satin panties and bra and put her hair into a pink-petaled shower cap. Although the rooms were well fanned, the air they stirred, pungent with the smell of tropical fruits and flowers, was warm and stifling. Perhaps if she were refreshed now she could manage to sleep. These late arrivals with dawn disembarkations were trying enough, but with her excitement revived, the intervening hours could be a nightmare.

She still missed Whitey to tell her thoughts to, Maudie's steadfast presence. Without them, and with all the new faces about her, she felt cut off from all that was familiar. If only Andy had been able to come—poor darling, he was suffering his own despair. Vic, of course, was a comfort . . .

. . . It was the disconnected feeling, she thought, looking at her tanned body and face, her blue eyes searching themselves in the mirror as the maid dried her. The journey had started out so well, so filled with gaiety and color, and she had loved all her companions, each for what they were . . .

Chris for his fine hands that plucked so delicately and sensitively the strings of his guitar, whose voice, when he sang, soothed or seduced her according to the occasion, and whose lovemaking had come about only as the outcome of a certain mood, in an unexpected place, a certain need for harmonizing body and emotion . . .

But it hadn't been realized as she imagined. All that Chris's beautiful hands on her body had evoked was gentle discord, an aching desire for Pierrot to take over. How could such gaps exist between expectation and fulfillment?

. . . Buddy she had invited because he was physically rugged and zestful, a joy to look at dressed or undressed and materially naïve—there had to be people to give to who enjoyed receiving . . .

But when she drew him closer, she found that he was just as earnest and thoughtful about sex, and that her delight in his tanned, muscular body was deflated by the intensity of his gratitude, his elevation of their sweaty communion to a great and solemn love.

Although she intensely despised the humorless Pierrot, she had a sudden glimmer of why he had dodged elaboration of pleasurable copulation. What a trial she must have been to him, what a tedium!

. . . Richard she had asked for the wonderful stories and jokes he had to tell. There was never an end to his anecdotes, and he had such good taste, such knowledgeability about human frailties, such compassion and understanding. She had never intended his good company to extend to her cabin. . . . But there was a certain rapport, particularly after a long day of sightseeing, when they had seemed the only two who took the ancient Middle East and East with an arm-in-arm maturity of vision—perhaps they were more of a vintage . . .

But he had had less authority in the bed. Marvelously humorous, very sweet and rather shy once he had shed his dashingly worn clothes to reveal a body disconcertingly pale below the sun-reddened line of his neck and heavily thickened at the waist and hips, he had been a kind of trusting mechanic, schooled by wives to press the right buttons, and, certain of their efficacy, gone ahead to his own abrupt, single-gasp end. One could only pat and comfort him, save him from his—or was it her?—failure.

. . . As for Vic—well, she muddled on with him because she was so fond of him. Only once had she felt a genuine response. She became increasingly guilty for keeping him from the invisible "Angie" and wished she could ship him back . . .

The rest of the party were meant to entertain each other; except for Claude and Lenny, old friends of Andy's whom she had virtually hired for their expertise in dating and assessing collector's items. They seemed very much in love and self-sufficient, and sometimes she wondered if they weren't the only ones in the party who knew anything about compatibility . . .

"Your negligee, madam?"

"No—I'll get right into bed. Ask Dimpkin to come in . . ."

"She has already gone to bed, Mrs. Kenelm. She feels the heat. I am only one on duty."

"Oh, well—good night, Anya. You can switch off the lights."

Lily lay back in the double bed in a printed cotton burnous of rich blue, one of a dozen in different colors purchased in Arabia, which in the heat she used in lieu of sheets. Without the engine vibration, there was a curious stillness. She could hear the faint lap of water, the sound of voices echoing mysteriously from shore, the creak of ropes, the occasional padding of a barefooted Sinhalese sailor past the curtained deck windows.

As she settled into the pillow, the scents of tropical fruits and flowers, the Arabian perfumes and Egyptian musks she had added to her own collection, sent her mind back over the past weeks in a dizzying kaleidoscope of scenes and scenery—deserts, mountains, lakes, canals, rivers, dams, pyramidal shapes of rock, statues, great columns and massive ruins, intricate fretwork and carvings, colorful tiles and mosaics, vast hotels, shimmering palaces, glittering pools and date-laden palm trees, veiled women, women who looked like moving tents, museums, art galleries, tombs, large treasures, miniature treasures, costumes of too many traditions, too varied to count, beautiful, high-spirited horses (she hoped Deedee would like the lovely Arabian animal she had had shipped), mounds of olives, figs, small, bitter tangerines, acres of marketplaces and bazáars, fantastic gardens, fountains, gateways, tawny earth and tawny dwellings hewn into rocks, islands, temples, mosques, caves, grottoes . . . cold, ancient interiors, hard, blazing sun, the hard, joggling rhythm of camels, camel caravans of strange hooded bedouins, brilliant parrakeets, peacocks, sudden lush oases, wavering mirages, and the ever obsequious traders, the perpetual exchange of money for man's versatile and creative artistry with materials of the earth . . .

"I'll have it. I'll take it. Send it to our hotel. Oh, I love it, I must have it! Yes, yes, yes!"

. . . And now the groaning trunks, the new trunks, the boxes in the hold filled with new possessions, not only for her, but for all of them . . .

And now—India. There would be the sumptuously woven silks for saris, saris of every rich hue and tint, brocades and fine cottons, slippers of tooled leather, and more scents, brass, silver, ivory and teak, and more exotic and wonderful musical instruments—and jewels, irresistible jewels . . .

She sighed deeply, turned onto her side, away from the filter of disturbing silver light. Where in it all had enjoyment dissolved, at what moment had she crossed the line of satiety and ceased to react, to care, to *desire?* And why, oh why? Everything in her still appreciated, was still aware of the beauty of the world and was grateful for her access to it, but in actuality it had gone flat, in fact it had dulled to numbness, coupled with guilt and regret that it should be so . . .

Turning restlessly to the other side of the bed, she opened the front of the burnous for more air; it seemed she could not breathe, find air . . .

Suddenly there was a gentle but sharp tap on her door. Her eyes blinked open, more relieved to be rid of her own mind than startled. "Who is it?" she called.

"Me—Vic."

Oh God—poor Vic—what she had done to *him* . . . ! "Go away, darling," she called. "I'm horribly tired, I must sleep . . . !"

When the door closed, she lay down hopefully, closed her eyes, but almost at once her lids rose. Her face turned to the window. Only a few more hours, she thought . . .

Penny Hammar laughed as she greeted the party on the steps to the great high-columned veranda of the Rajah's immense, minaret-topped residence in Tailapur. "This is great," she said, hugging and kissing Lily, shaking hands all round. "Come in and get refreshed—Ali will see to the cars. Please forgive Rao's not being here—he's had to see about some trouble with the water supply, but he'll be here for lunch."

The party followed her into a chandelier-festooned room too

vast to see all at once, so ornately overdecorated and over-furnished that it seemed more like the lounge of an immense baroque hotel with sitting arrangements for individual units scattered throughout, and a jungle graveyard of animal skins strewing the floor. Lily put on the fine handwoven shawl she had brought, having learned that heat could suddenly vanish in the sealed interiors of the East.

She could hardly believe the change in the essentially unattractive, sallow-complexioned woman whose only real claim to distinction had been the sheer extravagance of her clothes, jewels and clever hairstyles. In a shimmering green silk sari that glinted with gold and silver threads, a caste mark on her forehead, her darkish hair long and caught back behind her ears in a loose bun, her long earrings and two or three carved metal bangles her only ornaments, her face burnished by sun so that its flaws were muted, her ready smile showing seemingly much whiter teeth, she had, Lily thought, a near-radiance.

After some pleasantly spicy tea, the party was taken on a tour of some of the tremendous hillside estate that overlooked a crystalline blue lake on which there floated swans with jeweled collars. Peacocks strutted the lawns and every kind of tree and flower grew in exotic profusion as far as the eye could see. Inside, many of the rooms they peered into had high-arched ceilings decorated in mosaics made of mirrors and spangles and alabaster-paneled walls inlaid or carved in rich floral patterns.

Lily, walking along with the rest of the party, felt a stir of respect for the splendors achieved, made some mental notes for her own future use.

When Rao, the round-faced, smiling yet vaguely austere young Rajah appeared, he was almost a disappointment in his simplicity. No jeweled turban bound his head, and his high-collared white tunic was worn with plain, Westernized white trousers. He did not kiss Penny or show her any outward affection, but his dark eyes found hers constantly in warm communion, and once or twice Lily saw their hands touch.

At a simple lunch of only five courses, in which mainly French food and wine was served by the turbaned waiters, the party learned that although Penny and Rao lived a tremendously demanding and busy life, much like that of executives of a huge business, they were not very much bound by tradition. Occasional large tea parties, formal dinners—otherwise they could do as they pleased. To alleviate the conditions of the poor was one of their chosen ventures, and their plans in this direction were extremely ambitious.

"Which brings me to the subject of Swami Naharanda," Penny said, with a nod toward Lily. "I thought I'd run Lily out to his ashram after lunch, and that perhaps Rao could take the rest of you to do some sightseeing. That okay?"

Her American voice was obviously amusing to the group, and they all gave smiling assent. Vic nudged Lily. "Want me to come?"

She shook her head. Her eyes had the brightness of genuine excitement, and she was already tapping her foot, toying restlessly with her strands of mixed beads.

At last, she was sitting in the back of a sleek gray Rolls that Penny and Rao had brought back with them from a trip to England, where Rao had been educated at Cambridge University, "and, incidentally," Penny added, "where Rao and I met at a stuffy diplomatic function."

"Tell me more about Swami Naharanda. I read some of the clippings you sent, and bought a heap of books on the Holy Men of India."

"You don't need to know anything. You'll just meet the guy—and you'll *feel* it." Penny smiled serenely.

Lily looked at her, skeptical because of her wealth, now far greater than her own, yet tenaciously hopeful. After all, Penny had been hard-bitten, contemptuous of sentiment, anti-religious and not even particularly philosophical.

The car turned abruptly up a long road of hard-packed cow dung that wound about a tree-sprinkled hill. Lily leaned forward expectantly.

"It's not much of a setting," Penny said.

How calmly she sat, thought Lily, her hands folded, her smile easy, her eyes gentle.

"He's been much taken up by the West, but it doesn't touch him. He might be meditating—you might have to wait."

"Did you tell him who I was?"

Penny smiled. "He knows who you are."

Lily frowned. What did she mean?

As they wound finally to some gates, Lily noticed vultures drifting across the pale, mottled blue sky, and the hot breeze that stirred the tops of teak trees blew inward across her cheeks, fanned out wisps of her tightly bunned hair. She felt a wave of vague anxiety, as if she were about to be exposed, revealed as worse than her own worst suspicions.

"You know—the wild dogs don't howl here," Penny said. "They move closer during meditation."

"Really? Is that true?"

"How English you sound, Lily—still the Countess of Cambrook?" Her eyes teased.

"Not intentionally."

Now there were rows of log shacks on stilts, stark and precarious with floor-pad beds just visible. Here and there near-naked figures could be seen, as well as young people in a mixture of Western and Eastern clothes.

What on earth am I doing here? Lily thought, suddenly wishing she could turn and retreat.

A bigger log structure appeared now, surrounded with flowering plants. "Here we are," Penny said.

The driver opened the car door and helped them out. There was an odor of incense and wood smoke, a flat, rancid smell of oil that Lily had noticed on the drive through Bombay.

"Wait here," Penny said, and moved evenly toward the door, her sari rustling, her flat jeweled sandals slapping the hard dry earth.

Lily stood uncertainly, her light-blue silk shirtwaist dress with the full skirt feeling out of place, identifying her as foreign in fact and spirit. The sun bore down on her through the trees, making her perspire, turning her face and neck pink, and giving her a sharp thirst. There seemed no movement of life in this arid, sultry place other than the birds, the occasional darting presence of insects and small animals, a faint, perpetual tinkle of bells.

"Lily," said Penny, emerging with a look of bright anticipation, and beckoning. "The Master will see you now."

Lily moistened her lips, patted her hair, straightened her dress.

"I'll wait in the car, dear," said Penny.

Nodding, Lily went slowly inside.

It was cooler, very dim, an absolutely bare room except for a small raised platform surrounded with vases of flowers, a few large yellow cushions.

A small, long-haired, gray-bearded, nut-brown man in a white robe sat cross-legged on the platform. He waved a brown hand with whitish nails. "Please," he said in a gentle tenor.

Lily inferred that she was to sit on one of the cushions in front of him. She did this as gracefully as she could, wishing she had kept up her dancing and not allowed her legs to stiffen.

After she was settled, in the way nearest to his "lotus" position she could manage, her back straight, she showed that she was ready to speak. How very insignificant he looked, she thought, with a stab of embarrassment and doubt.

"Yes?" he said, in a low, soft singsong. He was so still he might have been one of the little statues that filled the temples she'd seen . . .

"Well—my name is Lily Boeker . . ."

"Your name is unimportant, except to you."

"Now that I'm here, I don't know what I want to say."

"Then don't say it."

He looked at her with eyes of infinite kindness, and Lily felt a sudden sense of timelessness, of deep, permeating peace. She felt a breath move out from within her, expelled on the absolutely soundless air.

After a few moments, she felt a slight smile form on her mouth. "I am of extreme material wealth, Swami Naharanda. I was born to it. Somehow, I have lost my way." Why did she speak in this formal way? It seemed appropriate . . .

"And do you *want* to find your way?"

Why, of course, she thought. But—did she, in fact—at *any* price? "I am not happy," she said. "I can find no real happiness."

The small old man nodded, his half-closed black-brown eyes widening as if to imbibe the essence of this thought.

"There is, of course, happiness. It arises only from self-awareness, awareness of Self, the knowing of the oneness of Spirit. When you have spiritual riches, you will have gained resolution and the joy you seek. Only then."

An emotion Lily had never known waved through her, bringing the sharp sting of tears to her eyes. "Yes," she breathed. And in that instant, going no further, she knew what the answer was to her life, to all life. "Yes . . . But how do I achieve this—self-awareness, this oneness?" she asked quickly.

He seemed to have left her. His eyes were closed. There was a smile on his mouth, curving it like a small arc. His hands were inert, just their thumbs and middle fingers touching.

She waited, afraid of disturbing him, yet anxious, oh so anxious for his words . . .

"It is a long hard discipline. Or—it is easy. It is both. To know, to surrender, to be."

His eyes did not open, and Lily tried to puzzle his words.

Sensing her confusion, he opened his eyes, gave the breath of a laugh. "The joy is like a fountain of infinite brilliance," he said, "like innumerable white birds released."

She waited.

"One must start wherever one is," he said, putting his fingertips together and moving them to and away from his face. "Start each minute again. When you want to find this oneness, when you want to find it more than you want anything else in life—then you will be ready to find it."

"But where am I? I've been given no religion, nothing but a vague Christian concept which seems to contradict itself, to be contradicted by everyone and everything I know!"

"Clean your mind like a slate. Ask who am I, what am I, what is the purpose of life, and what part of that life am I meant to play? Turn within for your answers. Listen, wait, and they will come—and more besides."

"They will definitely come?"

He nodded slowly, smiling softly. "Yes, to the degree that you listen. Always the revelation must await the attuned ear."

"And does my money stand in the way?"

"Only if you *think* it does. Money is nothing of itself. It does not act apart from the user."

"But I can't act apart from it!"

"An illusion."

"What would I have been like without it—how can I ever tell?"

"Whoever you think you were or are, you can only be Spirit, *as* you."

Suddenly he raised his hand. "There is no more to say. Come to me again when you have listened awhile and understood."

"But . . ." Lily stopped. She could see there was no use in speaking to him, his eyes were closed, he had finished.

She waited a few minutes in the silence, swamped in mysterious peace. After a while she rose, stood for a moment, then reached into her embroidered straw purse and brought out a checkbook and a gold pen. What could she leave him? she wondered. Should she speak to Penny and see how she went about it —or was this far from the concern of the small, holy man?

She felt crass, tasteless standing there thinking in these terms.

Suddenly he opened his eyes. "It will be used for spreading of the enlightenment," he said. "You can believe that." Smiling, he closed his eyes again.

Lily dated the check, wrote his name, signed, but hesitated still over the amount. Then, as if a sweet flower-scented breeze wafted through her mind, she stopped writing, left the amount blank.

Chapter 21

"I *must* get back to India!" Lily said, as she so often did, "see that guru again . . ."

"Yes, dear," murmured Vic.

"And make world news again, with another open check to the fakir?" said Chris, plucking a few gentle notes on his magnificently made guitar. "Or was it faker?"

"Can we go with you?" asked tall, red-headed Davey, and Elspeth, a young woman with soft brown curls and Beth's violet eyes, added, "Please, darling? I believe he was genuine—*honest,* or he'd have taken more than a couple of thou."

Lily gave a taut smile. At fifty-five her face had tightened onto the classic mold of her bone structure, become etched with fine lines that were somehow pleasant and appropriate. She wore her hair in a simple bun or French twist at all times now, and however gray it might have been was concealed by clever tinting that retained its ever-lighter shade of blond. Her eyes, despite the faint creeping around them, retained their ever-startling blue, and her body, at least in her clothes, more often than not her brilliantly colored saris, was that of a young girl.

"We'll see," she said.

The little group sat drinking after-dinner liqueurs on the awninged terrace of the huge, orange-tinted Grand Hotel overlooking the busy Grand Canal in Venice. By peering through the gathering dusk, past the busy boat traffic of high-powered gondolas and motorboats, they could just make out the twinkling lights of the *Sea Lily* among several other large boats out there in the harbor.

"I can't bear to go to this party tonight," Lily said, and with the words, she felt the old gloom she had suffered for so many months like ghostly fingers on her forehead. "In fact," she added, "I'm already tired of the palazzo—it's taking far too long, and the dampness is depressing." She thought of the Renaissance palace with its wide fronting of steps to the water, its statue-filled courtyard, the great history-laden rooms, three stories of them, every inch of every wall and ceiling pricelessly frescoed, decorated with ancient friezes, cornices and merlons, hung with Bellinis, Titians, Bordones, Tintorettos and Canalettos, vast, weighted red-velvet draperies and tapestries. To make it all light, dry, cheerful and sound had seemed at first so worthwhile, consumed her time and thoughts. She had loved the canal life, the bustle of motorboats, gondolas, vaporettos, the steamboats, and barges, the occasional big liner from which distant passengers, like little stick people, waved. She had loved all the mellowed squares and bridges, churches and old palaces brooding under the deep gold sunlight, and she had loved them at night in moonlight, in the shadowed intrigue of silver waters and black silhouettes, the dimly piercing lights that gave it all mysterious and secret dimensions, as if life had more to offer here in this place than anywhere else . . .

But the *dolce vita* parties, the incestuous shuffling and reshuffling of bed partners from the same pack of thrill-hunting jet-setters, had soon palled.

"I've had enough of everything," she said, sipping her Cointreau, her emeralds from India glinting in the deep V of her hooded black jersey pajama-dress. "Of everywhere."

Chris sipped, returned to his guitar, plucked soothingly. People at other tables gazed in wonder.

"Even me," said Elspeth, with her suggestive smile.

"Yes." Lily did not return the smile. Ever since Deedee had had the fatal hunting accident, been suddenly, abruptly removed from even the periphery of her life, she had felt nothing but revulsion for this lovely, honey-skinned girl who represented a brief, feverish belief that it was not men she had wanted all her life. . . . Then, too, had come the horrifying recognition that Elspeth looked like her own mother, Beth.

"You've been too much on the move," Vic said.

"They don't call you 'the rotating richling' for nothing, angel," Chris said, looking up a moment to grin at her. "Wonder you don't get dizzy hopping from one house or hotel to the other, one gala or sporting event, one party or ball to another—and the *distances!*"

"It's no more than anyone does these days," Lily said, signaling Davey to refill her glass. "It's the mobility of transportation, so many of us with planes, the shrinking world."

"You notice no one says 'How are you, Lily?' But 'Where are you going, Lily?' 'Where have you come from, Lily?' 'How long are you here for, Lily?'"

Lily kicked gently at his shin with her satin-sandaled foot, and puffed the sultry air, her lashes fluttering with ennui, or oppression, something like a deep velvet pall over her senses.

"You'll feel better tomorrow when we swim at the Lido," Davey said, patting her hand, avoiding the sharp edges of rings.

She looked into his hazel eyes, and felt a sense of déjà vu beyond description. How many younger man had lent her their love and companionship by now—she could hardly remember their names. It seemed the older she got, the more they loved her —or was it because she was that nearer to leaving them something worthwhile in her will? Perhaps that wasn't fair—perhaps it was that she could no longer bear older men, who reminded her of her own passing years.

. . . Even Vic was getting on now. Still, he was leaving soon, and she tried not to think about it—it had been her own ultimatum, a last gesture in his behalf.

"I'll enjoy swimming with you all at the Lido," she said, "and seeing all the charming, beautiful dreadful people, but I shan't feel better."

They all groaned, smiled. "You wish you were dead," they chorused.

She raised her chin so that her neck seemed longer, younger; her earrings swung and glittered. "I'm already that," she said.

"Oh, come on, Lily luv," Chris said, thrumming a discord, "what you need is to fall in love again. We'll have to find you someone."

"That's right!" Elspeth looked at him, and at the other two. "Why don't we try, set our minds to it!"

"Sure thing," said Davey, who had been a golf pro in Palm Beach. "We'll scout the joint."

"Tell us what you want," said Chris. "Tall, short, black, white, rich, poor?"

"Save your effort, my darling," Lily said, putting down her glass. "I'm through with all that. I looked, I didn't find, and my time has gone by."

Lily sat up, indicating she wanted her wrap. "Pay the bill, Vic," she said. "Chris, summon the boat."

"Are we or aren't we going to the party?" Elspeth said. She indicated the brilliant red satin dress Lily had given her, the borrowed diamonds.

"You look divine," Lily said reluctantly, avoiding her eyes.

"What about us?" Chris reminded her that they were all in evening clothes.

"Oh, all right!" Lily sighed, leaned into the chinchilla cape he held out. "But I'm not staying late."

The glass-enclosed *motoscafo* took them swiftly over the light-reflecting water, past mossy, crumbling but splendid houses with flower-hung balconies, under low-arched bridges, to the palazzo of Count and Countess Gioranos, a huge, rectangular building only guessed at in the dimness by the large striped awnings, striped gondola poles, dim lights in every window and a row of tied-up boats. They got out into the ink-blue darkness, Lily's jewels sparkling like a continuity of minute stars, and liveried footmen ran to help the two women onto the wet green steps. Once through the huge gold doors and inside the vast pink-and-blue hall, they followed the footmen up wide marble stairs with gilded ironwork banisters to an enormous room with a Tiepolo ceiling that was in all guidebooks on Venice, for Gioranos' had been in residence here since the sixteenth century. Great banks of flowers were everywhere, orchids, huge cages of shrilly twittering birds.

"I'm not staying late," Lily whispered.

"You said that," Vic whispered back.

She nodded, threw back her hood so that it draped below a back bare to the waist, revealing a large buckle of diamonds.

"My God," Lily whispered to Vic, after they had been greeted by the Count and Countess, and wandered among the magnificently dressed throng. "Same old faces. Same old couturiers. What are we doing here?"

"Start by dancing with me, darling."

Lily turned and moved into his familiar arms. He danced as badly as ever, she thought, but it didn't matter because she was so used to his peculiar steps by now that she could actually follow them. "I shall miss you very much," she told him.

"I won't go."

"You must."

"I don't see why—it's all too late for me as well."

"Rubbish. Still time to have children."

"God forbid. This world's no place—look at the young men slaughtered in the Six-Day War, and now in Vietnam—I'd never want a son."

"The world could be a better place by then."

He was silent, and she knew he suffered—still, she was no surer now than she had ever been that he loved her. The only sure test, she supposed, would be to lose all her money, to be without a material prop of any kind.

"I'm cutting in," said Chris.

He was so much smaller, making her feel tall and clumsy. What had she ever seen in him? Even his music palled now.

Her next dance, with Davey, was smooth, easy, fun. Davey had the same oiled movements on the dance floor as on the golf course. "You must go back to America soon," she told him, as he held her so tightly her feet almost lifted from the floor.

"Not until you command me," he said. "Even a share of you is better than the whole of any other female."

Lily frowned. She tried to reverse the feeling, to understand just how the spell worked—but before she had got anywhere, another man was asking her to dance. He was a duke, and it seemed she had met him at Ascot with Tony. She tried not to yawn at his conversation—did no one with a title have anything genuine to say? Or was it that the worth of whatever they said was canceled by their very position—as, undoubtedly, it was with her?

Soon she was dancing with others, and finding things to say to various women who no longer looked at her with uncomfortable awe—many fortunes in the sixties were catching up with hers . . .

It should have helped, she thought—but this, too, was too late. She held back yawns, felt herself becoming drawn and distant.

"Lily, Lily," said Elspeth, suddenly appearing with a bearded man. "Here's someone who says he's always wanted to meet you." She winked at the old cliché, but left Lily to fend for herself with the total stranger.

"I'm sorry," he said, laughing. "That's a terrible thing to do! I was only talking, saying that I thought you would be fascinating to know, and suddenly she whisked me over. I didn't even know she knew you!"

"Please. Explain not." Lily stood silently, denuded of small talk, but liking at once the obviously intelligent, obviously articulate man—with so much hair that she thought his only distinct feature was blueness of eyes.

"My name is Tanner St. Clare," he said. "I'm from London."

She supposed she would have to comment. "Are you visiting someone?" she asked.

He laughed. "Hardly. I'm staying at a tiny *pensione* on the Zattare—my two weeks' saved-up holiday. I met a nice couple in St. Mark's Square who offered to bring me along tonight to see how the . . . Sorry, again. Tactless."

Lily looked at him directly, her large eyes grayed by the massed candlelight. "I'd much rather know how *you* lived."

"It's dead boring, I assure you. I'm a writer by trade, but I work to eat. Night clerk in a Kensington hotel."

"Oh?" Her eyes brightened a little. "What do you write?"

"Now *you're* in the cliché group. I *try* to write good novels. Sometimes biographies."

"I see." What a pity he was so young, she thought—probably early thirties at the most. He was quite interesting . . .

"The strange coincidence is that I've followed your life with extreme fascination. I wasn't just talking when I said I wanted to meet you—not that I ever thought I *would!*"

"What in the world have you followed—all my disasters, the ghastly publicity, my obvious stupidity?"

"Well, yes—frankly. But I've wanted to know you, to understand how you felt, how it had all come about."

"As a character for one of your books?"

His broad, heavy shoulders shifted uneasily and he patted his knuckles to his gingerish beard. "Perhaps. Does that seem presumptuous?" His bright eyes questioned sharply.

She thought about it a moment. She felt no offense, only a gradual detached vision of herself standing apart, sharing his view. "Would it be an interesting story, worth bothering with? I mean, there's nothing much to say about being the richest girl in the world—in my day, mind you—that hasn't already been said."

He shook his head. "That's just the point. You could have been cemented into the cliché—you still must be an individual. *That's* what interests me."

She flicked the curled strands beside her ears, reached into her satin purse for her ebony-and-diamond cigarette case, lighter and holder. He watched her, not reaching to help, like a spectator of her movements.

"I didn't visualize you smoking," he said. "But I suppose you would."

"And I drink like a fish." She smiled, mitigating the statement. "Too much when I'm bored, lonely or desperate."

"You must often be those."

She looked at him, accepted the truth with a nod. "I don't want to discourage you, but several people have tried biographies of me, even thinly disguised novels."

"I know. Did you find any of them convincing, true?"

"No. No one's come near. One was libelous, another obscene. Actually, I'm sure it's impossible—too many contradictions. And the main point is that my money hasn't always made me unhappy—I've enjoyed it, too."

"You wouldn't want to be without it."

She made a silent whistle and shook her head. "Lord, no! It's become a recurring nightmare. I find myself walking along a street in this little town—no one knows who I am, or where I come from, or seems to see me. I sit down to order a meal and I haven't got a penny. My dress is a meager cotton thing and my shoes will hardly stay on my feet they're so worn. I try to tell the waiter that I not only can pay for the meal, but could buy the whole restaurant. He sneers, says, 'Oh, yeah'—and calls the police!" She stopped, shuddered, then broke out laughing. "There— I've never told that to anyone else."

He smiled in wonder, in preoccupation. "God—what a story it could be! What a challenge to a writer!"

There was a silence.

"Do you *really* want to know me?" she asked suddenly.

He looked at her solemnly. "Well, yes—I really would. But if you're talking about interviews . . ."

"I'm talking about staying with me, living in the place I happen to be, following my moods, getting to know the actual facts of my childhood, my marriages, my lovers, my thoughts."

Lily could not control the rise in her voice, but he was silent, his long look uncertain. "You don't know anything about me," he said. "I could be a thief, a murderer, a—"

"But I know you're not. Behind that beard and hair you're a clever, perceptive man, I can see that—and a genuine human being. Do you want to write a really good book, raise yourself from the rut, succeed?"

"Yes . . . That's my life's goal, to put it succinctly."

"Then?"

He frowned and smiled at the same time, considering the validity, the sense of the offer. "How would you suggest we go about it? I've got my ticket home, and when I get there, I'll be a month behind in my rent. I've only had three books published, none of them well reviewed, only speaking of 'great promise.'"

"Don't elaborate," she said. "You'll have to come to terms with taking money. Are you too proud? Have you got male vanity, hang-ups about unearned money taken from a woman?"

He held up a large, broad hand. "All of those."

"Then that's *your* problem. There's none with me. I'll pay you to be with me, a good solid subsidy you can stow away in your bank. I'll clothe, house and feed you and you'll be an honored ember of my entourage. But—there'll be strict application to the objective. Every day you'll be garnering impressions, asking me questions—I'll let you read letters, look through my scrapbooks . . ."

"Scrapbooks!"

She smiled at his eagerness. "Kept since I was a child—all my publicity photographs, everything that's ever happened to me—outwardly. The inward part will be your challenge."

"Lily—by the way, what last name do you use now?"

"I'm Lily Boeker—back to square one."

"That's interesting. Well, Lily—we must talk further. This would be a tremendous decision. I'd have to let the job go . . . I've got a girl friend I've been living with . . ."

"It's up to you. Entirely."

Lily felt a sudden pall—of course a man like this would never be alone—there would always be a woman to love him . . .

"Meanwhile, Lily—" He smiled. "Would you care to dance?"

"Love to." She moved into his arms. They were roomy, comfortable, his steps were moderately rhythmic, easy to follow. Was it Freud who had said that people who danced well together made good love together? As if it mattered . . . And why on earth should *that* thought cross her mind?

He put his cheek to hers. She felt herself relax.

Over his shoulder she was just conscious of four people watching her—Chris, Vic, Elspeth, Davey.

"It's all nonsense, Tanner," said Sarah Thornton, reaching for a towel and stepping out of the dingy, old-fashioned bathtub. "She just wants a new gigolo! You're presentable, virile—she's probably sex-starved, a nympho!"

Tanner lay back on the rumpled gray bedclothes and watched the tall, slim girl put on her green mini and brush out her waist-length dark hair. He wished he could come right out with the truth, that he had been looking for a reason to break with her for months. They had had good moments, but were on totally opposed wavelengths. He had longed to be alone again, free to write in some kind of order and peace. "What can I say? If I tell you it's not like that," he said, "you wouldn't believe me anyway."

She smiled at him slyly. "Come on, Tanner, confess—her money's got you by the short-and-curlies. You couldn't care less about writing the great definitive book on her!"

"I don't blame you for assuming that. My talent hasn't been much in evidence lately."

She sat on the edge of the bed. "Look, Tanny. I know you've had a long hard struggle and how much you loathe that hotel grind, but you aren't really going through with this moral corruption, are you?"

"You bet I am," he said. "In just over two hours."

She stared. "And what about me, the flat, everything?"

"You'll be all right, Sarah. You can stay here."

"Thank you very much."

He pressed her arm. "Sarah—you know damn well there were no commitments. And think—someday you'll pass W. H. Smith's window and see a big pile of my books, and you'll say, *I* knew him *when!*"

Sarah blinked back a suggestion of tears, but Tanner knew they were for herself. "Hand me my wallet," he said.

She got up with a guarded look of expectation, brought him the worn leather object, usually paper-flat except for a few frayed cards, now bulging.

Tanner drew out several ten-pound notes, held them up in front of her eyes. "Buy yourself that coat you were drizzling about," he said.

She took the money slowly, her eyes downcast.

"Looks good, doesn't it?"

For just a moment, Tanner thought she might give them back with some caustic comment, but she got up, threw them into her shabby leather purse, shouldered it and started for the door.

"I'll drop you a line when I know where I'll be," he said. "And I'll leave the keys—oh, and don't forget to pay the TV rental."

She paused. "Don't you forget to write a book," she said. "*Ciao.*"

Tanner looked at the closed door a moment, then sprang from

the bed. He could not remember ever having been so stimulated, so motivated, so totally committed! No more pacing about, he thought, drinking cups of filthy coffee, smoking cigarettes till his throat burned, or putting up any other of his excuses against getting on with it. He could hardly wait to start taking notes, to start working full-out! Titles filtered through his mind like music.

"Bring only what's important to you in your work, Tanner," Lily had written. "Get some clothes if you need them, but remember you'll have a cash reserve available." She had enclosed a check for a thousand pounds to cover "fares and expenses generally."

He packed with care, his few new clothes, some old, essential reference books, the red pen he thought brought him luck, his faithful portable typewriter, some notebooks. When he was there, he would buy a better tape recorder . . .

"We won't be staying here, Tanner," she had written. "Venice is beautiful beyond words, but I'm not at ease in the palazzo—I feel transient. Since you've guaranteed one year of your time, I thought I'd look for a house on the Isle of Picco. You may wonder why. Well, once we went ashore there from the yacht, and it's been on my mind ever since. I felt I could settle there on the great dramatic cliff looking over the Gulf of Naples, in sight of Vesuvius. I'd plant lovely gardens where none have grown before, terrace upon terrace down to the brilliant, glittering blue sea—I'd make it my final *raison d'être*. You see, I've always adored flowers, and learned so much from my gardeners in Long Island. This would keep me occupied while you were actually at work—for I don't intend to monopolize your time. You must feel *free!* And, above all, not even bound to produce a book at all if you don't feel there's one worth doing. Let's just think of our project as an experiment that, hopefully, can be interesting for us both. Yours, Lily."

When he had trimmed his hair and beard, was dressed and ready to leave, Tanner dialed his parents' home. "Well, Mum," he said, "this is to say *au revoir* for a while. Don't worry—I'll probably be hopping backwards and forwards. Lily's got a house here. I'll see you soon. Did you get the money? Good—now see that Dad doesn't kill himself at the garage. I'll send you more when I can. Mum—I'm *not* going to get involved with her, and it *isn't* opting out—it's a job of *work!* And you'll see—*this* time, success. Now take care of yourself, dear—yes, I'll send you my address. Goodbye for now."

When he hung up, Tanner thought of ringing his best friend and agent, Benjamin Hotchkiss, but it seemed extraneous—he had already explained it to him, been congratulated. "This could be the big break you deserve, Tan," Benjy had said. "Send me copy, as you do it, and I'll get cracking . . ."

Tanner pulled the sheets from the bed, rolled them up, straightened things as best he could, and with one last look around at all that symbolized unfulfilled promise, hard labor unrewarded and only a minimum of the inspiration and zest he felt capable of, he closed the door, went out into the rumbling Kensington traffic, hailed a taxi, put his bags inside.

"Heathrow, please," he said, and sat back, unable to help smiling.

Chapter 22

"I went into Maudie's room one day—I didn't think she was there. I've forgotten what I wanted. But she was there, and she was naked, quite naked. I'd never seen her naked. I remember thinking, good heavens, she's got a lovely body! It *was*, you know, darling. White and curved, beautiful, sort of athletic back, good breasts, nice waist, red hair down there. And I thought—oh, God, her body's never been appreciated, never even been *seen* by a man! She's never had a chance at life! I felt wicked, evil, a devourer of innocent life."

"That's good stuff." Tanner indicated the tape recorder between them on the top terrace of El Contento, and continued to sip his gin and tonic, his eyes on her face.

"Poor old darling Maudie—I never let her go. And I made her come out of retirement, all the way from Somerset to America, when I had my nervous breakdown—did I tell you that?"

Tanner nodded. "Just to sit beside you and occasionally call you 'dear' and 'Miss Lily.' And she did it by rote because she had grown a bit hazy mentally. Sometimes she talked to a little girl that wasn't there. It frightened you and you had to send her home."

"Yes. Did I tell you the bit about Whitey and Joel?"

"Yes—we've got enough on that relationship, I think."

Lily's deeply tanned and weathered face etched with smile lines. "Did I ever tell you about Vic reading sex books to learn techniques?"

Tanner laughed. "You did, my sweet. Graphically!"

"Ah, yes—I want to talk more about the guru. That was so nearly the turning point—I came so close to something, something . . ." Her voice faded, her eyes became distant.

"Poor baby."

Lily turned to look at him. He was so beautiful, she thought, a man of burnished gold, even the hair on his body catching the light of the sun, his eyes like the sea, a solid, substantial man for all seasons.

"I love you," she said, "so much."

He took her hand. "And I, you—more and more."

"But I'm so old, darling—sixty-three soon!"

"Don't be silly, I've caught up."

They laughed, neither of them wanting to remember that they had just celebrated his thirty-ninth birthday.

"Do you want to work?" she asked. "I've got a million things to do."

"Not yet—tell me about the bastard Pierrot."

Lily pressed hairpins primly into her bun, reached for her gardening hat. "You'll get excited . . ."

"No—I promise. I'm getting used to him."

Lily sat back in the brilliant bamboo chaise, crossed her thin brown legs, pulled her pale-blue denim skirt over her knees, closed the collar of her red-and-white cotton shirt.

Tanner put back his head and laughed. "No trust, eh?"

"Well—he's usually pretty good for a near-rape, my love."

"Not today—I'm lethargic. Too much wine with lunch."

"All right, what shall I tell?"

"About when you went to tell him lunch was ready, and he got you to make that 'commitment'!"

"Tanner St. Clare!" Lily took off one of her white-antelope gardening shoes and shot it at him.

"Mm," he said, "it's the bit I love. The way you hung over him . . . Darling, let's go inside . . ."

Lily looked at the bulge in his white swimming trunks and was full of wonder. That this husband she loved more than anything in the world should always want her so much after six years of marriage, seemed a dream out of time. Almost, almost, she had become convinced that she was lovable . . .

"Please?" he said, running his hand softly along her calf.

She closed her eyes, sighed involuntarily. He was the only man in her whole life, she thought, with the magic combination, the gift of lovemaking together with love itself. How was it possible that she had found him, so suddenly, so unexpectedly that night?

Or—was love always unexpected, was that its very essence?

She opened her eyes, reached for his hand. They walked past gardeners, servants, through the cool stone halls to her rooms.

He was the one to take the pins out of her hair so that it fell like light about her face and shoulders, he who undressed her, carried her to the vast low divan surrounded by Japanese screens. He seemed never to tire of her breasts, her thighs, the whole of her slender, still firm body.

"Do you ever think of that girl, Sarah?" she had asked him, and he had said, "Oh, her—never. She was senseless clay compared to you."

And what about all the others? None, he told her, could come close to her sensuality, so natural to her every move. "You were born for lovemaking!"

And when they lay together afterwards and talked, there was always so much to say—too much, she thought at times, and would send him off to get on with his writing.

Not much of this had been accomplished. In the big studio she had made for him, with every conceivable provision for his needs—he had even chosen which view he wanted—there were by now several filing cabinets filled with his notes and tapes. A secretary was at his command six days a week to keep up with his typing requirements. Of course, he wasn't always concerned with her book—he had written four short stories since being on the island, and sold two of them—mounds of the magazines that

had published them stood against the walls, and at Christmas
Lily had sent them out as greetings.

Not that it mattered. Getting a book done was *his* goal, not
hers—she was only thinking of him when she worried a little . . .

. . . On the other hand, he seemed so happy. Lying beside
him in a small pool of contented silence now, before they talked
again, she thought back over the years . . .

Their work had got off to a slow start—so many setbacks. . . .
Not only the delay in finding a house and getting physically settled in, but only a few weeks after he had arrived, Aunt Mirry had
cabled the news about Andy . . .

There was no hesitation on Tanner's part to go with her to
America. Vic had returned to England, Elspeth to Germany,
Davey to Long Island—only Chris remained, and Lily did not see
him fitting into the family scene. She had given him some money
to start a jazz group . . .

Tanner had been the pivot of those agonizing weeks. The way
he and Aunt Mirry had taken to each other was an unexpected
miracle: when Andy's fall from the penthouse roof transmuted
her poise to shattered grief, he was the only one who could reach
her. Walking with her along the pillared archways of the loggia,
or the beach shimmering beyond the leaning palms, he would
take her elbow and they would talk, talk—about Andy, about the
impenetrable mysteries of human character, of life itself.

Lily never knew exactly what Tanner would say to the aunt
she actually knew and understood so dimly, but somehow the
aging woman, who had become so cantankerous without Uncle
Will's softening presence (he had died suddenly one night at
dinner), was comforted, sustained, and even convinced that
Andy's plunge had been an accident.

"You have a gem here, my dear," she said to Lily, sternly,
accusingly. "Why couldn't you have married someone like him!"

Aunt Mirry had been loath to let Tanner go, and did all she
could to persuade him to make his home there. It was obvious
that in spite of all the people in her life, there had been no one
with whom she had communicated in such depth.

But since they were in America, it seemed logical to Lily to
show Tanner where she had been born and lived as a child, to
show him through the New York mansion (now, of course, a mu-

seum with attendants to point out the rooms and history of Wilbur Boeker).

Before they left Palm Beach, though, she had showed him the polo field, the very spot where her father had been killed, and Befred, the private Pullman car where Freddie had tried to rape her (still intact and kept as a showpiece on Aunt Mirry's grounds).

This firsthand illustration of her American years had almost overwhelmed Tanner. "I had no real idea of the scope of this project," he said. "Why, Palm Beach alone could take me a year to assimilate!"

When she showed him Long Island, the house, the gardens, her chalet, and described her early life, he groaned. "The mind boggles. I shan't know where to start!"

To round out the picture for him, she had introduced him to Coggy, but the flinty old man was by now hard of hearing and kept saying, "No more husbands, no more husbands." And "Live on your income, miss!"

His partners, three, now did his job, told them that they couldn't get the old man to stay home, that he was a nuisance sitting in the old Boeker office and refusing to stop figuring. They explained her taxation problems, and she listened, as she always did, without understanding.

"Is all well?" was all she wanted to know.

They said "not bad," and suggested that she become a Foundation, and she said that whatever that was, to go ahead, she would sign. They asked her to initial a sheaf of documents, wondered if she would be spending more time here in the United States . . .

"I doubt it," she said. "I've grown away from things here."

Having Tanner by her side, Lily had no trouble with nostalgia, none of the old yearning for Joel. She found that she could let go, live for today.

The only pang she had felt was for the doll's house. They had not gone to California.

"Next time," Tanner had said sensibly, for both of them. "You're bound to want to go back for visits."

"That's true."

And then, when they had got back to Europe, there was the

problem with the house in Cannes. There had been a fire, much damage to the lower levels. Tanner had discovered an unsuspected talent for organizing, for taking over at least her smaller decisions. "When the place is in order, rent it to responsible people," he had said. "You don't need to keep staff there doing nothing."

She had not thought of it; the solution seemed inspired.

Not long after that, they had decided they were in love, really in love, that it was not just passionate attraction, not just convenience or companionability—but all of it. Lily knew that Tanner would not propose—there was always that same old question of who had the money, and in his view, he had not yet got off the ground in his ambition.

So she asked him. Still, he took several months to make up his mind. In that time, he learned that he, too, was "hooked" on the great cool fortress of El Contento, which Lily had enlarged and decorated so exquisitely in a blend of Spanish, Japanese and modern, on growing magnolias, camellias, lilies, orchids, medinillas, roses, narcissi, campanulas, wild crocuses foreign to Picco, on taking part in the wine growing, the overseeing of the sundrenched groves of judas and oleanders.

Further, he loved the yacht, took an active interest in their cruising and was a natural host at all her social functions.

"All right," he said finally, "if you'll let me be your husband and not just an adjunct, and if you'll still bear in mind that I'm first and foremost a writer. There'll be a time when I simply disappear and get on with it. It'll seem selfish, but that's the nature of the beast."

"I couldn't understand more," Lily said.

And so they were married, in a brief, simple ceremony in the big sunken gardens that surrounded a small terra-cotta swimming pool and fountains. And, at last, Lily was happy. "It's come late in life," Lily would hear herself say, "very late. But it's been worth waiting for."

Stirring beside her now, Tanner yawned. "I think I'll have a doze," he said. "God, that sweet smell of jasmine—how I associate it with loving you!"

"You'll get right up this minute, my love," Lily said. "You've got to see Antonino about hauling the boulders for the shoreline wall."

"Oh, Lord, yes." Tanner sat, stretched, took her in his arms a moment. "I drown in beauty," he said, "hard as I try not to."

She kissed him, gave him a small push, then got up herself and worked her way back to where she had been before he had got her onto the subject of Pierrot. She smiled as she tied on the blue-scarfed gardening hat, picked up her long baskets of plants and tools and started quickly downward to one of the lower flower terraces by the sea.

Exchanging smiles, the gardeners watched her go. Over Vesuvius there hung the usual little green cloud. Far down below, a group of tourists was looking upward . . .

She waved.

"There she is!" said the tourist guide, "the owner of all this land, in fact a major portion of the island—the famous Lily Boeker. She's a Mrs. Tanner St. Clare now, but he's her fourth husband, and everyone knows her by her own name."

"I never heard of her," said a young girl in dark glasses and scarf.

"Nor have I," said a young man, flicking an ice-cream wrapper onto the rust-colored rock. "What's she famous *for?*"

The guide, a tall man with a dark, leathery face under a naval cap pushed far back on his head, grinned. "Well—she used to be the richest girl in the world. Always in the papers."

"I've never heard of her," the girl repeated.

"Figures. She's no chicken—and she lives pretty quiet these days."

"What are all those pink cottages?"

"Those belong to her servants."

"Servants!"

"You mean people still have that many?"

"You need 'em, I guess, if you have that much property."

"It shouldn't be allowed."

The group straggled on around the coastline.

Lily could have pinpointed the moment she knew something was wrong; one night she had awakened suddenly to find Tanner not in the bed, and when she had peered about the huge dim room, she had seen him standing, absolutely motionless, by one of the tall windows, gazing out to sea.

Some instinct had warned her not to speak. He had stood there so long that finally she had fallen off to sleep again, and in the morning he was beside her as usual, his heavy arm about her shoulders.

She tried not to imagine more than was indicated, but she never again settled into the same relaxed peace. And when she saw that hardly a night passed that he didn't roam, pace, stare from the window, she knew he had to be made to work; he was beginning to turn against his own evasions, his own procrastination, and soon he would turn against her.

Making excuses to leave him to it, she would vanish early and return late only to find that he was still out planting, or working with the men, or swimming, or out in one of the sailboats.

For the first time she realized just how much of an enemy such enjoyment of life was for him, just how much of a struggle it would be to shut himself off from all the absorbing and pleasurable activity and confine himself to a room, a desk, paper and typewriter.

One night, after their guests had gone, Lily took his hand and they wandered the upper terrace in the moonlight. The air was thick and sweetly pungent with flowers and a hint of salty, sultry wind. They could hear the water lapping and distant voices and music echoing over the rocks and cliffs.

Lily was wearing a sleeveless, starkly simple white dress, a lavish spread of diamonds, a tiny arrangement of them in the front of her smooth bun.

"You looked unbelievably beautiful tonight, Lily," Tanner said. "If only I could capture that beauty on paper—there's nothing harder than describing beauty."

"My darling—has the writing deserted you?" she asked softly.

He looked at her strangely. "I'm not sure. Why do you ask, precious?"

Her eyes opened into his, softly radiant with sympathy. "I'm not blind and insensible, my love."

"You mean, because I haven't been getting on with the book?"

"With *anything*. Your room's piled high with notes, but never a page of finished work."

He fell silent.

They walked to the end of the terrace, down flights of stone steps to another where white and pink asphodels seemed to nod at them as they passed. Lily's heart began to pound—she wondered if she had underestimated his conflict.

"There's only one way I can tell, Lily. I've found that I'm simply incapable of fighting myself here, with you. If I stay, I might just as well accept the fact. Relax and enjoy, as they say." He gave a self-deprecatory laugh. "So much for a lifetime of sweat and ambition."

"*If* you stay?" Lily's eyes seemed to grow larger, to engulf the light that fell across her face.

He paused, took her arms in a tight grip. "Perhaps it really isn't important," he said. "I don't know any more. Perhaps being your husband and companion, enjoying our lives together, *is* sufficient and valid justification for existence."

"Oh, Tanner, my love—can't you possibly combine them? I feel so responsible . . . !"

"Lily—what is one more wordsmith in the world—suppose I get a few things published?" He shrugged. "So what? Worms will eat them."

"Is that *you* talking?"

"I don't know that, either." He let her arms go, touched her chin, bent and kissed her. "Come on, forget it—we've got our shopping in Rome tomorrow, our visit to the Dompagni Cordovusos."

"But what did you mean by *if* I stay—was there an alternative in your mind?" she persisted.

He shook his head. "Not to worry."

"Oh, darling—you know I *will*."

"That's just it—I can't consider going—"

"Going?"

"To give it a try, my darling." He rubbed his face in hard impatience. "To clear up my head, Lily. To get my bearings. To *have* to work, to *need* money, to be *driven*, to have *incentive*, be *motivated*—sweet, sweet words! God, I've become a jellyfish, a hedonist, a souped-up gigolo—"

"You're my husband, darling! You're entitled to . . ."

"Balls. I'm sorry, darling—but I'm *entitled* to bugger-all."

"Tanner! Oh, my love, is that how you see all these good years?"

"No, of course not, Lily. The first few years could be called valid. Notes had to be taken. Your life had to be assimilated, put in perspective . . . Not that I've ever got one—you slipped away —and so did the goal, the desire, the ends and the means!"

"I see . . . Yes . . . Yes, you must go away for a few weeks! I could bear that, Tanner, and it would be right, good—I'll do anything I can to help."

"Lovey—a few weeks isn't any use whatever. I'd know I had an out, an escape route. No—it would have to be permanent. So you see, there it is—damned if I do, damned if I don't. Because I love you, Lily."

She felt that she was turning to stone, becoming riveted in the rock of the island. No breath would come. Her chest seemed to clamp shut, closing out oxygen . . .

"Lily? Are you all right?" He took her elbow, peered into her face.

She couldn't answer. She stared at him a moment, her eyes stark, then suddenly, without a sound, she collapsed.

"Oh, my darling, my dearest darling," Tanner murmured as he picked her up and ran with her toward the house.

The weeks passed slowly at El Contento, moved gradually into months. Tanner never mentioned the subject again, but Lily waited in pale expectation of doom. Her heart was no longer strong or reliable, and by doctor's orders her agile clambering from terrace to terrace had to be forgone for more flower arranging, supervising the gardeners, working out the menus and other matters with her staff from one of the upper terraces, often from her bed.

Tanner was left with most of the heavier tasks. He found that he lacked her quick perception with servants, her actual botanical knowledge garnered over the years, her sense of color, design, her broad vision, her ability to make immense, far-reaching decisions, to spend vast sums of money without a qualm of uncertainty. He came to realize that as an executive, she was her aunt's niece, that his ability in this regard was prosaic, plodding.

He did his best, and he got through the days, but life had taken a dull, unrewarding turn. On his own, without the savor of her company, her intense interest and sensitive reactions, the island itself, what it demanded, seemed sterile, totally unreal. What did it all matter? How could he ever have been bemused by it, enthralled . . . ? It was a grotesque prison of luxury and beauty. God, how he longed for ordinary people, easy laughter, noisy streets, a drink in a pub, his own desk in some plain but functional room with no particular view of anything . . .

He longed to find himself again—the old imperfect, battling outsider trying to get in, with no material security taken for granted!

Now and then he made a concerted effort to write. He found that he could sort, compile, clean the typewriter keys, improve his seating or lighting arrangement, shine up his new hornrims, wind his watch, get something to eat, drink or smoke—but he could not force his bottom to stay on the chair, his fingers on the keys.

Inevitably, he would give up and go to Lily. At least with her, he could be of some immediate use. She always looked up with that flash of blue eyes, that instant warm smile that lighted her still marvelously beautiful face—she surely would always be that beautiful even into very old age, he would think with a pang for the future. It was a surrender, but one that soothed them both, put their worlds to temporary rights.

Tanner let both physical and mental work slide. He put on weight, neglected to trim his beard. Lily teased him gently, called him "a big brown bear." She liked to just sit and look at him, fragile and somehow regal against her great mounds of pillows, or read to him from her pile of gardening books. In her lovely bed jackets or negligees, sometimes leaving her exquisitely maintained hair loose and thick around her shoulders, she seemed the princess of fairy tales grown only a little older.

The subject of a book about her, of trying to discern who or what she really was, would have been, or the meaning of her life, from all the material she had given him, all the thoughts, hopes, feelings she had unburdened over the years, was never discussed again. It was understood that neither of them had learned anything concrete; she had somehow vanished under dissection, like a cloud shape blown by the wind.

Tanner did start a rather promising poem about her, but it didn't get finished.

One close, humid night a storm suddenly broke over the vast cliff island. A gale howled about the house and terraces, bent the tall trees to the ground, sent rocks hurtling from cliff walls to the sea, whipped the sea itself to great froth-topped giants hurling themselves against the fortress shore. Lightning had forked across the window walls of Tanner's bedroom, keeping him wide awake, peculiarly tense . . .

The rising and falling wail of the wind seemed to strike deep into his own consciousness, to accuse, to tell him of life dissipated, values spurned, effort abandoned, of what might be a gift neglected, betrayed, lost . . .

Oh God, how could he stay here? How could he go on being this shell of a human being!

"Go!" the wind seemed to howl. "Go—no good can come of this—you've given her many years of happiness—go now, now, *now!*"

He had still been awake when the storm abated and the island was hot, still, calm again, a sharp, sweet perfume of washed earth and flowers drifting over his senses.

Lighting a cigarette, he sat for a long time thinking about Lily. He loved her, yes—but oftener than not these days, he felt the truth of his being with her was more gratitude, fondness, protectiveness, even pity.

Soon, he would be forty-one . . .

Leaving the question hanging uncomfortably, heavily unanswered, he fell into a torpid sleep.

In the morning, in the cleansed, sun-drenched air, he awakened with a sudden clarity. There was absolutely no question: he must face it out, tell her gently, gradually, but in the end definitely—he could not stay. He would explain to her that if he didn't go and get back to hard, slogging work, he would become a silly, useless old man who had never achieved what he set out to do, and that this was nothing short of living death. Surely she could understand this—the desire to earn what one got, to see reward arise logically, naturally, satisfyingly, from effort . . .

Yes, of course she would understand. Hard as it would be, she would not want to keep him, not want to see happen to him what had happened to her, the poor darling.

It would be a dreadful, shattering confrontation. But Lily would go on, Lily would be taken care of and find others willing to care for her.

He would start this very day, he thought, by taking the boat to the airport and flying over to London, just to look around and see where he might live, how he might go about his new, free life.

He would want nothing from her, except the few hundred pounds he had in a drawer, just to get him started.

He showered, shaved, put on a gray city suit, summoned Ernesto.

"Ernesto," he said. "I want you to take me to the airport at eleven. Please pack some stuff for a couple of days."

"Yes, signor." Ernesto nodded his dark head.

Suddenly, at the sound of raised voices, they both looked up . . .

"Mr. St. Clare! Mr. St. Clare!"

The two men looked at each other.

It was Fanny Dimpkin, followed by a maid, both of their faces distorted with horror.

"It's Madam," said Dimpkin. "Oh, Mr. St. Clare—it was terrible. We were just taking in her breakfast . . . She looked up, said something, then gasped and went horribly still . . ."

"Still?"

"Yes, sir—she's dead, Mr. St. Clare."

Tanner stood for a few moments, struck to numbness. Then he and the manservant followed the two women.

Lily's head had fallen to one side in a soft surround of loosened hair. The great blue eyes were wide, staring . . .

Tanner could not speak. He was immobile, his bearded face blank. After a few moments, he sighed deeply, reached down, gently closed the blue-veined white lids over the incredible light blue-green, of eyes seen for the last time.

"This was in her hand, Mr. St. Clare," Fanny Dimpkin said. She handed him a heavy gold-sealed white envelope with his name on it. "It's her will—I wonder if she knew she was going."

Like a man in a profound trance, Tanner sliced the seal with his forefinger, lifted out the contents. A letter was pinned to the formal document.

"Darling Tanner," it read, "I changed this recently without telling you because it is *you* who have given me the only real happiness in my life, and it is *you* that I want to have everything I own or have ever owned. Except for a few bequests to old friends or people who have been kind, some to charitable institutions, it is all yours, the Boeker inheritance, my dearest.

"I don't know when the day will be, but when it comes I know in my heart you will handle it with care and integrity—all the houses, the properties, the yacht, and investments, principal and income. You will also inherit Aunt Mirry's house, which was willed to me, when she passes on.

"You will have your work cut out to gather everything under control—I have been so careless with possessions, scattering and leaving them everywhere, particularly cars and all the treasures I've collected and sometimes not even uncrated.

"Try to contact Whitey. If she would, she could be of great help to you. Please do something with my doll's house—it would be enjoyable for children, a museum, some form of free display. Enlist Aunt Mirry—she will be invaluable. And, above all, go to see Coggy (if he's still around) and his associates. They will give you all the proper advice.

"My dearest, you will know by now that it isn't easy to be rich *and* have character—someone said it's the hardest test of all. But I do hope you will find you can have both. I do so want you to have a full and rewarding life. This is my last wish for you, my dearest, who gave meaning to at least some part of mine. Bless you always. Lily."

Tanner stood with the document in his hand.

Eventually, those about him turned away from the sight of tears streaming down his face.